Novels by Ellery Queen

The Roman Hat Mystery
The French Powder Mystery
The Dutch Shoe Mystery
The Greek Coffin Mystery
The Egyptian Cross Mystery
The American Gun Mystery
The Siamese Twin Mystery
The Chinese Orange Mystery
The Spanish Cape Mystery
Halfway House
The Door Between
The Devil to Pay
The Four of Hearts
The Dragon's Teeth
Calamity Town
There Was an Old Woman
The Murderer Is a Fox
Ten Days' Wonder
Cat of Many Tails
Double, Double
The Origin of Evil
The King Is Dead
The Scarlet Letters
The Glass Village
Inspector Queen's Own Case
The Finishing Stroke
The Player on the Other Side
And On the Eighth Day
The Fourth Side of the Triangle
A Study in Terror
Face to Face
The House of Brass
Cop Out
The Last Woman in His Life
A Fine and Private Place

Books of Short Stories by Ellery Queen

The Adventures of Ellery Queen
The *New* Adventures of Ellery Queen
The Casebook of Ellery Queen
Calendar of Crime
Q.B.I.: Queen's Bureau of Investigation
Queens Full
Q.E.D.: Queen's Experiments in Detection

Edited by Ellery Queen

Challenge to the Reader
101 Years' Entertainment
Sporting Blood
The Female of the Species
The Misadventures of Sherlock Holmes
Rogues' Gallery
Best Stories from *EQMM*
To the Queen's Taste
The Queen's Awards, 1946–1953
Murder by Experts
20th Century Detective Stories
Ellery Queen's Awards, 1954–1957
The Literature of Crime
Ellery Queen's Mystery Annuals: 13th-16th
Ellery Queen's Anthologies: 1960–1975
The Quintessence of Queen (*Edited by Anthony Boucher*)
To Be Read Before Midnight
Ellery Queen's Mystery Mix
Ellery Queen's Double Dozen
Ellery Queen's 20th Anniversary Annual
Ellery Queen's Crime Carousel
Ellery Queen's All-Star Lineup
Poetic Justice
Ellery Queen's Mystery Parade
Ellery Queen's Murder Menu
Ellery Queen's Minimysteries
Ellery Queen's Grand Slam
Ellery Queen's The Golden 13
Ellery Queen's Headliners
Ellery Queen's Mystery Bag
Ellery Queen's Crookbook
Ellery Queen's Murdercade

Ellery Queen's Mystery Magazine (35th Year)

True Crime by Ellery Queen

Ellery Queen's International Case Book
The Woman in the Case

Critical Works by Ellery Queen

The Detective Short Story
Queen's Quorum
In the Queens' Parlor

Under the Pseudonym of Barnaby Ross

The Tragedy of X
The Tragedy of Y
The Tragedy of Z
Drury Lane's Last Case

Ellery Queen's Murdercade

29th Mystery Annual

RANDOM HOUSE · NEW YORK

Ellery Queen's Murdercade

23 stories from
Ellery Queen's
Mystery Magazine

EDITED BY

Ellery Queen

Published in the United States by Random House, Inc., New York,
and simultaneously in Canada by
Random House of Canada Limited, Toronto.

Libary of Congress Cataloging in Publication Data

Queen, Ellery, pseud., comp.
Ellery Queen's murdercade.

(Mystery annual; 29)
CONTENTS: Davidson, A. The mad sniper.—Innes, M.
The memorial service.—Hoch, E. D. The most dangerous
man. [etc.]
1. Detective and mystery stories, American.
2. Detective and mystery stories, English. I. Ellery
Queen's mystery magazine. II. Title. III. Series:
EQMM annual; 29.
PZ1.A1E4 vol. 29 [PS648.D4] 823'.0872s [823'.0872]
ISBN 0-394-49674-4 74-29617

Manufactured in the United States of America

First Edition

Acknowledgments

The Editor hereby makes grateful acknowledgment to the following authors and authors' representatives for giving permission to reprint the material in this volume:

Isaac Asimov for *The Six Suspects*, © 1973 by Isaac Asimov.
Georges Borchardt, Inc., for *Trapped* by Ruth Rendell, © 1973 by Ruth Rendell.
Brandt & Brandt for *A Judicious Half Inch* by Ursula Curtiss, © 1973 by Ursula Curtiss.
Curtis Brown, Ltd., for *The Corruption of Officer Avakadian* by Stanley Ellin, © 1973 by Stanley Ellin.
Collins-Knowlton-Wing, Inc., for *The Memorial Service* by Michael Innes, © 1972 by Michael Innes.
John Cushman Associates, Inc., for *Fifty Years After* by Anthony Gilbert, © 1973 by Anthony Gilbert; and *How to Trap a Crook* by Julian Symons, © 1972 by Julian Symons.
Avram Davidson for *The Mad Sniper*, © 1972 by Avram Davidson.
Celia Fremlin for *If It's Got Your Number*, © 1973 by Celia Fremlin.
Elliot L. Gilbert for *The Sins of the Father*, © 1973 by Elliot L. Gilbert.
Edward D. Hoch for *The Most Dangerous Man*, © 1972 by Edward D. Hoch.
Mary Hocking for *Mr. Joslin's Journey*, © 1973 by Mary Hocking.
Philip MacDonald for *The Star of Starz*, © 1973 by Philip MacDonald.

Harold Matson Company, Inc., for *In an Outpost of Empire* by Jacob Hay, © 1973 by Jacob Hay; and *The Five Senses of Mrs. Craggs* by H. R. F. Keating, © 1973 by H. R. F. Keating.

Florence V. Mayberry for *In the Secret Hollow*, © 1973 by Florence V. Mayberry.

McIntosh & Otis, Inc., for *Who Dies, Who Lives?* by Patricia Highsmith, © 1973 by Patricia Highsmith.

Scott Meredith Literary Agency, Inc., for *See How They Run* by Robert Bloch, © 1973 by Robert Bloch; and *The Shooting of Curly Dan* by John Lutz, © 1973 by John Lutz.

William Miller for *Green Ink*, © 1973 by William Miller.

Harold Ober Associates, Inc., for *The Harlequin Tea Set* by Agatha Christie, © Agatha Christie 1971; and *Chapter and Verse* by Ngaio Marsh, © 1973 by Ngaio Marsh Limited.

Bill Pronzini for *Proof of Guilt*, © 1973 by Bill Pronzini.

Contents

Introduction

Dear Reader:

This is the twenty-ninth volume in the series of hardcover anthologies that have derived from *Ellery Queen's Mystery Magazine*. The first volume appeared in 1946, five years after the birth of *EQMM*, and a new one appeared every year thereafter until 1973, when the twenty-eighth volume, *Ellery Queen's Crookbook*, was scheduled to be published. But unexpectedly the publishers discontinued their trade-book division, and it was too late in the year to change publishers and still keep our record for annual publication intact. So 1973 became the first year since 1946 in which an *EQMM* hardcover anthology failed to appear.

We are happy to be back with Random House, who published the anthologies for nearly a decade, from 1958 through 1965, and *Crookbook* in 1974, and now brings you *Ellery Queen's Murdercade*, containing the best stories published in *EQMM* during 1973.

Murdercade. A new word? So far as we know, yes. But it has its precedents. There is cavalcade, a parade of people on horses or in horse-drawn vehicles. There is motorcade, a parade of people in automobiles. So why not murdercade?—a parade of people in murders.

True, not all the stories in this book deal with people involved in murders. But all the stories do revolve about crimes, and, to paraphrase the poet, if crime comes, can murder be far behind?

Cavalcade, motorcade, and murdercade suggest other rhyme words, and how they might apply generally to mystery stories and specifically to the stories in this collection. You will find, in the various writing styles, the tang and tart of orangeade and lemonade, with some sweetener, and plenty of fizz; in the diverse plots, the excitement of escapade, the danger of ambuscade, the mystery of jade; in the multifaceted people, everything from the gentleness of serenade to the explosiveness of hand grenade—but beware the false faces of masquerade; and in the manifold moods, the terrifying suspense of nightshade and the death hint of spade . . .

So, dear reader, get ready. The parade is about to begin—the bands and the floats are lining up. Take your seat in the front row of the reviewing stand. There, the Grand Marshal is coming into sight, and behind him—just turn the page—the first murder in the murdercade . . .

ELLERY QUEEN

Ellery Queen's Murdercade

THE MAD SNIPER

by Avram Davidson

Joe Gunnarson, who was a foreman at J. F. Guernsey's dried-fruit and dehydrated-vegetables plant, had troubles. Big ones. His son, his wife, his brother. And then there was that mysterious business of what was happening on the new part of the road that ran through the valley . . .

FOR two years the road through the valley had been in the making, and it had killed a man for each year. The first had been a construction employee whose piece of heavy equipment had toppled over on him. The second had defied the world to remove him from the house where he'd lived for fifty years—a traditional bit of Americana, complete with shotgun, rockingchair vigil, and photographers; but the old man had died of a heart attack before the deputies could lob in their first teargas shells.

But now, as Joe Gunnarson drove along the almost-finished road in the earliest dusk, he thought very little of the road and its history. There would be plenty of time for that. Time to reflect how the road would take him straight from home to work and straight back again, without delays at traffic lights, railroad crossings, or repairs—the old road was always being repaired, it had seemed. Time to reflect on who had lived where, but didn't any more because the new road ran right through the old homesites. And time to compare the disadvantage that he had to leave his car at the foot of the hill and climb up to his house with the advantage that on the old road he could park almost in his front yard.

Right now Joe Gunnarson was thinking about his troubles. The first was his little son, Jody, who had been sick when Joe left home this morning and who was almost certain to be sick when he got back: a pale, whining sort of child, who had inherited his face from his father but not, it seemed, his father's health. It was too bad he hadn't got his mother's looks instead of her metabolism. For Ella was trouble Number Two.

"Oh, leave me alone, Joe," she would say. "Bad enough I could hardly drag myself out of bed this morning"—retreating from Joe's comforting touch—"but the kid was crying the whole damned day. And as if *that* wasn't enough, your rotten brother—"

Was trouble Number Three. All his troubles were people, and the same ones all the time. Joe had a good job, his own health was vigorous. If only his wife and child were in better shape. If only his wife and brother got along together. Because Keith and Ella were at each other all the time, it seemed. Ideally Keith should be living somewhere else. But that was out of the question: he had no job, claimed (and it sounded reasonable) that he couldn't get one because—who knows?—he might be drafted.

So Keith slept late—which annoyed Ella; he sloped around the county in his old car that Joe had financed—which burned Ella up; and he came home as it pleased him, to eat big meals, for which, of course, he never paid—which enraged Ella.

"Let me alone, Joe. I said *NO!* Are you deaf? Do you know what that brother of yours said to me today?"

Joe sighed and the valley and hills grew darker and it was only with abrupt care that he kept from ramming into a car which had stopped on the road.

"My lord!" the man who belonged to the car kept saying. "My lord, I was shot at! Someone shot at me! Oh, my lord!" He was an ordinary man, middle-aged, in rumpled work clothes, and he had a Southwestern accent.

"Why would ennabodda wawnta do that to me? My lord, I was just drivin' aloeng and *peeng!*—there come that ol' bullet—right through *here*"—he put his finger through the hole—"an' hit right *here*—see that ol' dint? An' I heard it rattle around but now I cain't find it. Expect it might of fell out when I opened the door. Say, do you have a flashlight?"

Joe didn't. "Listen, what makes you sure it was a bullet? Couldn't it've been, say, a pebble that some car kicked up passing the other way?" Joe suggested.

The other man looked at him with an outraged expression that the shooting (if that was what it was) had failed to produce. "*Pebble?* Why, that wasn't no—now, you look here! No, never mind, you git aloeng about your own business. *I'm* goin' a drive in and *ree*port this to the Shurf. *Pebble! Oh,* my lord!"

Joe Gunnarson parked his car at the foot of the hill behind the house and climbed up the narrow path. Keith was lying on the floor in the living room, watching television. Ella poked at a pot on the stove, as if with intent to maim. Jody squatted in the doorway between the living room and the kitchen, sniffling.

"Funny thing happened as I was coming along the new part of the road," Joe said.

Keith said, "Ha, ha," his voice level, his face blank.

"You see, Joe? You see what I mean? That's how he is, only worse, the whole day long—fresh," moaned Ella. And little Jody kept reaching his hands for the piece of candy his father had brought "for after supper" until finally he spilled his milk. Joe pushed him back firmly and Jody began to cry.

"What do you want from the kid?" Keith asked. "He's hardly two years old. Get off his back, will you?" The little boy glared at his father. Joe sighed. After a minute he praised the supper (lying like a rug), but Ella just made an impatient noise. He went to bed early, but when he got up afterward, Keith was still on the living-room floor, smoking, watching the Late Late Show. And Ella, it turned out, was still in no better mood. Joe sighed again and went back to sleep.

Gunnarson worked for the J. F. Guernsey Corporation, an outfit which prepared and packaged dried fruit and dehydrated vegetables for manufacturers of other food products. It was a fairly small outfit—there were only four foremen, and Joe was one of them. In the row of big barnlike buildings Joe was happy and felt more at home than in his own house, though he didn't like to face that fact and pushed the thought away whenever it occurred to him.

"Funny thing happened to me last night when I was driving along the new part of the road," he said to the other foremen as they changed into their working clothes.

"Funny thing happened," he confided to the waitress at the lunchroom. It wasn't till he finished telling it to old Mr. Guernsey himself that a little voice between his ears said: Say, you're getting a lot of use out of this little incident. His face twisted as he had to admit it was true, and all he could think of in defense was to ask himself: Well, what else is there to talk about? They don't want to hear about my troubles. But it bothered him, so instead he started a conversation with the boss about cars.

"I see you got a last year's Chevy, just the same as mine, Mr. Guernsey," he said. "They sure get dusty—cars, I mean, about this time of year, and the whole road not all fixed yet. Why don't you get Manuel to give it a good cleanup?"

The old man pursed his mouth. "I *could* tell you that when I want your advice I'll ask for it," he began.

"Aw, now I—"

"But I know you mean well, Joe. So I'll just put it like this: at my age and in my position I can afford not to give a damn."

"Okay, Mr. G., I only—"

"If I want to spit on the floor, I spit on the floor. If I want to go without a tie, I go without a tie. And if I want to let my car get dusty, why, I *let* it get dusty."

"Okay, Mr. G., you're a hunderd percent right. Sorry I—"

"And now let's see the new onions that just came in." Mr. Guernsey closed the subject.

It wasn't till the day's work was finished that Joe gave another thought to the previous day's incident. It was in the shower that Bob La Motta, another foreman, mentioned it. Over the splashing and stomping and raucous yelling and singing Bob called over, "Hey, Joe! This old guy you were telling us about? Claim he had a *bullet* shot through his car and you claim, no, it was a pebble?"

Squeezing water out of his eyes, Joe yelled back, "I didn't say it *was* a pebble, I—"

" 'O Roe-za rosa Sanantone!' "

Gesturing to Bob that he couldn't hear what he was saying because of the noise, Joe finished his shower, dried, and dressed. La Motta came over and said, "So you were wrong, Joe. The deputies, they say it *was* a bullet."

Joe said that deputies had been known to be wrong before. Bob nodded sagely. *He* knew that. "But it happened again today. Lady from the city. Just driving along and—wham! Right through both back windows—a *bullet!* You can't mistake a bullethole in glass."

That was the second one.

The next day there were three more.

For the next two days the deputies scouted the hills to see who was—or who could be—sniping at cars on the road below. The answer as to who it could be was that it could be anybody. There were miles of road and many more miles of hills. But as to who actually was doing the sniping, they learned nothing.

For those two days and for two days after that nothing happened. And on the day after *that* someone fired six bullets into four different automobiles up and down the valley.

"Who in hell could be doing a thing like that?" Joe wondered aloud.

Ella had a prompt reply. "Some bum," she said. "The woods are full of them. They think the world owes them a living."

Keith swore. "Oh, get off my *back*, will ya?" he demanded.

"You going to let him talk to me like that?" Ella asked shrilly. And the battle was on again. Joe felt he'd had enough of it and made up his mind to ask Mr. Guernsey to find Keith a job even if it was uncertain how long he'd be able to hold it before he was drafted. No matter how low the pay, Joe would insist that his brother accept the job.

At least it would get him out of the house, give Ella a rest from quarreling with her brother-in-law, and let her pay more attention to the little boy. It would be nice to hear the kid laugh for a change instead of crying or whining. It was almost funny the way the same expression—pettish, annoyed, aggrieved—seemed to be on the faces of both uncle and nephew so much of the time, exaggerating the family resemblance between them.

"I think he must be a crackpot," Joe said, deliberately ignoring what had just passed between his wife and his brother. And the next day he wasn't surprised to see that the newspapers seemed to agree. Even the city newspapers had given it a three-column headline: *Who Is the Mad Sniper of the Valley?*

There were two uniformed deputies in the lunchroom one day during the week and Joe brought the matter up, asking them what they thought.

A thin sad-looking deputy said he thought maybe the papers were right. "Guy'd hafta be outa his mind to do a thing like that," he said. "He coulda killed somebody! I think it must be like they say, some poor fella like this here Mad Bomber back East that time, he figures he's got a kind of a grievance, and his mind snapped. Or maybe he was cracked all the time, only it took a nincident a some sort to bring it out inny open. If he'd only write a *note!* A *letter!* Then we could trap him like the Mad—"

The waitress pointed out that Jack the Ripper wrote enough notes to paper the walls at Scotland Yard, but they still never caught him. But the thin sad deputy said, "Yeah, well, but that was *years* ago, before the First World's War. Today—"

However, the other deputy, a heavier man with a small steady smile on his ruddy face, he didn't agree with his colleague or the papers.

"You want *my* opinion," he said, offering it without waiting to hear if it was wanted or not, "it's some punk kid. Nobuddy's doing it for revenge. If they was good enough ta hit the doggone ottamobiles, they'd be a good enough shot to of *killed* somebuddy by now. Right? No, it's some punk kid doing it for thrills, *my* opinion. Like playin' 'Chicken' with these hotrods. Prob'ly tryinna see how close they can git to hittin' the driver or the passenger without ackshly doin' it. Punk kids," he said, not stopping smiling. "Too soft onn'm. Otta bring back the wippin' post. Otta have one a them big ol' leather belts with brass studs in it. Git some a these punk kids," he said, smiling, "strip 'm down, an' git some blood out of 'm. Make 'm scream. Otta—"

But the waitress said he would make her scream in a minute, so would he please stop-pit? And the deputy, his smile neither larger nor smaller, said, "Why, sure."

Joe was about to ask Mr. Guernsey, after lunch, about a job for Keith, but the old man started talking first, and what was his theory? The same as the thin deputy's. Only Mr. G. had carried it a step further.

"Wouldn't be a bit surprised," he said, pinker than usual with the power of his idea, "but what it could be somebody who was kicked off his land when they put the new road through. Lot of people weren't a bit happy about that, you remember, Joe? Of course, in a way—now, don't get me wrong—but in a way you can't blame some of them. I'm not condoning violence, you understand. And we did need the new road—"

"We sure did," Joe said. "Before, I never knew if I was going to be late for work or not unless I started real early; or *when* I was going to get home. But now it's just like clockwork. Oh. Excuse me, Mr. G."

After a second the old man went on to say, "But it wasn't really fair the way they paid for it. They figured that every house of such-and-such a size is worth so much money. And that's all they'd *pay*. Didn't matter what improvements you'd put into the house—new paint, carpentry, plumbing, while your neighbor was letting his own place run down. No, same price for the both of you. So maybe somebody figured he was cheated and he got to brooding and now he's taking it out on just anyone who uses the new road."

Joe nodded slowly. "I wouldn't be surprised. You think you ought to tell the sheriff so maybe he could check up on everybody whose property was condemned for the new road?"

Old Mr. Guernsey's eyes and mouth grew o-shaped at the thought. "Do you suppose I really should, Joe?"

Joe's slow nod continued. "Well, I hate to be the cause of getting somebody into trouble, but—case like this? Yes. I really think so, uh huh."

And so he forgot all about asking about a job for Keith.

The next morning he got to work to find the place all excited, and the sheriff's officers' cars in the yard. "Burglary," Bob La Motta told him. "Broke into the office and smashed the cashbox, rifled the desks, stole a couple of typewriters and a radio and an adding machine and I don't know what else."

They heard old Mr. G. saying to the deputies loudly and sort of upset, "Of *course* I have ideas who did it. You really want to hear them or you going to give me the brush-off the way you did yesterday when I told you my ideas about the Mad Sniper?"

At this Joe immediately quit hanging around and summoned his men to work. If the boss had followed his advice and the result was that the boss was only embarrassed and made to look like a fool—why, then Joe didn't want to call any more attention to himself than he had to. He fell to on the peach-drying detail. Too bad, and it still seemed like a sound idea. However—

However, the solution to the burglary didn't take the sheriff's deputies very long, and this tended to diminish somewhat the value of the ex-homeowner's revenge theory in Joe's mind.

Not long before lunch, Manuel, the porter, buzzed up to the second floor on which the sulfur rooms were located and came over to Joe and his crew, very excited. "They caught 'im! The burglar! And you'll never guess who it was. Go ahead, guess."

"Miss Ponsonby?" someone offered, raising a laugh. Miss Ponsonby, who still wore a shirtwaist with a watch pinned to it, had been with the outfit as long as its founder, and was a model of all possible rectitude.

"No!" said Manuel disgustedly. "What're you, crazy? Miss Ponsonby! No—well, you wouldn't guess, so I'll tell you. It was Ray!"

This was certainly a surprise. Ray, the bookkeeper, a quiet young man who lived with his mother and played the organ in church. It was almost as unbelievable as if it had been Miss Ponsonby.

Manuel, his round face lit up by his news, explained. It seemed that Ray had been stealing money from the firm "all along." Why? No one knew exactly—at least, Manuel didn't know exactly—although several ribald and rather unlikely explanations were put forward by Joe's crew. The boss had caught him and had made him sign a confession.

He said to Ray, "I haven't made up my mind yet what I'll do."

The matter, not unnaturally, had preyed on Ray's mind, and he finally made up *his* mind what to do: steal the signed confession, quit his job, and deny everything he had admitted about his original crime.

Glancing into the sulfur room to see how the peaches were drying, Joe half asked and half suggested, "So he figured that while he was at it he might as well take the typewriters, the radio, and the other stuff."

But, according to Manuel, this wasn't just the way it was. "Ray said he figgered like this: If all he stole was the dockiment, they'd right away know who it was, see. So he figgered like this: If I steal alotta *other* stuff, they'll think it was a *real* burglary and so they won't suspeck *me*. See? He figgered like this—"

However poor Ray had figured, it threw his employer off the trail only long enough for him to discover the missing confession—which was, after all, an item most unlikely for any "real burglar" to have bothered with. And Mr. G. told his suspicion to the deputies, who (this time) listened. And Ray, jerked back into the *real* real world as soon as the uniforms confronted him, admitted All. He was now down at the jail, and so was the boss.

"He gunna press charges?"

"He say he hasn't made up his mind what to do yet."

Mr. Guernsey was reported to have remained in doubt all afternoon, and then decided it was his duty to discuss the matter with Ray's mother. Just a few minutes before quitting time he took off in his dusty car and headed down the valley for the home shared by Ray and his mother.

In the shower Bob La Motta asked Joe if he heard the latest about the Mad Sniper. "Whoever's car gits hit with a silver bullet is intitled to a free ticket to a vampire movie!"

Joe's mind was full of thoughts as he drove home in the

thickening blue dusk. So once again he almost missed observing a car by the side of the road—only this time someone was waving a flashlight. And this time he knew whose car it was.

"Keep moving, buddy, just keep on—I said, keep moving!"

"But that's my boss's car, Mr. Guernsey's, isn't it? He all right?"

The light was flashed in his eyes and stayed in his eyes. Joe, even before shading them, had recognized the voice of the heavy deputy and could imagine the smile. Then the light went back to the road.

"No, he ain't all right. He's dead. One a them bullets got 'im. You work for 'm, huh? What's *your* name?" He talked right on through Joe's cry of shock. A siren sounded. Another sheriff's car, light blinking rapidly and redly, came speeding down the road.

The old man lay fallen forward. Joe couldn't see his face. He felt this was just as well. "Bound to happen," said the thin sad deputy. "Sooner or later, you keep shooting at cars, you bound to kill somebody."

An idea sprang fully formed into Joe's mind, and without realizing, he began to think it out, aloud. "Suppose it wasn't an accident," he said. "Suppose a man wanted to kill a particular person, but he wasn't in a hurry. Suppose he wanted to cover his tracks in advance. Couldn't he start shooting at cars, not to hit anybody, but just to get across the idea that somebody—a maniac, maybe—was shooting at random? And then, when he *did* kill the man he wanted to, maybe then everybody *would* think it was an accident. Isn't that possible?"

No one made an answer. "But who," Joe cried, feeling genuine grief at the old man's death, unaware that he was asking the traditional, almost the ritual question—"Who would want to kill old Mr. Guernsey?"

In the headlights he could now see the half smile on the heavy deputy's face. "Not that sissy who was stealing from him, that's for sure," the officer said. "Besides, he's in jail. *You* worked for him—the old man have a girl friend on the side?"

Angrily Joe snapped, "He's a married man!"—then the sense of tense hit him—*was* a married man. Old Mrs. Guernsey, sweet and slow and childless—and tears formed in Joe's eyes.

The red-faced deputy snorted. "He's a married man! Buddy, you otta git wise! What's that gotta do with the Grand Army? Well, never mind, we'll find out. You better git movin'. We don't want no traffic block here. Come on, *come* on—"

Joe drove off. By and by he stopped seeing the road, except through a mist, half of grief, half of anger. He parked at the foot of the hill, knowing it was done clumsily, but not caring. He floundered his way up the path and threw open the door, aware that tears were running down his cheeks.

Ella and Keith were there, as usual, and he didn't know which one cried out first at seeing him come in, weeping. He felt half ashamed at feeling gratified that they were both so obviously upset at seeing him that way. They love me after all, he thought, moving forward and trying to smile at them to show he was really all right. Despite what they act like most of the time, they really love me.

It was a quick thought. It was replaced almost at once by another. What is the rifle doing in the kitchen where the baby can get at it? he was about to say. But then Keith got up, running, and he heard Ella scream at him, "You said he was dead! You said he was dead!"

And Joe looked at his wife's face and he looked at his brother's face and he understood what she meant and he understood everything that had happened and had been happening for quite some time.

But he didn't stand still as the understanding hit him. He moved, moved quickly, beating both Keith and Ella to the rifle, which was quite the worst piece of luck Keith and Ella had ever had.

THE MEMORIAL SERVICE

by Michael Innes

The memorial service for Christopher Brockbank, Q.C., who had died in an air disaster, was attended by family and dignitaries, the latter including Ministers of the Crown and the Lord Chief Justice. While the bishop was eulogizing the late Queen's Counsel, a strange event took place—perhaps the strangest event ever to occur during a memorial service of otherwise unflawed decorum.

You will find this story about Sir John Appleby, retired Commissioner of Metropolitan Police, a case of what might be called "macabre pertinacity." And as you might expect from Michael Innes, it is amusing, intelligent, sophisticated—in a phrase, "a civilized detective story" . . .

IN the fashionable church of St. Boniface in the Fields (mysteriously so named, since it was in the heart of London) a large and distinguished congregation was assembled to give thanks for the life of the late Christopher Brockbank, Q.C. The two newspaper reporters at the door, discreetly clad in unjournalistic black, had been busy receiving and recording all sorts of weighty names.

It was the sort of occasion on which sundry persons explained themselves as "representing" sundry other persons even more august than themselves or sundry institutions, corporations, charities, and learned bodies with which the deceased important individual had been associated.

Legal luminaries predominated. An acute observer (and there was at least one such present) might have remarked that a number of these did not settle in their pews, kneel, and bury their noses devoutly in their cupped hands without an exchange of glances in which a hint of whimsical humor fleetingly flickered. *All this for Chris Brockbank!* they appeared to be telling each other. *Just what would he have made of it?*

Sir John Appleby (our acute observer) was representing his successor as Commissioner of Metropolitan Police. For Brockbank long ago, and before he had transformed himself from a leading silk into a vigorous and somewhat eccentric legal reformer, had acknowledged his connections with Scotland Yard, and this fact had to be duly made known today.

Appleby possessed only a vague memory of the man, so that a certain artificiality attended his presence at the service. It hadn't seemed decent, however, to decline a request which was unlikely to occupy him for much more than twenty minutes—or thirty-five if one counted the time spent in scrambling into uniform and out again.

It would have been hard to tell that it wasn't something quite different—even a wedding—that was about to be transacted here. Gravity now and then there had to be, but on the whole a cheerful demeanor is held not improper on such occasions. The good fight had been fought, and there was nothing here for tears, nothing to wail or knock the breast for. Six weeks had passed, moreover, since Christopher Brockbank's death, and anybody much stunned by grief had thus had a substantial period in which to recover.

Whether there had been many such—that is, those stunned by grief—appeared doubtful. Brockbank had been unmarried, and now the front pew reserved for relations was occupied only by two elderly women, habited in old-fashioned and no doubt frequently exhibited mourning, whom somebody had identified for Appleby in a whisper as cousins of the dead man. If anything, they seemed to be rather enjoying their role. It was to be conjectured that they owned some quite obscure, although genteel, situation in society.

The truth is, nobody had ever heard of any Brockbank until Christopher, Q.C., had come along. In some corner of the globe, Appleby vaguely understood, there was a brother, Adrian Brockbank, who had also distinguished himself—as a lone yachtsman, it seemed. But the wandering Adrian had not, apparently, hoisted himself into a jet for the occasion.

The congregation had got to its feet and was listening to the singing of a psalm. It was well worth listening to, since the words were striking in themselves and the choir of St. Boniface's was justly celebrated. The congregation was, of course, in the expectation of playing a somewhat passive part. At such services it is understood that there is to be comparatively little scope for what, in other context, would be called audience participation.

Appleby looked about him. It was impressive that the Lord Chief Justice had turned up, and that he was flanked by two Ministers of the Crown. There were also two or three socially prominent dowagers, who were perhaps recalling passages with Christopher when he had been young as well as gay: these glanced from time to time in benevolent amusement at the two old creatures in the front pew.

Among the clergy, and wearing a very plain but very golden

pectoral cross, was a bishop who would presently ascend the pulpit and deliver a brief address. In the nave two elderly clubmen (as they ought probably to be called) of subdued raffish appearance were putting their heads together in muttered colloquy. These must connect with yet another aspect of the dead man's dead life: they were presumably laying a wager with one another on just how many minutes the eulogy would take.

The service proceeded with unflawed decorum. An anthem was sung. The bishop, ceremoniously conducted to his elevated perch, began his address. He lost no time in launching upon a character analysis of the late Queen's Counsel; it would have been possible to imagine an hourglass of the diminutive sort used to time the boiling of eggs as standing on the pulpit's edge beside him. The character analysis, although touching lightly once or twice on some endearing foible, was highly favorable in the main. The dead man, disposed in his private life to charity, humility, gentleness, and the study of English madrigals, had in his professional character been dedicated, stern, courageous, and passionately devoted to upholding, clarifying, and reforming his country's laws.

It was now that something slightly untoward occurred. A late arrival entered the church. An elderly man with a finely trimmed gray mustache, he was dressed with the exactest propriety for the occasion; that he was accustomed to such appearances was evident in the mere manner in which he contrived to carry a black silk hat, an umbrella, and a pair of gray kid gloves dexterously in his left hand while receiving from the hovering verger the printed service-sheet.

Not many of those present thought it becoming to turn their heads to see what was happening. But nobody, in fact, was cheated of a sight of the newcomer for long. He might have been expected (however accustomed to some position of prominence) to slip modestly into a pew near the west door. But this he did not do. He walked with quiet deliberation up the central aisle—very much (Appleby thought) as if he were an integral and expected part of the ritual which he was in fact indecorously troubling. He walked right up to the front pew and sat down beside Christopher Brockbank's female relatives.

There could be only one explanation. Here was the missing Adrian, brother of the dead man—to whom, indeed, in Appleby's recollection, he bore a strong family likeness. Perhaps the plane from Singapore or the Bahamas or wherever had been delayed; perhaps fog had caused it to be diverted from Heathrow to a more distant airport; thus rendered unavoidably tardy in his appearance, this much-traveled Brockbank had decided that he must afford a general indication of his presence, and move to the support of the ladies of the family, even at the cost of rendering an effect of considerable disturbance. It must have been, Appleby thought sympathetically, a difficult decision to make.

The bishop's eulogy went on. The new arrival listened with close attention to what must now be the tail end of it. And everybody else ought to have been doing the same thing.

But this was not so. The Lord Chief Justice had hastily removed one pair of spectacles, donned another, and directed on the fraternal appearance in the front pew the kind of gaze which for many years he had been accustomed to bring to bear on occupants of the dock at the Central Criminal Court. One of the Cabinet Ministers was looking frightened—which is something no Cabinet Minister should ever do.

Two of the dowagers were talking to one another in agitated and semi-audible whispers; a third appeared to be on the verge of hysterics. As for the bishop, he was so upset that he let the typescript of his carefully prepared allocution flutter to the floor below, with the result that he was promptly reduced to a peroration in terms of embarrassed improvisation.

But before even this was concluded, the brother of the late Christopher Brockbank behaved very strangely. He stood up, moved into the aisle, and bowed. He bowed, not toward the altar (which would have been very proper in itself), but to the bishop in his pulpit (which wasn't proper at all). He then turned, and retreated as he had come. Only, whereas on arriving he had kept his eyes decently directed to the floor, on departing he bowed to right and left as he walked—much like a monarch withdrawing from an audience chamber through a double file of respectful courtiers.

He paused only once, and that was beside the uniformed Appleby, on whom he directed a keen but momentary glance, before politely handing Appleby his service-sheet. Then he resumed his stately progress down the aisle until he reached the church door and vanished.

Somebody would possibly have followed a man so patently deranged, and therefore conceivably a danger to himself or others, had not the Rector of St. Boniface's thought it expedient to come to the rescue of the flustered bishop by promptly embarking on the prayers which, together with a hymn, were to conclude the service. These prayers (which are full of tremendous things) it would have been indecent to disturb. But a hymn is only a hymn, and it was quite plain that numerous members of the congregation were giving utterance not to the somewhat jejune sentiments this prayer proposed, but to various expressions, delivered more or less *sotto voce*, of indignation and stupefaction.

Moreover, the Lord Chief Justice was gesturing. He was gesturing at Appleby in a positively threatening way which Appleby understood perfectly. If Appleby bolted from this untoward and unseemly incident instead of reacting to it in some policemanlike fashion he would pretty well be treated as in contempt of court. This was why he found himself standing on the pavement outside St. Boniface's a couple of minutes later.

"Get *into* this thing," the Lord Chief Justice said imperiously, and pointed to his Rolls-Royce. "You, too," he said to the Home Secretary (who was one of the Ministers who had been giving thanks for the life of the deceased Brockbank). "We can't let such an *outrage* pass."

"Outrage?" Appleby queried, as he resignedly sat down in the car. "Wasn't it simply that Christopher Brockbank's brother is mildly dotty—nothing more?"

"Adrian mildly dotty! Damn it, Appleby, didn't you realize what he was doing? He was *impersonating* Christopher—nothing else. The mustache, those clothes, his entire bearing—they weren't remotely Adrian. They were Christopher *tout court*. Didn't you notice the reaction of those who knew Christopher well? Both those Brockbank brothers were given to brutal and tasteless practical jokes, but this was the *most* brutal and tasteless of the lot."

"They may well have been. In fact, I seem to remember hearing something of the sort about them. But if Adrian judged it funny to get himself up like Christopher while attending Christopher's memorial service, that seems to me entirely his own affair. I shall be surprised, Pomfret, if you can tell me he has broken the law." Appleby smiled at the eminent judge. "Although, of course, it wouldn't do for me not to believe what you say."

"I don't believe it was Adrian at all. It was Christopher's ghost." The Home Secretary endeavored to offer this in a whimsical manner. It was he who had been looking patently frightened ten minutes before, and he was trying to carry this off lightly now. "To turn up as a ghost for something like one's own funeral is a joke good enough to gratify any purgatorial spirit, I'd suppose. What we've witnessed is the kind of thing those psychic chaps call a veridical phantasm of the dead."

"I haven't set eyes on Christopher Brockbank for thirty years," Appleby said, "and his wandering brother Adrian I've never seen before. You say this well-groomed person bowing himself down the aisle in that crazy fashion was *very* like Christopher?"

"Very."

"Thoroughly scandalous," Lord Pomfret said. "*Not* to be tolerated. Appleby, you *must* look into it."

"My dear Chief Justice, I have no standing in such matters. This uniform is merely ornamental. I'm retired, as you know."

"Come, come." The Home Secretary laid a hand on Appleby's arm in a manner designed as wholly humorous. "Do as you're told, my boy."

"Do you know—perhaps I will. The ghost, or whatever, did distinguish me a little, after all. He stopped and handed me this." Appleby was still holding a superfluous service-sheet. "It was almost as if he was passing me the ball."

Much in the way of hard fact about Christopher Brockbank turned out not at all easy to come by. He proved to have been surprisingly wealthy. As the older of the two brothers he had inherited a substantial fortune, and to this he had added a second fortune earned at the Bar. Uninterested in becoming a judge, he had retired comparatively early, and for the greater part of the year lived in something like seclusion in the south of France. It was understood that this seclusion was in the interest of uninterrupted labor on a work of jurisprudence directed to some system of legal reform. The accident in which he had lost his life had been a large-scale air disaster in the Alpes-Maritimes. Surprisingly for a Q.C., he had died intestate, and his affairs were going to take a good deal of clearing up.

It was on the strength of no more than this amount of common knowledge, together with only a modicum of private inquiry, that Appleby eventually called on a bank manager in the City. "I understand from an official source," Appleby began blandly, "that the late Mr. Brockbank kept his private account in this country at your branch."

"That is certainly true." The bank manager nodded amiably. He had very clear views, Appleby conjectured, on what information was confidential and what was not. "He used to spare a few minutes to chat with me on the occasion of his quite infrequent visits. A delightful man."

"No doubt. It has occurred to me that, in addition to keeping an account with you, he may have been in the habit of lodging documents and so forth for safekeeping."

"Ah."

"I know you maintain some sort of strongroom for such purposes and I suppose your customers can hire strongboxes of one convenient size or another?"

"Yes, indeed, Sir John. Should you yourself ever have occasion—"

"Thank you. Brockbank did this?"

"Sir John, may I say that, when inquiries of this sort are judged expedient for one reason or another, a request—and it can scarcely be more than a request—is commonly preferred by one of the Law Officers of the Crown?" The manager paused, and found that this produced no more than a composed nod. "But no doubt there is little point in being sticky in the matter. Let me consult my appropriate file." He unlocked a drawer and rummaged. "Yes," he said. "It would appear that Brockbank had such a box."

"His executors haven't yet inquired about it?"

"Seemingly not."

"I'd like you to open it and let me examine the contents."

"My dear Sir John!" The manager was genuinely scandalized. "You can't believe—"

"But only in the most superficial way. I have an officer waiting in your outer office who would simply turn over these documents unopened and apply a very simple test to the envelopes or whatever the outer coverings may prove to be. He will not take, and I shall not take, the slightest interest in their contents."

For a moment the manager's hand hovered over his telephone. An appeal to higher authority—perhaps to the awful authority of the General Manager himself—was plainly in his mind. Then he took a deep breath.

"Very well," he said. "I suppose an adequate discretion will be observed?"

"Oh, most decidedly," Appleby said.

"So that, for a start, is that," Appleby murmured to the Lord Chief Justice an hour later.

"But surely, my dear Appleby, he would scarcely recognize you at a glance? The years have been passing over us, after all."

"That is all too true. But the point isn't material. There I was, dressed up for that formal occasion in the uniform of a high-ranking officer of the Metropolitan Police. He felt he could trust me to tumble to the thing."

"And you are quite sure? *Absolutely* sure? The fingerprints on that service-sheet *were* identical?"

"Beyond a shadow of doubt. Christopher Brockbank always deposited or withdrew documents from that strongbox in the presence of an official of the bank who was in a position to identify him beyond question. The man who attended Christopher Brockbank's memorial service was Christopher Brockbank himself."

"And he *wanted* the fact to be known?"

"He wanted the fact to be known."

"It makes *no* sense."

"What it makes is very good *nonsense.* And there is one kind of nonsense that Brockbank is on record as having a fondness for—the kind of nonsense one calls a practical joke. And I expect he had money on it."

"Money!" Lord Pomfret was outraged.

"Say a wager with one of his own kidney."

"We have been most *notoriously* abused." Something formidable had come into Pomfret's voice. One could almost imagine that high above his head in the chill London air the scales were trembling in the hand of the blindfolded figure of Justice which crowns the Central Criminal Court.

"I wouldn't deny it for a moment. But I come back to a point I've made before. You can't send a man down, Chief Justice, for attending his own memorial service. It just isn't a crime."

"But there must be *something* very like a crime in the hinterland of this impertinent buffoonery." Lord Pomfret had flushed darkly. "Steps have been taken to certify as dead a man who isn't dead at all."

"In a foreign country, and in the context of some hideous and, no doubt, vastly confused air crash. Possibly without any actual knowledge of the thing on Brockbank's own part. Possibly as a consequence of innocent error—error on top of which he has merely piled an audacious joke. A singularly tasteless joke, perhaps, but not one with jail at the end of it."

"We can get him. We can get him for *something*."

"I don't know what to make of that from a legal point of view." The retired Commissioner of Police made no bones about glancing at the Lord Chief Justice of England in frank amusement. "And there will be a good deal of laughter in court, wouldn't you say?"

"You're damn well *right!*" Not altogether unexpectedly, Lord Pomfret was suddenly laughing himself. "But what the devil is he going to do *now?* Just how is he proposing to come alive again?"

"With great respect, m'lud, I suggest your lordship is in some confusion." Appleby, watching his august interlocutor dive for a whiskey decanter and a siphon, was laughing, too. "Christopher Brockbank *is* alive. He's in a position, so to speak, in which no further action is necessary."

"Nor from us either? We *leave* him to it?"

"That I wouldn't say." Appleby was grave again. "I confess to being a little uneasy about the whole affair."

"The deuce you do!" Now on his feet, the Lord Chief Justice held the decanter poised in air. "Say when."

"Only a finger," Appleby said. "And I'll continue to look into the thing."

"With *discretion,* my dear fellow." Pomfret was suddenly almost like the bank manager.

"Oh, most decidedly," Appleby said.

Retired Police Commissioners don't go fossicking in France, and through the courtesy of his successor, Appleby received reports in due season. Hard on the air crash an elderly and distressed English gentleman had appeared on the scene of the disaster in a chauffeur-driven car. Presenting himself to the *chef de gendarmerie* who was in control of the rescue operations, he had explained that he was Adrian Brockbank, and that he had motored straight from Nice on hearing of the accident, since he had reason to suppose that his older brother, Mr. Christopher Brockbank, Q.C., had been on board the ill-fated plane. Could he be given any information about this?

It was explained to Mr. Adrian Brockbank that much confusion inevitably prevailed; that, as often happened on such sad occasions, there was no assurance that an entirely reliable list of passengers' names existed; and that certain necessarily painful and distressing attempts at identification were even then going on. Would Mr. Adrian Brockbank care to . . . ?

The inquirer steeled himself, and cared. Eventually he had been almost irrationally reluctant to admit the sad truth. A ring on the charred finger of one of the grim exhibits he had, indeed, formally deposed as being his brother's ring. But it seemed so tiny a piece of evidence! Might there not be more? A relevant article of baggage, perhaps, that had in part escaped the heat of the conflagration?

Not at the moment, it was explained to Mr. Adrian Brockbank. But something of that kind might yet turn up. As so often happened, debris was probably scattered over a very wide area. There was to be a systematic search at first light. With this information Mr. Adrian Brockbank and his chauffeur had departed to a nearby hotel for the night. And in the morning the somber expectation had been fulfilled.

Christopher Brockbank's brief case had been discovered, along with other detritus, in a field nearly a quarter of a mile away; and it contained a number of recent personal papers as well as Christopher's passport. Whereupon Adrian, formally identifying himself by producing his own passport and the testimony of his chauffeur, satisfied the requirements of French law by making a deposition before a magistrate. After that he made decent arrangements for the disposal of what could be called his brother's remains and then departed as he had come.

Such had been the report on the highly unsatisfactory death of Christopher Brockbank, Q.C.

All this, Appleby told himself, didn't remain exactly obscure once you took a straight look at it. Just as it wasn't Adrian who had turned up at the memorial service, so it hadn't been Adrian who had turned up at the grisly aftermath of that aerial holocaust. It had been Christopher on both occasions—and it was impossible to say that throughout the whole affair Adrian had played any positive role at all.

This was bizarre—but there was something that was mildly alarming as well. Christopher had *waited.* Equipped with a passport in the name of his brother, equipped no doubt with a passport in his own name, equipped with the brief case which he would eventually toss into an appropriate field—equipped with all this, Christopher had waited for a sufficiently substantial disaster within, say, a couple of hours' hard motoring of his French residence. He had certainly had to wait for months, more probably for years. A thoroughly macabre pertinacity had marked the attaining of his practical joke.

And hadn't the joker overreached himself? Could any place in society remain for a man who, with merely frivolous intent, had deliberately identified an unknown dead body as his own? It seemed not surprising that Christopher hadn't been heard of again since he had walked down that aisle, graciously bowing to a bewildered congregation. Perhaps he had very understandably lost his nerve.

But even if Adrian didn't come into the story at all, where was Adrian? He was almost certainly Christopher's heir, and yet even Christopher's English solicitors appeared to know nothing of his whereabouts. Perhaps they were just being more successfully cagey than that bank manager. Certainly they had, for the moment, nothing to say—except that Mr. Adrian Brockbank spent most of his time sailing the seven seas.

Appleby was coming to feel, not very rationally, that time was important. He had told Lord Pomfret he was uneasy—which had been injudicious, since he couldn't have explained why. Pomfret, however, had refrained from questioning him. And now he had the same uneasy feeling.

No Brockbank had died. But two Brockbanks might be described as lying low. There was about this the effect of an ominous lull.

And then Christopher Brockbank turned up.

He turned up on Appleby's urban doorstep and was shown in—looking precisely like the man who had put on the turn in St. Boniface's.

"My dear Appleby," he said, "I have ventured to call for the purpose of offering you an apology." Brockbank's address was easy and familiar; he might have been talking to someone he ran into every second week in one club or another.

"I don't need an apology. But I could do with an explanation."

"Ah, that—yes, indeed. But the apology must come first—for dragging you into the little joke. It started up in my mind like a creation, you know, just as I was walking out of that church. There on the service-sheet were my fingerprints, and there were you, who if handed the thing could be trusted to do as I have no doubt you have done. A sublimely simple way of proving I was still in the land of the living."

"I am delighted you are still with us." Appleby said this on a note of distinguishable irony. "And I accept your apology. And now, may the explanation of the little joke follow?"

"The explanation is that it has been designed as rather more than a little joke. My idea has been, in fact, to make a real impact on the complacency of some who are satisfied with the absurd inadequacy of many of our laws. That old fool Pomfret, for example. After all, I have been a legal reformer for some time."

"I see." Appleby really did see. "This exploit has been in the interest of highlighting the fact, or contention, that the law is hazardously lax as to adequately verifying the identity of deceased persons—that sort of thing?"

"Precisely that sort of thing. I shall have established—strikingly because of my ingenious prank—that in France and England alike—"

"Quite so, Mr. Brockbank. We need not linger on the worth of your intentions. But surely you have reflected of late on the extent to which you are likely to be in trouble, under French legal jurisdiction, if not under English? The deception you carried out on the occasion of that air disaster—"

"My dear Appleby, what can you be thinking of? That was my brother Adrian, was it not? This all begins from his proposing to bring off a better joke against *me* than I ever brought off against *him.* It is on the record, I suppose, that we have both rather gone in for that sort of thing. He was going to confront me with the pleasant position of my being legally dead. Well, I capped his joke by, you may say, concurring. I attended—I hope in a suitably devout manner—my own funeral and my own memorial service. So the laugh is going to be on him."

"Mr. Brockbank, I have seldom come across so impudent an imposture!" Appleby suddenly found himself as outraged as the Lord Chief Justice had been. "Whether your brother has, or has not, been remotely involved in this freakish and indecent affair I do not know. But I *do* know that six weeks ago in France you presented yourself as that brother on an occasion at which such clowning would have been wholly inconceivable"—Appleby paused, then took a calculated plunge—"to anybody bearing the character of a gentleman."

"I withdraw my apology." Christopher Brockbank had gone extremely pale. "As for what you allege—prove it. Or get somebody with a legitimate concern in my affairs to prove it. *You* have none."

"Then I scarcely see why you should be calling on me—except to discover how far I have penetrated to the truth of this nonsense. I am prepared to believe that you had some serious intention in the way of exposing the weakness of certain legal processes. I accept that notions of what is permissibly funny may differ as between one generation, or one coterie, and another. But your present pack of lies about the conduct of your own brother—lies which I must now suppose you are intending to make public—is a little too steep for me. Just what are you going to say to your brother when you meet?"

"I haven't decided yet. But I must do so, since I am on the point of running down to see him now."

"I beg your pardon?" Appleby stared incredulously at his visitor.

"I said I'm off to see Adrian. I must persuade him I'm not as dead as he has tried to represent me. In a way, he doesn't know that he has not, so to speak, liquidated me quite successfully. More than six weeks have gone by since his little turn over my supposed body and I haven't—so far as he knows—given a chirp. That must be puzzling him, wouldn't you say?"

"Possibly. Do I understand that your only public appearance has been at that deplorable memorial service?"

"Yes, it has. You may simply take it that it has amused me to lie low."

"You appear to me to be in love with your own mortality. Now more than ever it seems rich to die—that sort of thing. What if there's a general feeling, Mr. Brockbank, that your decease was a welcome event? You might have quite a task persuading a malicious world that you *are* alive; that you are *you,* in fact, and not some species of Tichborne Claimant."

"Ah, that's where those fingerprints come in. It's hardly a piece of evidence a conscientious policeman could suppress, eh?"

"No, it is not." Appleby was becoming impatient with this senseless conversation. "If your brother Adrian really played that trick at the scene of the disaster—which I do not believe for a moment—he will be gratified to learn that you have taken the consequences of his joke so seriously as to register your continued existence with the police."

"But I won't tell him what I did with that service-sheet." Christopher Brockbank gave a cunning chuckle. "Not till I'm sure he hasn't some further joke up his sleeve." He got to his feet. "And now I must be off on my brotherly visit."

"Far be it from me to detain you. But may I ask, Mr. Brockbank, where your brother is to be found?"

"Ah, that will doubtless become public property quite soon. Adrian is a minor celebrity in his way. But, just at the moment, I think I'll keep his whereabouts to myself."

The prediction proved accurate. The very next morning's papers carried the news that Adrian Brockbank's yacht had been sighted at anchor off Budleigh Salterton in Devon. It seemed probable that he had arrived unobtrusively in home waters several days earlier.

Appleby endeavored to absorb this as information of only moderate interest. Christopher Brockbank had had his practical joke, and it had involved a breach of the law in France if not in England. He had now gone off to join his nautical brother Adrian and crow over the manner in which he had taken Adrian's identity on himself at the inception of the imposture in the Alpes-Maritimes. Something like that must really be what was in Christopher's mind. And it was all very far from being Appleby's business; he ought to be indifferent as to whether those two professional jokers (as they appeared to have been) decided to laugh or quarrel over the thing. Let them fight it out.

But this line of thought didn't work. Several times in the course of the morning there came back into Appleby's head one particular statement that Christopher had made. It was a statement which just *might* be fraught with a consequence not pretty to think of. At noon Appleby got out his car and drove west.

Budleigh Salterton proved not to have a harbor. A few unimpressive craft were drawn up on a pebbly beach; far away on the horizon tankers and freighters plowed up and down the English Channel. The sea was otherwise empty except for a single yacht riding at anchor rather far out.

Binoculars didn't help to make anything of this. Where one might have expected to read the vessel's name a tarpaulin or small sail had been spread as if to dry. Appleby appealed to a bystander.

"Do you happen to know," he asked, "whose yacht that is?"

"I haven't any idea." The man addressed, although he appeared to be a resident of the place, was plainly without any nautical interest. "It has been here for some days—except that it went out at dusk yesterday evening and I happened to see it return at dawn this morning. But I did hear somebody say there was a rumor the fellow was one of those lone yachtsman types."

"Do you know where I can hire a rowboat?"

"Just down by that groyne, I believe."

"Thank you very much."

"May I come on aboard?" Appleby called out. Adrian Brockbank was very like his brother, even down to the neat gray mustache.

"Not if you're another of those infernal reporters."

"I'm not. I'm an infernal policeman. A retired one."

"You can come up if you like." And Adrian tossed down a small accommodation ladder. He had appeared only momentarily startled.

"Thank you." Appleby climbed and settled himself without ceremony on the gunwale. "Have you had any other visitors lately, Mr. Brockbank?"

"I see you know my name. Only a reporter, as I said. That was yesterday evening. But I persuaded him to clear out."

"What about your brother?"

"I beg your pardon?" Adrian stared.

"Your brother Christopher."

"Good God, Mr.—"

"Appleby. Sir John Appleby. Yes?"

"My brother Christopher was killed six weeks ago in an air crash. Your question is either ignorant or outrageous."

"That remains to be proved, sir. And I gather you have been on some extended cruise or other. Just how did you hear this sad news?"

"*Hear* it? Heaven and earth, man! It was I who actually identified Christopher's body. I'd sailed into Nice and tried to reach him by telephone. They said he was believed to have taken a plane for Paris. Then suddenly there was the news of this—"

"So you identified the body, made certain decent arrangements about it, and then went to sea again. Is that right?"

"It is right. But I'm damned if I know what entitles you—"

"And then, only a few days ago, there was your brother's memorial service at St. Boniface's in London. Do you say you attended it?"

"Certainly I attended it. But as I'd only just berthed here and had to get hold of the right clothes, I was a bit late for the occasion."

"I see. Then you came straight back here?"

"Obviously I did. I don't like fuss. I've been lying low."

"That's something that appears to run in your family. And so, very decidedly, does something else."

"May I ask what that is?" Adrian was now eyeing Appleby narrowly.

"A rash fondness for ingenious but quite vulnerable lies. Mr. Brockbank, your brother Christopher, having somehow got wind of your arrival here at Budleigh, came down yesterday evening and—I don't doubt—rowed out to see you just as I have done. It was something quite out of the blue. I don't know where you've come from, but you certainly haven't been receiving English news on the way. And here, suddenly, was your brother, chock-full of the craziest of his practical jokes. He'd resolved to attend his own memorial service, partly for the sheer hell of it, and partly to dramatize what he considered some sort of loophole in the law. He'd plotted the thing ingeniously enough, and it had involved his impersonating you at the scene of an air crash. He told you all this in exuberant detail. *You* had been made to appear the practical joker—this was the best part of *his* joke—and as a result he was officially dead until he chose to come alive again."

Appleby paused. "Mr. Brockbank," he went on quietly, "you decided that he never *would* so choose."

"This is the most outrageous—"

"Please don't interrupt. What you said to yourself was this: if Christopher wanted to be dead, let him damned well *be* dead—and let his large fortune pass to his next of kin, yourself. It was all so simple, was it not? Lie Number One: *you* had sworn to the identity of the dead man. Lie Number Two: *you* had been just in time for the memorial service. Your story would be simple and plausible. The true story, supposing anybody should tumble to it, would be too fantastic to be believed. Have I succeeded in stating the matter with some succinctness? And accuracy?"

"You have a kind of professional glibness, Sir John." Adrian said this coolly. "I suppose that for most of your days you've been concocting yarns like this. But it won't wash, you know—it won't wash at all. You are reckoning that, at every step, it will be possible to collect some scrap of circumstantial evidence against me, and that these will add up. But they won't—not to anything like the total that would persuade a jury of such nonsense. My poor brother met an accidental death in France and I identified his body—and that's that."

"On the contrary, your brother was murdered by you on this yacht yesterday evening—doubtless sewed up in canvas along with whatever miscellaneous heavy metal objects you could find on board—and thrown over the side, far out at sea, last night."

"Far out at sea?" Adrian repeated the words ironically. "Awkward, that. A body is rather a useful exhibit, is it not, when a thin case has to be proved?"

"Mr. Brockbank, you entirely mistake the matter. There is absolute proof that your brother Christopher, alive and well, attended his own memorial service. It is a proof which, I know, he proposed to withhold from you for a time—which was a pity. But the evidence, which I need not particularize, is safely in my possession."

"Dear me!" Adrian made a casual gesture which somehow didn't match his suddenly alert look and tautened frame. "And is this evidence in the possession of anybody else?"

"Yes, of several people. Otherwise, I'm bound to say, I shouldn't be here alone with you, Mr. Brockbank, in this secluded situation. But it hasn't, I repeat, been evidence in *your* possession. For it wasn't in your brother's mind to mention its existence to you just at present. He was keeping it up *his* sleeve in case you proved to have something further up *your* sleeve. Rather a muzzy notion, perhaps, but understandable when Brockbank is sparring with Brockbank. It is evidence, incidentally, which was entirely and ingeniously devised by your brother himself."

Appleby paused. "I may just say that his fingerprints come into it. Irrefutable things, you know."

There was a long silence, and then Adrian Brockbank, who had also been perched on a gunwale, stood up.

"If I may slip below for a moment," he said, "I think I can turn up something which will put an end to this whole absurd affair."

"As you please," said Appleby.

It was only after another pause that Appleby had spoken. He might have been staring with interest at some small smudge of smoke on the horizon. For a couple of long minutes he continued immobile, somberly waiting. For a further minute he continued to wait—even after the revolver shot had rung out.

Then Appleby rose with a small sigh and sought the late Adrian Brockbank below.

THE MOST DANGEROUS MAN

by Edward D. Hoch

"Like a spider in the centre of its web" . . .

THE professor glanced up from the desk where a new treatise on the binomial theorem lay open before him. His ears had detected a noise upon the landing—not loud, but enough to sharpen his senses. When it was repeated, he rose from the chair and walked across the room to the bolted door.

"Who is it?" he asked.

"Dwiggins, Professor! Open the door!"

The bolt was pulled back and the professor turned up the gas-flame a bit higher. "You arrived sooner than I had expected. Did all go well?"

Dwiggins was a slender man with black bushy hair and side-whiskers. His special value was his innate ability to assume the guise of a bumbling tradesman. The professor had known and used him many times in the past, always with success.

"It was perfect, Professor," reported Dwiggins. "I arranged a meeting with Archibald Andrews and told him of my needs. He agreed quite readily when I revealed the sum of money I was willing to pay."

"Capital, Dwiggins!" The professor drew a small note-book from his pocket and made a check mark. Then, with the tip of the pencil running down a list of names, he said, "We will have a final meeting to-morrow evening. Make certain everyone is in attendance."

"Right you are, Professor!"

When he was alone once more, the tall pale man hurried to the window and watched the progress of Dwiggins along the opposite curb. His deeply-sunken eyes scanned the alleyways, searching for a police-agent who might be following the bushy-haired man, but he saw no one. Thus far, nothing had happened to endanger his master plan.

The flickering gas-flames cast an uncertain glow over the five men who gathered in the professor's quarters the following evening. They were a mixed lot, drawn from various walks of life, but each had been chosen carefully for his special skills and accomplishments. Seated next to Dwiggins was Coxe, the notorious bank robber, and by his side was Quinn, an expert with a knife who proudly boasted of having been a police suspect in their search for Jack the Ripper only two years earlier. Moran, the former army colonel, was present too, along with Jenkins, a street ruffian especially adept in the handling of horses.

"Now, now," said the professor, peering and blinking at the men before him. "We must get to the business at hand."

"Will it be to-morrow?" asked Coxe.

The professor nodded. "To-morrow, the twenty-third of January, the City and Suburban Bank will make its regular Friday morning delivery of money to its branches. A two-horse van will enter the alleyway off Farringdon Street shortly after nine o'clock to-morrow morning, and proceed to the rear entrance of the bank. The flat of one Archibald Andrews overlooks this alley, and our Mr. Dwiggins has been most successful in luring said Andrews away from his flat for the entire morning. Tell us how it was accomplished, Dwiggins."

The bushy-haired man was quick to oblige. "I approached Andrews yesterday afternoon. Knowing him to be temporarily unemployed, I presented myself as a spice merchant with expectations of setting up a small shop in Oxford Street. I offered to pay him ten pounds if he would spend Friday morning visiting a list of shops and noting the prices charged for a variety of spices. He is to begin at Covent Garden Market promptly at eight, which should keep him far enough from his rooms in Farringdon Street."

"Tut, tut!" said the professor, shaking his head sadly. "I fear that Archibald Andrews will learn more about the price of spices than he really needs to know. Coxe, you should have no trouble with the door to his lodgings. You and Quinn will enter the rooms at precisely half-past eight, and station yourselves at the windows overlooking the alley. When the two-horse van arrives for the money, you will open the windows and prepare to jump. As I explained earlier, there is no manner in which the robbery can be executed while the money is being loaded. The armed guards will be on the alert for trouble. And once it leaves the alley to move through the crowded London streets it will once again be safe from our hands. The one weak link in the chain occurs at the precise instant the van is locked and starts out of the alley. The armed guards will have entered a carriage to travel ahead of the van, and the van itself will be travelling so slowly that you two can easily drop onto it from Mr. Andrews's second-storey windows."

"Excuse me, Professor," said Coxe. "I understand all that, but what will the two guards in the carriage do when they realise we have intercepted the van?"

The professor merely smiled, blinking his puckered eyes. "Everything is attended to. Jenkins here will be near at hand, in the guise of a hansom driver. At the proper moment his horse will appear to go out of control, and will carry the hansom cab between the guards' carriage and the van. Quinn will kill the driver of the van, and you will turn it in the opposite direction on Farringdon Street, away from the carriage. If the guards are able to get clear of the hansom and pursue you, Moran will be waiting with his air-gun."

"Where will you be?" asked Quinn.

"Dwiggins and I will be waiting close by. Once you are on your way, we will follow." He turned and took a cut-glass decanter from the sideboard. "Now, gentlemen, I suggest a bit of wine to toast the success of our endeavour on the morrow."

When Archibald Andrews left the doorway of his lodgings just before eight o'clock the following morning, Dwiggins and the professor were watching from across the street. It was a raw, blustery January morning, and the professor had turned up the collar of his greatcoat against the sharpness of the wind.

"Running like clockwork," Dwiggins commented as he watched Andrews go off down the street.

"Good, good!" The professor slipped a watch from his inner pocket and snapped open the lid. "Coxe and Quinn should be starting out now."

They waited, watching the movement of shop-girls and clerks along the busy street. Then, at half-past the hour, the professor saw his two confederates enter the street door to Archibald Andrews's lodgings. Dwiggins returned from his rounds to report. "Coxe and Quinn are in the flat, Professor. I saw them by the windows."

"And Moran?"

"He has just arrived and stationed himself across the street from the alley. The air-gun is hidden in his walking-stick."

"Jenkins?"

"His hansom is parked near-by."

The professor nodded. All was well.

At six minutes after nine o'clock, the two-horse van appeared and turned into the alley. A carriage drew up behind it and discharged two uniformed guards. The professor's face was oscillating slowly from side to side, in a curiously reptilian fashion, as he watched.

They waited while the minutes ticked by and the professor's sharp eyes scanned the passers-by for any sign of trouble. There seemed nothing unusual until—

"Dwiggins!"

"What is it, Professor?"

"That man hurrying through the crowd across the street—is it Archibald Andrews, returning so soon to his lodgings?"

"Bloody right it is!"

"Come on, we must stop him."

They crossed the street quickly, and Dwiggins called out, "Here now! I hired you to do a job for me!"

Archibald Andrews stopped in his tracks, looking from one to the other. "I—I—"

"Speak up, man!" urged Dwiggins. "This is my partner in the spice shop. Do you have the prices for us?"

"No, sir," muttered Andrews. "That is, you see, it seemed like a great deal of money for you to pay. I mentioned it to a friend of mine last evening—a physician who rooms with a consulting detective of sorts. He suggested something odd might be afoot."

"Quickly," snarled the professor. "If he comes here—"

But already there was movement in the alley. The guards' carriage had moved away, and the two-horse van was starting out with its precious cargo. As the professor watched, he saw Coxe and Quinn throw back the shutters and drop through the windows onto the roof of the van.

In the same instant there came the sound of police whistles, and suddenly the van seemed alive with uniformed bobbies. Coxe and Quinn were seized by a dozen strong arms.

"Quickly!" the professor told Dwiggins. "We must make our escape!"

"What about the others?"

But it was too late for them. Jenkins, abandoning his hansom for flight on foot, was in the clasp of a tall, sharp-featured man whose long white fingers seemed to clutch like steel.

"It is too late for them," the professor decided. "We can only hope that Moran was able to make good his escape."

"How did the police discover our plans so quickly?"

"That man is a devil!—that tall one who had Jenkins in his grip! As soon as he discovered that Andrews's lodgings overlooked the alley by the bank, he must have known we were luring the man away for a number of hours while we used his flat to reach the money-van."

"All that because I offered Andrews ten pounds?" Dwiggins followed the professor down a side street, away from the bustle of the crowds. "Who is this man that outwitted us?"

"His name is Sherlock Holmes," answered Professor Moriarty. "He is the most dangerous man in London."

CHAPTER AND VERSE: *The Little Copplestone Mystery*

by Ngaio Marsh

In the August 1946 issue of Ellery Queen's Mystery Magazine *we published "I Can Find My Way Out," a novelette about Inspector Roderick (Rory) Alleyn, the famous detective created by Ngaio Marsh. In our January 1948 issue we published another novelette about Inspector Alleyn—"Death on the Air." And to the best of our knowledge, and to the best of Ngaio Marsh's memory at that time, these were the only two stories about Inspector Alleyn that Ngaio Marsh ever wrote in shorter-than-novel length.*

Ah, knowledge, ah, memory . . . In 1972 we had occasion to write to Dame Ngaio, and in her reply she hinted at the existence of a third Inspector Alleyn novelette. Well, you can imagine: letters flew back and forth, and now, after more than a quarter of a century since the last appearance of Alleyn in EQMM, *we are privileged to give you that elusive third novelette . . .*

If a story about cold-blooded crimes can possibly be called charming, Dame Ngaio Marsh's "Chapter and Verse" is exactly that—a mixture of multiple murder, an old and rare Bible, eighteenth- and nineteenth-century genealogy, and as interesting a group of characters as you have ever sifted for suspects—with Alleyn (now Superintendent) at the top of his form . . .

WHEN the telephone rang, Troy came in, sun-dazzled, from the cottage garden to answer it, hoping it would be a call from London.

"Oh," said a strange voice uncertainly. "May I speak to Superintendent Alleyn, if you please?"

"I'm sorry. He's away."

"Oh, dear!" said the voice, crestfallen. "Er—would that be—am I speaking to Mrs. Alleyn?"

"Yes."

"Oh. Yes. Well, it's Timothy Bates here, Mrs. Alleyn. You don't know me," the voice confessed wistfully, "but I had the pleasure several years ago of meeting your husband. In New Zealand. And he did say that if I ever came home I was to get in touch, and when I heard quite by accident that you were here—well, I *was* excited. But, alas, no good after all."

"I *am* sorry," Troy said. "He'll be back, I hope, on Sunday night. Perhaps—"

"Will he! Come, *that's* something! Because here I am at the Star and Garter, you see, and so—" The voice trailed away again.

"Yes, indeed. He'll be delighted," Troy said, hoping that he would.

"I'm a bookman," the voice confided. "Old books, you know.

He used to come into my shop. It was always such a pleasure."

"But, of course!" Troy exclaimed. "I remember perfectly now. He's often talked about it."

"*Has* he? Has he, really! Well, you see, Mrs. Alleyn, I'm here on business. Not to *sell* anything, please don't think that, but on a voyage of discovery; almost, one might say, of detection, and I think it might amuse him. He has such an eye for the curious. Not," the voice hurriedly amended, "in the trade sense. I mean curious in the sense of mysterious and unusual. But I mustn't bore you."

Troy assured him that he was not boring her and indeed it was true. The voice was so much colored by odd little overtones that she found herself quite drawn to its owner. "I know where you are," he was saying. "Your house was pointed out to me."

After that there was nothing to do but ask him to visit. He seemed to cheer up prodigiously. "May I? May I, really? Now?"

"Why not?" Troy said. "You'll be here in five minutes."

She heard a little crow of delight before he hung up the receiver.

He turned out to be exactly like his voice—a short, middle-aged, bespectacled man, rather untidily dressed. As he came up the path she saw that with both arms he clutched to his stomach an enormous Bible. He was thrown into a fever over the difficulty of removing his cap.

"How ridiculous!" he exclaimed. "Forgive me! One moment."

He laid his burden tenderly on a garden seat. "There!" he cried. "Now! How do you do!"

Troy took him indoors and gave him a drink. He chose sherry and sat in the window seat with his Bible beside him. "You'll wonder," he said, "why I've appeared with this unusual piece of baggage. I *do* trust it arouses your curiosity."

He went into a long excitable explanation. It appeared that the Bible was an old and rare one that he had picked up in a job lot of books in New Zealand. All this time he kept it under his square little hands as if it might open of its own accord and spoil his story.

"Because," he said, "the *really* exciting thing to me is *not* its undoubted authenticity but—" He made a conspiratorial face at Troy and suddenly opened the Bible. "Look!" he invited.

He displayed the flyleaf. Troy saw that it was almost filled with entries in a minute, faded copperplate handwriting.

"The top," Mr. Bates cried. "Top left-hand. Look at *that.*"

Troy read: "*Crabtree Farm at Little Copplestone in the County of Kent.* Why, it comes from our village!"

"Ah, ha! So it does. Now, the entries, my dear Mrs. Alleyn. The entries."

They were the recorded births and deaths of a family named Wagstaff, beginning in 1705 and ending in 1870 with the birth of William James Wagstaff. Here they broke off but were followed by three further entries, close together.

Stewart Shakespeare Hadet. Died: Tuesday, 5th April, 1779. 2nd Samuel 1.10.

Naomi Balbus Hadet. Died: Saturday, 13th August, 1779. Jeremiah 50.24.

Peter Rook Hadet. Died: Monday, 12th September, 1779. Ezekiel 7.6.

Troy looked up to find Mr. Bates's gaze fixed on her. "And what," Mr. Bates asked, "my dear Mrs. Alleyn, do you make of *that?*"

"Well," she said cautiously, "I know about Crabtree Farm. There's the farm itself, owned by Mr. De'ath, and there's Crabtree House, belonging to Miss Hart, and—yes, I fancy I've heard they both belonged originally to a family named Wagstaff."

"You are perfectly right. Now! What about the Hadets? What about *them?*"

"I've never heard of a family named Hadet in Little Copplestone. But—"

"Of course you haven't. For the very good reason that there never have been any Hadets in Little Copplestone."

Child could spot it... De'ath (odd enow) has in Hadet— an anagram.

"Perhaps in New Zealand, then?"

"The dates, my dear Mrs. Alleyn, the dates! New Zealand was not colonized in 1779. Look closer. Do you see the sequence of double dots—ditto marks—under the address? Meaning, of course, 'also of Crabtree Farm at Little Copplestone in the County of Kent'."

"I suppose so."

"Of course you do. And how right you are. Now! You have noticed that throughout there are biblical references. For the Wagstaffs they are the usual pious offerings. You need not trouble yourself with them. But consult the text awarded to the three Hadets. Just you look *them* up! I've put markers."

He threw himself back with an air of triumph and sipped his sherry. Troy turned over the heavy bulk of pages to the first marker. "Second of Samuel, one, ten," Mr. Bates prompted, closing his eyes.

The verse had been faintly underlined.

"So I stood upon him," Troy read, *"and slew him."*

"That's Stewart Shakespeare Hadet's valedictory," said Mr. Bates. "Next!"

The next was at the 50th chapter of Jeremiah, verse 24: *"I have laid a snare for thee and thou are taken."*

Troy looked at Mr. Bates. His eyes were still closed and he was smiling faintly.

"That was Naomi Balbus Hadet," he said. "Now for Peter Rook Hadet. Ezekiel, seven, six."

The pages flopped back to the last marker.

"An end is come, the end is come: it watcheth for thee; behold it is come."

Troy shut the Bible.

"How very unpleasant," she said.

"And how very intriguing, don't you think?" And when she didn't answer, "Quite up your husband's street, it seemed to me."

"I'm afraid," Troy said, "that even Rory's investigations don't go back to 1779."

"What a pity!" Mr. Bates cried gaily.

"Do I gather that you conclude from all this that there was dirty work among the Hadets in 1779?"

"I don't know, but I'm dying to find out. *Dying* to. Thank you, I should enjoy another glass. Delicious!"

He had settled down so cosily and seemed to be enjoying himself so much that Troy was constrained to ask him to stay to lunch.

"Miss Hart's coming," she said. "She's the one who bought Crabtree House from the Wagstaffs. If there's any gossip to be picked up in Copplestone, Miss Hart's the one for it. She's coming about a painting she wants me to donate to the Harvest Festival raffle."

Mr. Bates was greatly excited. "Who knows!" he cried. "A Wagstaff in the hand may be worth two Hadets in the bush. I am your slave forever, my dear Mrs. Alleyn!"

Miss Hart was a lady of perhaps sixty-seven years. On meeting Mr. Bates she seemed to imply that some explanation should be advanced for Troy receiving a gentleman caller in her husband's absence. When the Bible was produced, she immediately accepted it in this light, glanced with professional expertise at the inscriptions and fastened on the Wagstaffs.

"No doubt," said Miss Hart, "it was their family Bible and much good it did them. A most eccentric lot they were. Very unsound. Very unsound, indeed. Especially Old Jimmy."

"Who," Mr. Bates asked greedily, "was Old Jimmy?"

Miss Hart jabbed her forefinger at the last of the Wagstaff entries. "William James Wagstaff. Born 1870. And died, although it doesn't say so, in April, 1921. Nobody was left to complete the entry, of course. Unless you count the niece, which I don't. Baggage, if ever I saw one."

"The niece?"

"Fanny Wagstaff. Orphan. Old Jimmy brought her up. Dragged would be the better word. Drunken old reprobate he was and he came to a drunkard's end. They said he beat her *and* I daresay she needed it." Miss Hart lowered her voice to a whisper and confided in Troy. "Not a *nice* girl. You know what I mean."

Troy, feeling it was expected of her, nodded portentously.

"A drunken end, did you say?" prompted Mr. Bates.

"Certainly. On a Saturday night after Market. Fell through the top-landing stair rail in his nightshirt and split his skull on the flagstoned hall."

"And your father bought it, then, after Old Jimmy died?" Troy ventured.

"Bought the house and garden. Richard De'ath took the farm. He'd been after it for years—wanted it to round off his own place. He and Old Jimmy were at daggers-drawn over *that* business. And, of course, Richard being an atheist, over the Seven Seals."

"I beg your pardon?" Mr. Bates asked.

"Blasphemous!" Miss Hart shouted. "That's what it was, rank blasphemy. It was a sect that Wagstaff founded. If the rector had known his business he'd have had him excommunicated for it."

Miss Hart was prevented from elaborating this theory by the appearance at the window of an enormous woman, stuffily encased in black, with a face like a full moon.

"Anybody at home?" the newcomer playfully chanted. "Telegram for a lucky girl! Come and get it!"

It was Mrs. Simpson, the village postmistress. Miss Hart said, "Well, *really!*" and gave an acid laugh.

"Sorry, I'm sure," said Mrs. Simpson, staring at the Bible which lay under her nose on the window seat. "I didn't realize there was company. Thought I'd pop it in as I was passing."

Troy read the telegram while Mrs. Simpson, panting, sank heavily on the window ledge and eyed Mr. Bates, who had drawn back in confusion. "I'm no good in the heat," she told him. "Slays me."

"Thank you so much, Mrs. Simpson," Troy said. "No answer."

"Righty-ho. Cheerie-bye," said Mrs. Simpson and with another stare at Mr. Bates and the Bible, and a derisive grin at Miss Hart, she waddled away.

"It's from Rory," Troy said. "He'll be home on Sunday evening."

"*As* that woman will no doubt inform the village," Miss Hart pronounced. "A busybody of the first water and ought to be taught her place. Did you ever!"

She fulminated throughout luncheon and it was with difficulty that Troy and Mr. Bates persuaded her to finish her story of the last of the Wagstaffs. It appeared that Old Jimmy had died intestate, his niece succeeding. She had at once announced her intention of selling everything and had left the district to pursue, Miss Hart suggested, a life of freedom, no doubt in London or even in Paris. Miss Hart wouldn't, and didn't want to, know. On the subject of the Hadets, however, she was uninformed and showed no inclination to look up the marked Bible references attached to them.

After luncheon Troy showed Miss Hart three of her paintings, any one of which would have commanded a high price at an exhibition of contemporary art, and Miss Hart chose the one that, in her own phrase, really did look like something. She insisted that Troy and Mr. Bates accompany her to the parish hall where Mr. Bates would meet the rector, an authority on village folklore. Troy in person must hand over her painting to be raffled.

Troy would have declined this honor if Mr. Bates had not retired behind Miss Hart and made a series of beseeching gestures and grimaces. They set out therefore in Miss Hart's car which was crammed with vegetables for the Harvest Festival decorations.

"And if the woman Simpson thinks she's going to hog the lectern with *her* pumpkins," said Miss Hart, "she's in for a shock. Hah!"

St. Cuthbert's was an ancient parish church round whose flanks the tiny village nestled. Its tower, an immensely high one, was said to be unique. Nearby was the parish hall where Miss Hart pulled up with a masterful jerk.

Troy and Mr. Bates helped her unload some of her lesser marrows to be offered for sale within. They were observed by a truculent-looking man in tweeds who grinned at Miss Hart. "Burnt offerings," he jeered, "for the tribal gods, I perceive." It was Mr. Richard De'ath, the atheist. Miss Hart cut him dead and led the way into the hall.

Here they found the rector, with a crimson-faced elderly man and a clutch of ladies engaged in preparing for the morrow's sale.

The rector was a thin gentle person, obviously frightened of Miss Hart and timidly delighted by Troy. On being shown the Bible he became excited and dived at once into the story of Old Jimmy Wagstaff.

"Intemperate, I'm afraid, in everything," sighed the rector. "Indeed, it would not be too much to say that he both preached and drank hellfire. He *did* preach, on Saturday nights at the crossroads outside the Star and Garter. Drunken, blasphemous nonsense it was and although he used to talk about his followers, the only one he could claim was his niece, Fanny, who was probably too much under his thumb to refuse him."

"Edward Pilbrow," Miss Hart announced, jerking her head at the elderly man who had come quite close to them. "Drowned him with his bell. They had a fight over it. Deaf as a post," she added, catching sight of Mr. Bates's startled expression. "He's the verger now. *And* the town crier."

"What!" Mr. Bates exclaimed.

"Oh, yes," the rector explained. "The village is endowed with a town crier." He went over to Mr. Pilbrow, who at once cupped his hand round his ear. The rector yelled into it.

"When did you start crying, Edward?"

"Twenty-ninth September, 'twenty-one," Mr. Pilbrow roared back.

"I thought so."

There was something in their manner that made it difficult to remember, Troy thought, that they were talking about events that were almost fifty years back in the past. Even the year 1779 evidently seemed to them to be not so long ago, but, alas, none of them knew of any Hadets.

"By all means," the rector invited Mr. Bates, "consult the church records, but I can assure you—no Hadets. Never any Hadets."

Troy saw an expression of extreme obstinacy settle round Mr. Bates's mouth.

The rector invited him to look at the church and as they both seemed to expect Troy to tag along, she did so. In the lane they once more encountered Mr. Richard De'ath out of whose pocket protruded a paper-wrapped bottle. He touched his cap to Troy and glared at the rector, who turned pink and said, "Afternoon, De'ath," and hurried on.

Mr. Bates whispered imploringly to Troy, "*Would* you mind? I *do* so want to have a word—" and she was obliged to introduce him. It was not a successful encounter. Mr. Bates no sooner broached the topic of his Bible, which he still carried, than Mr. De'ath burst into an alcoholic diatribe against superstition, and on the mention of Old Jimmy Wagstaff, worked himself up into such a state of reminiscent fury that Mr. Bates was glad to hurry away with Troy.

They overtook the rector in the churchyard, now bathed in the golden opulence of an already westering sun.

"There they all lie," the rector said, waving a fatherly hand at the company of headstones. "All your Wagstaffs, right back to the sixteenth century. But no Hadets, Mr. Bates, I assure you."

They stood looking up at the spire. Pigeons flew in and out of a balcony far above their heads. At their feet was a little flagged area edged by a low coping. Mr. Bates stepped forward and the rector laid a hand on his arm.

"Not there," he said. "Do you mind?"

"Don't!" bellowed Mr. Pilbrow from the rear. "Don't you set foot on them bloody stones, Mister."

Mr. Bates backed away.

"Edward's not swearing," the rector mildly explained. "He is to be taken, alas, literally. A sad and dreadful story, Mr. Bates."

"Indeed?" Mr. Bates asked eagerly.

"Indeed, yes. Some time ago, in the very year we have been discussing—1921, you know—one of our girls, a very beautiful girl she was, named Ruth Wall, fell from the balcony of the tower and was, of course, killed. She used to go up there to feed the pigeons and it was thought that in leaning over the low balustrade she overbalanced."

"Ah!" Mr. Pilbrow roared with considerable relish, evidently guessing the purport of the rector's speech. "Terrible, terrible! And 'er sweetheart after 'er, too. Terrible!"

"Oh, no!" Troy protested.

The rector made a dabbing gesture to subdue Mr. Pilbrow. "I wish he wouldn't," he said. "Yes. It was a few days later. A lad called Simon Castle. They were to be married. People said it must be suicide but—it may have been wrong of me—I couldn't bring myself—in short, he lies beside her over there. If you would care to look."

For a minute or two they stood before the headstones.

"Ruth Wall. Spinster of this Parish. 1903–1921. *I will extend peace to her like a river.*"

"Simon Castle. Bachelor of this Parish. 1900–1921. *And God shall wipe away all tears from their eyes.*"

The afternoon having by now worn on, and the others having excused themselves, Mr. Bates remained alone in the churchyard, clutching his Bible and staring at the headstones. The light of the hunter's zeal still gleamed in his eyes.

Troy didn't see Mr. Bates again until Sunday night service when, on her way up the aisle, she passed him, sitting in the rearmost pew. She was amused to observe that his gigantic Bible was under the seat.

"*We plow the fields,*" sang the choir, "*and scatter—*" Mrs. Simpson roared away on the organ, the smell of assorted greengrocery rising like some humble incense. Everybody in Little Copplestone except Mr. Richard De'ath was there for the Harvest Festival. At last the rector stepped over Miss Hart's biggest pumpkin and ascended the pulpit, Edward Pilbrow switched off all the lights except one and they settled down for the sermon.

"A sower went forth to sow," announced the rector. He spoke simply and well but somehow Troy's attention wandered. She found herself wondering where, through the centuries, the succeeding generations of Wagstaffs had sat until Old Jimmy took to his freakish practices; and whether Ruth Wall and Simon Castle, poor things, had shared the same hymnbook and held hands during the sermon; and whether, after all, Stewart Shakespeare Hadet and Peter Rook Hadet had not, in 1779, occupied some dark corner of the church and been unaccountably forgotten.

Here we are, Troy thought drowsily, and there, outside in the churchyard, are all the others going back and back—

She saw a girl, bright in the evening sunlight, reach from a balcony toward a multitude of wings. She was falling—dreadfully—into nothingness. Troy woke with a sickening jerk.

"—on stony ground," the rector was saying. Troy listened guiltily to the rest of the sermon.

Mr. Bates emerged on the balcony. He laid his Bible on the coping and looked at the moonlit tree tops and the churchyard so dreadfully far below. He heard someone coming up the stairway. Torchlight danced on the door jamb.

"You were quick," said the visitor.

"I am all eagerness and, I confess, puzzlement."

"It had to be here, on the spot. If you *really* want to find out—"

"But I do, I do!"

"We haven't much time. You've brought the Bible?"

"You particularly asked—"

"If you'd open it at Ezekiel, chapter twelve. I'll shine my torch."

Mr. Bates opened the Bible.

"The thirteenth verse. There!"

Mr. Bates leaned forward. The Bible tipped and moved.

"Look out!" the voice urged.

Mr. Bates was scarcely aware of the thrust. He felt the page tear as the book sank under his hands. The last thing he heard was the beating of a multitude of wings.

"—and forevermore," said the rector in a changed voice, facing east. The congregation got to its feet. He announced the last hymn. Mrs. Simpson made a preliminary rumble and Troy groped in her pocket for the collection plate. Presently they all filed out into the autumnal moonlight.

It was coldish in the churchyard. People stood about in groups. One or two had already moved through the lychgate. Troy heard a voice, which she recognized as that of Mr. De'ath. "I suppose," it jeered, "you all know you've been assisting at a fertility rite."

"Drunk as usual, Dick De'ath," somebody returned without rancor. There was a general laugh.

They had all begun to move away when, from the shadows at the base of the church tower, there arose a great cry. They stood, transfixed, turned toward the voice.

Out of the shadows came the rector in his cassock. When Troy saw his face she thought he must be ill and went to him.

"No, no!" he said. "Not a woman! Edward! Where's Edward Pilbrow?"

Behind him, at the foot of the tower, was a pool of darkness; but Troy, having come closer, could see within it a figure, broken like a puppet on the flagstones. An eddy of night air stole round the church and fluttered a page of the giant Bible that lay pinned beneath the head.

It was nine o'clock when Troy heard the car pull up outside the cottage. She saw her husband coming up the path and ran to meet him, as if they had been parted for months.

He said, "This is mighty gratifying!" And then, "Hullo, my love. What's the matter?"

As she tumbled out her story, filled with relief at telling him, a large man with uncommonly bright eyes came up behind them.

"Listen to this, Fox," Roderick Alleyn said. "We're in demand, it seems." He put his arm through Troy's and closed his hand round hers. "Let's go indoors, shall we? Here's Fox, darling, come for a nice bucolic rest. Can we give him a bed?"

Troy pulled herself together and greeted Inspector Fox. Presently she was able to give them a coherent account of the evening's tragedy. When she had finished, Alleyn said, "Poor little Bates. He was a nice little bloke." He put his hand on Troy's. "You need a drink," he said, "and so, by the way, do we."

While he was getting the drinks he asked quite casually, "You've had a shock and a beastly one at that, but there's something else, isn't there?"

"Yes," Troy swallowed hard, "there is. They're all saying it's an accident."

"Yes?"

"And, Rory, I don't think it is."

Mr. Fox cleared his throat. "Fancy," he said.

"Suicide?" Alleyn suggested, bringing her drink to her.

"No. Certainly not."

"A bit of rough stuff, then?"

"You sound as if you're asking about the sort of weather we've been having."

"Well, darling, you don't expect Fox and me to go into hysterics. Why not an accident?"

"He knew all about the other accidents, he *knew* it was dangerous. And then the oddness of it, Rory. To leave the Harvest Festival service and climb the tower in the dark, carrying that enormous Bible!"

"And he was hell-bent on tracing these Hadets?"

"Yes. He kept saying you'd be interested. He actually brought a copy of the entries for you."

"Have you got it?"

She found it for him. "The selected texts," he said, "are pretty rum, aren't they, Br'er Fox?" and handed it over.

"Very vindictive," said Mr. Fox.

"Mr. Bates thought it was in your line," Troy said.

"The devil he did! What's been done about this?"

"The village policeman was in the church. They sent for the doctor. And—well, you see, Mr. Bates had talked a lot about you and they hope you'll be able to tell them something about him—whom they should get in touch with and so on."

"Have they moved him?"

"They weren't going to until the doctor had seen him."

Alleyn pulled his wife's ear and looked at Fox. "Do you fancy a stroll through the village, Foxkin?"

"There's a lovely moon," Fox said bitterly and got to his feet.

The moon was high in the heavens when they came to the base of the tower and it shone on a group of four men—the rector, Richard De'ath, Edward Pilbrow, and Sergeant Botting, the village constable. When they saw Alleyn and Fox, they separated and revealed a fifth, who was kneeling by the body of Timothy Bates.

"Kind of you to come," the rector said, shaking hands with Alleyn. "And a great relief to all of us."

Their manner indicated that Alleyn's arrival would remove a sense of personal responsibility. "If you'd like to have a look—?" the doctor said.

The broken body lay huddled on its side. The head rested on the open Bible. The right hand, rigid in cadaveric spasm, clutched a torn page. Alleyn knelt and Fox came closer with the torch. At the top of the page Alleyn saw the word Ezekiel and a little farther down, Chapter 12.

Using the tip of his finger Alleyn straightened the page. "Look," he said, and pointed to the thirteenth verse. "*My net also will I spread upon him and he shall be taken in my snare.*"

The words had been faintly underlined in mauve.

Alleyn stood up and looked round the circle of faces.

"Well," the doctor said, "we'd better see about moving him."

Alleyn said, "I don't think he should be moved just yet."

"Not!" the rector cried out. "But surely—to leave him like this—I mean, after this terrible accident—"

"It has yet to be proved," Alleyn said, "that it was an accident."

There was a sharp sound from Richard De'ath.

"—and I fancy," Alleyn went on, glancing at De'ath, "that it's going to take quite a lot of proving."

After that, events, as Fox observed with resignation, took the course that was to be expected. The local Superintendent said that under the circumstances it would be silly not to ask Alleyn to carry on, the Chief Constable agreed, and appropriate instructions came through from Scotland Yard. The rest of the night was spent in routine procedure. The body having been photographed and the Bible set aside for fingerprinting, both were removed and arrangements put in hand for the inquest.

At dawn Alleyn and Fox climbed the tower. The winding stair brought them to an extremely narrow doorway through which they saw the countryside lying vaporous in the faint light. Fox was about to go through to the balcony when Alleyn stopped him and pointed to the door jambs. They were covered with a growth of stonecrop.

About three feet from the floor this had been brushed off over a space of perhaps four inches and fragments of the microscopic plant hung from the scars. From among these, on either side, Alleyn removed morsels of dark-colored thread. "And here," he sighed, "as sure as fate, we go again. O Lord, O Lord!"

They stepped through to the balcony and there was a sudden whirr and beating of wings as a company of pigeons flew out of the tower. The balcony was narrow and the balustrade indeed very low. "If there's any looking over," Alleyn said, "you, my dear Foxkin, may do it."

Nevertheless he leaned over the balustrade and presently knelt beside it. "Look at this. Bates rested the open Bible here—blow me down flat if he didn't! There's a powder of leather where it scraped on the stone and a fragment where it tore. It must have been moved—outward. Now, why, *why*?"

"Shoved it accidentally with his knees, then made a grab and overbalanced?"

"But why put the open Bible there? To read by moonlight? *My net also will I spread upon him and he shall be taken in my snare.* Are you going to tell me he underlined it and then dived overboard?"

"I'm not going to tell you anything," Fox grunted and then: "That old chap Edward Pilbrow's down below swabbing the stones. He looks like a beetle."

"Let him look like a rhinoceros if he wants to, but for the love of Mike don't leer over the edge—you give me the willies. Here, let's pick this stuff up before it blows away."

They salvaged the scraps of leather and put them in an envelope. Since there was nothing more to do, they went down and out through the vestry and so home to breakfast.

"Darling," Alleyn told his wife, "you've landed us with a snorter."

"Then you *do* think—?"

"There's a certain degree of fishiness. Now, see here, wouldn't *somebody* have noticed little Bates get up and go out? I know he sat all alone on the back bench, but wasn't there *someone*?"

"The rector?"

"No. I asked him. Too intent on his sermon, it seems."

"Mrs. Simpson? If she looks through her little red curtain she faces the nave."

"We'd better call on her, Fox. I'll take the opportunity to send a couple of cables to New Zealand. She's fat, jolly, keeps the shop-cum-postoffice, and is supposed to read all the postcards. Just your cup of tea. You're dynamite with postmistresses. Away we go."

Mrs. Simpson sat behind her counter doing a crossword puzzle and refreshing herself with licorice. She welcomed Alleyn with enthusiasm. He introduced Fox and then he retired to a corner to write out his cables.

"What a catastrophe!" Mrs. Simpson said, plunging straight into the tragedy. "Shocking! As nice a little gentleman as you'd wish to meet, Mr. Fox. Typical New Zealander. Pick him a mile away and a friend of Mr. Alleyn's, I'm told, and if I've said it once I've said it a hundred times, Mr. Fox, they ought to have put something up to prevent it. Wire netting or a bit of ironwork; but, no, they let it go on from year to year and now see what's happened—history repeating itself and giving the village a bad name. Terrible!"

Fox bought a packet of tobacco from Mrs. Simpson and paid her a number of compliments on the layout of her shop, modulating from there into an appreciation of the village. He said that one always found such pleasant company in small communities. Mrs. Simpson was impressed and offered him a piece of licorice.

"As for pleasant company," she chuckled, "that's as may be, though by and large I suppose I mustn't grumble. I'm a cockney and a stranger here myself, Mr. Fox. Only twenty-four years and that doesn't go for anything with this lot."

"Ah," Fox said, "then you wouldn't recollect the former tragedies. Though to be sure," he added, "you wouldn't do that in any case, being much too young, if you'll excuse the liberty, Mrs. Simpson."

After this classic opening Alleyn was not surprised to hear Mrs. Simpson embark on a retrospective survey of life in Little

Copplestone. She was particularly lively on Miss Hart, who, she hinted, had had her eye on Mr. Richard De'ath for many a long day.

"As far back as when Old Jimmy Wagstaff died, which was why she was so set on getting the next-door house; but Mr. De'ath never looked at anybody except Ruth Wall, and her head-over-heels in love with young Castle, which together with her falling to her destruction when feeding pigeons led Mr. De'ath to forsake religion and take to drink, which he has done something cruel ever since.

"They do say he's got a terrible temper, Mr. Fox, and it's well known he give Old Jimmy Wagstaff a thrashing on account of straying cattle and threatened young Castle, saying if he couldn't have Ruth, nobody else would, but fair's fair and personally I've never seen him anything but nice-mannered, drunk or sober. Speak as you find's my motto and always has been, but these old maids, when they take a fancy they get it pitiful hard. You wouldn't know a word of nine letters meaning 'pale-faced lure like a sprat in a fishy story,' would you?"

Fox was speechless, but Alleyn, emerging with his cables, suggested "whitebait."

"Correct!" shouted Mrs. Simpson. "Fits like a glove. Although it's not a bit like a sprat and a quarter the size. Cheating, I call it. Still, it fits." She licked her indelible pencil and triumphantly added it to her crossword.

They managed to lead her back to Timothy Bates. Fox, professing a passionate interest in organ music, was able to extract from her that when the rector began his sermon she had in fact dimly observed someone move out of the back bench and through the doors. "He must have walked round the church and in through the vestry and little did I think he was going to his death," Mrs. Simpson said with considerable relish and a sigh like an earthquake.

"You didn't happen to hear him in the vestry?" Fox ventured, but it appeared that the door from the vestry into the organ loft was shut and Mrs. Simpson, having settled herself to enjoy the sermon with, as she shamelessly admitted, a bag of chocolates, was not in a position to notice.

Alleyn gave her his two cables: the first to Timothy Bates's partner in New Zealand and the second to one of his own colleagues in that country asking for any available information about relatives of the late William James Wagstaff of Little Copplestone, Kent, possibly resident in New Zealand after 1921, and of any persons of the name of Peter Rook Hadet or Naomi Balbus Hadet.

Mrs. Simpson agitatedly checked over the cables, professional etiquette and burning curiosity struggling together in her enormous bosom. She restrained herself, however, merely observing that an event of this sort set you thinking, didn't it?

"And no doubt," Alleyn said as they walked up the lane, "she'll be telling her customers that the next stop's bloodhounds and manacles."

"Quite a tidy armful of lady, isn't she, Mr. Alleyn?" Fox calmly rejoined.

The inquest was at 10:20 in the smoking room of the Star and Garter. With half an hour in hand, Alleyn and Fox visited the churchyard. Alleyn gave particular attention to the headstones of Old Jimmy Wagstaff, Ruth Wall, and Simon Castle. "No mention of the month or day," he said. And after a moment: "I wonder. We must ask the rector."

"No need to ask the rector," said a voice behind them. It was Miss Hart. She must have come soundlessly across the soft turf. Her air was truculent. "Though why," she said, "it should be of interest, I'm sure I don't know. Ruth Wall died on August thirteenth, 1921. It was a Saturday."

"You've a remarkable memory," Alleyn observed.

"Not as good as it sounds. That Saturday afternoon I came to do the flowers in the church. I found her and I'm not likely ever to forget it. Young Castle went the same way almost a month later.

September twelfth. In my opinion there was never a more glaring case of suicide. I believe," Miss Hart said harshly, "in facing facts."

"She was a beautiful girl, wasn't she?"

"I'm no judge of beauty. She set the men by the ears. *He* was a fine-looking young fellow. Fanny Wagstaff did her best to get *him.*"

"Had Ruth Wall," Alleyn asked, "other admirers?"

Miss Hart didn't answer and he turned to her. Her face was blotted with an unlovely flush. "She ruined two men's lives, if you want to know. Castle and Richard De'ath," said Miss Hart. She turned on her heel and without another word marched away.

"September twelfth," Alleyn murmured. "That would be a Monday, Br'er Fox."

"So it would," Fox agreed, after a short calculation, "so it would. Quite a coincidence."

"Or not, as the case may be. I'm going to take a gamble on this one. Come on."

They left the churchyard and walked down the lane, overtaking Edward Pilbrow on the way. He was wearing his town crier's coat and hat and carrying his bell by the clapper. He manifested great excitement when he saw them.

"Hey!" he shouted, "what's this I hear? Murder's the game, is it? What a go! Come on, gents, let's have it. Did 'e fall or was 'e pushed? Hor, hor, hor! Come on."

"Not till after the inquest," Alleyn shouted.

"Do we get a look at the body?"

"Shut up," Mr. Fox bellowed suddenly.

"I got to know, haven't I? It'll be the smartest bit of crying I ever done, this will! I reckon I might get on the telly with this. 'Town crier tells old-world village death stalks the churchyard.' Hor, hor, hor!"

"Let us," Alleyn whispered, "leave this horrible old man."

They quickened their stride and arrived at the pub, to be met with covert glances and dead silence.

The smoking room was crowded for the inquest. Everybody was there, including Mrs. Simpson who sat in the back row with her candies and her crossword puzzle. It went through very quickly. The rector deposed to finding the body. Richard De'ath, sober and less truculent than usual, was questioned as to his sojourn outside the churchyard and said he'd noticed nothing unusual apart from hearing a disturbance among the pigeons roosting in the balcony. From where he stood, he said, he couldn't see the face of the tower.

An open verdict was recorded.

Alleyn had invited the rector, Miss Hart, Mrs. Simpson, Richard De'ath, and, reluctantly, Edward Pilbrow, to join him in the Bar-Parlor and had arranged with the landlord that nobody else would be admitted. The Public Bar, as a result, drove a roaring trade.

When they had all been served and the hatch closed, Alleyn walked into the middle of the room and raised his hand. It was the slightest of gestures but it secured their attention.

He said, "I think you must all realize that we are not satisfied this was an accident. The evidence against accident has been collected piecemeal from the persons in this room and I am going to put it before you. If I go wrong I want you to correct me. I ask you to do this with absolute frankness, even if you are obliged to implicate someone who you would say was the last person in the world to be capable of a crime of violence."

He waited. Pilbrow, who had come very close, had his ear cupped in his hand. The rector looked vaguely horrified. Richard De'ath suddenly gulped down his double whiskey. Miss Hart coughed over her lemonade and Mrs. Simpson avidly popped a peppermint cream in her mouth and took a swig of her port-and-raspberry.

Alleyn nodded to Fox, who laid Mr. Bates's Bible, open at the flyleaf, on the table before him.

"The case," Alleyn said, "hinges on this book. You have all seen the entries. I remind you of the recorded deaths in 1779 of the three Hadets—Stewart Shakespeare, Naomi Balbus, and Peter Rook. To each of these is attached a biblical text suggesting that they met their death by violence. There have never been any Hadets in this village and the days of the week are wrong for the given dates. They are right, however, for the year 1921 and *they fit the deaths,* all by falling from a height, of William Wagstaff, Ruth Wall, and Simon Castle.

"By analogy the Christian names agree. William suggests Shakespeare. Naomi—Ruth; Balbus—a wall. Simon—Peter; and a Rook is a Castle in chess. And Hadet," Alleyn said without emphasis, "is an anagram of Death."

"Balderdash!" Miss Hart cried out in an unrecognizable voice.

"No, it's not," said Mrs. Simpson. "It's jolly good crossword stuff."

"Wicked balderdash. Richard!"

De'ath said, "Be quiet. Let him go on."

"We believe," Alleyn said, "that these three people met their deaths by one hand. Motive is a secondary consideration, but it is present in several instances, predominantly in one. Who had cause to wish the death of these three people? Someone whom old Wagstaff had bullied and to whom he had left his money and who killed him for it. Someone who was infatuated with Simon Castle and bitterly jealous of Ruth Wall. Someone who hoped, as an heiress, to win Castle for herself and who, failing, was determined nobody else should have him. Wagstaff's orphaned niece—Fanny Wagstaff."

There were cries of relief from all but one of his hearers. He went on. "Fanny Wagstaff sold everything, disappeared, and was never heard of again in the village. But twenty-four years later she returned, and has remained here ever since."

A glass crashed to the floor and a chair overturned as the vast bulk of the postmistress rose to confront him.

"Lies! *Lies!*" screamed Mrs. Simpson.

"Did you sell everything again, before leaving New Zealand?" he asked as Fox moved forward. "Including the Bible, Miss Wagstaff?"

"But," Troy said, "how could you be so sure?"

"She was the only one who could leave her place in the church unobserved. She was the the only one fat enough to rub her hips against the narrow door jambs. She uses an indelible pencil. We presume she arranged to meet Bates on the balcony, giving a cock-and-bull promise to tell him something nobody else knew about the Hadets. She indicated the text with her pencil, gave the Bible a shove, and, as he leaned out to grab it, tipped him over the edge.

"In talking about 1921 she forgot herself and described the events as if she had been there. She called Bates a typical New Zealander but gave herself out to be a Londoner. She said whitebait are only a quarter of the size of sprats. New Zealand whitebait are—English whitebait are about the same size.

"And as we've now discovered, she didn't send my cables. Of course she thought poor little Bates was hot on her tracks, especially when she learned that he'd come here to see me. She's got the kind of crossword-puzzle mind that would think up the biblical clues, and would get no end of a kick in writing them in. She's overwhelmingly conceited and vindictive."

"Still—"

"I know. Not good enough if we'd played the waiting game. But good enough to try shock tactics. We caught her off her guard and she cracked up."

"Not," Mr. Fox said, "a nice type of woman."

Alleyn strolled to the gate and looked up the lane to the church. The spire shone golden in the evening sun.

"The rector," Alleyn said, "tells me he's going to do something about the balcony."

"Mrs. Simpson, née Wagstaff," Fox remarked, "suggested wire netting."

"And she ought to know," Alleyn said and turned back to the cottage.

A JUDICIOUS HALF INCH

by Ursula Curtiss

Ursula Curtiss' "A Judicious Half Inch" exudes a profound sense of evil. You can hear it, see it, feel it, almost smell and taste it . . . A subtly told story with touch after touch of warning . . .

HADDON saw the thing beginning to take shape before his very eyes on a day in July which seemed cloudless in every respect. He could even put an exact time to it, because he had just picked up his watch from the glass-topped table, timing the end of his therapeutic swim in his aunt's pool. It was exactly 1:45 P.M. when Chrissie Menlo slipped through the row of young trees that bounded the property to the north.

She was wearing a pink-and-white bikini that made her look a tiny sixteen rather than the six she was. All of her, in fact—her pointed petal-like face, her straight swinging ash-blonde hair, the setting of her light-gray eyes—gave her the air of an adult looked at through the wrong end of binoculars. Haddon, who had a basic distrust of young children who were always clean and impeccably dressed and who nipped deftly around at cocktail parties proffering canapés and bowls of nuts, disliked her heartily.

"May I go in now, Mr. Haddon?" asked Chrissie, cocking her head prettily. "You've finished your swim."

"In fifteen minutes," said Haddon, implacable.

Chrissie cast a rebellious glance at the pool, pear-shaped, still quaking bluely from Haddon's exit. "Why does it have to be two o'clock?"

They had been over this ground many times before, and Haddon shrugged. "You know the rules," he said.

They were not his aunt's rules, as implied, but his own, and he was proud of them; the rules' very arbitrariness—that Chrissie and her brother Harvey could swim between two and three o'clock every other day—gave them the stamp of authenticity. His Aunt Ellen, in Spain for the summer, could hardly be appealed to.

Strong measures of self-defense were required with the Menlo children. They had evidently been brought up in the belief that they brightened the lives of all around them, and were welcome on any and every occasion for hours at a time. They sparkled with the conviction of their own worth, had been well tutored in the material value of things, and were as formidably boring as adults.

Haddon, whose recent leg wound in Vietnam had healed stiffly and imperfectly, had grown thorny when it became apparent soon after his arrival here that the Menlo parents were prepared, indulgently, to let him be their babysitter and pool guard for the summer. "He's depressed about his leg," he imagined them saying to each other, "and the children will take his mind off it."

Chrissie usually wheedled, however vainly. Today she did not. Dropping sociably down in another lawn chair she said, "My

Granny's coming tonight, from New York. That's my mommy's mother, not my other grandmother. She doesn't like to be called Granny."

"I don't blame her," said Haddon with feeling.

Chrissie gave herself a little hug in what seemed an essence of feminine malice. "Daddy said why did that damned old crone have to come now?"

It was clearly a direct quote, and Haddon was mildly diverted in spite of himself. "He didn't say this to your mother, I take it."

"Oh, no, he said it to his very own self," said Chrissie, widening her eyes in astonished recollection, "and he hit his desk. He must have hurt his hand. I asked him why he hit his desk and he said he just suddenly got mad at it." She giggled, glancing archly at Haddon. "Isn't that silly, getting mad at a desk?"

It was the kind of question, demanding the kind of response, that raised Haddon's hackles. He was almost pleased at the arrival of nine-year-old Harvey—brown, somewhat fat, with a large hearty face which would someday beam at Chamber of Commerce dinners. It was the boy's habit to inquire ceremoniously about Haddon's leg once every day, and he did so now.

"Will it ever get well?" asked Chrissie, not to be outdone in solicitude, and Harvey said reprovingly, "It's better than *no* leg. Right?"

"It's two minutes after two," said Haddon with inflection, and closed his eyes. Monumental splashes an instant later told him the children had dived in.

Perhaps because of his very annoyance at having his blessings counted for him so unctuously, his leg set up a gnawing ache. He lay consciously still in a dappling of coolness and warmth; presently, in a strange way lulled by the familiar pain, he almost slept. Birds twittered high in the branches of the sheltering cottonwood, mercifully absorbing the children's shrieks as they jumped and tussled in the water. Harvey's voice, when it came, seemed channeled startlingly into Haddon's ear, but the boy was only hanging onto the deck at the deep end of the pool, kicking his feet idly and saying, "Did Chrissie tell you about our grandmother?"

"She's coming tonight. Yes."

"That's not our grandmother who has a place at Lake Tahoe, though."

"With stables," added Chrissie, who had bobbed up beside her brother.

Both of them stared at Haddon with a kind of triumphant challenge. In command of this pool he might be, but could he ever possibly match a place at Lake Tahoe, with stables? Haddon's leg went on hurting. He said kindly, "There is absolutely nothing wrong with having stables on your property if they're kept clean. Horses have to stay somewhere, you know." And before their stunned faces could recover, "If you must dive for stones, use bigger ones. Pebbles get into the filter."

Harvey was of a more forgiving nature than Chrissie. He said as he wrapped his corpulence in a towel at the end of the swim, "I guess we'll be seeing you at six o'clock, Mr. Haddon. Mom said you were coming over for cocktails."

Haddon had forgotten about this invitation, acceded to three days earlier because there had seemed no graceful way of getting out of it. "Oh, I doubt it. With your grandmother coming—"

"Mom said to remind you 'specially," said Harvey, bestowing a keys-of-the-kingdom look, and Chrissie, still cool but wanting him to have a taste of the delights in store, said, "I'm going to wear my nurse's costume that I got for my birthday, because Granny's never seen it, and Harvey's going to show her his bow and arrows."

"The arrows have rubber caps on them, for now," said Harvey at an involuntary expression on Haddon's face. "Because they could be very dangerous. Well, so long, Mr. Haddon. Thanks for the swim."

They skipped off hand in hand, a practice Haddon knew he should regard as charming but which he looked on sourly instead.

He plunged back into the pool and swam steadily for half an hour, alternating crawl, breaststroke, sidestroke, backstroke in obedience to his doctor's instructions. Stretched out to dry on the concrete deck, he watched the sunny marblings of the disturbed water and saw, detachedly, a different and unpleasant pattern: the "damned old crone" coming "now"; the angry fist striking the desk; the bow and arrows; even, ridiculous though it seemed, the diminutive nurse's uniform.

Most significant of all was the fact that Menlo, apparently believing himself to be alone, had spoken that casually vicious phrase aloud. To do that he must have been driven indeed.

Apart from their being the parents of such children, the Menlos were pleasant enough. Barbara Menlo was a tall slender thirty, with short dark hair, an extremely long neck, and willowy shoulders. Her husband, Richard, was a good ten years older, with a face that belonged on a public-relations man, which he was—faintly humorous, horn-rimmed-and-eyeglassed, confident.

"Granny" was a surprise.

Haddon didn't know what he had expected of this relative, clearly downgraded in the children's eyes, but he was somehow startled to find Mrs. Fielding thin, tanned, calm, and very smartly dressed. It was only simple mathematics that placed her in her early fifties.

Damned old crone? Far from it, in any accepted sense, so that was the terminology of violent personal dislike, or bitter resentment. Or, coupled with the word *now*, fear.

Cocktails were on the patio. "We have to take advantage of this weather while we can," explained Barbara Menlo to her mother, "because it really blows in August and every tumbleweed in New Mexico winds up right here. And it clouds over regularly at four o'clock, although"—she turned, smiling—"I suppose I shouldn't be telling you all this, Mr. Haddon."

"Lessen the shock," said Haddon mildly. He glanced at Mrs. Fielding. "Do you live in Manhattan—the home of the brave?"

"Yonkers. Very different," said Mrs. Fielding. "Very small-towny, in a nice sense, if you've lived there as long as I have. Although now I—"

"Don't shoot the bartender, he's doing his best," said Menlo cheerily, gathering glasses out of startled hands. "Where's Florence Nightingale with something edible, may I ask? *Chrissie!*" he roared, and out she came, backing carefully through the sliding glass doors from the living room with a silver bowl of nuts and a plate of crackers and dip. She wore a navy cape over a child-sized white uniform, and a frilled cap which gave her the look of a ministering angel. She said reproachfully, "It's *medicine,* Daddy."

"Sorry about that, Nurse," said Menlo jovially. "Where's Harv?"

"Out putting up his target, of course," said Chrissie, indicating with her chin, and indeed a small figure could be seen in the distance, toiling back from the ditch bank at the end of the Menlo property. "Would you like some of these, Granny?"

"That's 'Grandmama,' " said Barbara in a steely voice. " 'Would you like some of these, Grandmama'?"

Chrissie inclined her prettily capped head and said, "I'm sorry, Grandmama. Would you?" and Mrs. Fielding inspected the offerings with none of the flustered overgratitude sometimes drawn forth from otherwise sensible adults on such occasions. "I will have a nut," she said pleasantly. "Thank you, Chrissie." Obscurely, Haddon felt like cheering.

"We're all going to a horse show tomorrow," said Chrissie, coming around to Haddon. "All Palominos, they're the prettiest horses, and they only have it once a year. Would you like to come?"

"Actually we're not, sweetie," said Barbara, looking faintly worried. "Daddy and Grandmama have some kind of mysterious appointment in the morning, so they'll be using the car. But there's an Appaloosa show next week, and I'm sure we can get to—"

"I hate Appaloosas," interrupted Chrissie in a clear steady

voice, "and Daddy promised. Daddy . . . ?" Always neat, she set down her burdens with care and departed into the house.

Barbara said without much apology, "She's such a single-minded child. As a matter of fact, the horse show doesn't begin until eleven, so I suppose there's a chance—"

But Haddon's attention was on Mrs. Fielding, who had unobtrusively taken a pill from a small silver box in her purse and was gathering herself as if to rise. He said, "May I get you some water?" and she gave him a smile and nodded.

Haddon had been in the house before, and wended his way through the glass doors and angled to his right. Even if he hadn't known where the kitchen was, the tap of cracked ice and the sound of running water would have told him. From this perspective only a short stretch of counter was visible, with the drinks tray and Menlo's hands measuring and pouring Scotch over the ice in four glasses. There was also the entranced voice of Chrissie, obviously picking up an earlier thread: ". . . just a teensy-weensy bit sick?"

Menlo, finished with his bartending duties, raised a hand with the thumb and forefinger a judicious half inch apart. "Oh, about that much."

Out of sight, Chrissie giggled, a smothered spillover of excitement that affected Haddon like a fingernail drawn across a blackboard. There was something in the kitchen, he would have sworn it, that didn't belong among squares of late sunlight on the brick-patterned vinyl floor, the bowl of fruit, the blue pottery jar full of nasturtiums.

Menlo gave him an unruffled smile when Haddon explained his errand, but Chrissie's hand had gone swiftly to her mouth. She jumped up at once and offered to bring the glass of water to her grandmother, but just then Haddon would not have trusted her with crumbs for a sparrow. He wondered, as he followed his host outside, what kind of pills Mrs. Fielding took, and why.

Twenty minutes later she told him. The Menlos seemed to take it for granted their guests were chafing to see Harvey's prowess with bow and arrow, and struck out energetically into the field at the sound of a distant hail. Haddon and Mrs. Fielding followed more slowly, and even before she said, "I think this is far enough for me," he had guessed that her calm was really a careful and necessary pacing.

"Heart," she said in a crisp dismissive tone, as though to apologize for public pill-swallowing. "Nothing very alarming, so long as I'm careful. As a matter of fact, though, I'm much more excited than I'm supposed to be, right now . . . You look like a good secret-keeper, Mr. Haddon."

Haddon assured her he was—and moved reflexively as Harvey, twenty-five feet away and apparently checking up on the attention of his audience, turned squarely around with his bow at full stretch. Sunlight shot along the length of the arrow, including the metal tip.

Menlo bellowed, "Damn it, Harv, watch that thing!" and after a second Harvey pivoted obediently and then released the arrow. Even from a distance its impact on the target was formidable, and Mrs. Fielding gave a little shudder.

"I hope they don't intend to let him aim that at birds . . . As I was saying, Mr. Haddon, Barbara doesn't know it yet because I want to surprise her, but I think I'm going to be coming out here to live. She's my only child, you know, and we've always been close. My doctor was afraid of this altitude for me, but he's found a medication that he thinks will lick that. I've been keeping my fingers crossed for a year, while Richard's been making some investments for me and looking around for a small house."

"And that's your appointment for tomorrow," said Haddon, smiling at her; her pleasure was contagious.

"Yes, he thinks he's found what I want. I really don't know what you make of me, confiding all my plans like this, but I had to tell someone."

"I won't say a word," promised Haddon, but as soon as he had spoken he felt a chill flash over him. With the mention of investments, Menlo's furious *now* might well be explained: how often before had men appropriated money entrusted to them, assuring themselves that there would be plenty of time to replace it? Or was Haddon merely prejudiced, largely because he didn't like the children? And even if he was right in his impression of a sharpening pattern, how could he, a near-stranger to this likable woman, warn her in a way which would not seem mad or monstrous or both?

Harvey had sent off his other arrows and was packing up his target while the Menlos and little navy-and-white Chrissie, anchoring her frilly cap with one hand, started back toward them. "I hope Chrissie won't let that uniform go to her head," said Haddon, choosing his words with care. "I have a little niece"—this was a firm and fluent lie—"who thought she could really dispense medicine, and made the whole family ill for a week."

Mrs. Fielding gazed at him thoughtfully. "Oh, I'm sure Chrissie wouldn't do anything like that," she said.

Haddon was pressed to stay for dinner, but he went home. For the rest of the evening he told himself variously that he had a suspicious mind; that it was impossible to guarantee the safety of another person, especially someone you had barely met; that Barbara Menlo must know, in a general way, of investments made for her mother by her husband over the course of a year. He also convinced himself that, the change in altitude notwithstanding, Mrs. Fielding's heart condition could hardly be such that her sudden death would pass unquestioned.

The ambulance left the Menlo driveway at 9:30 the next morning, but the police cars were there for another hour. It was not until five o'clock that afternoon that Haddon learned the exact sequence of events.

Chrissie (getting the last bit of mileage out of her nurse's costume, reflected Haddon grimly) had dispensed chocolate-covered mints after dinner, and they had all retired early in deference to Mrs. Fielding's fatigue. In the morning Barbara Menlo had tiptoed out of the bedroom to wake her mother, deciding to give her husband another twenty minutes of sleep while she started breakfast, and then gone back to rouse him, and could not.

It was several hours too late for that.

And Chrissie had come skipping along the carpeted hall outside the door which her mother had instinctively closed, her gray eyes full of mischief. "I think we're going to be able to go to the horse show after all," she said, "because"—she held her lifted thumb and forefinger a judicious half inch apart—"Daddy's going to be just a teensy-weensy bit sick."

HOW TO TRAP A CROOK

by Julian Symons

The American businessman and art collector was no fool when it came to buying a genuine Corot. But there was no harm in being doubly sure. So it was obviously a case for the connoisseurship of Max van Galen, "the greatest expert on Corot outside France"—and for the criminological connoisseurship of Francis Quarles . . .

A PRETTY little swindle, Francis Quarles said afterward, one that showed how the most intelligent of detectives can be made to look like a fool. But in telling the story, which involved at one point his own distinct discomfiture, Quarles retained the air of imperturbable self-esteem that infuriated so many of his acquaintances.

The affair began, as Quarles told it, when Charles Henderson was brought by Molly Player into Quarles's office with the big window overlooking Trafalgar Square. Henderson was a big, ruddy, conservatively dressed American.

"Mr. Quarles, you may not know who I am—"

Quarles held up a hand. "I should think it very remiss not to have *Who's Who in America* on my shelves, and after your telephone call not to consult it. You are the president of the Porkette Manufacturing and Canning Company, you have a wife and three children, an apartment in New York, and a house on Long Island. You are known colloquially as Porkette Henderson. The financial section of the *Times* tells me that you are here to find new retail outlets for Porkette. Correct so far?"

"Correct but irrelevant," Henderson said. It is unusual for a detective to be disliked by a client, but as Quarles realized, Henderson obviously disliked him from the start. Was it the rather extravagantly Edwardian cut of the detective's jacket, the large diamond ring he wore, or simply his air of knowing beforehand what you were about to say? Whatever the reason, Quarles sensed the antagonism and responded to it. As Henderson's manner became more brisk and businesslike, Quarles's appeared more esthetically languid.

"I suspect I may be about to be conned, and my friend Willard Monteith—"

"The Chicago attorney."

"Yes. Willard told me you'd helped him in a matter relating to a dispute about a picture."

"An attempt to provide a provenance for a fake Matisse, yes. A flight to Paris, a chat with a couple of colleagues there, and the matter was settled."

"Willard reckoned you knew your way about the art world."

Henderson's gaze shifted to the picture above Quarles's desk. "That's a nice Utrillo."

"Yves Poirier of the Galerie Poirier gave it to me after I had recovered his wife's three kidnaped cats."

"I like to think I've got the finest private collection of nineteenth-century paintings in New York," Henderson said. "And every time I come over I try to add to it. Have you heard of a man named Charles Scrutton?"

"The Scrutton Gallery, just off New Bond Street. I know him slightly, only slightly."

"He's offered me a Corot landscape. It's done in that typical silvery Corot style. And the price is reasonable, very reasonable."

"And you are asking for my advice. Simple, Mr. Henderson. I said I knew Scrutton only slightly, but I know his reputation well enough. Don't buy from him. Or if you must buy, get the provenance of the picture established beyond doubt—speak to its former owner yourself if possible—"

"Mr. Quarles." Beneath his silver crew cut Henderson's face was red with annoyance. "I am not totally stupid about buying pictures, and I know Scrutton's reputation. At the same time I'm not convinced that I shouldn't buy from him."

"He has never been convicted, or even charged with anything, that's true."

"More than that, I know a couple of people who have bought pictures from him with which they're perfectly happy. They swear Scrutton's absolutely honest."

Quarles's bulky shoulders shrugged under the Edwardian jacket. "If you are not interested in my advice I don't see how I can help you."

"Willard said you were friendly with Max van Galen. I suppose he's just about the greatest expert on Corot and Manet outside France. If it was possible to get van Galen to take a look at this Corot of Scrutton's, I'd be grateful."

"Why not ask him yourself?"

"I've tried." Henderson's face grew redder. "I never even got to talk to him. His secretary said Professor van Galen was too busy to deal with personal requests. You know he's Professor of Fine Art at London University."

"So you want me to arrange something for you that you can't do yourself? Just to make it clear."

Henderson glared. "I'll pay you for your services."

Quarles held up the hand on which the diamond ring glinted. "That doesn't arise. This will be for amusement only." He spoke to Molly in the outer office. "Molly, see if you can get me Max van Galen. In person. Thank you."

He smiled blandly at Henderson, who got up and looked out of the window at Nelson on his column and the lions below. The telephone rang, and Quarles spoke.

"Max? Francis Quarles. I'm very well, and how are you? No, nothing like that, just what may be an entertaining little problem concerning a Corot. An American acquaintance of mine has been offered one. By Charles Scrutton." A pause, and then Quarles laughed. "I've told him that, but he is not deterred. Is there any chance you might be able to look at it yourself? Of course you're busy, Max, but the walk to New Bond Street will do you good." He put his hand over the receiver. "When are you seeing Scrutton, to decide about the picture?"

"Eleven o'clock tomorrow."

"Could you be there at eleven fifteen tomorrow morning, Max? Marvelous. Yes, I'll promise that." He put down the telephone. "Max is a great man for fish. I promised him lunch at Prunier's after we'd looked at the picture. That will be at your expense."

Henderson grunted. "Why did you say eleven fifteen to him instead of eleven?"

"Because it will give Scrutton time to make his sales pitch for the picture and to guarantee its genuineness. Our objects are not identical, Mr. Henderson. You want to make sure that you are not conned. For me, this should be a simple demonstration of how to trap a crook."

"You're convinced Scrutton will try to put something over on me?"

"Of course. From his point of view that's the object of the exercise."

Henderson and Quarles got out of the taxi. The façade said *Charles Scrutton, Fine Art* in elegant lettering. In the window was a single small painting of a mill and trees, labeled *17th Century Dutch School.*

Inside the gallery a sleek assistant advanced and then retreated as Henderson identified himself. Charles Scrutton came forward with hand outstretched. He was a tall florid man with thick muttonchop whiskers, and he wore a suit of powerful checks. His manner was bluffly rural. He looked as little like an art dealer as it was possible to imagine.

"Mr. Henderson." He paused fractionally before giving Quarles a firm handshake. "And Francis Quarles, isn't it? I think we last met at that party for the Whistler exhibition."

"Mr. Quarles is interested," Henderson said. "He has a fine Utrillo on his office wall. He wanted to see this Corot."

"There it is," Scrutton switched on a light, illuminating a picture which showed rocks, trees, and a stream. The two men stood looking at it. Quarles could not have told whether it was by Corot or by one of a dozen other French artists.

"It's Corot's style, all right," Henderson said.

Scrutton pulled at his muttonchop whiskers. "Mr. Henderson, I'm not going to sell you this picture."

"You mean you've got another buyer?" Henderson flushed angrily. "I call that—"

"I won't sell it to you because it is not a genuine Corot. I'm very much afraid it's from Dr. Jousseaume's collection. You've heard of Jousseaume? He made a tremendous collection of Corot paintings and drawings. When he died in 1923 they were let loose on the market and three-quarters of them turned out to be fakes, done especially for the doctor's benefit. Like other dealers I watch out for things from the Jousseaume collection and try to avoid them, but every so often you get caught. I've checked this one thoroughly, and I'm afraid there's no doubt about it." He gave them a ruefully comical glance. "It doesn't often happen, but this time Charles Scrutton's been had."

Quarles asked, "As a matter of interest, what will you do with the painting now?"

"Put it in a sale as 'attributed to Corot' or 'in the manner of Corot,' for whatever it will fetch. That won't be much." The telephone rang. The assistant murmured something to Scrutton, who excused himself and left them.

Henderson turned to Quarles. "A simple demonstration of how to trap a crook, eh? How about that, Quarles? Admit you were wrong."

Before the detective could reply the door opened and Max van Galen came into the gallery.

The art expert was a short squat man with a hurried, jerky walk, and the wide mouth and popping eyes of a frog. His voice was a frog's croak.

"Quarles, how are you, nice to see you again." He gave a perfunctory handshake and a popeyed stare at Henderson, and said, "Now, where's this picture you want me to look at?"

Scrutton came back and said, "Professor, this is a pleasure. And an honor. You don't know me, but I recognize you. I'm Charles Scrutton."

Van Galen allowed his hand to be pumped. "The picture."

Henderson spoke in some confusion. "Mr. Scrutton, I may as well admit I asked the Professor to come along here and check on the picture. I'm not feeling too proud of myself at the moment."

"*You* asked?" Van Galen snapped at him. "I don't know you. I spoke to Francis Quarles here."

Quarles said, "The point is that Mr. Scrutton has discovered that the painting is not genuine and has very properly withdrawn it."

"It's one of the Jousseaume lot, I'm afraid. See for yourself."

Scrutton switched on the light above the painting again. Van Galen took a magnifying glass from his pocket, glanced at the painting, and immediately put the glass back.

"A close inspection is not necessary. This is a very poor piece of work. I am surprised you should have bought it."

"We all make mistakes," Scrutton said cheerfully. His glance moved quickly from one to the other of them. "Professor van Galen, since you're here I should like to ask you a favor. A couple of days ago I acquired another picture, which I do believe to be a genuine Corot. Would you care to give your opinion of it?"

"I am always ready to look at a picture."

"I'm grateful. Jordan, will you get that little Corot landscape?" Scrutton said to Henderson, "I couldn't offer you this picture because at the time you got in touch with me I didn't possess it."

Jordan returned with a picture which he stood on a small table. It showed a snowy landscape, with a small house in the background and a man standing beside it. The four of them looked at it.

"Full of charm, don't you think?" Scrutton said. "It's called 'Winter Landscape.' Rather like the Lincolnshire fen country, where I was brought up."

"This is a different matter from that other—affair." Van Galen bent over, examining the picture closely under his magnifying glass. He put away the glass and went on looking, then straightened up with a sigh of pleasure, and said simply, "Yes."

"It's a genuine Corot?" the American asked.

"It is a very good Corot, a lovely picture. It is a pleasure to see it."

"Mr. Scrutton, would you like to put a price on that picture?"

"If you'll just come into my office, we can talk about it."

Henderson paused at the office door and said with heavy irony, "You don't have any doubts, Quarles?"

"As far as I'm concerned, Max van Galen's word is law."

"And of course you're not an art expert yourself."

"I'm not an art expert," Quarles agreed.

Van Galen rubbed his hands. "I am looking forward to lunch. Are plovers' eggs in season?"

Quarles was standing beside the picture, with his back to van Galen. "I doubt it. You may have to settle for caviar as an opening course." He turned. "There's no doubt about the authenticity of this Corot?"

Van Galen laughed. "You know the definition of being positive? To be mistaken at the top of your voice. An expert learns to be careful. But I should be prepared to offer a sporting bet of twenty to one that this is a genuine Corot. You didn't expect this to happen?"

Before Quarles could reply, Henderson and Scrutton returned. "Can I take it with me?" the American asked. "I want to do a little gloating in my suite at the Savoy."

"I'd sooner send it along—there are customs forms to complete, and so on."

"I should like to take it now, Mr. Scrutton. You have my check."

Scrutton hesitated, then said, "Yes, of course. Jordan, will you pack up this picture for Mr. Henderson." The sleek assistant came forward and took the Corot. "It's a pleasure to sell something to a man who's going to enjoy it."

"I'm very very happy." A smile spread over Henderson's face. "Are you happy, Quarles?"

"I'm glad you've got what you wanted." Quarles strolled about the gallery, looking at the other pictures. He turned as Jordan came back with the picture wrapped in heavy paper. "I thought it was charming, as Scrutton said."

"Pleased you approve of my choice."

"So charming that I should like to see it again." Scrutton stared at him. "Would you unwrap it, please?"

"What the hell d'you mean, what are you talking about? Jordan, stop him."

Quarles was already at the wrapping paper, tearing it away. There was an undignified scuffle, and then the picture was

evealed. It showed a snowy landscape, with a small house in the
ackground and a man standing beside it.

"Are you off your head, Quarles?" Henderson asked. "That's
ny picture."

"It is not your picture." Quarles moved quickly across to the
oom where Jordan had taken the Corot, went in, and came out
vith another picture in his hands showing the same scene. "*This* is
our Corot. If you'll just lift that telephone and ring for the police,
Max, I'll make sure that Mr. Scrutton stays here."

"It was a neat variation on an old trick," Quarles said. "He
ained your confidence by denouncing an obvious fake, then
howed the genuine Corot, and then substituted the copy. Max
eing there was a stroke of luck for him, because his authentica-
ion left you without the shadow of a doubt. You wouldn't have
othered about any further examination, would you?"

A chastened Henderson shook his head. Van Galen said through
mouthful of caviar, "It was a very good copy. Carefully done. I
hould have needed a close examination to be sure about it."

"That's what I don't understand," Henderson said hesitantly.
"You knew it was a copy immediately, Quarles. That seems like
nagic to me. How did you do it?"

"A genuine, a perfect lobster bisque." Quarles looked at his
mpty plate with regret. "I knew there must be some trick
nvolved, you see."

"So?"

"So I marked the frame of the genuine Corot on the back with a
ross, while you were making your deal with Scrutton. There was
o cross on the frame of the other one."

Henderson looked disappointed. "I see. Really very simple."

"But of course. Didn't I tell you it would be a simple
lemonstration of how to trap a crook?"

SEE HOW THEY RUN

by Robert Bloch

The phrase "crime story" means something different to Robert Bloch—something different from what it means to every other writer of crime stories. You will see what we mean when you read "See How They Run" . . .

We have often wondered: Has Robert Bloch ever written a story that doesn't have something special about it? . . .

APRIL 2nd

Okay, Doc, you win.

I'll keep my promise and make regular entries, but damned if

I'll start out with a heading like *Dear Diary*. Or *Dear Doctor*, either. You want me to tell it like it is? Okay, but the way it is right now, Doc, beware. If you've got any ideas about wading in my stream of consciousness, just watch out for the alligators.

I know what you're thinking. "Here's a professional writer who claims he has a writer's block. Get him to keep a diary and he'll be writing in spite of himself. Then he'll see how wrong he is." Right, Doc? Write, Doc?

Only that's not my real problem. My hangup is the exact opposite—antithetical, if you're looking for something fancy. Logorrhea. Verbosity. Two-bit words from a dime-a-dozen writer? But that's what they always say at the studio: writers are a dime a dozen.

Okay, so here's your dime. Run out and buy me a dozen writers. Let's see—I'll have two Hemingways, one Thomas Wolfe, a James Joyce, a couple of Homers if they're fresh, and six William Shakespeares.

I almost said it to Gerber when he dropped me from the show. But what's the use? Those producers have only one idea. They point at the parking lot and say, "I'm driving the Caddy and you're driving the Volks." Sure. If you're so smart, why aren't you rich?

Call it a rationalization if you like. You shrinks are great at pinning labels on everything. Pin the tail on the donkey, that's the name of the game, and the patient is always the jackass. Pardon me, it's not "patient," it's "analysand." For fifty bucks an hour you can afford to dream up a fancy word. And for fifty bucks an hour I can't afford not to word up some fancy dreams.

If that's what you want from me, forget it. There are no dreams. Not any more. Once upon a time (as we writers say) there was a dream. A dream about coming out to Hollywood and cracking the television market. Write for comedy shows, make big money in your spare time this new easy way, buy a fancy pad with a big swimming pool, and live it up until you settle down with a cute little chick.

Dreams are nothing to worry about. It's only when they come true that you've got trouble. Then you find out that the comedy isn't funny any more, the big money disappears, and the swimming pool turns into a stream of consciousness. Even a cute little chick like Jean changes to something else. It's not a dream any more, it's a nightmare, and it's real.

There's a problem for you, Doc. Cure me of reality.

April 5th

A little-known historical fact. Shortly after being wounded in Peru, Pizarro, always a master of understatement, wrote that he was Incapacitated.

Damn it, Doc, I say it's funny! I don't buy your theory about puns being a form of oral aggression. Because I'm not the aggressive type.

Hostile, yes. Why shouldn't I be? Fired off the show after three seasons of sweating blood for Gerber and that lousy no-talent comic of his. Lou Lane couldn't get a job as M.C. in a laundromat until I started writing his material and now he's Mr. Neilsen himself, to hear him tell it.

But that's not going to trigger me into doing anything foolish. I don't have to. One season without me and he'll be back where he belongs—a parking attendant in a Drive-In Mortuary. Curb Service. We Pick Up and Deliver. Ha, ha.

Gerber gave me the same pitch; my stuff is getting sour. We don't want black comedy. It's nasty, and this is a family-type show. Okay, so maybe it was my way of releasing tension, getting it out of my system—catharsis, isn't that the term? And it made me come on a little too strong. Which is where you get into the act. Blow my mind for me, put me back on the track, and I'll get myself another assignment and make with the family-type funnies again.

Meanwhile, no problems. Jean is bringing in the bread. I never figured it that way when we got married. At first I thought her singing was a gag and I went along with it. Let the voice coach keep her busy while I was working on the show—give her something to do for a hobby. Even when she took the first few club dates it was still Amateur Night as far as I was concerned. But then they hit her with the recording contract, and after the singles came the album, etc. My little chick turned into a canary.

Funny about Jean. Such a nothing when I met her. Very good in the looks department but aside from that, nothing. It's the singing that made the difference. Finding her voice was like finding herself. All of a sudden, confidence.

Of course I'm proud of her but it still shakes me up a little. The way she takes over, like insisting I see a psychiatrist. Not that I'm hacked about it, I know she's only doing it for my own good, but it's hard to get used to. Like last night at the Guild screening, her agent introduced us to some friends of his—"I want you to meet Jean Norman and her husband."

Second billing. That's not for me, Doc. I'm a big boy now. The last thing I need is an identity crisis, right? And as long as we're playing true confessions, I might as well admit Jean has one point—I've been hitting the bottle a little too hard lately, since I got canned.

I didn't mention it at our last session, but this is the main reason she made me come to you. She says alcohol is my security blanket. Maybe taking it away would fix things. Or would it?

One man's security blanket is another man's shroud.

April 7th

You stupid jerk. What do you mean, alcoholism is only a symptom?

First of all, I'm not an alcoholic. Sure I drink, maybe I drink a lot, everybody drinks in this business. It's either that or pot or hard drugs and I'm not going to freak out and mess up my life. But you've got to have something to keep your head together and just because I belt a few doesn't mean I'm an alcoholic.

But for the sake of argument, suppose it does? You call it a symptom. A symptom of *what*?

Suppose you tell me that little thing. Sitting back in that overstuffed chair with your hands folded on your overstuffed gut and letting me do all the talking—let's hear you spill something for a change. What is it you suspect, Mr. Judge, Mr. Jury, Mr. Prosecuting Attorney, Mr. Executioner? What's the charge—heterosexuality in the first degree?

I'm not asking for sympathy. I get plenty of that from Jean. Too much. I'm up to here on the oh-you-poor-baby routine. I don't want tolerance or understanding or any of that phony jive. Just give me a few facts for a change. I'm tired of Jean playing Mommy and I'm tired of you playing Big Daddy. What I want is some real help, you've got to help me help me please please help me.

April 9th

Two resolutions.

Number one, I'm not going to drink any more. I'm quitting as of now, flat-out. I was stoned when I wrote that last entry and all I had to do was read it today when I'm sober to see what I've been doing to myself. So no more drinking. Not now or ever.

Number two. From now on I'm not showing this to Dr. Moss. I'll cooperate with him completely during therapy sessions but that's it. There's such a thing as invasion of privacy. And after what happened today I'm not going to lay myself wide open again. Particularly without an anesthetic, and I've just given that up.

If I keep on writing everything down it will be for my own information, a matter of personal record. Of course I won't tell him that. He'd come up with some fancy psychiatric zinger, meaning I'm talking to myself. I've got it figured out—the shrinks are all authority figures and they use their labels as putdowns. Who needs it?

All I need is to keep track of what's happening, when things start to get confused. Like they did at the session today.

First of all, this hypnotherapy bit.

As long as this is just between me and myself I'll admit the whole idea of being hypnotized always scared me. And if I had any suspicion the old creep was trying to put me under I'd have cut out of there in two seconds flat.

But he caught me off guard. I was on the couch and supposed to say whatever came into my head. Only I drew a blank, couldn't think of anything. Emotional exhaustion, he said, and turned down the lights. Why not close my eyes and relax? Not go to sleep, just daydream a little. Daydreams are sometimes more important than those that come in sleep. In fact he didn't want me to fall asleep, so if I'd concentrate on his voice and let everything hang loose—

He got to me. I didn't feel I was losing control, no panic, I knew where I was and everything, but he got to me. He must have, because he kept talking about memory. How memory is our own personal form of time travel, a vehicle to carry us back, way back to earliest childhood, didn't I agree? And I said yes, it can carry us back, carry me back, back to old Virginny.

Then I started to hum something I hadn't thought about in years. And he said what's that, it sounds like a nursery rhyme, and I said that's right, Doc, don't you know it, *Three Blind Mice.*

Why don't you sing the words for me, he said. So I started.

Three blind mice, three blind mice,
See how they run, see how they run!
They all ran after the farmer's wife,
Did you ever see such a sight in your life
As three blind mice, three blind mice?

"Very nice," he said. "But didn't you leave out a line?"

"What line?" I said. All at once, for no reason at all, I could feel myself getting very uptight. "That's the song. My old lady sang that to me when I was a baby. I wouldn't forget a thing like that. What line?"

He started to sing it to me.

They all ran after the farmer's wife,
She cut off their heads with a carving knife,

Then it happened.

It wasn't like remembering. It was happening. Right now, all over again.

Late at night. Cold. Wind blowing. I wake up. I want a drink of water. Everyone asleep. Dark. I go into the kitchen.

Then I hear the noise. Like a tapping on the floor. It scares me. I turn on the light and I see it. In the corner behind the door. The trap. Something moving in it. All gray and furry and flopping up and down.

The mouse. Its paw is caught in the trap and it can't get loose. Maybe I can help. I pick up the trap and push the spring back. I hold the mouse. It wiggles and squeaks and that scares me more. I don't want to hurt it, just put it outside so it can run away. But it wiggles and squeaks and then it bites me.

When I see the blood on my finger I'm not scared any more. I get mad. All I want to do is help and it bites me. Dirty little thing. Squeaking at me with its eyes shut. Blind. Three Blind Mice. Farmer's wife.

There. On the sink. The carving knife.

It tries to bite me again. I'll fix it. I take the knife. And I cut, I drop the knife, and I start to scream.

I was screaming again, thirty years later, and I opened my eyes and there I was in Dr. Moss's office, bawling like a kid.

"How old were you?" Dr. Moss said.

"Seven."

It just popped out. I hadn't remembered how old I was, hadn't remembered what happened—it was all blacked out of my mind, just like the line in the nursery rhyme.

But I remember now. I remember everything. My old lady finding the mouse head in the trash can and then beating the hell out of me. I think that's what made me sick, not the bite, even though the doctor who came and gave me the shot said it was infection that caused the fever. I was laid up in bed for two weeks. When I'd wake up screaming from the nightmares, my old lady used to come in and hold me and tell me how sorry she was. She always told me how sorry she was—after she did something to me.

I guess that's when I really started to hate her. No wonder I built so many of Lou Lane's routines on mother and mother-in-law gags. Oral aggression? Could be. All these years and I never knew it, never realized how I hated her. I still hate her now, hate her—

What I need is a drink.

April 23rd

Two weeks since I wrote the last entry. I told Dr. Moss I quit keeping a diary and he believed me. I told Dr. Moss a lot of things besides that, and whether he believed me or not I don't know. Not that I care one way or the other. I don't believe everything he tells *me,* either.

Hebephrenic schizophrenia. Now there's a real grabber.

Meaning certain personality types, confronted with a stress situation they can't handle, revert to childhood or infantile behavior levels.

I looked it up the other day after I got a peek at Moss's notes, but if that's what he thinks, then he's the one who's flipped.

Dr. Moss has a thing about words like flipped, nuts, crazy. Mental disturbance, that's his speed.

That and regression. He's hung up on regression. No more hypnosis—I told him that was out, absolutely—and he got the message. But he uses other techniques like free association, and they seem to work. What really happens is that I talk myself into remembering, talk my way back into the past.

I've come up with some weirdies. Like not drinking a glass of milk until I was five years old—my old lady let me drink that formula stuff out of the bottle and there was a big hassle over it when I went to kindergarten and wouldn't touch my milk any other way. Then she clouted me one and said I made her ashamed when she had to explain to the teacher, and she took the bottle away. But it was her fault in the first place. I'm beginning to understand why I hated her.

My old man wasn't any prize, either. Whenever we had company over for dinner he'd come out with things I'd said to him, all the dumb kid stuff you say when you don't know any better, and everybody would laugh. Hard to realize kids get embarrassed, too, until you remember the way it was. The old man kept needling me to make stupid cracks just so he could take bows for repeating them to his buddies. No wonder you forget things like that—it hurts too much to remember.

It still hurts.

Of course there were good memories, too. When you're a kid, most of the time you don't give a damn about anything, you don't worry about the future, you don't even understand the real meaning of things like pain and death—and that's worth remembering.

I always seem to start out that way in our sessions but then Moss steers me into the other stuff. Catharsis, he says, it's good for you. Let it all hang out. Okay, I'm cooperating, but when we finish up with one of those children's hours I'm ready to go home and have a nice, big drink.

Jean is starting to bug me about it again. We had another hassle last night when she came home from the club date. Singing, that's all she's really interested in nowadays, never has any time for me.

Okay, so that's her business, why doesn't she mind it and let me alone? So I was stoned, so what? I tried to tell her about the therapy, how I was hurting and how a drink helped. "Why don't you grow up?" she said. "A little pain never hurt anyone."

Sometimes I think they're all crazy.

April 25th

They're crazy, all right.

Jean calling Dr. Moss and telling him I was back on the bottle again.

"On the bottle," I said, when he told me about it. "What kind of talk is that? You'd think she was my mother and I was her baby."

"Isn't that what you think?" Moss said.

I just looked at him. I didn't know what to say. This was one time when he did all the talking.

He started out very quietly, about how he'd hoped therapy would help us make certain discoveries together. And over a period of time I'd begin to understand the meaning of the pattern I'd established in my life. Only it hadn't seemed to work out that way, and while as a general thing he didn't care to run the risk of inducing psychic trauma, in this case it seemed indicated that he clarify the situation for me.

That part I can remember, almost word for word, because it made sense. But what he told me after that is all mixed up.

Like saying I have an oral fixation on the bottle because it represents the formula bottle my mother took away from me when I was a kid. And the reason I got into comedy writing was to reproduce the situation where my father used to tell people all my funny remarks—because even if they laughed it meant I was getting attention, and I wanted attention. But at the same time I resented my father taking the credit for amusing them, just like I resented Lou Lane making it big because of what I wrote for him. That's why I blew the job, writing material he couldn't use. I wanted him to use it and bomb out, because I hated him. Lou Lane had become a father image and I hated my father.

I remember looking at Dr. Moss and thinking he has to be crazy. Only a crazy shrink could come up with things like that.

He was really wild. Talking about my old lady. How I hated her so much when I was a kid I had to displace my feelings—transfer them to something else so I wouldn't feel so guilty about it.

Like the time I got up for a drink of water. I really wanted my bottle back, but my mother wouldn't give it to me. And maybe the bottle was a symbol of something she gave my father. Hearing them was what really woke me up and I hated her for that most of all.

Then I went into the kitchen and saw the mouse. The mouse reminded me of the nursery rhyme and the nursery rhyme reminded me of my mother. I took the knife, but I didn't want to kill the mouse. In my mind I was really killing my mother—

That's when I hit him. Right in his dirty mouth.

Nobody talks about my mother that way.

Apr 29

Better this way. Don't need Moss. Don't need therapy. Do it myself.

Been doing it. Regression. Take a little drink, take a little trip. Little trip down memory lane.

Not to the bad things. Good things. All the warm soft memories. The time I was in bed with the fever and mother came in with the ice cream on the tray. And my father bringing me that toy.

That's what's nice about remembering. Best thing in the world. There was a poem we used to read in school. I still remember it. "Backward, turn backward, O time in your flight, make me a child again just for tonight!" Well, no problem. A few drinks and away you go. Little oil for the old time machine.

When Jean found out about Dr. Moss she blew her stack. I had to call him up right away and apologize, she screamed.

"To hell with that," I said. "I don't need him any more. I can work this thing out for myself."

"Maybe you'll have to," Jean said.

Then she told me about Vegas. Lounge date, three weeks on the Strip. All excited because this means she's really made it—the big time. Lou Lane is playing the big room and he called her agent and told her it was all set.

"Wait a minute," I said. "Lou Lane set this up for you?"

"He's been a good friend," Jean told me. "All through this he's kept in touch, because he's worried about you. He'd be your friend, too, if you'd only let him."

Sure he would. With friends like that you don't need enemies. My eyes were opening fast. No wonder he squawked to Gerber and got me off the show. So he could move in on Jean. He had it set up, all right. The two of them, playing Vegas together. Jean in the lounge, him in the big room, and then, after the show—

For a moment there I was so shook up I couldn't see straight and I don't know what I would have done if I could. But I mean I really couldn't see straight because I started to cry. And then she was holding me and it was all right again. She'd cancel the Vegas date and stay here with me, we'd work this out together. But I had to promise her one thing—no more drinking.

I promised. The way she got to me I would have promised her anything.

So I watched her clean out the bar and then she went into town to see her agent.

It's a lie, of course. She could have picked up the phone and called him from here. So she's doing something else.

Like going straight to Lou Lane and spilling everything to him. I can just hear her. "Don't worry, darling, I had to beg off this time or he'd get too suspicious. But what's three weeks in Vegas when we've got a whole lifetime ahead of us?" And then the two of them get together—

No. I'm not going to think about it. I don't have to think about it, there are other things, better things.

That's why I took the bottle. The one she didn't know about when she cleaned out the bar, the one I had stashed away in the basement.

I'm not going to worry any more. She can't tell me what to do. Take a little drink, take a little trip. That's all there is to it.

I'm home free.

Later

She broke the bottle.

She came in and saw me and grabbed the bottle away from me

and she broke it. I know she's mad because she ran into the kitchen and slammed the door. Why the kitchen?

Extension phone there.

Wonder if she'll try to call Dr. Moss.

Aprel 30

I was a bad boy.
The Dr. come. he sed what did you do.
I sed she took the bottel away.
He saw it on the floor the knive
I had to do it I sed.
He saw blood.
Like the mouse he sed.
No not a mouse. A canarry.
dont look in the trash can I sed
But he did.

FIFTY YEARS AFTER

by Anthony Gilbert

Once again we cannot resist saying it: Anthony Gilbert wrote a kind of crime story all her own; no one else in or out of the mystery field writes quite the same way about quite the same people . . . Here is the story of what happened fifty years ago in the home of Admiral Webb, at Number 4 Frederick Street in St. Charles-on-Sea, as seen through the eyes of Lily, one of the servants in the house—the story of Admiral Webb's ward, Vicky, the vital vivacious Vicky, the alluring and radiant Vicky, a girl "made for joy" . . .

WHEN I saw the house where the terrible thing happened, fifty years after the event, it scarcely seemed to have changed at all: a high narrow house sadly in need of a new coat of paint. In those days Admiral Webb had bought it for his wife and the three daughters whom Mrs. Webb hadn't contrived to marry off. Small chance they'll have here, the neighbors had said, for St. Charles-on-Sea had been born middle-aged.

The daughters were Miss Maude, the showy one in the splendid hats and flying scarves and Bohemian airs; she was once stopped on the High Street by an artist who wanted to paint her. In lieu of a husband she had her lawn tennis and croquet and was a member of the Bridge Club.

Miss Sarah was the religious one, and pretty Miss Meg was a real storybook daughter-at-home. Miss Meg paid calls with her mother in the hired carriage, arranged flowers, pottered about the garden. She was a wonderful dressmaker, made all her own clothes, but she never made so much as a smicket for Vicky.

Vicky was Victoria Gaye who burst into the household with all the suddenness of a bomb. One morning the Admiral received a letter with a London postmark, and for once he failed to go to his window chair in the club and play the chess tournament he was expected to win—chess was his passion, as gardening was Mrs. Webb's and religion Miss Sarah's.

About five o'clock he returned home, bringing with him a little girl of thirteen or so, small and dark, wearing a sailor suit much too young for her. Her luggage was one of those straw baskets that girls have when they first go out to service, before they graduate to a tin trunk.

"This is Victoria Gaye," he said. "Her mother and I were cousins, but when we were young we were more like brother and sister."

It seemed Mrs. Gaye had made a late improvident marriage, her husband had left her, and she had been eking out a wretched living copying music and teaching piano lessons to small children.

She had succumbed suddenly to some kind of heart condition, abandoning Vicky to the world.

"But fortunately the landlady found my address in Caroline's book and wrote to me," the Admiral wound up.

"I do not recall your mentioning her," said Mrs. Webb. She was short and solid, rather like the old Queen, with an alexandrine fringe, and she ruled her household with a rod of iron.

"Oh, Caroline was younger than I and inevitably our paths diverged. But she remembered she had a cousin. And now," he added to Vicky, who hadn't yet opened her mouth, "you will have cousins, too."

I seldom saw Mrs. Webb flabbergasted, but she was flabbergasted then.

"You have invited her here for a visit?" Not a welcoming word, mark you.

"This is to be her home," explained the Admiral in his bluff naval way. "It will be good to have something young about the house again."

"Our daughters," began Mrs. Webb, but he laughed and said, "They'll be pleased as Punch to have a younger sister to cosset." He really believed it. He smiled at Vicky and said, "This is Lily. She will show you the room that is to be yours. I daresay it'll not take long to get it shipshape."

It was an awkward situation from the start. Vicky—she asked me to call her that from the outset—was too young for anyone in that household except the Admiral. Miss Maude looked through her, Miss Sarah spent more time than ever wearing out the knees of her skirts praying in cold churches for the newcomer's soul, and to Miss Meg she was a mystery she couldn't hope to solve. They all shelved her conveniently.

But for the Admiral she'd have had a pretty poor time, with Mrs. Webb treating her like Little Orphan Annie and looking surprised each morning to find she was still on the premises. But the Admiral took to her from the beginning, and not just because he'd known her mother. He used to take her walking in the Garth—the big gardens opposite the house—when he came back from mornings at his club, and often on to tea at Anderson's, the famous pastry cooks whose wedding cakes were popular all over the county. If it was wet and he had no afternoon engagement, he taught her to play chess; he'd never been successful with his own girls, but he said she was as sharp as a man—a great compliment in those days.

When the question of her education cropped up, Mrs. Webb was all for sending her away to boarding school; there were no local schools because there were no local children, except during holiday periods when grandchildren came to visit. But once again the Admiral had his way.

"This is virtually the first settled home Victoria has had. Her days of being badgered from pillar to post are over."

Eventually a governess was decided on, and Letitia Bagguley joined the household. I was fascinated by her name before ever I saw her. She was nearly as dark as Vicky, with curly black hair and eyes as bright as a bird's. She was part Irish, I think, and she wasn't Mrs. Webb's choice—she had preferred a sober middle-aged woman named Sharman—but the Admiral said, "We are all old fogeys here—let her have someone young."

Miss Bagguley was twenty-two, which was practically childhood in St. Charles. When I saw the two of them together, I thought, Dynamite!—and was amazed that no one but myself seemed to notice. But to Mrs. Webb a governess was a governess, as impersonal as the housemaid or the postman.

I don't know how good a governess Miss Bagguley was, but she was very good for Vicky in other ways.

"You don't want to stay in Sleepy Hollow all your life," she'd say. "Life's for living."

She brought a bicycle with her and I had mine, and we used to run with Vicky, one of us on each side, in the lane behind the houses until Vicky could balance by herself. As soon as the

Admiral saw she could ride he bought her a bicycle of her own and she and Miss Bagguley would go soaring over the Downs which were wild and free in those days half a century ago.

"Is that child learning anything?" Mrs. Webb would demand.

And the Admiral would say, "She is learning to be happy."

Sometimes, when I had my afternoon off and Alfred couldn't meet me, I would go up to the Downs, too, and we would all have a cottage tea together. Mrs. Webb didn't know about it, of course; she never thought of Vicky as the equal of her own daughters, but she wouldn't have allowed her to have tea with a servant. (Alfred was my young man; we'd been keeping company for two years and as soon as he got a raise we would get married; but he didn't mean us to start in two rooms in his mother's house. What's worth having is worth waiting for, he said.)

Other times, when Miss Bagguley had her free afternoons—and she made friends the way a bear scents out honey—Vicky would come slipping down to the kitchen. Mrs. Skimpole, the cook, and Edwardes, the parlormaid, used to sit in the servants' sitting room in the front, but I never felt comfortable there; they were both so old. Vicky would sit with me and help me with darning and mending and we bought paper patterns and made her blouses—she'd have had little enough if she'd depended on Mrs. Webb.

"You must remember you will have to earn your own living," Mrs. Webb told Vicky. "Perhaps you could teach young children."

But Vicky laughed and said the only children she'd want to teach would be her own, though how she expected to meet a young man in Frederick Street I couldn't imagine. She'd never even catch sight of one over the banisters. Mind you, Miss Bagguley did her best—she took chances that Miss Sharman would never even have considered. Once, when I was out with Alfred, I saw the two of them at a beach café having tea with two men, neither of them quite as young as they'd like to be, but all laughing and chattering and Vicky smiling to beat the band. I recognized the men—part of the pierrot troupe that came to St.

Charles every summer and performed on the beach. The daughters wouldn't have paid threepence for a chair, but Miss Bagguley did, and—well, it was never hard for her to make friends.

Another time she'd take Vicky on the pier—ninepence including the price of a ticket for the current entertainment (the Admiral was generous with pocket money and Vicky was a natural spendthrift). They'd put coppers in the slot machines, playing football or horseracing. Vicky loved it.

I think, in the light of what happened later, Miss B. must have been glad she'd given the girl so much happiness. For you'd have said Vicky was made for joy. When that first surface lack of assurance had worn off and she knew the Admiral was on her side, she sparkled with vitality. Miss Sarah tried to cash in by asking her to keep some of her high spirits for God's service. No one else, except the Admiral, seemed to notice.

Vicky was sixteen when something happened that broke the whole pattern of affairs. Miss Bagguley's mother was suddenly taken ill and Letitia had to go up and look after her business; she had a boardinghouse in Cheshire and boardinghouses don't run themselves.

"She must go as soon as we can make arrangements," said Mrs. Webb.

"She must go today," said the Admiral and he ordered a fly and saw her off from the station.

"You must continue to study by yourself," Mrs. Webb told Vicky.

"There is no sense in lessons," Vicky told her. "How does knowing the principal products of the countries of Europe or the names of the chief rivers help one to live?"

"Even if you only teach small children," said Miss Maude carelessly, "you will need to know something. Parents expect value for their money." She was getting a bit long in the tooth now, past thirty and still on the hunt.

"Perhaps she could be a children's nurse," suggested Miss Meg, who was a nice girl, but not very well furnished upstairs.

But the Admiral said he regarded her as one of his own and wasn't going to have her cleaning nurseries and black-leading grates. He never understood—none of them did—that provided she was happy Vicky didn't care what she had to do. With Miss Bagguley out of the way for weeks—for Mrs. Bagguley didn't improve as they'd hoped—Vicky was like a dog without a tail. I blame the family for what followed. None of them put herself out to make her feel at home, and she was left to find her own entertainment.

Vicky spent long afternoons up on the Downs with her bicycle, bringing back flowers which she put into a bit of rough ground at the foot of Mrs. Webb's garden, so it was as though the woodland had crept in from the back lane. She worked in the garden, too; no one let her touch the plants, but she gathered the fallen leaves between two wooden boards and dumped them on the compost heap, and dealt with the weeds in a fashion Miss Meg never would. Miss Meg was fussy about her appearance—well, it was all she had. Weed-killer might hurt her hands that she needed for piano practise. Vicky worked in the garden like a little gnome.

Then the Admiral became ill, going out one cold day insufficiently wrapped up, and the ensuing chill settled in his lungs. He was such a hale well-built fellow you could never think of him as being an elderly man, marching down to the club every morning and back up the hill to lunch, round to the Chess Centre or the library, and taking Vicky to the Garth and on to tea. It was somehow shocking he should be ill.

In those days hospitals were for the poor; sick folk were nursed in their own home in the Admiral's stratum of society. Sir George Gosheron, the biggest doctor in the county, was called in, and his carriage and pair stood outside the door every day for a fortnight. Mrs. Webb wouldn't have Vicky in the sickroom, and Mrs. Skimpole wouldn't have her in the kitchen. She was left very much to her own devices. One day I crossed the Garth and she was sitting on a seat talking to a young man who'd never called at

No. 4 and laughing in a way that would put the sun into a November sky.

Then the Admiral took a turn for the worse and Sir George sent a nurse in, which always makes extra work for the staff, since she couldn't eat with the family and wouldn't eat in the kitchen and had to have separate trays.

Then Miss Bagguley wrote, asking for her bits and pieces, and Mrs. Webb sent them back. "Isn't Letty coming back?" Vicky cried, and Mrs. Webb said, "You are almost seventeen. You don't require a governess any longer."

They never seemed to ask what she did with herself during the days. They should blame themselves for that.

The blow when it fell shocked everyone. The Admiral was still convalescent, the nurse had gone. He used to ask for Vicky to read to him—he was still sleeping in the spare room—or play chess on the big black-and-white board. Mrs. Webb started paying calls again, and Miss Sarah had a novena in gratitude for her father's recovery. Miss Maude took up golf.

One morning Vicky couldn't keep her breakfast down. "Something you have eaten has disagreed with you," said Mrs. Webb. "All those sweets—"

Two days later she fainted in the Admiral's room and he insisted on sending for Dr. Bunn. He was the more homey little doctor whom Mrs. Webb had for the servants.

"It is only growing pains," Mrs. Webb said. "A tonic perhaps—"

But I could have told them better. No one, not even Vicky, anticipated Dr. Bunn's diagnosis.

"The girl is six weeks' pregnant," he said, and to Vicky, "Didn't you even suspect?"

In those days mothers were very guarded about what they told their daughters. I doubt if anyone had tried to tell Vicky the facts of life, and I, who could have done so, wouldn't have dared; I should have got my notice right off. I daresay Miss Bagguley would have said something if it hadn't been for her mother's sudden illness, but everyone was very prudish fifty years ago. I'd seen my mother have four children after me, so I didn't have to be told.

Mrs. Webb, I heard, said only two things and they were both questions.

"Victoria, is this possible?" and "Will he marry you?"

"How can he?" asked Vicky. "He was only here for a holiday." She had no notion where he might be now. I wondered if he might be the young man I had seen her talking with in the Garth.

Young and ignorant and passionate, it must have been easy to sweep her off her feet. According to her, he was very little older than herself.

"He was the first truly young person I had ever known," she said.

"Getting into trouble like a housemaid," said Miss Maude, who didn't believe that housemaids had any feelings, just as anglers tell you fish don't feel anything with the hook in their throat.

"Didn't you think of waiting for marriage?" I asked her, but she said, "I didn't think at all. Oh, Lily, I was in love. Tomorrow didn't exist, everything was today."

Mrs. Webb, of course, wanted her out of the house hey presto. "We must consider our own daughters," she told the Admiral.

"Our daughters are young women," said the Admiral. "If they had paid Vicky a little more attention this need never have occurred."

"You would blame your own daughters sooner than that—that waif," shrilled Mrs. Webb.

"She is no waif. She is our responsibility. We are all to blame, Kate."

"But what will people say?" she demanded. I had gone to the Admiral's room with a glass of hot lemon tea; neither of them paid the least attention to me.

"I should not concern myself with gossip," the Admiral said simply. "Now we must think how we can best help her."

"She cannot stay here," Mrs. Webb insisted.

"This is her home."

"She has qualified for a different sort of home. I believe there is a society in London—"

"You would make a present of Vicky's trouble to a *society?*"

"We must think of the future. She cannot stay here and some plan must be evolved for her and the child. And what will others say?"

Mind you, I knew it wasn't so unusual as Mrs. Webb made out. There were plenty of cases where ladies suddenly found that their young daughters had developed a bit of "lung trouble"—the doctor recommends Switzerland, just for a few months, the air, you see. My mother, who had been in service before her marriage, had told me. "And if funds wouldn't run to Switzerland, then there would be an old nurse in the background. It was astounding how many of these old nurses were scattered about in remote country districts." "What happened to the babies?" I asked. "Oh," said my mother, "no one ever spoke of them. They were farmed out or fostered." Abortion wasn't the fashionable thing in those days, except among the poor, and they mostly worked it themselves with domestic means.

It seemed for the first two or three weeks that Vicky actually believed she could have her baby and bring it back to Frederick Street. "I would look after it myself," she said. "Mrs. Webb insists that I shall give him up." She always spoke of the child as a son. "But he will be the first thing all my own that I have ever had. I have worn other people's clothes, lived in other people's houses—"

"A child without a father," I said, but she interrupted fiercely, "I had a father and what use was he to me? He was always going away and my mother was ashamed. Well, if I can't have him here—I remember once my mother had a situation as sewing-maid in a children's home because she was allowed to have me with her. If the Admiral would help me till I am able to work—you said yourself, Lily, I'm as good at darning and patching as you, and I can make children's clothes—I wouldn't mind what I did."

"Does Miss Victoria talk to you, Lily?" Mrs. Webb asked me. "I hope you don't encourage her in her foolish fancies."

And to Vicky she said, "When you are through this piece of trouble you can find some employment, but not if you have an encumbrance."

In the kitchen there wasn't much sympathy shown for the girl. "Made her bed, let her lie on it," said Mrs. Skimpole.

"Maybe she won't come to term," said Edwardes comfortably. "Best for everyone if she don't."

"Might as well take a dose of salts and be done with it," said the under-housemaid pertly.

Salts of lemon was a common way out of trouble for girls who'd fallen into it. Easy to come by—you said you wanted it to clean a straw hat—a penn'orth or two-penn'orth over the counter and no questions asked.

"These silly girls," said Mrs. Skimpole. "If they knew what they were letting themselves in for—" But she boxed the under-housemaid's ears just the same. "We don't want any of that talk," she said.

"Well, I'm sure you keep it conspicuous enough in the housemaid's cupboard," sniveled the girl.

Of course, the talk had already started. Whispers, nudges, glances when the Admiral took Vicky through the Garth. Mrs. Webb saw them all. Mind you, she knew the Admiral had never had any but paternal feelings for the girl, but others were less nice in their thoughts, and Vicky was like a plump dark little partridge, with an allure I don't think she knew she possessed. Of course, the Admiral was well on in his sixties and she was barely seventeen, but it's happened before.

I caught sight of Mrs. Webb's face when the Admiral said they were responsible and at least partly to blame. It made me think of a line of poetry in a book Vicky had: "Each eye shrank up to a serpent's eye . . ." Mrs. Webb realized what people were saying. She'd never forgive Vicky for causing that.

Mrs. Webb was going to London—to see a friend, she said; but everybody seemed to know she would be talking to someone about Vicky's condition. A foolish girl in my household has disgraced herself, that was what she would say, never a word about the girl being her husband's ward. She talked to Vicky in the little schoolroom before she went, and on the way out she left orders that Miss Victoria not be permitted to bother the Admiral, and she wasn't to go out of the house.

After Mrs. Webb departed, the postman brought the day's second mail delivery. There was a letter for Vicky in bold black handwriting and with a Cheshire postmark, so I knew Vicky had disobeyed Mrs. Webb and told Miss Bagguley the truth. I ran up to the schoolroom, the letter in my hand. Vicky was doing nothing, just staring into space; this morning all hope had gone out of her face.

"I thought you would never come, Lily," she said. "She has got everything panned out, is going to make arrangements for a place for me to go while I am waiting for the baby. I could stay here, Lily, I feel well and strong, and there's plenty I could do; but she won't ever let me come back or mention the baby. A lady she knows will find me suitable accommodations when it is born, and then I must look for a situation and put the past out of my mind. As if one could, Lily. The past is part of the present."

When I showed her the letter she brightened. "Perhaps Letty can suggest something. I had to tell her, Lily. I must have someone on my side."

I heard Miss Maude calling me, so I couldn't wait and I didn't see Vicky again till I took up her lunch; now she was transformed, her eyes bright, her face full of hope again.

"I knew she would help me, Lily! She writes that as soon as I am strong again, I can go to her and bring the child. I could be of use there, Lily, sewing and cooking."

I wondered how much Miss B. had told her mother; it doesn't do a boardinghouse any good when it's known there's a "love child" on the premises. And if it cried in the night and disturbed the boarders—but I couldn't say a word to blot out that radiance. Only, "Babies take up a lot of time, Vicky," I warned her and she laughed, and said, "What does it matter, Lily? I shall have all the time there is."

After lunch she came down saying she couldn't stay in that little box of a room all afternoon; she knew about the embargo on her going out, but Mrs. Webb couldn't object to her doing some work in the garden. The weeds needed attention, I admitted that. Miss Meg got very lazy without her mother to drive her.

Mrs. Webb came back earlier than anyone anticipated and asked at once for Vicky. I had to say she was out in the garden. "Doing the weeding," I added.

"You are sure she has not gone out through the little gate in the wall?"

I had forgotten about the little gate. We used to go through it when Miss Bagguley and I were teaching Vicky to ride. But I said, no, she thought the garden could do with some attention. She would be putting down weed-killer and hunting up the slugs, jobs Miss Meg wouldn't do.

"I'll tell her you are back, madam," I said, but she told me she would go and talk to Vicky among the weeds. Perhaps she thought it would be more private there, and she had things to say not fit for the Admiral's ears. She didn't even go in to see how he was, she was in that much of a hurry to get things settled.

They were down there a long time; then Vicky came helter-skelter up the path as if a bear was after her, her hair flying.

"Do you know what she did, Lily? She trampled all my little garden, she grubbed up the flowers, she said they were weeds and had no part in a civilized place. And she thinks of me as a weed, too, and she would grub me up if she could. But she won't win—I still have one shot left in my locker."

When I took up her supper she wouldn't look at the tray; she just sat there, her chin on her palm, Miss Bagguley's letter clenched in her hand.

When I took the Admiral and Mrs. Webb their milky drinks that night, I put another glass on the tray and two of Mrs. Skimpole's freshly baked fruit scones, thickly plastered with butter. Mrs. Webb noticed them, of course.

"Who are those for, Lily?"

I explained about Vicky eating no supper.

"Tell her to come down here and fetch them for herself. Perhaps by this time she will be able to see reason."

But Vicky wouldn't budge. "I would rather die of starvation," she said. So in the end I took the tray up and left it with her, saying, "You should try to sleep. Things always look better in the morning."

But not for Vicky. I slipped up with a cup of tea I had sneaked from Mrs. Webb's pot—the schoolroom wasn't supposed to have morning tea; but the minute I saw that dreadful contorted face I knew Vicky wouldn't ever be wanting tea again. I stood by the bed; my hands opened and the cup fell through, and I felt the hot tea spurt on my stocking. Then I was tearing wildly down the stairs to the Admiral's room. I never thought to go to her.

I never saw an old gentleman move so fast as he did when he saw my face.

"Is it Miss Victoria?"

"Oh, sir," I gasped. "I'm afraid she's done herself a mischief."

He was out of bed in a flash, tying the cord of his dressing gown. He made me come with him up the stairs, but on the landing he told me to wait. He went in alone and seemed to be a long time. When he came out he had put on twenty years; for the first time I saw him as an old man. He locked the door and put the key in his pocket. I saw him put his hand over his eyes.

"How could she?" he whispered. "How could she?"

I remembered the talk about the salts of lemon, and I, too, thought, How could she? But it wasn't Vicky I had in mind.

The Admiral straightened himself. "Get your hat and coat, Lily," he said. "I will give you a note for Dr. Bunn. Be sure to bring him back—and say nothing to anyone."

I ran all the way to Dr. Bunn's office. It was still not much past eight, the time for the kitchen breakfast; but he was down and having his in the morning room. The maid told me he couldn't be interrupted, but I cried that I had come from the Admiral, it was urgent. Dr. Bunn must have heard me for he came out of the morning room, a napkin bunched in his hand.

When he had read the Admiral's note he sent the maid to call for John to bring round the carriage, and took me into the morning room where he made me drink a cup of tea. He would have laced it with brandy, but I said "No, thank you, sir," Alfred being temperance.

When we got back to Frederick Street everybody must have heard what had happened—at least, they knew I had run for the doctor.

"I don't know anything," I told them, fighting dizziness. I took some tea and a piece of bread into the pantry. Edwardes said, "Let her be." But I could hardly bear the pantry either; Vicky seemed everywhere here.

Presently the bell rang and I was sent for, to go upstairs. Mrs. Webb and the doctor were in the morning room. She looked as soft as something carved in stone. She didn't attach much value to Dr. Bunn but here he was giving orders in her house. For he was telling me he couldn't give a death certificate because in his opinion it wasn't a natural death; he was warning me the police would ask questions. "All you have to do, Lily, is answer them truthfully. If you don't know the answer, say so. Don't offer speculations or guesses." And he quoted that bit from the Bible: "Let your yea be yea and your nay nay."

Mrs. Webb said, "I doubt whether my housemaid could tell the authorities more about Victoria than my husband and myself," and Dr. Bunn said, "She is young, too, you understand."

There was a coroner's inquest and I had to give evidence. I

remembered what Dr. Bunn had said and just answered yes and no. I did wonder how Vicky could have done such a thing—it was weed-killer, you see, so it must have been a spur-of-the-minute decision—in the light of Miss Bagguley's letter; but I wasn't asked about that, so I didn't mention it.

In fact, the letter wasn't mentioned from start to finish. I kept seeing the Admiral with his hand over his eyes, saying, "How could she? How could she?" There hadn't been any suicide note, and they brought in the usual verdict about the balance of Vicky's mind being disturbed.

Directly after the funeral Alfred got news of his raise and he made me give in my notice and we went nearly a hundred miles from Frederick Street and I hadn't been back from that day to this—but I never forgot Vicky . . .

I heard myself give a great gusty sigh and I thought how daft I must look, standing there in a sort of dream and staring at an unoccupied old house. I stepped back smartish and nearly tripped a gentleman coming down the hill. He muttered something about damn-fool women, but didn't stop.

I looked across the road. The railings that used to make the Garth look so dignified were gone, but there was a seat on the pavement, for the road rises steeply here and elderly folk are glad of a chance to rest.

I crossed over and sat down. There was a lady sitting at the other end, and when I saw her she made me think of the house again; she looked like some outdated fashion plate. A fur maxicoat that made you think of all the kittens you'd loved and lost, a round fur turban, a pink wool scarf tucked into the neck, and high laced-up shoes. Her hair was a suspiciously bright black and her cheeks unusually red, but she couldn't have faked the brightness in her eyes. I saw she was another like myself, and as Vicky would have been if she had lived to grow old; whatever you lose there's always something left.

She must have been watching me, for after a minute she leaned forward to say, "You are interested in Number Four?"

"I used to live there," I said. "That is," I corrected myself sharply, "I was in service there in Admiral Webb's day."

"Then you will remember the scandal?"

"I thought it would be forgotten by now," I said. The Admiral had died some ten years later, forty years ago, and they were all gone now, even the daughters.

"There's some won't be forgotten," the lady said.

I looked at her again. I didn't believe it! "Miss Bagguley?"

"Mrs. Emerson now. I married after my mother died—twelve years I had and enough. I don't know why people make so much fuss over marriage. You're Lily, aren't you? I knew you at once. You haven't changed, just grown older."

"Do you live here now?"

"In a little boardinghouse near the front. I often come and sit here, wondering if I'll ever know the truth. Could you tell me, Lily? About my letter, I mean."

I drew a deep breath. "There was no letter mentioned."

"I know. I read all the newspapers. What did she do with it, Lily? And don't try and pretend it didn't come, for she sent me a card—the last thing she wrote to anyone, I suppose—and put it in that box on the wall at the back. I'd have helped her, she knew I would, so why did she take the stuff? It wasn't just her, Lily, it was her baby. The way she wrote about that child—"

"Mrs. Webb was going to separate them; she being a minor, you see, she had no powers."

"Vicky would never believe that. She had me, and the Admiral would have stood by her. No, I can't believe it."

"The Admiral couldn't believe it, not at first. He stood there whispering, 'How could she? How could she?' But he hadn't seen your letter."

"You think Vicky destroyed it?"

"Why should she do that?" I asked. "But it vanished—no one

knows where. She couldn't have burned it, there was no fire in the schoolroom."

"Perhaps it was to someone else's interest that the letter should disappear. I think if the police had seen that letter, there would have been a different verdict."

I said, bemused, "You think Mrs. Webb destroyed it?"

"I think she'd not have hesitated. But did she have the opportunity? Vicky didn't come down from the schoolroom—that was established—and Mrs. Webb didn't go up. You wouldn't have destroyed it, Lily—so who does that leave?"

"There is only the Admiral, but he—"

"You said he was a long time in the room. It would take a few minutes to read that letter."

"But why should *he* wish to destroy it?"

"Because no one who knew Vicky and had read that letter would believe she'd have taken poison. And did Mrs. Webb see Vicky bring the poison into the house? If so, why didn't she stop her? No, no, Vicky wasn't the only one who had access to the weed-killer."

"You can't think what you're saying, Miss Bagguley."

"Someone put it into the milk or, more likely, into the scones. It wasn't you. Who else had the opportunity?"

I remembered the tray left with Mrs. Webb while I went up to urge Vicky to come down. But I still couldn't take it in.

"The Admiral," I demurred. "You think he saw the letter and took it?"

"There was no one else."

"But why should he destroy it? It would have vindicated Vicky."

"Some victories are not worth their cost. At whose expense could he have vindicated her? A man doesn't accuse his own wife and name his own children as the daughters of a murderess."

I still felt quite dazed. "But why?" I said it again, "*Why?*"

"Because Vicky living would always be a danger to her. Vicky would have defeated her enemies and had the child; she would have brought it down to show to the Admiral. She would have been a perpetual thorn in Mrs. Webb's side, and of course it was humiliating for an old battle-ax like that to be defeated by a girl who scarcely had a name. Oh, I've wondered sometimes if the police guessed more than they let on, but there was no actual proof, and with the letter gone—you said nothing of it, Lily."

"Dr. Bunn told me only to answer their questions, to volunteer nothing."

"Perhaps he had doubts, too. Oh, never blame the Admiral. Nothing he could have said then would have brought Vicky back, and it's the living who count."

"But they stayed together for more than ten years," I protested. "If he knew all that time—"

"Ah, but she couldn't be sure. She would know what she was, but she could never be certain how much he knew or suspected. Think of it, Lily. Ten years sharing the same room, sitting at the same table, walking beside him to church, never sure when the sword might fall or if it was just your own sense of guilt that made you wait for it. For ten years, Lily. Satan himself couldn't have thought of a better revenge.

"They say that before he died she had shrunk into a shriveled little creature. And—you remember how she used to lay down the law—well, if she got too vocal he would simply look at her and she would dry up like a sudden storm, not a patter of a drop. Man has designed some pretty ingenious torments for his fellow-man, but the Bench of Bishops couldn't have thought up a greater punishment than that. She must often have envied Vicky lying quiet in her grave." She drew a deep breath. "Ten years, Lily. And three hundred and sixty-five days to every year."

She was smiling to herself, then suddenly she stood up. "Come and have lunch with me—I'm going to Anderson's. The dining room there hasn't changed either. There we can recall the happy past. To me, you see, to me Vicky's never been really dead; a spirit like hers is unquenchable."

So we took arms and walked down the hill, two old women remembering the one who would never be old.

THE SINS OF THE FATHER

by Elliot L. Gilbert

"Rumors had begun almost at once about the things that happened at the old mansion—unspeakable things" . . .

A WOMAN would have to be crazy to marry Kirk Martineau.

That, at any rate, was the opinion of the villagers. Normally such an opinion would be suspect. Any woman coming as a stranger into a remote town to marry its wealthiest citizen would naturally provoke some hostility.

In the small seaside town of East Hallam, however, the hostility was mixed with sympathy for the slight blonde girl who had arrived only a few months before from a distant state to be the new mistress of Martineau House.

Money was all very well as a motive for marriage. There was no need to lecture the inhabitants of East Hallam on the advantages of a fine old house and a rich husband. But when the house was the old Martineau place, perched gloomily on a headland jutting out to sea, and when the rich husband was Kirk Martineau . . .

There were those charitable souls in town who claimed that a son should not be abominated for the sins of his father. But the sins they had in mind were ordinary ones, things like drunkenness or larceny or even a good, clean, angry murder.

When the father was Duncan Martineau, however, even Christian charity was strained to the breaking point.

There were still plenty of people around town who remembered the night old Duncan had killed his wife. When that first mistress of Martineau House, also a slight blonde girl, had arrived, many years before, to live with her new husband on his secluded estate by the sea, rumors had begun almost at once about the things that happened at the old mansion—unspeakable things to which only a perverse imagination could give the name of love.

True, the woman had never complained, but this only made the matter worse. On her infrequent trips to town no one could miss the signs of abuse she bore proudly on her arms and shoulders and throat, like grim badges of achievement.

This went on for more than a year, during which time the boy Kirk was born and the pale wife of Duncan Martineau visibly declined. So badly, indeed, did things appear to be going with her toward the end that the women of the town had taken to visiting her, in the face of old Duncan's clear disapproval, to give the poor girl every opportunity to ask for help if she wanted it and to let the angry husband know that his behavior was being watched.

All these precautions failed. One day Duncan Martineau came into town and announced that his wife had run away.

Though the girl had had every reason to leave her tormentor, no one believed the story. Tales had long circulated about violent midnight rites conducted behind the old mansion on a sunken terrace paved with flat square white stones. If on one of these occasions the bloody ritual had got out of hand, it would have been a simple enough matter for the husband to take the body of his wife out to sea and sink it where it could never be found.

The townspeople had demanded an investigation, and everything inside and outside the old house, especially the infamous white paved terrace, had been searched with unusual thoroughness and a mounting air of expectancy. It was reasoned that so violent a crime must have left a trace—a last message, perhaps, or a bloodstain—which old Duncan had failed to remove.

But no trace of murder was found. The old house contained no messages, and the flat white stones, which would have been indelibly marked by the least spot of blood spilled on them, were clean. Duncan Martineau had gone on living in the gloomy mansion as the years passed and his son grew up under his cruel eye.

At no point was there ever any rebellion by the boy against the fate which both the tutelage of his father and the expectations of the village had prepared for him. When at last Duncan died and young Kirk became master of Martineau House, the townspeople of East Hallam knew what to expect.

The arrival of the slight blonde wife caused no surprise. Neither, in the weeks that followed, did the growing evidence of mistreatment of the girl or the recurrence of rumors about unholy midnight rites.

In the end Kirk Martineau did what his heritage and training had taught him to do. The white stones of the sunken terrace, over which he bore the slim mutilated body of his young wife toward its deep sea grave, gleamed coldly in the moonlight.

The same stones awaited his solitary return. On one of them there was a memento of the evening's work. All that night and all the following day the young husband labored to clean away the bright splash of blood from the stone.

But nothing would remove the stain.

Panic beat at his mind. In the village, he knew, the women who had spied on him ever since his return to East Hallam with his bride would soon be setting out on their daily visit. When they did not find the girl, they would search the house, discover the flat bloody stone, and surmise the truth.

What should he do? To cleanse the bloodstain was impossible. To remove the stone itself would raise unanswerable questions. In the end he was inspired by his deadly danger both with an idea and with the strength to carry it out.

Even as the voices of the villagers approached the house, Kirk Martineau, for a moment sublimely strong, pried the flat white paving stone from where it was imbedded in the earth and turned it over so that it fit exactly, undetectably, into its depression.

When the women reached him minutes later, he was staring at the old, nearly faded bloodstain on the square stone at his feet.

MR. JOSLIN'S JOURNEY

by Mary Hocking

All right, we've said it before and we'll say it again: we're suckers for a good railway-compartment story. Put even a small group of people—in this instance, only three—in a hot, narrow compartment en route to Lahore, India, and a most dramatic situation can develop. This one is a beauty! . . .

MR. JOSLIN was a missionary. A dedicated one. Only a dedicated missionary could have endured the discomfort of ten years in a remote area of Peshawar, to say nothing of the disillusions involved in the close study of a people so durably resilient to betterment in any form.

Mr. Joslin stood on the railway platform and surveyed his companions through the swirl of dust rising from the cracked dirt roads which led down to the station. He was a fastidious man, and ten years in Peshawar had done nothing to make him less sensitive. The stench from the open sewers was as appalling to him as it had been on the first day he arrived in this place; the heat he found more exhausting, the insects more intolerable. As for the people . . .

A denser cloud of dust in the distance heralded the arrival of the train. Mr. Joslin braced his muscles and reminded himself that he was British and must be prepared to die fighting for his rights. Fight he certainly must. A film unit wishing to shoot a particularly lurid scene from the Indian Mutiny could have wished for nothing better than the tumult which would ensue as soon as the train drew into the platform.

Mr. Joslin, who was a timid man by nature, closed his eyes, lowered his head, and charged the train, holding his suitcase before him like a battering ram. Determination, however, counted for little against the wiry agility of the other contestants, and Mr. Joslin, in spite of his gallantry, would have been swept away on the tide had it not been for two men who had already gained entry to one compartment and were engaged in beating off all comers. Since the train stood high above the platform, the two men had the advantage and the insurgents moved off to join the assault on the next carriage. Mr. Joslin was left gasping like a fish stranded on a beach after a wave had receded.

The two men stood in the doorway and laughed. They were, Mr. Joslin noted, particularly rapscallion specimens of one of the more belligerent of the hill tribes. Their behavior was not to be tolerated. There was plenty of room in the compartment—even in England it would have seated six with comfort.

Mr. Joslin advanced firmly, holding his suitcase in front of him. He mounted the steps. The two men stood aside. Mr. Joslin, perspiring and short of breath, sat down, feeling rather gratified. Natural authority, he thought as he mopped himself with a handkerchief, will always tell.

The train started. Mr. Joslin had noticed before that when there were only one or two people on a platform the train stood there for a very long time, as though disappointed at not being in greater demand and hoping that by delay it might drum up a little more business; whereas when the platform was crowded, the train appeared to be embarrassed by its popularity and made a quick exit. There was a great deal of screaming and shouting now, as the train moved out, but the platform was empty, which meant that those who had not herded into a compartment must be hanging like ants to the outside or have fallen onto the track.

Mr. Joslin had never actually seen anyone run over by a train, but he was not convinced that this did not happen and felt disquieted by every lurch and bump.

The two men had settled down in the corner seats at the other end of the narrow compartment. Mr. Joslin, who knew the area from which they came, had no difficulty in understanding the silly remarks they were making about his appearance. The remarks were accompanied by sly glances to see how he responded. Mr. Joslin responded by opening his copy of the *Daily Telegraph* and studying it with poker-faced detachment.

He was going home on leave, and his leave started the moment he set foot on the train. He had no intention of letting these fellows know that he spoke their language. He loved his fellow human beings, whatever their color or creed, but at the moment he needed a rest from their company, and the last thing he wanted to do was to enter into conversation.

Nevertheless, as he scanned the paper he allowed himself occasional surreptitious glances at his two companions. A colorful people, these hill folk—arrogant, predatory, but undeniably splendid; the bone structure was remarkably fine and the faces were intensely alive; the skin had a dark lustre, the eyes were brilliant. The eyes of these men had an almost hypnotic quality.

Mr. Joslin found it difficult to concentrate on the *Daily Telegraph.*

The train jerked along the tortuous track, and sun and shadow played on the faces of his companions, giving them something of the dramatic quality of men in a Rembrandt painting. The train rumbled on. Time passed and Mr. Joslin began to feel rather less poetic. It was toward noon and the heat was building up; soon the compartment would be like a furnace. The seats were not made of leather, but of some substitute material which had extraordinary properties; after he had been sitting on it for a while it appeared to draw itself together, like a huge fist slowly clenching so that fingers of steel seemed to close on Mr. Joslin's thin buttocks. Excruciating agony completely absorbed Mr. Joslin for a time.

His companions chattered, but only odd words registered. Mr. Joslin writhed, squirmed, and sweated. After some time, however, the very oddness of the words which came to him from the other end of the compartment made Mr. Joslin become more attentive in spite of his agony. He concentrated. It took only a few moments to realize that the two men were talking business and that their business was murder.

They were regular travelers on this train, working their own system which, as Mr. Joslin had seen demonstrated, involved getting into an empty compartment and fending off the invading hordes until a suitable victim appeared. Mr. Joslin, outraged by this monstrous conspiracy, thanked God he had been put in a position where he could denounce such villains and possibly save the lives of many innocent wayfarers. As soon as he arrived in Lahore . . .

"—he is rich American, Kamal. He wears the glasses with rims of steel, and he will carry much money with him."

At this point Mr. Joslin realized that it was his own murder which was under discussion. The question which appeared to be at issue was *how* he was to be dispatched. It was not clear whether or not they had decided *when.*

Mr. Joslin offered some rather more urgent prayers to God and turned a page of the *Daily Telegraph;* the flimsy paper made this at the best of times an awkward process so that his nervousness was not conspicuous.

"The knife, the knife." The man on the seat opposite crooned the word.

"There will be too much blood." His companion was sorrowful, gentle, persuasive. His subsequent words made it apparent that he had no objection to the letting of blood but was afraid it would soil any banknotes which might adorn Mr. Joslin's person.

"Kamal, Kamal." The knife man was deeply offended by the suggestion that an artist of his caliber should perform so crudely as to damage valuable goods, wherever they might be disposed. He leaned forward, the better to plead his cause. "After the last time you cannot refuse." His eyes were open very wide and his gaunt face shone with a mixture of fear, anger, and a terrible eagerness as he pleaded for the supremacy of the knife. His companion, a highly unstable character who giggled a lot, was in favor of strangulation.

Mr. Joslin thought, I must look for the communication cord. This presented problems. He was transported back to his school-days. Scripture lessons had been given by the Headmaster, who had had a formidable ability to note when any one of the twenty boys in the class glanced at the clock. Anyone so doing was punished immediately. The need to locate the position of the cord, and the fear of punishment, momentarily drove all other considerations from Mr. Joslin's mind. His whole life depended on the exact timing of this glance.

"Quicker, so much quicker." The knife man caressed the words as though wooing a lover.

"A long neck, like a chicken." His companion pressed his claim no less ardently.

A mosquito zoomed between Mr. Joslin and the *Daily Tele-graph.* He took out his handkerchief and swished it in the air. As usual, the mosquito escaped unharmed. But Mr. Joslin had gained a clear view of the communication cord: it had been fenced round by an amateurishly contrived, but undoubtedly effective, wire cage.

Mr. Joslin took out his ballpoint pen and folded the *Daily Telegraph* on his knee, the crossword facing upward. He scribbled in the margin the possibilities open to him.

1. Jump. But suppose the door handle stuck?

2. Set fire—to what? His own clothing was quite unsuitable, being of a slow-burning material, and he could hardly suppose his companions would sit quietly while he set fire to either their garments or their beards. Also, he was a nonsmoker and had no matches.

3. Wait until the next stop and get out. Much the most attractive solution, provided they had not already decided to kill him before the next stop. All in all, Mr. Joslin did not think he could wait to find out.

4. Frighten them off. But how? He was aware, having spent some time among them, that they were subject to irrational fears. Now, thinking about it, he was not sure to what extent their fears *were* irrational. They were certainly irrational to Mr. Joslin, but it was not inconceivable that to them there was some kind of logical pattern.

He peered at them, his eyelids lowered. They were leaning toward each other as though drawn together over a fire, their faces suffused with light, and there was a radiance about them which in any other circumstances would have made them almost beautiful.

It was difficult to decide what would frighten them. Were he, for example, to stand on his head, burst into tears, and then proceed to undress, this would be quite sufficient to convince the occupants of an English railway carriage that he was a dangerous lunatic. He could not be sure what effect such behavior would have on these men. In any case, he could not go through with such a performance, even to save his life.

"No, no! We leave him under the seat, Hadram, that is much simpler."

Mr. Joslin supposed he could stab them with a pin and then tell them that the tip of the pin was poisoned. The giggling man said, "But the blood, Hadram, the blood," and the knife man replied, "See how withered he is! He will not bleed much."

Once having stabbed them with the pin, Mr. Joslin could tell them he possessed the antidote which he would give to them provided he was alive by the time the train reached the next station.

The train rumbled on, the men discussing murder, Mr. Joslin pondering poison. Beyond the window the sun sparked on rock, and white dust eddied from the track and settled in a thin pall on the floor of the compartment. The two men had stopped talking; they were looking at Mr. Joslin. His heart missed a beat. Then there was blackness. The roar of the train was muffled and the compartment was filled with fumes. A tunnel.

Under cover of the coughing and hawking which ensued, Mr. Joslin tried the handle of the door and pushed. Nothing happened. The door was jammed. The fumes, however, had reminded him forcibly of a factor which he had so far overlooked. The window was also jammed—but it was wide-open. A swallow dive through the window now appeared to be Mr. Joslin's only means of escape. He was not athletic, but he had heard of people performing astonishing feats of agility when spurred on by fear.

The train emerged from the tunnel, a steep wall of rock on the far side, light, air, and nothing else on Mr. Joslin's side. Mr. Joslin leaned forward gingerly and squinted down. A long, long way below he could see the tips of trees like tiny exclamation marks scored on the sheer rock face.

Mr. Joslin had a bad head for heights. He took out his handkerchief and mopped his brow. It took a considerable effort of will to hold himself together. He was still alive—he must cling to this consolation; it must mean the two men were waiting for the right moment. What would they consider to be the right moment? After the next stop? Or just before the next stop, so that they would not have long to travel with evidence of their crime and could make a quick getaway in the crowd which would inevitably besiege the carriage. If only he could remember what *was* the next stop.

In any case, he could not risk waiting for that. He must do something at once. The open window. He must throw his suitcase through the window. He should have thought of that before! Once they were robbed of their spoils, he would be of no further interest to them. Or were they so unbalanced that they would kill him for what little money he might have on his person? In which case, it would be an unnecessary extravagance to part with his suitcase.

Mr. Joslin was becoming very confused. He tried desperately to clarify his thoughts. The giggling man said, "All right, Hadram, my dear Hadram, it shall be the knife." The knife man got to his feet and Mr. Joslin's thoughts clarified marvelously.

Before he knew what he was doing, he dropped the heavy suitcase on the floor and suddenly the knife man was sitting down again, nursing one crushed bare foot. Mr. Joslin knelt before the suitcase. He smiled at the knife man. He smiled at the giggling man as well, so that he should feel included in the situation. While he was smiling, his fingers pressed the catch, then threw back the lid of the suitcase to reveal the mysteries of Mr. Joslin's wardrobe.

Mr. Joslin took out a shirt and laid it across the knees of the knife man; to his companion he presented a pair of pants and a tie. Neither man seemed impressed. It occurred to Mr. Joslin that more panache was required in this display. He unfolded the shirt and made a clumsy attempt to drape it across the chest of the knife man. He picked up the pair of pants; there was not much one could do with a pair of pants, but he waved them slowly and, he hoped, enticingly in front of the other man, who had now stopped giggling.

Mr. Joslin burrowed in his case and found a dressing gown in yellow and mauve cotton which his daughter had sent to him and which he had considered too deplorable ever to be worn. Now, however, he was glad of its gaudy colors. He held it tantalizingly in front of the two men. Apparently they did not like it either. They were both sitting well back in their corners, obviously suspicious and unsure what this performance signified. Mr. Joslin, who had no clear idea himself what his performance signified, draped the dressing gown over the right shoulder of the knife man.

He was sorry he had given the tie to the man who favored strangulation, but decided not to draw attention to it by withdrawing the gift. He made haste to cover the tie with a pair of khaki drill shorts. He had now come to his medicines which he had sandwiched between the clothes in order to protect the bottles.

Mr. Joslin believed in being prepared for all eventualities and his supply of medicines was extensive; there were a lot of bottles. He was about to push them to one side when a brown hand reached forward and grasped one of the bottles. The knife man had decided to join in the game. He held the bottle up to the light, shook it, then pretended, without unstoppering it, to quaff the contents, an act which was accompanied by a vigorous rubbing of the stomach and much rolling of the eyes. He played the game better than Mr. Joslin.

His companion then grabbed a large bottle of pills which he rattled like castanets about his head; he had begun to giggle in a way which Mr. Joslin felt was altogether too uncontrolled. The knife man was now getting rid of the bottles by the simple method of tossing them through the window. Mr. Joslin could see that if he did not regain control, the suitcase would soon be emptied and the game finished. The knife man was already behaving as though he was conducting a search rather than playing a game.

Mr. Joslin grasped a pair of trousers and endeavored, by pushing his hands into the legs, to manipulate them in the manner of a puppetmaster, making the trousers perform a grotesque dance on the remaining contents of the suitcase. The giggling man, who seemed the more easily diverted of the two, appeared to be fascinated by this and made a shy gesture indicating, as Mr. Joslin thought, that he would like to try. Mr. Joslin gave him the trousers and then realized that it was the belt which had caught the man's attention.

The knife man, Mr. Joslin now saw with horror, was unpacking his shaving kit. The train lurched, swayed, and bumped, and Mr. Joslin was thrown forward. The knife man momentarily lost his hold on the shaving kit. Mr. Joslin delved frantically and unearthed the precious roll of silk which he was taking home as a present for his daughter. He wound it round his body and, wiggling in what he hoped was an attention-provoking manner, he rotated slowly and found himself facing the astonished gaze of an English army officer. The train had reached the next stop.

Relief was too much for Mr. Joslin. He stumbled forward, tripped over the silk, and landed on his knees at the feet of his savior, gibbering incoherently.

The army officer said, "Disgusting!" and a voice from the platform said, "Fellah ought to be horsewhipped."

The army officer thrust Mr. Joslin aside and began to collect the contents of the case which were festooned about the persons of Mr. Joslin's tormentors. Mr. Joslin, who was not quite clear what was happening, murmured, "Very kind." The army officer whipped the silk from Mr. Joslin's midriff and stuffed it and the garments into the suitcase. He then shut the case and threw it onto the platform.

Mr. Joslin cried, "No, no!"

The army officer said sternly, "Get out before I throw you out."

"You don't understand—"

"I understand only too well!"

The army officer took Mr. Joslin by the shoulders and booted him out of the carriage, informing him as he did so that he was a rotten little pervert and a disgrace to his country. By the time Mr. Joslin had picked himself up, the train was moving out. The army officer had said goodbye to his friend and had moved away from the window, but the two hill men were there, laughing and waving at Mr. Joslin.

The terrible suspicion came to Mr. Joslin that he had been the victim, not of an attempted murder, but of a particularly cruel practical joke. Perhaps the two hill men were even now telling the army officer how they had hoodwinked and terrified the little missionary. Mr. Joslin hoped the army officer did not speak their language. Cowardice, he was sure, would rate even more contempt than perversion in the army officer's view. Mr. Joslin sat on his suitcase and began to cry.

There was no other train to Lahore that day, so Mr. Joslin had plenty of time to meditate on his humiliation. When the train came the next day, he traveled in extreme discomfort in a very crowded carriage. He had by now missed his plane. There had been a strike and all the planes were full. He had small hope of getting a seat when he presented himself at the airport.

In fact, however, he was lucky. The clerk at the reservations counter informed him that one seat was available: it had been reserved by a Major Carruthers who had had the misfortune to be murdered in a railway carriage the previous day.

The clerk handed the ticket to Mr. Joslin and wished him a good journey.

IN AN OUTPOST OF EMPIRE

by Jacob Hay

Another of Jacob Hay's stories about "the demanding profession of international diplomacy," and as always it is beautifully written and utterly charming . . .

IT never ceased to delight Bootworthy that his Residency should be, year in and year out, officially described by Her Britannic Majesty's Foreign Office as a hardship post (and, strictly unofficially, of course, as one of those posts reserved for that dimmish few whose superiors had quietly given them up as dead losses in the demanding profession of international diplomacy).

Superficially, the facts supported the Foreign Office, and the "hardship" rating guaranteed that nobody in his right skull would ever voluntarily seek to replace Bootworthy.

Of all the Trucial States that lie along the southern coast of the Persian Gulf, none is bleaker and more forbidding in aspect than the minuscule Sheikhdom of Qad al Akh, the capital (and only) city and chief port of which is Gad Hufel, where the incumbent ruler, Sheikh Ibn Sadak (affectionately known as "The Damned") governs, with an iron hand and a kind of benign ferocity, his 32,500 (give or take a few dozen) profoundly apathetic subjects.

The products of this seemingly dismal land have historically included poor quality pearls, a species of date from which several millennia of unskilled cultivation have effectively removed any trace of flavor, and a breed of camels notable throughout the Arabian Peninsula for their ungovernable tempers. The climate has been accurately described as intolerable, with an average rainfall of .01 inch per decade.

But it is not oil which accounts for the relative prosperity of Qad al Akh. There is oil on every side, to be sure, and there is almost certainly oil beneath the drab and sandy wastes of Qad al Akh; but Sheikh Ibn Sadak, like his father, Hassan the Wise, and his father's father, Abdul the Mad, has resolutely declined to explore this possibility. "Any fool," he has often been quoted as saying, "can be lucky enough to have oil under the ground, but he is thrice blessed of Allah whose oases bloom with the joy of mankind and the dreams of Paradise."

The reference is not, alas, to the dates, but to what a majority of the world's experts consider to be the finest *Cannabis sativa* grown anywhere in the world. It is this minination's sole export, and its cultivation, in a string of oases bordering on the Empty Quarter, is a monopoly of the ruling family which, over the years, has plowed the profits of this enterprise back into wives, concubines, improvements to the vast royal palace at Gad Hufel, and what may be the largest privately owned fleet of Rolls-Royce limousines between Bahrein and Oman.

The abundance of *Cannabis sativa* allows the entire population of Qad al Akh to spend their lives quietly stoned, thus insuring a tranquillity rare in that oft-troubled area. To have this amiable situation disturbed by the heavy boots, bulldozers, and drilling rigs of the world's oil prospectors was, in the view of the Sheikhs of Qad al Akh, unthinkable.

The British Residency in Gad Hufel, established in the nineteenth century during the reign of Queen Victoria, had become irrelevant and immaterial as early as 1912, but the British Foreign Office is slow to change, and the Residency was allowed, almost absent-mindedly, to continue its vague and useless existence, housed in an enormous echoing granite villa overlooking Gad Hufel's Marine Parade (Sheikh Abdul the Mad had been a staunch admirer of the Widow of Windsor, and had so renamed what had formerly been The Street of the Dead Camel) and the waters of the Persian Gulf.

At the time of the events described in this narrative the Residency's British staff had been reduced to a total of four. They were: The Hon. Adrian Bootworthy, the Resident; Major Fergus, The MacNaughton of That Ilk, the military attaché and military adviser to Sheikh Ibn Sadat; Mr. Cyprian Pertwee, M.A. (Oxon.), the cultural attaché and personal tutor to Prince Gamal, eldest legitimate son of Ibn Sadak; and Pte. Hubert Rumples, Major MacNaughton's batman, who also served as the Residency's majordomo, supervising the large and lethargic staff of native servants. Each (with the exception of Pte. Rumples, whose record was spotless) had been assigned to Qad al Akh for the kind of reasons that got people assigned to Qad al Akh.

Thus, Adrian Bootworthy had been singled out when, as a Third Secretary at the British Embassy in Stockholm, he had somehow mismanaged his dessert spoon as to send an icy globule of lemon sherbet spinning into the awesome decolletage of the wife of the Swedish Foreign Minister at an Embassy luncheon. Major, The MacNaughton of That Ilk, had gravely troubled his superiors in Whitehall when he had turned his company of Scots Guards to the *right* (as opposed to the left) on marching out of the forecourt of Buck House on the completion of the Changing of the Guard, resulting in a traffic tie-up which took five hours to untangle, since the London police were totally unprepared for this unprecedented troop movement. It was not a court-martial offense, but it marked the Major as Qad al Akh material. Cyprian Pertwee, while deemed sound on such subjects as the works of Bach and Purcell, the paintings of Rembrandt and Gainsborough, and English Literature in general, had cut himself off from the academic and cultural mainstream by his singleminded insistence that the Earth was, in fact, quite flat, as any fool could plainly see.

Perhaps happily all were bachelors, with no close family ties to call them home. Their paychecks arrived with praiseworthy regularity, and they were in general agreement that, despite the heat, disease, poverty, and polluted water, life in Gad Hufel was not at all bad. From time to time the even tenor of Residency life was interrupted by an invitation to dine at the palace of Ibn Sadak. These affairs were regarded much as were natural disasters, and entailed scooping up great greasy chunks of roasted lamb in one's right hand, occasionally coming across the odd eyeball—a supreme delicacy—with the consequence that after such banquets the neon-lit dining chamber ended up looking like serious bomb damage in a sewage-disposal plant.

So an invitation to the palace was a duty to be borne as bravely as the diarrhea which inevitably followed. This affliction, however, could be endured, even dismissed, by a few puffs on a pipe packed with Grade A No. 1 Royal Special Reserve Hashish, of which each member of the staff received a five-pound, gift-wrapped box on the occasion of the Sheikh's birthday.

The day-to-day operations of the Residency were left largely in the hands of Pte. Rumples, who was unique in Qad al Akh in being a pearl of great price. In the course of his duties he had managed to teach Mohammed, the native cook, to prepare such homely delicacies as roast camel, brown Windsor soup, and trifle. He had taught the houseboys how to make a proper taut-sheeted bed and how to bone boots to a mirror finish.

Like his superiors, Pte. Rumples was a bachelor, a condition he assuaged with a variety of hobbies. He was addicted to painting by the numbers, purchasing his kits from the United States, with the result that the Residency numbered among its various assortments a number of his meticulous renditions of Van Gogh, Gauguin, and Renoir (his was a catholic taste), and during his first few years in the Sheikhdom he had found satisfaction in the construction of plastic model airplanes, but it was a short-lived satisfaction, since the planes tended to melt, Dali-style, in the shimmering heat of Gad Hufel.

His real satisfaction came, however, from his splendid collection of true-crime magazines, especially those published in the United States, and in this area of study he was something of an expert. He knew, and could describe in excruciating detail, the exact circumstances surrounding the betrayal of John Dillinger by the Woman in Red, and he had theories as to the fate of Judge Carter.

From time to time his superiors would urge upon him the advantages and delights of sampling some less sordid type of literature: Bootworthy strongly recommended the plays of William Shakespeare; Cyprian Pertwee suggested that he might find pleasure in the writings of James Joyce, while The MacNaughton felt that Rumples might improve himself culturally and professionally by a study of the writings of Clauswitz. But Pte. Rumples continued to remain faithful to his true tales of crime and criminals.

"You never can tell, sir," he would reply to his superiors when they chided him for his simplistic tastes in reading, "but it might come in handy some fine day."

It was an argument for which his superiors could find no ready rebuttal.

What was to disturb this placid way of life was a development none could have foreseen, and this was the discovery of *Cannabis sativa* by increasingly affluent American college students and their bored suburban parents. It did not take long for the word to pass among them that out of the East, from somewhere in far Araby, there came a *Cannabis* of such exquisite excellence as to make the Mexican variety seem like so much inflammable breakfast cereal, and the domestic product beneath contempt. It was reputed to travel by camel and dhow from the shores of the Persian Gulf via Naples to the New World, and it was, of course, the incomparable harvest of the oases of Qad al Akh.

American sales soared to heights undreamed of, and in the light of this spectacular benefaction, although no Sheikh of Qad al Akh had ever traveled beyond his own borders, Ibn Sadak announced his intentions of dispatching Prince Gamal, accompanied by Cyprian Pertwee, as tutor and chaperon, to the United States to see what manner of land this was that gave so bounteously of its wealth into the coffers of the Sheikhdom.

"Congratulations, Cyprian," Bootworthy said to his colleague, on hearing the news. "They always say that travel broadens."

"We shall fall off the edge, mark you my words," Pertwee replied moodily, his expression somber.

"Nonsense, old boy," protested Major MacNaughton heartily, as the three of them sat on the Residency's veranda enjoying their daily sundowner, with Pte. Rumples hovering discreetly in the background, smart in his white mess jacket. "If the Royal Navy can get there, as I understand they do from time to time, so jolly well can you. You must send us the occasional postcard. Rumples! I see the Resident's glass is empty."

"Sah!" barked Pte. Rumples, and leaped to his duty.

So, in due course, Prince Gamal and Mr. Pertwee, accompanied by a mountain of luggage, took dhow for Bahrein, whence they would begin their journey by a chartered airliner to the United States. The use of air transportation had considerably soothed and eased Mr. Pertwee's mind, since it meant that if they were unlucky enough to fly out over the edge of the Earth, it would still be possible to turn around and fly back to safety.

"We shall miss Pertwee," Bootworthy observed gravely as he and The MacNaughton of That Ilk repaired to The Prince Consort Hotel, the only establishment of its sort in the Sheikhdom, which had been built as an exact replica of a Scottish castle, a photograph of which Sheikh Abdul the Mad, still in the thrall of Queen Victoria, had seen and admired in *The London Illustrated News* for the week of April 12, 1901. It had been intended to house distinguished foreign visitors, and was the only place in Gad Hufel where alcohol might be consumed in public.

"Cuts the garrison by one-third," mused The MacNaughton in professional appreciation of the situation. "But we shall carry on, of course."

"Of course," agreed Bootworthy, signaling a waiter to fetch tea.

Under the hotel's portecochère Pte. Rumples, in pith helmet and starched khakis, waited in patient dignity behind the steering wheel of the 1927 Daimler which was the Resident's official limousine.

Events now followed quickly, one upon the other.

Barely a week later there appeared in the shallow badly silted harbor of Gad Hufel a gleaming white yacht flying the colors of the Italian Republic, which anchored only long enough to send its launch to shore. Lounging luxuriously along the elegantly leather-upholstered stern bench was a swarthy man wearing a creamy Panama hat and a pair of alligator-hide shoes, between which stretched a suit of electric-blue silk, such as the best tailors in Rome can turn out, set off by a shirt of midnight blue and a hugely knotted orange cravat.

From the balcony of the British Residency two pairs of binoculars followed the progress of the launch from yacht to Gad Hufel's solitary stone quay, for it was not just every year that a yacht steamed into harbor to discharge a passenger, and the Residency was appropriately interested.

In short order the newcomer proceeded to reserve the entire second floor, including the Royale Suite, of The Prince Consort Hotel. On the hotel's registry he signed himself boldly, "Giovanni Caliaferi," and gave his residence as Naples, Italy.

In this wise there arrived in Qad al Akh one Johnny Cauliflower, as he was better known to the U.S. Federal Bureau of Investigation, which had been largely instrumental in arrangements for his deportation from the United States to his homeland, and Interpol, which kept a wary eye on his comings and goings after his return to his native Naples.

Less than twenty-four hours later Bootworthy and The MacNaughton were summoned to the palace for an audience with Ibn Sadak at the unusual hour of three P.M., a time during which 99.44 percent of Gad Hufel was taking its postluncheon nap, an hour when the palace was not likely to be filled with a muttering mob of suppliants seeking the Sheikh's favors, when the palace's long corridors were deserted.

The Ibn Sadak who received the Britons in his audience hall was not the princely figure to which they were accustomed: the vulturine features were pale and waxy, and the amber worry-beads clicked through his beringed fingers with the nervous rattle of a miniature machine gun. Beside the Sheikh, in a wood-framed, canvas, officer's campaign chair set on a level with the regal throne, sprawled Johnny Cauliflower who, seen at close range, looked something like a cross between Dean Martin and Victor Mature, with overtones of George Raft and Edward G. Robinson in their prime. A toothpick dangled from the sensual lips, and the black eyes were hooded and dangerous beneath the black brows that contrasted dramatically with the distinguished gray at the temples.

"Gentlemen," began Ibn Sadak without preamble, after the Englishmen had bowed their respects, "permit me to introduce Signor Caliaferi. Signor Caliaferi is—" The Sheikh hesitated.

"An expediter," Johnny Cauliflower supplied graciously. "I get things done, 'fya unnehstan whaddeye mean."

"—er, yes," Ibn Sadak resumed edgily. "He has—ah—brought with him a communication which will explain his presence here, and although it is addressed to me I think you should read it, since it comes from your colleague, Mr. Pertwee." With which Ibn Sadak extended a sheet of notepaper toward Bootworthy.

"My dear Sheikh," Bootworthy read, "the bearer of this letter is a Signor Caliaferi, who is the representative of an Italo-American consortium of businessmen, of which His Highness, Prince Gamal, and I are presently the involuntary guests somewhere in the United States. It is the consortium's desire to improve the economy of Qad al Akh by the increased production, more scientific processing, and modern packaging and shipping techniques of *Cannabis sativa,* of which project Signor Caliaferi is to have sole charge. While His Highness and I are presently comfortable, albeit with only limited freedom of movement, we have been advised that our condition could change drastically if Signor Caliaferi's suggestions are not carried out to the letter. Otherwise, we have been assured that we will, in the colorful language of our hosts, 'end up with wooden overcoats,' whatever that may mean. I have the honour to remain, Your Highness, your obedient servant,

Cyprian Pertwee, M.A."

"Hmmm," said Bootworthy, passing the letter to The MacNaughton, who read it carefully, brushing a finger beneath his flaring Guards mustache as he absorbed the contents.

"Hmmm," said The MacNaughton.

"My frens and me, we kinda figured this whole operation could use a little American know-how," Johnny Cauliflower explained, shifting his toothpick. "Natcherly, we gotta charge like a consultant's fee, y'unnerstan. The Sheek here says you're his top advisers, so I wanned you gents to read this letter so's you could advise him to do like I say, or"—and here Mr. Cauliflower drew a lean forefinger gracefully across his cravat—"else."

"Else, eh?" Bootworthy murmured.

"Else," repeated Johnny Cauliflower coldly.

Returned to their Residency, Bootworthy and The MacNaughton sat down to assess the situation over whiskey and soda. That the situation was fraught with problems was unhappily clear. An American takeover of *Cannabis sativa* production would be as disruptive as the discovery of oil under the fertile oases of Guq and Guq Guq (in the matter of place names, the natives of Qad al Akh have historically displayed little or no imagination), where the finest *Cannabis* grew. Obviously, something would have to be done.

"We must fight fire with fire," declared Bootworthy, when Pte. Rumples had brought them a second round of drinks.

"Adapt ourselves to the native ways," said The MacNaughton, recalling what he had learned at Sandhurst of Braddock's Defeat. "Adopt their methods, as it were."

"One wonders how the late Al Capone might have responded to a similar challenge." Bootworthy's tone was thoughtful, and then grew angry. "What's more, MacNaughton, this is no ordinary challenge: this, my dear chap, is a challenge to British authority. It must be met."

"Only a few years ago one might have called for a destroyer and a platoon of Royal Marines," replied The MacNaughton wistfully, "but with Aden gone . . ." He left his sentence sadly unfinished. "Nonetheless, Bootworthy, I take your point. One sees one's duty clear. We must act, and with dispatch."

"By George, I think I've got it!" exclaimed Bootworthy, his lean face flushing with unaccustomed excitement. "Rumples! A word with you."

"Sah!" barked Pte. Rumples, stamping to attention.

Sheikh Ibn Sadak had listened with growing unease at dinner that same evening as Johnny Cauliflower had outlined his plans for the future, among them a new cement-block processing and packaging plant, together with a corrugated-steel, prefabricated warehouse and the construction of an airstrip for air freight operations. The Sheikh was consequently much relieved when

Johnny encountered his first lamb's eye and abruptly decided to take a constitutional from the palace back to The Prince Consort Hotel to regain his composure in the sickly breeze which blew inland every evening from the Persian Gulf.

This job, Johnny decided as he strolled through the dusk, was not going to be the soft touch he and his associates had initially envisioned. Finding an eyeball in the lamb stew can be a distracting experience, and it was doubtless by reason of this distraction that Johnny did not observe the approach of the towering 1927 Daimler limousine until it drew alongside him, its light extinguished.

"Okay, pal," growled Pte. Rumples out of the side of his mouth, "this here is it. Get inna back." Even in the dimly lighted street Johnny could see that the speaker of these words held a revolver of imposing size and that it was pointed steadily at his islet of Langerhans, which would make for a very painful wound. Dumbfounded, Johnny crawled into the Daimler's back seat, where two still figures awaited him. Johnny had a sudden sense of *déjà vu,* especially when another gun barrel was pressed firmly into the area of his McBirney's point, another anatomically unsuitable target.

"Whaddahell izzis?" he asked hoarsely, knowing full well what the hell it was.

"Sorry to trouble you, my dear fellow," replied Bootworthy, and these were the last words Johnny was to hear for some time as The MacNaughton of That Ilk bashed him briskly over the skull with the butt of his service Webley, which he had spent most of the early evening in cleaning and polishing to a proper Guards sheen.

Johnny Cauliflower's first sensation on recovering consciousness was that his feet had unaccountably fallen asleep, and he unconsciously wiggled his toes to restore their circulation. This led to the discovery that his feet felt curiously heavy. He found he was seated on a wooden chair in the middle of an otherwise unfurnished room, illuminated by a single naked light bulb dependent from the ceiling.

He glanced down at where his feet should have been and saw that the bottoms of his flawlessly tailored trousers disappeared into the flat round gray surface of a tubful of a substance he could not immediately identify.

"Hey!" he yelled, as realization dawned.

"Ah," said a pleased voice from the shadows behind his chair. "He's come to. A very skillful blow, my dear MacNaughton, I must say."

"Hey!" yelled Johnny Cauliflower yet again, as Adrian Bootworthy and The MacNaughton emerged to stand in front of his chair and peer down at him with kindly curiosity.

The MacNaughton stooped and rapped the substance encasing Johnny's feet with his knuckles. "Quite hard," he announced, arising. "Good show, Rumples; nicely poured."

"Sah!" came the answering yelp from the shadows.

"You should be quite comfortable, Signor," Bootworthy told his guest. "There is a bucket beside your chair to accommodate the requirements of nature, and, of course, you will be fed a simple but nourishing diet."

Bootworthy paused, then walked to the wall facing Johnny's chair, from which protruded the open end of a large pipe. "The chamber we now occupy," he resumed, his voice professorial, "is a cistern, formerly used to contain sea water which, due to the scarcity of potable fresh water, was employed in laundering and floor scrubbing. This pipe runs from the Residency beneath the Marine Parade to a point under the waters of the harbor. The inlet valve is controlled from the floor above us. Do I make myself clear?"

Johnny Cauliflower glowered fiercely and remained silent.

"Splendid, splendid," Bootworthy went on, beaming. "Well, when we leave you I shall admit, oh, say, six inches of water into this chamber—I'm afraid you'll find it a trifle odoriferous, with lots of bits and pieces floating about—while you can be thinking about the sort of message you will be sending to your colleagues back in the United States ordering the immediate return of Prince Gamal and Mr. Pertwee to Qad al Akh. Oh, and I shouldn't brood overmuch about those bits and pieces; not good for the old morale. Brekkie at seven ack-emma. Until then, good night."

Some minutes later a horrible gray stream began vomiting steadily into the cistern and continued to flow until Johnny was surrounded by a turgid pool of unspeakably aromatic fluid six inches deep, at which point it stopped.

Precisely at seven A.M. the following morning a trap door in the ceiling directly above Johnny's chair opened to disclose the face of Pte. Rumples. "Breakfast is served," he said formally, and lowered a tray to Johnny's waiting, outstretched hands. Johnny took the tray and put it in his lap as the trap door gently closed. Kippers and one slice of toast with marmalade. Across the room the water pipe belched, gurgled, and began doing its thing.

At eight A.M. the trap door was lifted again, this time to reveal the features of Adrian Bootworthy, who wore an expression of concern. "Ready with your message, old chap?" he called into the depths. But Johnny remained adamantly silent. He had not eaten his kippers. Seeing this, Bootworthy tutted and said, "Mustn't neglect our digestions, my dear fellow," as Rumples reappeared to lower the rope with which to raise Johnny's breakfast tray.

It was not for nothing that Johnny Cauliflower was known to his intimates as "Hard Nose," and it was not a lack of determination which had won him his fearsome reputation in and subsequent deportation from the American underworld; but his character weakened when the surface of the pool in which he sat immobile reached the level of his knees that afternoon, and weakened still further when the water pipe choked briefly and then disgorged several objects which defied analysis by the rational mind. The spirit which had once aroused the admiration of the late Dutch Schultz and Legs Diamond finally cracked when the water level reached the bottom of Johnny's rib cage. His mighty shouts of surrender would have halted a Roman legion in mid-charge.

"Excellent decision, Caliaferi, and quite wise," Bootworthy called down when the trap door had been thrown open. "I say, MacNaughton! Caliaferi here's ready to send his message. Have you got that damned wireless transmitter working yet?" Then, as an afterthought, "Rumples, do you have the foggiest idea how we can get this poor devil out of there?"

It was, as the poet wrote, a famous victory. Three days later Prince Gamal and Cyprian Pertwee were once again safely in Gad Hufel. Johnny Cauliflower, his feet still encased in their concrete galosh, had been hoisted aboard a dhow bound for Oman and given a hammer and chisel wherewith to chip himself free during what might otherwise be a boring voyage; and peace and quiet reigned once more in the Sheikhdom of Qad al Akh.

"It was really most frightfully clever of you all," Cyprian Pertwee declared in heartfelt tones as the staff of Her Britannic Majesty's Residency gathered for their first evening sundowner after what had undeniably been a touching reunion.

"It was nothing, actually," Bootworthy understated modestly, in the finest tradition of the Foreign Office.

"Simply took the blighter in the flank, by God," said Major, The MacNaughton of That Ilk, taking an appreciative gulp of his drink. "The Brigade did the same thing at Waterloo, if memory serves."

Bootworthy rose from the depths of his rattan armchair and stood to attention in the shadows of the Residency veranda, his glass raised.

"Gentlemen, the Queen," he toasted.

"The Queen," echoed his two companions, and Pte. Rumples added, "God bless 'er," ever so quietly.

High overhead from the absurd crenellated tower which was the Residency's most inexplicable architectural feature the red, white, and blue St. Andrew's crosses of the British flag fluttered bravely against the darkening dusk.

Another outpost of Empire had defied and survived yet another in the endless succession of challenges to the might and majesty of the Crown.

THE HARLEQUIN TEA SET

by Agatha Christie

"The Harlequin Tea Set" is about Harley Quin, the mystical detective who seems always to be "passing by" when there is trouble or tragedy impending. Harley Quin—"someone who might turn up anywhere and who, if he did turn up, was always an announcement that something was going to happen." From words that Mr. Quin utters, Mr. Satterthwaite gets ideas. He sees things that otherwise he would not see, imagines things that otherwise he would not imagine, finds out things that otherwise would elude him. Mr. Quin is, in a phrase, a detective-maker, and Mr. Satterthwaite is that rare, perhaps unique, "Watson" who becomes a detective in his own right.

And there is one more aspect of the Harley Quin stories that, so far as we know, has never been noted—at least, never been commented on in print. The Harley Quin adventures-in-detection are, as distinguished from "dying message" stories, what might be called "living message" stories. You will see what we mean when you read Dame Agatha Christie's novelette of love and death—and other crucial matters . . .

MR. SATTERTHWAITE clucked twice in vexation. Whether right in his assumption or not, he was more and more convinced that cars nowadays broke down far more frequently than they used to do. The only cars he trusted were old friends who had survived the test of time. They had their little idiosyncrasies, but you knew about those, provided for them, fulfilled their wants before they became too acute.

But new cars! Full of new gadgets, different kinds of windows, an instrument panel newly and differently arranged, handsome in their glistening wood but, being unfamiliar, your groping hand hovered uneasily over fog lights, windshield wipers, choke, et cetera. All these things with knobs in a place you didn't expect them. And when your gleaming new purchase failed in performance, your local garage uttered the intensely irritating words, "Teething troubles. Splendid car, sir, these roadsters Super Superbos. All the latest accessories. But bound to have their teething troubles, you know." As though a car was a baby.

But Mr. Satterthwaite, being now at an advanced age, was strongly of the opinion that a new car ought to be fully adult. Tested, inspected, and its teething troubles already dealt with before it came into its purchaser's possession.

Mr. Satterthwaite was on his way to pay a weekend visit to friends in the country. His new car had already, on the way from London, given certain symptoms of discomfort, and was now drawn up in a garage waiting for the diagnosis and how long it would take before he could resume progress toward his destination. His chauffeur was in consultation with a mechanic. Mr. Satterthwaite sat, striving for patience. He had assured his hosts, on the telephone the night before, that he would be arriving in good time for tea. He would reach Doverton Kingsbourne, he assured them, well before four.

He clucked again in irritation and tried to turn his thoughts to something pleasant. It was no good sitting here in a state of acute irritation, frequently consulting his wrist watch, clucking once more and giving, he had to realize, a very good imitation of a hen pleased with its prowess in laying an egg.

Yes. Something pleasant. Yes, now hadn't there been something—something he had noticed as they were driving along. Not very long ago. Something that he had seen through the window which had pleased and excited him. But before he had had time to think about it, the car's misbehavior had become more pronounced and a rapid visit to the nearest service station had been inevitable.

What was it he had seen? On the left—no, on the right. Yes, on the right as they drove slowly through the village street. Next door to a post office. Yes, he was quite sure of that. Next door to a post office because the sight of the post office had given him the idea of telephoning to the Addisons to break the news that he might be slightly late in his arrival. The post office. A village post office. And next to it—yes, definitely, next to it, next door or if not next door the door after.

Something that had stirred old memories, and he had wanted—just what was it that he had wanted? Oh, dear, it would come to him presently. It was mixed up with a color. Several colors. Yes, a color or colors. Or a word. Some definite word that had stirred memories, thoughts, pleasures gone by, excitement, recalling something that had been vivid and alive. Something which he himself had not only seen but observed. No, he had done more.

He had taken part. Taken part in what, and why, and where? All sorts of places. The answer came quickly at the last thought. All sorts of places.

On an island? In Corsica? At Monte Carlo watching the croupier spinning his roulette wheel? A house in the country? All sorts of places. And he had been there, and someone else. Yes, someone else. It all tied up with that. He was getting there at last. If he could just— He was interrupted at that moment by the chauffeur coming to the window with the garage mechanic in tow.

"Won't be long now, sir," the chauffeur assured Mr. Satterthwaite cheerfully. "Matter of ten minutes or so. Not more."

"Nothing seriously wrong," said the mechanic, in a low, hoarse, country voice. "Teething troubles, as you might say."

Mr. Satterthwaite did not cluck this time. He gnashed his teeth. A phrase he had often read in books and which in old age he seemed to have got into the habit of doing himself, owing, perhaps, to the slight looseness of his upper plate. Really, teething trouble! Toothache. Teeth gnashing. False teeth. One's whole life centered, he thought, about teeth.

"Doverton Kingsbourne's only a few miles away," said the chauffeur, "and they've a taxi here. You could go on in that, sir, and I'd bring the car along later as soon as it's fixed up."

"No!" said Mr. Satterthwaite.

He said the word explosively and both the chauffeur and the mechanic looked startled. Mr. Satterthwaite's eyes were sparkling. His voice was clear and decisive. Memory had come to him.

"I propose," he said, "to walk along the road we have just come by. When the car is ready, you will pick me up there. The Harlequin Café, I think it is called."

"It's not much of a place, sir," the mechanic advised.

"That is where I shall be," said Mr. Satterthwaite, speaking with a kind of regal autocracy.

He walked off briskly. The two men stared after him.

"Don't know what's got into him," said the chauffeur. "Never seen him like that before."

The village of Kingsbourne Ducis did not live up to the Old World grandeur of its name. It was a smallish village consisting of one street. A few houses. Shops that were dotted rather unevenly, sometimes betraying the fact that they were houses which had been turned into shops or that they were shops which now existed as houses without any industrial intentions.

It was not particularly Old World or beautiful. It was just simple and rather unobtrusive. Perhaps that was why, thought Mr. Satterthwaite, that dash of brilliant color had caught his eye. Ah, here he was at the post office. The post office was a simply functioning post office with a mailbox outside, a display of some newspapers and some postcards, and surely, next to it—yes, there was the sign up above. The Harlequin Café.

A sudden qualm struck Mr. Satterthwaite. Really, he was getting too old. He had fancies. Why should that one word stir his heart? *Harlequin.*

The mechanic at the service station had been quite right. It did not look like a place in which one would really be tempted to have a meal. A snack perhaps. A morning coffee. Then why? But he suddenly realized why. Because the café—or perhaps one could better put it as the house that sheltered the café—was in two portions.

One side of it had small tables with chairs around them ready for patrons who came here to eat. But the other side was a shop. A shop that sold china. It was not an antique shop. It had no little shelves of glass vases or mugs. It was a shop that sold modern goods, and the show window that gave on the street was at the present moment housing every shade of the rainbow. A tea set of largish cups and saucers, each one of a different color. Blue, red, yellow, green, pink, purple.

Really, Mr. Satterthwaite thought, a wonderful show of color. No wonder it had struck his eye as the car had passed slowly beside the pavement, looking ahead for any sign of a garage or service station. It was labeled with a large card: *A Harlequin Tea Set.*

It was the word *harlequin*, of course, which had remained fixed in Mr. Satterthwaite's mind, although just far enough back in his mind so that it had been difficult to recall it. The gay colors. The harlequin colors. And he had thought, wondered, had the absurd but exciting idea that in some way here was a call to him. To him specially. Here, perhaps, eating a meal or purchasing cups and saucers might be his own old friend, Mr. Harley Quin.

How many years was it since he had last seen Mr. Quin? A large number of years. Was it the day he had seen Mr. Quin walking away from him down a country lane? Lovers' Lane they had called it. He had always expected to see Mr. Quin again, once a year at least. Possibly twice a year. But no. That had not happened.

And so today he had had the wonderful and surprising idea that here, in the village of Kingsbourne Ducis, he might once again find Mr. Harley Quin.

"Absurd of me," said Mr. Satterthwaite, "quite absurd of me. Really, the ideas one has as one gets old!"

He had missed Mr. Quin. Missed something that had been one of the most exciting things in the late years of his life. Someone who might turn up anywhere and who, if he did turn up, was always an announcement that something was going to happen. Something that was going to happen to him.

No, that was not quite right. Not *to* him, but through him. That was the exciting part. Just from the words that Mr. Quin might utter. Words. From things he might show him, ideas would come to Mr. Satterthwaite. He would see things, he would imagine things, he would find out things. He would deal with something that needed to be dealt with. And opposite him would sit Mr. Quin, perhaps smiling approval. Something that Mr. Quin said would start the flow of ideas, but the active person would be he himself. He, Mr. Satterthwaite. The man with so many old friends. A man among whose friends had been duchesses, an occasional bishop, people who counted.

Especially, he had to admit, people who had counted in the

social world. Because, after all, Mr. Satterthwaite had always been a snob. He had liked duchesses, he had liked knowing old families, families who had represented the landed gentry of England for several generations. And he had had, too, an interest in young people not necessarily socially important. Young people who were in trouble, who were in love, who were unhappy, who needed help. Because of Mr. Quin, Mr. Satterthwaite was enabled to give help.

And now, like an idiot, he was looking into an unprepossessing village café and a shop for modern china and tea sets and casseroles no doubt.

"All the same," said Mr. Satterthwaite to himself, "I must go in. Now that I've been foolish enough to walk back here, I must go in just—well, just in case. They'll be longer, I expect, doing the car than they say. It will be more than ten minutes. Just in case there is anything interesting inside."

He looked once more at the window full of china. He appreciated suddenly that it was good china. Well made. A good modern product. He looked back into the past, remembering. The Duchess of Leith, he remembered. What a wonderful old lady she had been. How kind she had been to her maid on the occasion of a very rough sea voyage to the island of Corsica. She had ministered to her with the kindliness of a ministering angel and only on the next day had she resumed her autocratic, bullying manner which the domestics of those days had seemed able to stand without any sign of rebellion.

Maria. Yes, that's what the Duchess' name had been. Dear old Maria Leith. Ah, well. She had died some years ago. But she had had a harlequin breakfast set, he remembered. Yes. Big round cups in different colors. Black. Yellow, red, and a particularly pernicious shade of puce. Puce, he thought, must have been a favorite color of hers. She had had a Rockingham tea set, he remembered, in which the predominating color had been puce decorated with gold.

"Ah," sighed Mr. Satterthwaite, "those were the days. Well, I suppose I'd better go in. Perhaps order a cup of coffee or something. It will be very full of milk, I expect, and possibly already sweetened. But still, one has to pass the time."

He went in. The café side was practically empty. It was early, Mr. Satterthwaite supposed, for people to want cups of tea. And anyway, very few people did want cups of tea nowadays. Except, that is, occasionally elderly people in their own homes. There was a young couple in the far window and two women gossiping at a table against the back wall.

"I said to her," one of them was saying, "I said you can't do that sort of thing. No, it's not the sort of thing that I'll put up with, and I said the same to Henry and he agreed with me."

It shot through Mr. Satterthwaite's mind that Henry must have rather a hard life and that no doubt he had found it always wise to agree, whatever was put up to him. A most unattractive woman with a most unattractive friend. He turned his attention to the other side of the building, murmuring, "May I look around?"

There was quite a pleasant woman in charge and she said, "Oh, yes, sir. We've got a good stock at present."

Mr. Satterthwaite looked at the colored cups, picked up one or two of them, examined the milk jug, picked up a china zebra and considered it, examined some ashtrays of a fairly pleasing pattern. He heard chairs being pushed back and, turning his head, noted that the two middle-aged women still discussing former grievances had paid their bill and were now leaving the shop.

As they went out of the door, a tall man in a dark suit came in. He sat down at the table which they had just vacated. His back was to Mr. Satterthwaite, who thought that he had an attractive back. Lean, strong, well muscled, but rather dark and sinister-looking because there was very little light in the shop.

Mr. Satterthwaite looked back again at the ashtrays. "I might buy an ashtray so as not to cause a disappointment to the shop owner," he thought. As he did so, the sun came out suddenly.

He had not realized that the shop had looked dim because of the lack of sunshine. The sun must have been under a cloud for some time. It had clouded over, he remembered, at about the time they had got to the service station. But now there was this sudden burst of sunlight. It caught up the colors of the china through a colored glass window of somewhat ecclesiastical pattern which must, Mr. Satterthwaite thought, have been left over in the original Victorian house.

The sun came through the window and lit up the dingy café. In some curious way it also lit up the back of the man who had just sat down there. Instead of a dark black silhouette, there was now a festoon of colors. Red and blue and yellow. And suddenly Mr. Satterthwaite realized that he was looking at exactly what he had hoped to find. His intuition had not played him false. He knew who had just come in and sat down there. He knew so well that he had no need to wait until he could look at the face.

He turned his back on the china, went back into the café, round the corner of the table, and sat down opposite the man who had just come in.

"Mr. Quin," said Mr. Satterthwaite. "I knew somehow it was going to be you."

Mr. Quin smiled. "You always know so many things."

"It's a long time since I've seen you," said Mr. Satterthwaite.

"Does time matter?" said Mr. Quin.

"Perhaps not. You may be right. Perhaps not."

"May I offer you some refreshment?"

"Is there any refreshment to be had?" said Mr. Satterthwaite doubtfully. "I suppose you must have come in for that purpose."

"One is never quite sure of one's purpose, is one?" said Mr. Quin.

"I am so pleased to see you again," said Mr. Satterthwaite. "I'd almost forgotten, you know. I mean forgotten the way you talk, the things you say. The things you make me think of, the things you make me do."

"I make you do? You are so wrong. You have always known yourself just what you wanted to do and why you want to do them and why you know so well that they have to be done."

"I only feel that when you are here."

"Oh, no," said Mr. Quin lightly. "I have nothing to do with it. I am just, as I've often told you, I am just passing by. That is all."

"Today you are passing by through Kingsbourne Ducis."

"And you are not passing by. You are going to a definite place. Am I right?"

"I'm going to see a very old friend. A friend I have not seen for a good many years. He's old now. Somewhat crippled. He has had one stroke. He has recovered from it quite well, but one never knows."

"Does he live by himself?"

"Not now, I am glad to say. His family have come back from abroad, what is left of his family, that is. They have been living with him now for some months. I am glad to be able to see them again all together. Those, that's to say, that I have seen before, and those that I have not seen."

"You mean children?"

"Children and grandchildren." Mr. Satterthwaite sighed. Just for a moment he was sad that he had had no children and no grandchildren and no great-grandchildren himself. He did not usually regret it at all.

"They have some special Turkish coffee here," said Mr. Quin. "Really good of its kind. Everything else is, as you have guessed, rather unpalatable. But one can always have a cup of Turkish coffee, can one not? Let us have one because I suppose you will soon have to get on with your pilgrimage, or whatever it is."

In the doorway came a small black dog. He came and sat down by the table and looked up at Mr. Quin.

"Your dog?" said Mr. Satterthwaite.

"Yes. Let me introduce you to Hermes." He stroked the black dog's head. "Coffee," he said. "Tell Ali."

The black dog walked from the table through a door at the back of the shop. They heard him give a short incisive bark. Presently he reappeared and with him came a young man with a very dark complexion, wearing an emerald green pullover.

"Coffee, Ali," said Mr. Quin. "Two coffees."

"Turkish coffee. That's right, isn't it, sir?" He smiled and disappeared.

The dog sat down again.

"Tell me," said Mr. Satterthwaite, "tell me where you've been and what you have been doing and why I have not seen you for so long."

"I have just told you that time really means nothing. It is clear in my mind and I think it is clear in yours the occasion when we last met."

"A very tragic occasion," said Mr. Satterthwaite. "I do not really like to think of it."

"Because of death? But death is not always a tragedy. I have told you that before."

"No," said Mr. Satterthwaite, "perhaps that death—the one we are both thinking of—was not a tragedy. But all the same—"

"But all the same it is life that really matters. You are quite right, of course," said Mr. Quin. "Quite right. It is life that matters. We do not want someone young, someone who is happy, or could be happy, to die. Neither of us wants that, do we? That is the reason why we must always save a life when the command comes."

"Have you a command for me?"

"Me—a command for you?" Harley Quin's long sad face brightened into its peculiarly charming smile. "I have no commands for *you,* Mr. Satterthwaite. I have never had commands. You yourself know things, see things, know what to do, do them. It has nothing to do with me."

"Oh, yes, it has," said Mr. Satterthwaite. "You're not going to change my mind on that point. But tell me. Where have you been during what it is too short to call time?"

"Well, I have been here and there. In different countries, different climates, different adventures. But mostly, as usual, just passing by. I think it is more for you to tell me not only what you have been doing but what you are going to do now. More about where you are going. Who you are going to meet. Your friends, what they are like."

"Of course I will tell you. I should enjoy telling you because I have been thinking about these friends I am going to. When you have not seen a family for a long time, when you have not been closely connected with them for many years, it is always a nervous moment when you are going to resume old friendships and old ties."

"You are so right," said Mr. Quin.

The Turkish coffee was brought in little cups of oriental pattern. Ali placed them with a smile and departed. Mr. Satterthwaite sipped approvingly.

"As sweet as love, as black as night, and as hot as hell. That is the old Arab phrase, isn't it?"

Harley smiled and nodded.

"Yes," said Mr. Satterthwaite, "I must tell you where I am going, though what I am doing hardly matters. I am going to renew old friendships, to make acquaintance with the younger generation. Tom Addison, as I have said, is a very old friend of mine. We did many things together in our young days. Then, as often happens, life parted us. He was in the Diplomatic Service, went abroad for several foreign posts in turn. Sometimes I went and stayed with him, sometimes I saw him when he was home in England. One of his early posts was in Spain. He married a Spanish girl, a very beautiful, dark girl called Pilar. He loved her very much."

"They had children?"

"Two daughters. A fair-haired baby like her father, called Lily, and a second daughter, Maria, who took after her Spanish mother. I was Lily's godfather. Naturally, I did not see either of the children very often. Two or three times a year I either gave a party for Lily or went to see her at her school. She was a sweet and lovely person. Very devoted to her father and he was very devoted to her.

"But in between these meetings, these revivals of friendship, we went through some difficult times. My contemporaries and I had difficulties in meeting through the war years. Lily married a pilot in the Air Force. A fighter pilot. Until the other day I had even forgotten his name. Simon Gilliatt. Squadron Leader Gilliatt."

"He was killed in the war?"

"No, no. He came through safely. After the war he resigned from the Air Force and he and Lily went out to Kenya, as so many did. They settled there and they lived very happily. They had a son, a little boy called Roland. Later when he was at school in England I saw him once or twice. The last time, I think, was when he was twelve years old. A nice boy. He had red hair like his father. I've not seen him since, so I am looking forward to seeing him today. He is twenty-three—twenty-four now. Time goes on so."

"Is he married?"

"No. Well, not yet."

"Ah. Prospects of marriage?"

"Well, I wondered from something Tom Addison said in his letter. There is a girl cousin. The younger daughter Maria married the local doctor. I never knew her very well. It was rather sad. She died in childbirth. Her little girl was called Inez, a family name chosen by her Spanish grandmother. As it happens, I have only seen Inez once since she grew up. A dark Spanish type very much like her grandmother. But I am boring you with all this."

"No. I want to hear it. It is very interesting to me."

"I wonder why," said Mr. Satterthwaite.

He looked at Mr. Quin with that slight air of suspicion which sometimes came to him.

"You want to know all about this family. Why?"

"So that I can picture it, perhaps, in my mind."

"Well, this house I am going to, Doverton Kingsbourne it is called. It is quite a beautiful old house. Not so spectacular as to invite tourists or to be open to visitors on special days. Just a quiet country house to be lived in by an Englishman who has served his country and comes back to enjoy a mellow life when the age of retirement comes. Tom was always fond of country life. He enjoyed fishing. He was a good shot and we had very happy days together in the family home of his boyhood.

"I spent many of my own holidays as a boy at Doverton Kingsbourne. And all through my life I have had that image in my mind. No place like Doverton Kingsbourne. No other house to touch it. Every time I drove near it I would make a detour and just pass to see the view through a gap in the trees of the long lane that runs in front of the house, glimpses of the river where we used to fish, and of the house itself. And I would remember all the things Tom and I did together. He has been a man of action. A man who has done things. And I—I have just been an old bachelor."

"You have been more than that," said Mr. Quin. "You have been a man who made friends, who had many friends, and who has served his friends well."

"Well, if I can think that. Perhaps you are being too kind."

"Not at all. You are very good company besides. The stories you can tell, the things you've seen, the places you have visited. The curious things that have happened in your life. You could write a whole book on them," said Mr. Quin.

"I should make you the main character in it if I did."

"No, you would not," said Mr. Quin. "I am the one who passes by. That is all. But go on. Tell me more."

"Well, this is just a family chronicle that I'm telling you. As I say, there were long periods when I did not see any of them. But they have been always my old friends. I saw Tom and Pilar until the time when Pilar died—she died rather young, unfortunately. Lily, my godchild, and Inez, the quiet doctor's daughter who lives in the village with her father—"

"How old is the daughter?"

"Inez is nineteen or twenty, I think. I shall be glad to make friends with her."

"So it is on the whole a happy chronicle?"

"Not entirely. Lily, my godchild—the one who went to Kenya

with her husband—was killed there in an automobile accident. She left behind her a baby of barely a year old, little Roland. Simon, her husband, was quite broken-hearted. They were an unusually happy couple. However, the best thing happened to him that could happen, I suppose. He married again, a young widow who was the widow of a squadron leader, a friend of his, and who also had been left with a baby the same age. Little Timothy and little Roland had only two or three months in age between them.

"Simon's marriage, I believe, has been quite happy though I've not seen them, of course, because they continued to live in Kenya. The boys were brought up like brothers. They went to the same school in England and spent their holidays usually in Kenya. I have not seen them, of course, for many years. Well, you know what has happened in Kenya. Some people have managed to stay on. Some people, friends of mine, have gone to Western Australia and have settled happily there with their families. Some have come home to this country.

"Simon Gilliatt and his wife and their two children left Kenya. It was not the same to them and so they came home and accepted the invitation that has always been given them and renewed every year by old Tom Addison. They have come, his son-in-law, his son-in-law's second wife, and the two children, now grown-up boys, or rather, young men. They have come to live as a family and they are happy. Tom's other grandchild, Inez Horton, as I told you, lives in the village with her father, the doctor, and she spends a good deal of her time, I gather, at Doverton Kingsbourne with Tom Addison, who is very devoted to his granddaughter.

"They sound all very happy together there. He has urged me several times to come there and see. Meet them all again. And so I accepted the invitation. Just for a weekend. It will be sad in some ways to see dear old Tom again, somewhat crippled, with perhaps not a very long expectation of life but still cheerful and gay, as far as I can make out. And to see also the old house again. Doverton Kingsbourne. Tied up with all my boyish memories. When one has not lived a very eventful life, when nothing has happened to one personally, and that is true of me, the things that remain with you are the friends, the houses, and the things you did as a child and a boy and a young man. There is only one thing that worries me."

"You should not be worried. What is it that worries you?"

"That I might be—disappointed. The house one remembers, one has dreams of, when one might come to see it again it would not be as you remembered it or dreamed it. A new wing would have been added, the garden would have been altered, all sorts of things can have happened to it. It is a very long time, really, since I have been there."

"I think your memories will go with you," said Mr. Quin. "I am glad you are going there."

"I have an idea," said Mr. Satterthwaite. "Come with me. Come with me on this visit. You need not fear you'll not be welcome. Dear Tom Addison is the most hospitable fellow in the world. Any friend of mine would immediately be a friend of his. Come with me. You must. I insist."

Making an impulsive gesture, Mr. Satterthwaite nearly knocked his coffee cup off the table. He caught it just in time.

At that moment the shop door was pushed open, ringing its old-fashioned bell as it did so. A middle-aged woman came in. She was slightly out of breath and looked somewhat hot. She was good-looking still, with a head of auburn hair only just touched here and there with gray. She had that clear ivory-colored skin that so often goes with reddish hair and blue eyes, and she had kept her figure well. The newcomer glanced round the café and turned into the china shop.

"Oh!" she exclaimed, "you've still got some of the harlequin cups."

"Yes, Mrs. Gilliatt, we had a new stock arrived in yesterday."

"Oh, I'm so pleased. I really have been very worried. I rushed down here. I took one of the boys' motorbikes. They'd gone off somewhere and I couldn't find either of them. But I really had to do something. There was an unfortunate accident this morning with some of the cups and we've got people arriving for tea and a party this afternoon. So if you can give me a blue and a green and perhaps I'd better have another red one as well, in case. That's the worst of these different-colored cups, isn't it?"

"Well, I know they do say as it's a disadvantage and you can't always replace the particular color you want."

Mr. Satterthwaite's head had gone over his shoulder now and he was looking with some interest at what was going on. Mrs. Gilliatt, the shop woman had said. But of course. He realized it now. This must be—he rose from his seat, half hesitating, and then took a few steps into the shop.

"Excuse me," he said, "but are you Mrs. Gilliatt from Doverton Kingsbourne?"

"Oh, yes. I am Beryl Gilliatt. Do you—I mean . . . ?"

She looked at him, wrinkling her brows a little. An attractive woman, Mr. Satterthwaite thought. Rather a hard face, perhaps, but competent. So this was Simon Gilliatt's second wife. She hadn't the beauty of Lily, but she seemed an attractive woman, pleasant and efficient. Suddenly a smile came to Mrs. Gilliatt's face.

"I do believe—yes, of course. My father-in-law, Tom, has a photograph of you and you must be the guest we are expecting this afternoon. You must be Mr. Satterthwaite."

"Exactly," said Mr. Satterthwaite. "But I shall have to apologize for being so much later in arriving than I said. But unfortunately my car has had a breakdown. It's in the garage now being attended to."

"Oh, how miserable for you. What a shame. But it's not teatime yet. Don't worry. We've put it off, anyway. As you probably heard, I ran down to replace a few cups which unfortunately got swept off a table this morning. Whenever one has anyone to lunch or tea or dinner, something like that always happens."

"There you are, Mrs. Gilliatt," said the shop woman. "I'll wrap them up in here. Shall I put them in a box for you?"

"No, if you'll just put some paper around them and put them in this shopping bag of mine, they'll be quite all right."

"If you are returning to Doverton Kingsbourne," said Mr. Satterthwaite, "I could give you a lift in my car. It will be arriving from the garage any moment now."

"That's very kind of you. I wish really I could accept. But I've simply got to take the motorbike back. The boys will be miserable without it. They're going somewhere this evening."

"Let me introduce you," said Mr. Satterthwaite. He turned toward Mr. Quin, who had risen to his feet and was now standing quite near. "This is an old friend of mine, Mr. Harley Quin, whom I have just happened to run across here. I've been trying to persuade him to come along to Doverton Kingsbourne. Would it be possible, do you think, for Tom to put up another guest for tonight?"

"Oh, I'm sure it would be quite all right," said Beryl Gilliatt. "I'm sure he'd be delighted to see another friend of yours. Perhaps it's a friend of his as well."

"No," said Mr. Quin, "I've never met Mr. Addison, though I've often heard my friend, Mr. Satterthwaite, speak of him."

"Well, then, do let Mr. Satterthwaite bring you. We should be delighted."

"I am very sorry," said Mr. Quin. "Unfortunately, I have another engagement. Indeed"—he looked at his watch—"I must start for it immediately. I am late already, which is what comes of meeting old friends."

"Here you are, Mrs. Gilliatt," said the saleswoman. "It'll be quite all right, I think, in your bag."

Beryl Gilliatt put the parcel carefully into the bag she was carrying, then said to Mr. Satterthwaite, "Well, see you presently. Tea isn't until quarter past five, so don't worry. I'm so pleased to meet you at last, having heard so much about you always both from Simon and from my father-in-law."

She said a hurried goodbye to Mr. Quin and went out of the shop.

"Bit of a hurry she's in, isn't she," said the shop woman, "but she's always like that. Gets through a lot in a day, I'd say."

The sound of the motorcycle outside was heard as it revved up.

"Quite a character, isn't she?" said Mr. Satterthwaite.

"It would seem so," said Mr. Quin.

"And I really can't persuade you?"

"I'm only passing by," said Mr. Quin.

"And when shall I see you again?"

"Oh, it will not be very long," said Mr. Quin. "I think you will recognize me when you do see me."

"Have you nothing more to tell me? Nothing more to explain?"

"To explain what?"

"To explain why I have met you here."

"You are a man of considerable knowledge," said Mr. Quin. "One word might mean something to you. I think it would and it might come in useful."

"What word?"

"Daltonism," said Mr. Quin. He smiled.

"I don't think—" Mr. Satterthwaite frowned for a moment. "Yes. Yes, I do know, only just for the moment I can't remember."

"Goodbye for the present," said Mr. Quin. "Here is your car."

At that moment the car was pulling up by the post-office door. Mr. Satterthwaite went out to it. He was anxious not to waste more time and keep his hosts waiting longer than need be. But he was sad all the same at saying goodbye to his friend.

"There is nothing I can do for you?" he said, and his tone was almost wistful.

"Nothing you can do for *me*."

"For someone else?"

"I think so. Very likely."

"I hope I know what you mean."

"I have the utmost faith in you," said Mr. Quin. "You always know things. You are very quick to observe and to know the meaning of things. You have not changed, I assure you."

His hand rested for a moment on Mr. Satterthwaite's shoulder, then he walked out and proceeded briskly down the village street in the opposite direction to Doverton Kingsbourne. Mr. Satterthwaite got into his car.

"I hope we won't have any more trouble," he said.

His chauffeur reassured him. "It's no distance from here, sir. Three or four miles at most, and she's running beautifully now."

Mr. Satterthwaite said, "Daltonism." It still didn't mean anything to him, but yet he felt it should. It was a word he'd heard used before.

"Doverton Kingsbourne," said Mr. Satterthwaite to himself. He said it softly under his breath. The two words still meant to him what they had always meant. A place of joyous reunion, a place to which he couldn't get too quickly. A place where he was going to enjoy himself, even though so many of those whom he had known would not be there any longer. But Tom would be there. His old friend, Tom, and he thought again of the grass and the lake and the river and the things they had done together as boys.

Tea was set out on the lawn. Steps led out from the French windows in the drawing room and down to where a big copper beech at one side and a cedar of Lebanon on the other made the setting for the afternoon scene. There were two painted and carved white tables and various garden chairs. Upright ones with colored cushions and lounging ones where you could lean back and stretch your feet out and sleep, if you wished to do so. Some of them had hoods over them to guard against the sun.

It was a beautiful early evening and the green of the grass was a soft deep color. The golden light came through the copper beech, and the cedar showed the lines of its beauty against a soft pinkish-golden sky.

Tom Addison was waiting for his guest in a long basket chair, his feet up. Mr. Satterthwaite noted with some amusement what he remembered from many other occasions of meeting his host: he had comfortable bedroom slippers suited to his slightly swollen gouty feet, and the shoes were odd ones. One red and one green.

Good old Tom, thought Mr. Satterthwaite, he hasn't changed. Just the same. And he thought, "What an idiot I am. Of course I know what that word meant. Why didn't I think of it at once?"

"Thought you were never going to turn up, you old devil," said Tom Addison.

He was still a handsome old man. He had a broad face with deep-set twinkling gray eyes; his shoulders were still square and gave him a look of power. Every line in his face seemed a line of good humor and of affectionate welcome. "He never changes," thought Mr. Satterthwaite.

"Can't get up to greet you," said Tom Addison. "Takes two strong men and a stick to get me on my feet. Now, do you know our little crowd, or don't you? You know Simon, of course."

"Of course I do. It's a good few years since I've seen you, but you haven't changed much."

Squadron Leader Simon Gilliatt was a lean, handsome man with a mop of red hair.

"Sorry you never came to see us when we were in Kenya," he said. "You'd have enjoyed yourself. Lots of things we could have shown you. Ah, well, one can't see what the future may bring. I thought I'd lay my bones in that country."

"We've got a very nice churchyard here," said Tom Addison. "Nobody's ruined our church yet by restoring it and we haven't very much new building round about, so there's plenty of room in the churchyard still."

"What a gloomy conversation you're having," said Beryl Gilliatt, smiling. "These are our boys," she said, "but you know them already, don't you, Mr. Satterthwaite?"

"I don't think I'd have known them now," said Mr. Satterthwaite.

Indeed, the last time he had seen the two boys was on a day when he had taken them out from their prep school. Although there was no blood relationship between them—they had had different fathers and mothers—yet the boys could have been, and often were, taken for brothers. They were about the same height and both had red hair, Roland, presumably, having inherited it from his father and Timothy from his auburn-haired mother. There seemed also to be a kind of comradeship between them.

Yet really, Mr. Satterthwaite thought, they were very different. The difference was clearer now when they were, he supposed, between twenty-two and twenty-five years old. He could see no resemblance in Roland to his grandfather. Nor apart from his red hair did he look like his father.

Mr. Satterthwaite had wondered sometimes whether the boy would look like Lily, his dead mother. But there again he could see little resemblance. If anything, Timothy looked more as a son of Lily's might have looked. The fair skin and the high forehead and a delicacy of bone structure.

At his elbow a soft deep voice said, "I'm Inez. I don't expect you remember me. It was quite a long time ago when I saw you."

A beautiful girl, Mr. Satterthwaite thought at once. A dark type. He cast his mind back a long way to the days when he had come to be best man at Tom Addison's wedding to Pilar. She showed her Spanish blood, he thought—the carriage of her head and the dark aristocratic beauty.

Her father, Dr. Horton, was standing just behind her. He looked much older than when Mr. Satterthwaite had seen him last. A nice man and kindly. A good general practitioner, unambitious but reliable and devoted, Mr. Satterthwaite thought, to his daughter. He was obviously immensely proud of her.

Mr. Satterthwaite felt an enormous happiness creeping over him. All these people, although some of them strange to him, seemed like friends he had always known. The dark beautiful girl, the two red-haired boys, Beryl Gilliatt, fussing over the tea tray, arranging cups and saucers, beckoning to a maid from the house to bring out cakes and plates of sandwiches. A splendid tea. There were chairs that pulled up to the tables so that you could sit comfortably eating all you wanted to eat. The boys settled themselves, inviting Mr. Satterthwaite to sit between them.

He was pleased at that. He had already planned in his own

mind that it was the boys he wanted to talk to first, to see how much they recalled to him Tom Addison in the old days, and he thought, "Lily. How I wish Lily could be here now."

Here he was, thought Mr. Satterthwaite, here he was back in his boyhood. Here where he had come and been welcomed by Tom's father and mother, an aunt or so, too, and a great-uncle and cousins. And now, well, there were not so many in this family, but it *was* a family. Tom in his bedroom slippers, one red, one green, old but still merry and happy. Happy in those who were around him.

And here was Doverton just, or almost just, as it had been. Not quite so well kept up, perhaps, but the lawn was in good condition. And down there he could see the gleam of the river through the trees, and the trees, too. More trees than there had been. And the house needing, perhaps, another coat of paint but not too badly.

After all, Tom Addison was a rich man. Well provided for, owning a large quantity of land. A man with simple tastes who spent enough to keep his place up but was not a spendthrift in other ways. He seldom traveled or went abroad nowadays, but he entertained. Not big parties, just friends. Friends who came to stay, friends who usually had some connection going back into the past. A friendly house.

He turned a little in his chair, drawing it away from the table so that he could see better the view down to the river. Down there was the mill, of course, and beyond the other side were fields. And in one of the fields, it amused him to see a kind of scarecrow, a dark figure on which birds were settling on the straw. Just for a moment he thought it looked like Mr. Harley Quin. Perhaps, thought Mr. Satterthwaite, it *is* my friend Mr. Quin. It was an absurd idea, and yet, if someone had piled up the scarecrow and tried to make it look like Mr. Quin, it could have had the sort of slender elegance that was foreign to most scarecrows.

"Are you looking at our scarecrow?" said Timothy. "We've got a name for him, you know. We call him Mr. Harley Barley."

"Do you indeed," said Mr. Satterthwaite. "Dear me, I find that very interesting."

"Why do you find it interesting?" said Roland, with some curiosity.

"Well, because it rather resembles someone I know, whose name happens to be Harley. His first name, that is."

The boys began singing, "Harley Barley stands on guard, Harley Barley takes things hard. Guards the ricks and guards the hay, Keeps the trespassers away."

"Cucumber sandwich, Mr. Satterthwaite?" said Beryl Gilliatt. "Or do you prefer a homemade pâté one?"

Mr. Satterthwaite accepted the homemade pâté. She deposited by his side a puce cup, the same color as he had admired in the shop. How gay it looked, all that tea set on the table. Yellow, red, blue, green, and all the rest of it.

He wondered if each one had their favorite color. Timothy, he noticed, had a red cup, Roland had a yellow one. Beside Timothy's cup was an object Mr. Satterthwaite could not at first identify. Then he saw it was a meerschaum pipe. It was years since Mr. Satterthwaite had thought of or seen a meerschaum pipe.

Roland, noticing what he was looking at, said, "Tim brought that back from Germany when he went. He's smoking his pipe all the time."

"Don't you smoke, Roland?"

"No. I'm not one for smoking. I don't smoke cigarettes and I don't smoke pot either."

Inez came to the table and sat down the other side of him. Both the young men pressed food on her. They started a laughing conversation together.

Mr. Satterthwaite felt very happy among these young people. Not that they took very much notice of him apart from their natural politeness. But he liked hearing them. He liked, too, making up his judgment about them. He thought, he was almost sure, that both the young men were in love with Inez. Well, it was not surprising. Propinquity brings these things about.

Both had come to live here with their grandfather. A beautiful girl, Roland's first cousin, was living almost next door. Mr. Satterthwaite turned his head. He could just see the house through the trees where it poked up from the road just beyond the front gate. That was the same house that Dr. Horton had lived in last time he came here, seven or eight years ago.

He looked at Inez. He wondered which of the two young men she preferred or whether her affections were already engaged elsewhere. There was no special reason why she should fall in love with one of these two attractive young specimens of the male race.

Having eaten as much as he wanted, Mr. Satterthwaite drew his chair back, altering its angle a little so that he could look all round him.

Mrs. Gilliatt was still busy. Very much the housewife, he thought, making perhaps rather more of a fuss than she need of domesticity. Continually offering people cakes, taking their cups away and replenishing them, handing things round. Somehow, he thought, it would be more pleasant and more informal if she let people help themselves. He wished she was not so busy a hostess.

He looked up to the place where Tom Addison lay stretched out in his chair. Tom Addison was also watching Beryl Gilliatt. Mr. Satterthwaite thought to himself, "He doesn't like her. No. Tom doesn't like her. Well, perhaps that's to be expected." After all, Beryl had taken the place of his own daughter, of Simon Gilliatt's first wife, Lily. "My beautiful Lily," thought Mr. Satterthwaite again, and wondered why for some reason he felt that although he could not see anyone like her, yet Lily in some strange way was here. She was here at this tea party.

"I suppose one begins to imagine these things as one gets old," said Mr. Satterthwaite to himself. "After all, why shouldn't Lily be here to see her son."

He looked affectionately at Timothy and then suddenly realized that he was not looking at Lily's son. Roland was Lily's son. Timothy was Beryl's son.

"I believe Lily knows I'm here. I believe she'd like to speak to me," thought Mr. Satterthwaite. "Oh, dear, oh, dear, I mustn't start imagining foolish things."

For some reason he looked again at the scarecrow. It didn't look like a scarecrow now. It looked like Mr. Harley Quin. Some tricks of the light, of the sunset, were providing it with color, and there was a black dog like Hermes chasing the birds.

"Color," thought Mr. Satterthwaite, and looked again at the table and the tea set and the people having tea. "Why am I here?" said Mr. Satterthwaite to himself. "Why am I here and what ought I to be doing? There's a reason."

Now he knew there was some crisis affecting all these people—or only some of them. Beryl Gilliatt? She was nervous about something. On edge. Tom? Nothing wrong with Tom. He wasn't affected. A lucky man to own this beauty, to own Doverton and to have a grandson, so that when he died all this would come to Roland. Yes, all this would be Roland's. Was Tom hoping that Roland would marry Inez? Or would he have a fear of first cousins marrying? "Nothing must happen," said Mr. Satterthwaite, "nothing must happen. I must prevent it."

Really, his thoughts were the thoughts of a madman. A peaceful scene. A tea set. The varying colors of the harlequin cups. He looked at the white meerschaum pipe lying against the red of the cup. Beryl Gilliatt said something to Timothy. Timothy nodded, got up, and went off toward the house. Beryl removed some empty plates from the table, adjusted a chair or two, murmured something to Roland, who went across and offered a frosted cake to Dr. Horton.

Mr. Satterthwaite watched her. He saw the sweep of her sleeve as she passed the table. He saw a red cup get pushed off the table. It broke on the iron feet of a chair. He heard her little exclamation as she picked up the bits. She went to the tea tray, came back, and placed on the table a pale blue cup and saucer. She replaced the meerschaum pipe, putting it close against it. She brought the teapot and poured tea, then she moved away.

The table was untenanted now. Inez also had got up and left it. Gone to speak to her grandfather. "I don't understand," said Mr. Satterthwaite to himself. "Something's going to happen. What's going to happen?"

A table with different-colored cups and—yes, Timothy, his red hair glowing in the sun. Red hair glowing with that same tint, that attractive sideways wave that Simon Gilliatt's hair had always had. Timothy, coming back, standing a moment, looking at the table with a slightly puzzled eye, then going to where the meerschaum pipe rested against the pale blue cup.

Inez came back then. She laughed suddenly and said, "Timothy, you're drinking your tea out of the wrong cup. The blue cup's mine. Yours is the red one."

And Timothy said, "Don't be silly, Inez, I know my own cup. It's got sugar in it and you won't like it. Nonsense. This is my cup. The meerschaum's up against it."

It came to Mr. Satterthwaite then. A shock. Was he mad? Was he imagining things? Was any of this real?

He got up. He walked quickly toward the table, and as Timothy raised the blue cup to his lips he shouted.

"Don't drink that!" he called. "Don't drink it, I say."

Timothy turned a surprised face. Mr. Satterthwaite turned his head. Dr. Horton, rather startled, got up from his seat and was coming near.

"What's the matter, Satterthwaite?"

"That cup. There's something wrong about it," said Mr. Satterthwaite. "Don't let the boy drink from it."

Horton stared at it. "My dear fellow—"

"I know what I'm saying. The red cup was his," said Mr. Satterthwaite, "and the red cup's broken. It's been replaced with a blue one. He doesn't know the red from blue, does he?"

Dr. Horton looked puzzled. "D'you mean—d'you mean—like Tom?"

"Tom Addison. He's color-blind. You know that, don't you?"

"Oh, yes, of course. We all know that. That's why he's got odd shoes on today. He never knows red from green."

"This boy is the same."

"But—but surely not. Anyway, there's never been any sign of it in—in Roland."

"There might be, though, mightn't there?" said Mr. Satterthwaite. "I'm right in thinking—Daltonism. That's what they call it, don't they?"

"It was a name they used to call it by, yes."

"It's not inherited by a female, but it passes through the female. Lily wasn't color-blind, but Lily's son might easily be color-blind."

"But, my dear Satterthwaite, Timothy isn't Lily's son. Roland is Lily's son. I know they're rather alike. Same age, same color hair, but—well, perhaps you don't remember."

"No," said Mr. Satterthwaite, "I shouldn't have remembered. But I know now. I can see the resemblance, too. Roland's Beryl's son. They were both babies, weren't they, when Simon remarried. It is very easy for a woman looking after two babies, especially if both of them were going to have red hair. Timothy's Lily's son and Roland is Beryl's son. Beryl's and Christopher Eden's. There is no reason why he should be color-blind. I know it, I tell you. I know it!"

He saw Dr. Horton's eyes go from one to the other. Timothy, not catching what they said but holding the blue cup and looking puzzled.

"I saw her buy it," said Mr. Satterthwaite. "Listen to me, man. You've known me for some years. You know that I don't make mistakes if I say a thing positively."

"Quite true. I've never known you make a mistake."

"Take that cup away from him," said Mr. Satterthwaite. "Take it to an analytic chemist and find out what's in it. I saw that woman buy that cup. She bought it in the village shop. She knew then that she was going to break a red cup, replace it by a blue, and that Timothy would never know that the colors were different."

"I think you're mad, Satterthwaite. But all the same I'm going to do what you say."

He advanced on the table, stretched out a hand to the blue cup.

"Do you mind letting me have a look at that?" said Dr. Horton.

"Of course," said Timothy. He looked slightly surprised.

"I think there's a flaw in the china, here, you know. Rather interesting."

Beryl came across the lawn. She came quickly and sharply.

"What are you doing? What's the matter? What is happening?"

"Nothing's the matter," said Dr. Horton cheerfully. "I just want to show the boys a little experiment I'm going to make with a cup of tea."

He was looking at her very closely and he saw the expression of fear, of terror. Mr. Satterthwaite saw the change of countenance.

"Would you like to come with me, Satterthwaite? Just a little experiment, you know. A matter of testing porcelain and different qualities in it nowadays. A very interesting discovery was made lately."

Chatting, he walked along the grass. Mr. Satterthwaite followed him, and the two young men, chatting to each other, followed.

"What's the Doc up to now, Roly?" said Timothy.

"I don't know," said Roland. "He seems to have got some very extraordinary ideas. Oh, well, we shall hear about it later, I expect. Let's go and get our bikes."

Beryl Gilliatt turned abruptly. She retraced her steps rapidly up the lawn toward the house. Tom Addison called to her, "Anything the matter, Beryl?"

"Something I'd forgotten," said Beryl Gilliatt. "That's all."

Tom Addison looked inquiringly toward Simon Gilliatt. "Anything wrong with your wife?" he said.

"Beryl? Oh, no, not that I know of. I expect it's some little thing or other that she's forgotten. Nothing I can do for you, Beryl?" he called.

"No. No, I'll be back later." She turned her head half sideways, looking at the old man lying back in the chair. She spoke suddenly and vehemently. "You silly old fool. You've got the wrong shoes on again today. They don't match. Do you know you've got one shoe that's red and one shoe that's green?"

"Ah, done it again, have I?" said Tom Addison. "They look exactly the same color to me, you know. It's odd, isn't it, but there it is."

She went past him, her steps quickening.

Presently Mr. Satterthwaite and Dr. Horton reached the gate that led out into the roadway. They heard a motorcycle speeding along.

"She's gone," said Dr. Horton. "She's run for it. We ought to have stopped her, I suppose. Do you think she'll come back?"

"No," said Mr. Satterthwaite, "I don't think she'll come back. Perhaps," he said thoughtfully, "it's best that way."

"You mean?"

"It's an old house," said Mr. Satterthwaite. "An old family. A good family. A lot of good people in it. One doesn't want trouble, scandal, brought on it. Best to let her go, I think."

"Tom Addison never liked her," said Dr. Horton. "Never. He was always polite and kind but he didn't like her."

"And there's the boy to think of," said Mr. Satterthwaite.

"The boy. You mean?"

"The other boy. Roland. This way he needn't know about what his mother was trying to do."

"Why on earth did she do it?"

"You've no doubt now that she did," said Mr. Satterthwaite.

"No. I've no doubt now. I saw her face, Satterthwaite, when she looked at me. I knew then that what you'd said was truth. But why?"

"Greed, I suppose," said Mr. Satterthwaite. "She hadn't any

money of her own, I believe. Her first husband, Christopher Eden, was a nice chap by all accounts but he hadn't anything in the way of means. But Tom Addison's grandchild has big money coming to him. A lot of money. Property all around here has appreciated enormously. I've no doubt Tom Addison will leave the bulk of what he has to his grandson. She wanted it for her own son, and through her own son, of course, for herself. She is a greedy woman."

Mr. Satterthwaite turned his head back suddenly.

"Something's on fire over there," he said.

"Good lord, so it is. Oh, it's the scarecrow down in the field. Some young chap or other's set fire to it, I suppose. But there's nothing to worry about. There are no ricks or anything anywhere near. It'll just burn itself out."

"Yes," said Mr. Satterthwaite. "Well, you go on, Doctor. You don't need me to help you in your tests."

"I've no doubt of what I shall find. I don't mean the exact substance, but I have come to your belief that this blue cup holds death."

Mr. Satterthwaite had turned back through the gate. He was going now down in the direction where the scarecrow was burning. Behind it was the sunset. A remarkable sunset that evening. Its colors illuminated the air round it, illuminated the burning scarecrow.

"So that's the way you've chosen to go," said Mr. Satterthwaite.

He looked slightly startled then, for in the neighborhood of the flames he saw the tall slight figure of a woman. A woman dressed in some pale mother-of-pearl coloring. She was walking in the direction of Mr. Satterthwaite. He stopped, watching.

"Lily," he said. "Lily."

He saw her quite plainly now. It was Lily walking toward him. Too far away for him to see her face but he knew very well who it was. Just for a moment or two he wondered whether anyone else would see her or whether the sight was only for him. He said, not very loud, only in a whisper, "It's all right, Lily, your son is safe."

She stopped then. She raised one hand to her lips. He didn't see her smile, but he knew she was smiling. She kissed her hand and waved it to him and then she turned. She walked back toward where the scarecrow was disintegrating into a mass of ashes.

"She's going away again," said Mr. Satterthwaite to himself. "She's going away with him. They're walking away together. They belong to the same world, of course. They only come—those sort of people—they only come when it's a case of love or death or both."

He wouldn't see Lily again, he supposed, but he wondered how soon he would meet Mr. Quin again. He went back across the lawn toward the tea table and the harlequin tea set, and beyond that, to his old friend Tom Addison. Beryl wouldn't come back. He was sure of it. Doverton Kingsbourne was safe again.

Across the lawn came the small black dog in flying leaps. It came to Mr. Satterthwaite, panting a little and wagging its tail. Through its collar was twisted a scrap of paper. Mr. Satterthwaite stooped and detached it.

On it in colored letters was written a message:

CONGRATULATIONS!
TO OUR NEXT MEETING

H.Q.

"Thank you, Hermes," said Mr. Satterthwaite, and watched the black dog flying across the meadow to rejoin the two figures that he knew were there but could no longer see.

WHO DIES, WHO LIVES?

by Patricia Highsmith

How long does hate have to fester before it bursts into murder? Seventeen years—is that long enough? Dr. Stephen McCullough toyed with the idea . . .

One of Patricia Highsmith's most delicate probings into the hearts and minds of people . . .

DR. STEPHEN McCULLOUGH had a first-class compartment to himself on the express from Paris to Geneva. He sat browsing in one of the medical quarterlies he had brought from America, but he was not concentrating. He was toying with the idea of murder. That was why he had taken the train instead of flying, to give himself time to think or perhaps merely to dream.

He was a serious man of forty-five, a little overweight, with a prominent and spreading nose, a brown mustache, brown-rimmed glasses, a receding hairline. His eyebrows were tense with an inward anxiety, which his patients often thought a concern with their problems. Actually, he was unhappily married, and though he refused to quarrel with Lillian—that meant answer her back—there was discord between them.

In Paris yesterday he had answered Lillian back, and on a ridiculous matter about whether he or she would return an evening bag to a shop on the Rue Royale, a bag Lillian had decided she did not want. He had been angry not because he had had to take the bag back, but because he had agreed, in a weak moment fifteen minutes before, to visit Roger Fane in Geneva.

"Go and see him, Steve," Lillian had said yesterday morning. "You're so close to Geneva now, why not? Think of the pleasure it would give Roger."

What pleasure? Why? But Dr. McCullough had rung Roger at the American Embassy in Geneva, and Roger had been very friendly—much too friendly, of course—and had said that Stephen must come and stay a few days and that he had plenty of room to put him up. Dr. McCullough had agreed to spend one night. Then he was going to fly to Rome to join Lillian.

Dr. McCullough detested Roger Fane. It was the kind of hatred that time does nothing to diminish. Roger Fane, seventeen years ago, had married the woman Dr. McCullough loved. Margaret. Margaret had died a year ago in an automobile accident on an Alpine road.

Roger Fane was smug, cautious, mightily pleased with himself, and not very intelligent. Seventeen years ago Roger Fane had told Margaret that he, Stephen McCullough, was having a secret affair with another girl. Nothing was further from the truth, but before Stephen could prove anything, Margaret had married Roger. Dr. McCullough had not expected the marriage to last, but it had, and finally Dr. McCullough had married Lillian, whose face resembled Margaret's a little, but that was the only similarity. In the past seventeen years Dr. McCullough had seen Roger and Margaret perhaps three times when they had come to New York on short trips. He had not seen Roger since Margaret's death.

Now as the train shot through the French countryside Dr. McCullough reflected on the satisfaction that murdering Roger Fane would give him. He had never before thought of murdering anybody, but yesterday evening while he was taking a bath in the Paris hotel, after the telephone conversation with Roger, a thought had come to him in regard to murder: most murderers were caught because they left some clue, despite their efforts to erase all the clues. Many murderers wanted to be caught, the doctor realized, and unconsciously planted a clue that led the police straight to them. In the Leopold and Loeb case one of them had dropped his glasses at the scene, for instance.

But suppose a murderer deliberately left a dozen clues, practically down to his calling card? It seemed to Dr. McCullough that the very obviousness of it would throw off suspicion. Especially if the person were a man like himself, well thought of, a non-violent type. Also, there'd be no motive that anyone could see, because Dr. McCullough had never even told Lillian that he had loved the woman Roger Fane had married. Of course, a few of his old friends knew it, but Dr. McCullough hadn't mentioned Margaret or Roger Fane in a decade.

He imagined Roger's apartment as formal and gloomy, perhaps with a servant prowling about full time, a servant who slept in. A servant would complicate things. Let's say there wasn't a servant who slept in, that he and Roger would be having a nightcap in the living room or in Roger's study, and then just before saying good night, Dr. McCullough would pick up a heavy paperweight or a big vase and—then he would calmly take his leave. Of course, the bed should be slept in, since he was supposed to stay the night, so perhaps the morning would be better for the crime than the evening. The essential thing was to leave quietly and at the time he was supposed to leave. But the doctor found himself unable to plot in much detail after all.

Roger Fane's street in Geneva looked just as Dr. McCullough had imagined it—a narrow curving street that combined business establishments with old private dwellings—and it was not too well lighted when Dr. McCullough's taxi entered it at nine P.M.; yet in law-abiding Switzerland, the doctor supposed, dark streets held few dangers for anyone. The front door buzzed in response to his ring, and Dr. McCullough opened it. The door was as heavy as a bank vault's door.

"Hello!" Roger's voice called cheerily down the stairwell. "Come up! I'm on the third floor. Fourth to you, I suppose."

"Be right there," Dr. McCullough said, shy about raising his voice in the presence of the closed doors on either side of the hall. He had telephoned Roger a few minutes before from the railway station, because Roger had said he would meet him. Roger had apologized and said he had been held up at a meeting at his office, and would Steve mind hopping a taxi and coming right over? Dr. McCullough suspected that Roger had not been held up at all, but simply hadn't wanted to show him the courtesy of being at the station.

"Well, well, Steve!" said Roger, pumping Dr. McCullough's hand. "It's great to see you again. Come in, come in. Is that thing heavy?" Roger made a pass at the doctor's suitcase, but the doctor caught it up first.

"Not at all. Good to see you again, Roger." He went into the apartment.

There were oriental rugs, ornate lamps that gave off dim light. It was even stuffier than Dr. McCullough had anticipated. Roger looked a trifle thinner. He was shorter than the doctor, and had sparse blond hair. His weak face perpetually smiled. Both had eaten dinner, so they drank Scotch in the living room.

"So you're joining Lillian in Rome tomorrow," said Roger. "Sorry you won't be staying longer. I'd intended to drive you out to the country tomorrow evening to meet a friend of mine. A woman," Roger added with a smile.

"Oh? Too bad. Yes, I'll be off on the one o'clock plane tomorrow afternoon. I made the reservation from Paris." Dr. McCullough found himself speaking automatically. Strangely, he felt a little drunk, though he'd taken only a couple of sips of his Scotch. It was because of the falsity of the situation, he thought, the falsity of his being here at all, of his pretending friendship or at least friendliness. And Roger's smile irked him, so merry and yet so forced.

Roger hadn't referred to Margaret, though Dr. McCullough had not seen him since she died. But then, neither had the doctor referred to her, even to give a few words of condolence. And already, it seemed, Roger had another female interest. Roger was just over forty, still trim of figure and bright of eye. And Margaret, that jewel among women, was just something that had come his way, stayed a while, and departed, Dr. McCullough supposed. Roger looked not at all bereaved.

The doctor detested Roger fully as much as he had on the train, but the reality of Roger Fane was somewhat dismaying. If Stephen killed him, he would have to touch him, or feel the resistance of his flesh to the object he hit him with. And what was the servant situation?

As if Roger read his mind, he said, "I've a girl who comes in to clean every morning at ten and leaves at twelve. If you want her to do anything for you—wash and iron a shirt or something like that—don't hesitate. She's very fast, or can be if you ask her. Her name's Yvonne."

Then the telephone rang. Roger spoke in French. His face fell slightly as he agreed to do something that the other person was asking him to do.

Roger said to the doctor, "Of all the irritating things! I've got to catch the seven o'clock plane to Zurich tomorrow. Some visiting fireman's being welcomed at a breakfast. So, old man, I suppose I'll be gone before you're out of bed."

"Oh!" Dr. McCullough found himself chuckling. "You think doctors aren't used to early calls? Of course I'll get up to say goodbye and see you off."

Roger's smile widened slightly. "Well, we'll see. I certainly won't wake you for it. Make yourself at home and I'll leave a note for Yvonne to prepare coffee and rolls. Or would you like a more substantial brunch around eleven?"

Dr. McCullough was not thinking about what Roger was saying. He had just noticed a rectangular marble pen-and-pencil holder on the desk where the telephone stood. He was looking at Roger's high and faintly pink forehead.

"Oh, brunch," said the doctor vaguely. "No, no, for goodness sake. They feed you enough on the plane."

And then his thoughts leaped to Lillian and the quarrel yesterday in Paris. Hostility smoldered in him. Had Roger ever quarreled with Margaret? Dr. McCullough could not imagine Margaret being unfair, being mean. It was no wonder Roger's face looked relaxed and untroubled.

"A penny for your thoughts," said Roger, getting up to replenish his glass.

The doctor's glass was still half full.

"I suppose I'm a bit tired," said Dr. McCullough, and passed his hand across his forehead. When he lifted his head again, he saw a photograph of Margaret which he had not noticed before on the top of the highboy on his right. Margaret in her twenties, as she had looked when Roger married her, as she had looked when the doctor had so loved her. Dr. McCullough looked suddenly at Roger. His hatred returned in a wave that left him physically weak.

"I suppose I'd better turn in," he said, setting his glass carefully on the little table in front of him and standing up. Roger had showed him his bedroom.

"Sure you wouldn't like a spot of brandy?" asked Roger. "You look all in." Roger smiled cockily, standing very straight.

The tide of the doctor's anger flowed back. He picked up the marble slab with one hand, and before Roger could step back, smashed him in the forehead with its base. It was a blow that would kill, the doctor knew. Roger fell and without even a last twitch lay still and limp.

The doctor set the marble holder back where it had been, picked up the pen and pencil, which had fallen, replaced them, then wiped the marble with his handkerchief where his fingers had touched it and also the pen and pencil. Roger's forehead was bleeding slightly. He felt Roger's still warm wrist and found no pulse. Then he went down the hall to his own room.

He awakened the next morning at 8:15, after a mediocre night's sleep. He showered in the bathroom between his room and Roger's bedroom, shaved, dressed, and left the house at a quarter past nine. A hall went from his room past the kitchen to the apartment door; it had not been necessary to cross the living room, and even if he had glanced into the living room, Roger's body would have been out of sight to him. Dr. McCullough had not glanced in.

At 5:30 P.M. he was in Rome, riding in a taxi from the airport to the Hotel Majestic where Lillian awaited him. Lillian was out, however. The doctor had some coffee sent up, and it was then that he noticed his brief case was missing. He had wanted to lie on the bed and drink coffee and read his medical quarterlies. Now he remembered distinctly: for some reason he had carried his brief case into Roger's living room last evening.

This did not disturb him at all. It was exactly what he would have done on purpose if he had thought of it. His name and his New York address were written in the slot of the brief case. And Dr. McCullough supposed that Roger had written his name in full in some engagement book along with the time of his arrival.

He found Lillian in good humor. She had bought a lot of things in the Via Condotti. They had dinner and then took a carozza ride through the Villa Borghese, to the Piazza di Spagna and the

Piazza del Populo. If there were anything in the papers about Roger, Dr. McCullough was ignorant of it. He bought only the Paris *Herald-Tribune*, which was a morning paper.

The news came the next morning as he and Lillian were breakfasting at Donay's in the Via Veneto. It was in the Paris *Herald-Tribune*, and there was a picture of Roger Fane on the front page, a serious, official picture of him in a wing collar.

"Good Lord!" said Lillian. "Why, it happened the night you were there!"

Looking over her shoulder, Dr. McCullough pretended surprise. " '—died some time between eight P.M. and three A.M.,' " the doctor read. "I said good night to him about eleven, I think, then went into my room."

"You didn't *hear* anything?"

"No. My room was down a hall. I closed my door."

"And the next morning. You didn't—"

"I told you, Roger had to catch a seven o'clock plane. I assumed he was gone. I left the house around nine."

"And all the time he was lying dead in the living room!" Lillian said with a gasp. "Steve! Why, this is terrible!"

Was it, Dr. McCullough wondered. Was it so terrible for her? Her voice did not sound really concerned. He looked into her wide eyes. "It's certainly terrible—but I'm not responsible, God knows. Don't worry about it, Lillian."

The police were at the Hotel Majestic when they returned, waiting for Dr. McCullough in the lobby. They were both plainclothes Swiss police, and they spoke English. They interviewed Dr. McCullough at a table in a corner of the lobby. Lillian had, at Dr. McCullough's insistence, gone up to their room.

Dr. McCullough had wondered why the police had not come for him hours earlier than this—it was so simple to check the passenger lists of planes leaving Geneva—but he soon found out why. The maid Yvonne had not come to clean yesterday morning, so Roger Fane's body had not been discovered until six P.M yesterday, when his office had become alarmed at his absence and sent someone around to his apartment to investigate.

"This is your brief case, I think," said the slender blond officer with a smile, opening a large paper bag he had been carrying under his arm.

"Yes, thank you very much. I realized today that I'd left it." The doctor took it and placed it on his lap.

The two Swiss watched him quietly.

"This is very shocking," Dr. McCullough said. "It's hard for me to realize." He was impatient for them to make their charge—if they were going to—and ask him to return to Geneva with them. They both seemed almost in awe of him.

"How well did you know Mr. Fane?" asked the other officer.

"Not too well. I've known him many years, but we were never close friends. I hadn't seen him in five years, I think." Dr. McCullough spoke steadily and in his usual tone.

"Mr. Fane was still fully dressed, so he had not gone to bed. You are sure you heard no disturbance that night?"

"I did not," the doctor answered for the second time. A silence. "Have you any clues as to who might have done it?"

"Oh, yes, yes," the blond man said matter-of-factly. "We suspect the brother of the maid Yvonne. He was drunk that night and hasn't an alibi for the time of the crime. He and his sister live together and that night he went off with his sister's batch of keys—among which was the key to Mr. Fane's apartment. He didn't come back until nearly noon yesterday. Yvonne was worried about him, which is why she didn't go to Mr. Fane's apartment yesterday—that plus the fact she couldn't have got in. She tried to telephone at eight thirty yesterday morning to say she wouldn't be coming, but she got no answer. We've questioned the brother Anton. He's a ne'er-do-well." The officer shrugged.

Dr. McCullough remembered hearing the telephone ring at eight thirty. "But—what was the motive?"

"Oh—resentment. Robbery maybe if he'd been sober enough to

find anything to take. He's a case for a psychiatrist or an alcoholic ward. Mr. Fane knew him, so he might have let him into the apartment, or he could have walked in, since he had the key. Yvonne said that Mr. Fane had been trying for months to get her to live apart from her brother. Her brother beats her and takes her money. Mr. Fane had spoken to the brother a couple of times, and it's on our record that Mr. Fane once had to call the police to get Anton out of the apartment when he came there looking for his sister. That incident happened at nine in the evening, an hour when his sister is never there. You see how off his head he is."

Dr. McCullough cleared his throat and asked, "Has Anton confessed?"

"Oh, the same as. Poor chap, I really don't think he knows what he's doing half the time. But at least in Switzerland there's no capital punishment. He'll have enough time to dry out in jail, all right." He glanced at his colleague and they both stood up. "Thank you very much, Dr. McCullough."

"You're very welcome," said the doctor. "Thank you for the brief case."

Dr. McCullough went upstairs with his brief case to his room.

"What did they say?" Lillian asked as he came in.

"They think the brother of the maid did it," said Dr. McCullough. "Fellow who's an alcoholic and who seems to have had it in for Roger. Some ne'er-do-well."

Frowning, he went into the bathroom to wash his hands. He suddenly detested himself, detested Lillian's long sigh, an "Ah-h" of relief.

"Thank God, thank God!" Lillian said. "Do you know what this would have meant if they'd—if they'd have accused *you?*" she asked in a softer voice, as if the walls had ears, and she came closer to the bathroom door.

"Certainly," Dr. McCullough said, and felt a burst of anger in his blood. "I'd have had a hell of a time proving I was innocent, since I was right there at the time."

"Exactly. You couldn't have proved you were innocent. Thank

God for this Anton, whoever he is." Her small face glowed, her eyes twinkled. "A ne'er-do-well. Ha! He did us some good!" She laughed shrilly and turned on one heel.

"I don't see why you have to gloat," he said, drying his hands carefully. "It's a sad story."

"Sadder than if they'd blamed you? Don't be so—so altruistic, dear. Or rather, think of us. Husband kills old rival-in-love after—let's see—seventeen years, isn't it? And after eleven years of marriage to another woman. The torch still burns high. Do you think I'd like that?"

"Lillian, what're you talking about?" He came out of the bathroom scowling.

"You know exactly. You think I don't know you were in love with Margaret? *Still* are? You think I don't know you killed Roger?" Her gray eyes looked at him with a wild challenge. Her head was tipped to one side, her hands on her hips.

He felt tongue-tied, paralyzed. They stared at each other for perhaps fifteen seconds, while his mind moved tentatively over the abyss her words had just spread before him. He hadn't known that she still thought of Margaret. Of course she'd known about Margaret. But who had kept the story alive in her mind? Perhaps he had by his silence, the doctor realized. But the future was what mattered. Now she had something to hold over his head, something by which she could control him forever. "My dear, you are mistaken."

But Lillian with a toss of her head walked away, and the doctor knew he had not won.

Absolutely nothing was said about the matter the rest of the day. They lunched, spent a leisurely hour in the Vatican museum, but Dr. McCullough's mind was on things other than Michelangelo's paintings. He was going to go to Geneva and confess the thing, not for decency's sake or because his conscience bothered him, but because Lillian's attitude was insupportable. It was less supportable than a long stretch in prison.

He managed to get away long enough to make a telephone call

at five P.M. There was a plane to Geneva at 7:20 P.M. At 6:15 P.M. he left their hotel room empty-handed and took a taxi to Ciampino Airport. He had his passport and Travelers Cheques.

He arrived in Geneva before eleven that evening and called the police. At first they were not willing to tell him the whereabouts of the man accused of murdering Roger Fane; but Dr. McCullough gave his name and said he had some important information, and then the Swiss police told him where Anton Carpeaux was being held. Dr. McCullough took a taxi to what seemed the outskirts of Geneva. It was a new white building, not at all like a prison.

Here he was greeted by one of the plainclothes officers who had come to see him, the blond one. "Dr. McCullough," he said with a faint smile. "You have some information, you say? I am afraid it is a little late."

"Oh? Why?"

"Anton Carpeaux has just killed himself—by bashing his head against the wall of his cell. Just twenty minutes ago." The man gave a hopeless shrug.

"Good God," Dr. McCullough said softly.

"But what was your information?"

The doctor hesitated. The words wouldn't come. And then he realized that it was cowardice and shame that kept him silent. He had never felt so worthless in his life, and he felt infinitely lower than the drunken ne'er-do-well who had killed himself. "I'd rather not. In this case—I mean—it's so all over, isn't it? It was something else against Anton—but what's the use now? It's bad enough—"

"Yes, I suppose so," said the Swiss.

"So—I'll say good night."

"Good night, Dr. McCullough."

Then the doctor walked on into the night, aimlessly. He felt a curious emptiness, a nothingness in himself that was not like any mood he had ever known. His plan for murder had succeeded, but it had dragged worse tragedies in its wake. Anton Carpeaux. And

* Obvious Swiss do not have much in way of serious crime. Police in others countries would have heard "information" first, No?

Lillian. In a strange way he had killed himself just as much as he had killed Roger Fane.

Half an hour later he stood on a formal bridge looking down at the black water of Lake Leman. He stared down a long while and imagined his body toppling over and over, striking the water with not much of a splash, sinking. He stared hard at the blackness that looked so solid but would be so yielding, so willing to swallow him into death. But he hadn't even the courage or the despair for suicide.

One day, however, he would, he knew. One day when the planes of cowardice and courage met at the proper angle. And that day would be a surprise to him and to everyone else who knew him. Then his hands that gripped the stone parapet pushed him back, and the doctor walked on heavily. He would see about a hotel for tonight, and tomorrow arrange to get back to Rome. He was now a dead man, a walking dead man.

THE SHOOTING OF CURLY DAN;
or, The Gandy Dancers' Lament

by John Lutz

A story that reads like American folklore . . .

OLLIE ROBINSON was my great-great-grandfather, and he didn't know himself how old he was or where he was born. He was a smart man, but he didn't have much education, and he kept to himself most of the time because of how the other kids would make fun of him. When I was younger I used to laugh at him myself, then all of a sudden one day I got to thinking, I was thirteen, and he was—what? 113? But I had found out that when he told a story, it was worth listening to, because he was a man who'd done things and been places and met people.

One night when Mom and Dad weren't home he told me the story of Curly Dan's murder that happened when Grandpa Ollie—that's what I called him—was a gandy dancer for the Alton and Southern Railroad. That railroad is gone now, and so are gandy dancers, I expect. Grandpa Ollie didn't tell me how long ago it happened, but it had to be a long, long time. It didn't matter to him, though, because for Grandpa Ollie, sitting there half crippled in his cane chair, chin stuck out and skin loose and wrinkled like an old dollar bill, the past was sometimes right there all around him.

I was sitting near his chair, listening to the even in-and-out rhythm of his breathing and thinking he was asleep. Way off somebody was beating on something metal with a hammer, and maybe that's what kept him from dozing off like he usually did. But he wasn't asleep, and he began talking to me in a voice clearer than his usual voice—younger-sounding, like he was really back there living what he was telling me, living it all over again . . .

All the railroads had crews of gandy dancers in them days (Grandpa Ollie began), eight or ten strong men to a crew and a caller. I was a gandy dancer for three years with the A & S, but I guess you don't know what a gandy dancer be. When trains go over and over a set of rails, them rails gets crooked and outa line with each other, and somebody's got to set 'em straight again. They got a machine does it now, but then it was done like most things, with sweat and muscle.

There was nine men on each Alton and Southern line crew, 'long with a line chief usually. The company engine would drop us off way out where the rails didn't have no care for a long time and we'd walk along carryin' our pry bars while the line chief kept his eye on the rails that needed work done on 'em. There was a flat cart with water and tools that we pushed along with us, 'cause we done other work besides just truin' the rails. Sometimes we'd have to take a hammer and drive loose spikes, or shovel earth under a section of roadbedding that had give way.

The day Curly Dan was killed we didn't have a line boss, like we didn't sometimes the day before payday, 'cause the foreman, he be workin' on the payroll and paperwork, and he figured ol' Ivy Joe was good enough to be caller and boss both. The line boss and his crew was over on a section of track the other side of a rise, close enough so we could hear the ringin' of their steel and sometimes their voices.

Ivy Joe, that wasn't his true name, but his initials was I. V., so that's what we called him. Now we'd walk along the track, carryin' our pry bars, till Joe spotted a place needed work. Our pry bars was about five feet long and tempered steel, kinda curved and flattened on one end. When we wanted to line track we'd stand in a row 'longside it and put the flattened ends of the bars under the rail. Then, like the big boss always told us, everything depended on rhythm. Nine men had to move like one. That's where Ivy Joe's callin' came in, and he was the best caller the A & S ever had.

When we all had our pry bars 'neath the rail, ready to use 'em like long levers, that's when Ivy Joe started callin' and we'd all tap the rail in rhythm. Then at the last of his chant he'd raise his voice sudden and we'd all put our backs in it together and there'd be a loud ring of steel and we'd move that rail. Over and over we'd do it till the rails was true, then we'd walk on downtrack to the next bad spot.

It were a hot day when the murder happened, and we hadn't had a water break since middle mornin' and the sun was near high. Steel was ringin' and Ivy Joe was callin' the rhythm:

Tell me line boss eyes be blind
How he gonna tell if the rails in line?

And we'd all pull back together and strike steel in rhythm to inch the rail over. We stopped for a water break after that bad section were trued and I can tell you ain't none of us didn't need it.

Then we worked on ahead, leavin' the water and tool cart sittin' behind as usual till we found another bad place. We was workin' hard on a bend in the rails for some time 'fore Ivy Joe noticed Curly Dan wasn't with us.

"Where that Curly Dan?" he says, standin' with his big fists on his hips. "You know, Slim?"

Slim Deacon was the one helped Curly Dan read letters from Albany. His lean body kinda bent and he shook his head.

"Chaney?"

Chaney were a big man, always grinnin', and he grinned wider and shrugged his heavy shoulders.

"Ollie," Ivy Joe says to me, "you run on back to the tool cart an' see if that lazy Curly Dan be layin' out on us."

I took out runnin', listenin' to the ringin' rhythm of the line crew across the rise while my feet hit the ties.

When I rounded the bend and ran a ways, there be Curly Dan, layin' on his side, kinda curled up around the water jug that was still sittin' on the ground. His blue shirt back were covered with blood where he'd been shot, the bullet goin' clear through, and when I got closer I could see he'd been shot in the back of the head, too, like someone wanted to make sure he be dead.

Everything seemed unnatural quiet and still there. Even the water just below the top of the jug were as calm and still as Curly Dan hisself.

I run back halfway round the bend, yellin' and wavin', and the rest of the crew followed me back to Curly Dan's body. For a while we all stood and stared, lookin' from one to the other.

"How come we didn't hear no shot?" Arky said. He was a short wide man from Arkansas that always had a blade of grass in his teeth.

Ivy Joe looked round him towards the rise and a grove of trees. " 'Cause the killer timed his shot with the rhythm," he says. "Brogan's crew be workin' over the rise when we was here, and when they hit steel hard is when the killer pulled the trigger from the trees over there."

Then Ivy Joe walks over to the grove of trees and a while later comes back holdin' a pistol. "It be a small gun," he said, "and I found where the brush was flattened down where the killer was hidin'." Then he looked real close at the body, standin' there holdin' the pistol and thinkin'. "Load Curly Dan onto the tool cart," he said, and we did that and put up the tools and water jug that was still layin' there from our last work break. Kelly, a bowlegged man with a big mustache, and a man name of Tall Al slid Curly Dan well to the back so's he wouldn't get blood on any of the tools.

"What we gonna do now?" Chaney asked, standin' with his arms crossed.

"We gonna work," Ivy Joe told him. "We gonna work on." And we went on down the tracks.

"Who'd have any reason to shoot Curly Dan?" Ben Zebo said while we was walkin' back to where we'd left off workin'.

Nobody answered 'cause everybody know'd who. There was three men on the crew coulda done it for reason. Chaney was sweet on Curly's little gal, Molly Ann Parker, who'd been all his till Curly Dan took her over. And a man named Handy Billy Grover, he was awful sweet on her too, and he and Curly Dan'd had a fight about her just a few days ago. If any of 'em had any sense they'd just waited, 'cause Molly Ann woulda come round to 'em again. Then there was Arky, who Curly Dan owed fifty dollars to, and who'd been in a argument with him last week over Curly Dan not payin' up.

Ivy Joe know'd all these things, but he didn't say any of 'em as we kept on walkin' 'long the tracks, listenin' to Brogan's crew ringin' steel on the return line over the rise. Kelly with the big mustache was laggin' behind us, pushin' the cart along the tracks real slow and keepin' his distance from Curly Dan.

We got to where we was linin' track, took our places again along the outside rail, and slid our pry bars under the steel. Ivy Joe started to clink his bar in rhythm and sing like always.

Work be hard but I ain' gonna moan
Work my han's 'til I see de bone!

Steel rung and we moved that rail 'bout an inch. It were a song Ivy Joe'd sung lots before and we was all in rhythm, pullin' hard and together.

'Long the bend we was workin' was the worst section of track on the Alton and Southern but for the Gibsey Hill, and we could look ahead in the sun and see rail shimmerin' outa line for a long ways. We worked on and sweat was runnin' down us all.

Somebody hide an' shoot Curly Dan
Shame to kill dat young good man!

All the while Ivy Joe sang we was tappin' rhythm on the steel, all together and bendin' our backs to it at the last when he'd raise his fine voice. Movin' rail, we was, and then walkin' on to more rail. The sun be high and hot as I ever felt it, and we was all walkin'-weary soon, throats dry and eyes burnin' with sweat. I seen Arky in front of me, staggerin' some as we walk on down the line.

"When we gonna stop for water?" Chaney yelled, but Ivy Joe, he didn't hear and kept right on workin'.

Somebody on de railroad crew
Know how to shoot when the rhythm do!

And the steel clang together like one clang, all through the song, then loud like to make your head hurt.

We work on for must've been hours like that, in kind of a daze like you'd get when Ivy Joe was callin' rhythm. We was all tired and achin', and I remember how my back felt like it was blazin' and it pained me to lean. Still we kept the rhythm, 'cause the job, it be all rhythm.

There be sorrow for Molly Ann
Somebody done gone an' shoot her man!

I pulled up and back on my pry bar, feelin' a pain down my stomach, and the rail hardly move and I heard a little clink just a eyewink after the other men had pulled hard together.

"Water," Handy Billy called out, and we all called out for

water. Billy's clothes was stickin' to him and his face be all swollen where he kept wipin' his sleeve to keep the sweat outa his eyes.

Someone here he done hang back
Kill Curly Dan when we move downtrack!

Much pain as there be, we still tried to keep up the rhythm. My mouth was dry as sand and the pain almost kept me from straightenin' as the steel rang, and again I heard that clang of a pry bar outta time.

One man kill fo' a woman's all
Now a rope gonna stop his fall!

"I got to have water!" Handy Billy yelled again with his voice all cracked when the steel ring, and I could hardly hear if there was a late ring that time.

The heat be risin' from the ground, and I know'd any time I was gonna fall flat on my face, but we worked on, gaspin' for breath and tryin' to ignore the achin'. Then again there was a late ring of steel, this time later than before, and there was a thuddin' sound too, and we turned and seen the last man in the crew layin' out on the ties with his chest heavin'.

Ivy Joe walked on back and looked down at him. "You the one killed Curly Dan, Chaney," he said like he know'd for sure.

Chaney just looked up at him and kinda croaked.

Then Ivy Joe let us all have water, but not Chaney. Ivy Joe standed over him with the ladle full after everybody else drunk. He let a few drops fall down on Chaney's forehead.

"You killed him," Ivy Joe said again.

"I done it," Chaney said in a raw voice. "I done it to get Molly Ann, an' I used her gun. Danny, he had it comin' to him!" He raised up a hand what was all bloody and blistered like everybody else. "Now gimme some water!"

Ivy Joe let him drink then, and I didn't think Chaney was ever gonna stop drinkin'.

"How'd you know it were him?" Handy Billy asked, wonderin' on his luck at bein' Molly Ann's one and only again. "It didn't have to be a railroad man to time his shot with the rhythm."

"It be a railroad man," Ivy Joe said. "That's why he left the gun, so's we wouldn't find it on him. I know'd it was prob'ly one of three men at first: Arky, Chaney, or you, Handy Billy. I figured it wasn't Arky that shot a man who owed him money, 'cause it's day before payday. Least he'd do is wait a day or two."

Ivy Joe looked back towards where we come from. "Instead of linin' up for water, the killer hid in them trees during water break, seein' Curly Dan was last in line for a drink, then picked him off when the rest of us was walkin' away uptrack. Then he caught up with us 'fore we missed him and was there to help us move track."

"But it coulda been somebody else," Billy said. "It coulda been somebody from the crew over the rise."

"I know'd it were someone from our crew," Ivy Joe said, " 'cause of the way Curly Dan was layin' curled round the water jug where he'd been drinkin'. He musta been shot first in the back, then fell, 'cause the bullet come out the front and there were no hole in the jug, or the jug wouldn't be full like we found it.

"Now from that distance a shot in the head is a funny way to make sure you done finished a man off, but that's where Curly Dan was shot again while he were layin' there on the ground. Why in the head? Like I said, so's not to break the water jug and lose our water. So then I know'd the killer was on our crew and was the only one hadn't had a water break since early mornin'. In this heat, first man to drop from thirst would likely be Curly Dan's killer. And when it were Chaney that dropped first I *know'd.*"

Ivy Joe sent a man on ahead, and we stayed where we was till a whistle blowed and smoke raised up and the big company engine come on down those straight true rails to take Chaney back to the company yards. To take him back where by and by the hangman be waitin' for him.

Then we started workin' again.

TRAPPED

by Ruth Rendell

What might happen when a discharged employee's wife invites her husband's former employer to dinner, and the employer, who was solely responsible for the husband's dismissal, is foolish enough to accept the invitation? To an isolated Victorian house? On a stormy night? And the employer with a bad heart condition? And what was all this talk about Macbeth? . . .

THEY had been very pressing and at last, on the third time of asking, he had accepted. Resignedly, almost fatalistically, he had agreed to dine with them. But as he began the long drive out of London he thought petulantly that they ought to have had the tact to drop the acquaintanceship altogether.

No other employee he had sacked had ever made such approaches to him. Threats, yes. Several had threatened him and one had even tried blackmail, but no one had ever had the effrontery to invite him to dinner. It wasn't done. A discreet man wouldn't have done it. But of course Hugo Crouch wasn't a discreet man and that, among other things, was why he had been sacked.

He knew why they had asked him. They wanted to hold a court of inquiry, to have the whole thing out in the open. Knowing this, he had suggested they meet in a restaurant and at his expense. They couldn't harangue a man in a public restaurant and he wouldn't be at their mercy. But they had insisted he come to their house and in the end he had agreed. He was an elderly man with a heart condition; it was sixteen miles' slow driving from his flat to their house—monstrous on a filthy February night—but he would show them he could take it. The Chairman of the Board of Fraser's would show them he couldn't be intimidated by a bumptious do-gooder like Hugo Crouch, and he would cope with the situation just as he had coped in the past with the blackmailer.

By the time he reached the outskirts of the Forest, the rain was coming down so hard that he had to put his windshield wipers on at top speed, and he felt more than ever thankful that he had this new car with all its efficient gadgets. Certainly the firm wouldn't have been able to buy it if he had kept Hugo Crouch on a month longer. If he had acquiesced to all Hugo's demands he would still be stuck with that old Daimler and he would never have managed that winter cruise. Hugo had been a real thorn in the firm's flesh what with his extravagance and his choosing to live in a house in the middle of Epping Forest. And it was in the middle, totally isolated, not even on the edge of one of the Forest villages. The general manager of Fraser's had to be within reach, on call. Burying oneself out here had been ridiculous.

The car's powerful headlights showed a dark winding lane

ahead, the gray tree trunks making it appear like some somber pillared corridor. And this picture was cut off every few seconds by a curtain of rain, to reappear with the sweep of the wipers. Fortunately he had been here once before, otherwise he might have passed the high brick wall and the wooden gates behind which stood the Crouch house, the peak-roofed Victorian villa, drab, shabby, and to his eyes quite hideous. Anyone who put a demolition order on this house would be doing a service to the environment, he thought as he drove in through the gates.

There wasn't a single light showing. He remembered that they lived in the rear, but they might have put a light on in front to greet him. But for his car headlights, he wouldn't have been able to see his way at all.

Clutching the box of peppermint creams he had brought for Elizabeth Crouch, he splashed across the almost flooded paving, under eaves from which water poured as from a row of taps, and made for the front door which happened to be—which *would* be—at the far side of the house. It was hard to tell where their garden and the Forest began, for no demarcation was visible. Nothing was visible but black rain-lashed branches, faintly illuminated by a dim glow showing through the transom over the door.

He rang the bell hard, keeping his finger on it, hoping the rain hadn't got through his coat to his hundred-guinea suit. A jet of water struck the back of his neck, sending a shiver through him, and then the door opened.

"Duncan! You must be soaked. Have you had a dreadful journey?"

He gasped out, "Awful, awful!" and ducked into the dry sanctuary of the hall. "What a night!" He thrust the chocolates at her and gave her his hand. Then he remembered that in the old days they always used to kiss. Well, he never minded kissing a pretty woman and it hadn't been her fault. "How are you, Elizabeth?" he said after their cheeks had touched.

"I'm fine. Let me take your coat. I'll take it into the kitchen and dry it. Hugo's in the sitting room. You remember your way, don't you?"

Down a long passage, he recalled, that was never properly lighted and wasn't heated at all. The whole place cried out for central heating. He was by now extremely cold and he couldn't help thinking of his flat where the radiators got so hot that you had to open the windows even in February and where, had he been at home, his housekeeper would at this moment be placing before him a portion of hot paté, to be followed by Poulet San Josef. Elizabeth Crouch, he recalled, was rather a poor cook.

Outside the sitting room door he paused, girding himself for the encounter. He hadn't set eyes on Hugo Crouch since the man marched out of the office in a huff because he, Duncan Fraser, Chairman of Fraser's, had tentatively suggested that Crouch might be happier in another job.

Well, the sooner the first words were over the better. Very few men in his position, he thought, would let the matter weigh on their minds at all or have his sensitivity. Very few, for that matter, would have come here at all.

He would be genial, casual, perhaps a little avuncular. Above all, he would avoid at any cost the subject of Hugo's dismissal. They wouldn't be able to make him talk about it if he was determined not to; ultimately the politeness of hosts to guest would put up a barrier to stop them.

He opened the door, smiling pleasantly, achieving a merry twinkle in his eye. "Well, here I am, Hugo! I've made it."

Hugo wore a very sour look, the kind of look Duncan had often seen on his face when some more than usually extravagant order of his had been countermanded. He didn't smile. He gave Duncan his hand gravely and asked him what he would like to drink.

Duncan looked quickly around the room which hadn't changed and was still furnished with rather grim Victorian pieces. There was, at any rate, a huge fire of logs burning in the grate.

"Ah, yes, a drink," he said, rubbing his hands together. He didn't dare ask for whiskey, which he would have liked best, because his doctor had forbidden it. "A little dry Vermouth?"

"I'm afraid I don't have any Vermouth."

This rejoinder, though spoken quite lightly, though he had even expected something of the sort, gave Duncan a slight shock. It put him on his mettle and yet it jolted him. He had known, of course, that they would start on him quickly, but he hadn't anticipated the first move coming so fast. All right, let the man remind him he couldn't afford fancy drinks because he had lost his job. He, Duncan, wouldn't be drawn. "Sherry, then," he said. "You do have sherry?"

"Oh, yes, we have sherry. Come and sit by the fire."

As soon as he was seated in front of those blazing logs and had begun to thaw out, he decided to pursue the conversation along the lines of the weather. It was the only subject he could think of to break the ice until Elizabeth came in, and they were doing quite well at it, moving into such sidelines as floods in East Anglia and crashes in motorway fog, when she appeared and sat next to him.

"We haven't asked anyone else, Duncan. We wanted to have you to ourselves."

A pointless remark, he thought, under the circumstances. Naturally, they hadn't asked anyone else. The presence of other guests would have defeated their purpose. But perhaps it hadn't been so pointless, after all. It could be an opening maneuver.

"Delightful," he said.

"We've got such a lot to talk about. I thought it would be nicer this way."

"Much nicer." Such a lot to talk about? There was only one thing she could mean by that. But she needn't think—silent Hugo sitting there with his grim moody face needn't think—that he would help them along an inch of the way. If they were going to get onto the subject they would have to do all the spadework themselves.

"We were just saying," he said, "how tragic all these motorway crashes are. Now I feel all this could be stopped by a very simple method."

He outlined the simple method but he could tell they weren't really interested and he wasn't surprised when Elizabeth said, "That's fascinating, Duncan, but let's talk about you. What have you been doing lately?"

Controlling the business your husband nearly ruined. "Oh, this and that," he said. "Nothing much."

"Did you go on a cruise this winter?"

"Er—yes, yes I did. The Caribbean, as a matter of fact."

"That's nice. I'm sure the change did you good."

Implying he needed having good done to him, of course. She had only got onto cruises so that she could point out that some people couldn't afford them.

"I had a real rest," he said heartily. "I must just tell you about a most amusing thing that happened to me on the way home." He told them but it didn't sound very amusing and although Elizabeth smiled half-heartedly, Hugo didn't. "Well, it seemed funny at the time," he said.

"We can eat in five minutes," said Elizabeth. "Tell me, Duncan, did you buy that villa you were so keen on in the South of France?"

"Oh, yes, I bought it." She was looking at him very curiously, very impertinently really, waiting for him to apologize for spending his own money, he supposed. "Listen to that rain," he said. "It hasn't let up at all."

They agreed that it hadn't and a silence fell. He could tell from the glance they exchanged—he was very astute in these matters—that they knew they had been balked for the time being. And they both looked pretty fed-up, he thought triumphantly. But the woman was weighing in again and a bit nearer the bone this time.

"Who do you think we ran into last week, Duncan? John Church."

The man who had done that printing for Fraser's a couple of

years back. He had got the order, Duncan remembered, just about the time of Hugo's promotion. He sat tight as he drank the last of his sherry.

"He told us he'd been in the hospital for months and lost quite a lot of business. I felt so—"

"I wonder if I might wash my hands," Duncan asked firmly. "If you could just tell me where the bathroom is?"

"Of course." She looked disappointed, as well she might. "It's the door facing you at the top of the stairs."

Duncan made his way to the bathroom. He mustn't think he was going to get off the hook as easily as that. They would be bound to start in on him again during the meal. Very likely they thought the dinner table a good place to hold an inquest. Still, he'd be ready for them; he'd done rather well up to now.

They were both waiting for him at the foot of the stairs to lead him into the dining room and again he saw the woman give her husband one of those looks that are the equivalent of prompting nudges. Hugo was probably getting cold feet. In these cases, of course, it was always the women who were more aggressive. Duncan gave a swift glance at the table and the plate of hors d'oeuvres—sardines, anchovies, and artichoke hearts, none of which he liked.

"I'm afraid you've been to a great deal of trouble, Elizabeth," he said graciously.

She gave him a dazzling smile. He had forgotten that smile of hers—how it lit her whole face, her eyes as flashing blue as a kingfisher's plumage. " 'The labor we delight in,' " she said, " 'physics pain.' "

"Ah, *Macbeth*." Good, an excellent topic to get them through the first course. "Do you know, the only time we three ever went to the theater together was to see *Macbeth*?"

"I remember," she said. "Bread, Duncan?"

"Thank you. I saw a splendid performance of *Macbeth* by that Polish company last week. Perhaps you've seen it?"

"We haven't been to the theater at all this winter," said Hugo.

She must have kicked him under the table to prompt that one. Duncan took no notice. He told them in detail about the Polish *Macbeth,* although such was his mounting tenseness that he couldn't remember half the names of the characters or, for that matter, the names of any of the actors.

"I wish Keith could have seen it," she said. "It's the play for his exam."

She was going to force him to ask after her sons and be told they had had to take them away from that absurdly expensive boarding school. Well, he wouldn't. Rude it might be, but he wouldn't ask.

"I don't think you ever met our children, Duncan?"

"No, I didn't."

"They'll be home for half-term holiday next week. I'm so delighted that their holiday happens to coincide with mine."

"Yours?" he said suspiciously.

"Elizabeth has gone back to teaching."

"Really?" said Duncan. "No, I won't have any more, thank you. That was delicious. Let me give you a hand. If I could carry something—?"

"Please don't trouble. I can manage." She looked rather offended. "If you two will excuse me I'll see to the main course."

He was left alone with Hugo in the chilly dining room. He shifted his legs from under the tablecloth to bring them closer to the one-bar electric heater. Hugo began to struggle with the cork of the wine bottle. Unable to extract it, he cursed under his breath.

"Let me try."

"I'll be able to cope quite well, thanks, if you don't watch me," said Hugo sharply, and then, irrelevantly if you didn't know that nothing those two said was irrelevant, "I'm taking a course in accountancy."

"As a wine waiter, Hugo," said Duncan, "you make a very good accountant, ha ha!"

Hugo didn't laugh. He got the cork out at last. "I think I'll do all right. I was always reasonably good at figures."

"So you were, so you were. And more than reasonably good." That was true. It had been with personnel that the man had been so abysmally bad giving junior executives and typists ideas above their station. "I'm sure you'll do well."

Why didn't the woman come back? It must have been ten minutes since she had gone off to the kitchen down those miles of hallways. His own wife, long dead, would have got that main course into serving dishes before they had sat down to the hors d'oeuvres.

"Get a qualification, that's the thing," Duncan said. In the distance he heard the wheels of a serving table coming. It was a more welcome sound than that of the wheels of a train one has awaited for an hour on a cold platform. He didn't like the woman but anything was better than being alone with Hugo.

Why not get it over now, he thought, before they began on the amazingly small roasted chicken which had appeared? He managed a smile. He said, "I can tell you've both faced the situation squarely. I'm quite sure, Hugo, you'll look back on all this when you're a successful accountant and thank God you and Fraser's parted company."

And that ought to be that. They had put him through their inquisition and now perhaps they would let him eat in peace this overcooked mess that passed for a dinner. At last they would talk of something else, not leave it to him who had been making the conversation all the evening.

But instead of further conversation, there was a deep silence. No one seemed to have anything to say. And although Duncan, working manfully at his chicken wing, racked his brains for a topic, he could think of nothing. Their house, his flat, the employees at Fraser's, his new car, the high cost of living, her job, Hugo's course, Christmas past, summer to come—all these subjects must inevitably lead by a direct or indirect route back to Hugo's dismissal. And Duncan saw with irritable despair that *all* subjects would lead to it because he was he and they were they and the dismissal lay between them like an unavoidable specter at their dismal feast.

From time to time he lifted his eyes from his plate, hoping that she would respond to that famous smile of his, that smile that was growing stiff with insincere use; but each time he looked at her he saw that she was staring fixedly at him, eating hardly anything, her expression concentrated, and somehow dogged. And her eyes had lost their kingfisher flash. They were dull and dead like smoky glass.

So they hadn't had enough then, she and her subdued and morose husband? They wanted to see him abject, not merely referring with open frankness to the dismissal as he had, but explaining it, apologizing. Well, they should have his explanation. There was no escape.

Carefully he placed his knife and fork side by side on his empty plate. Precisely, but very politely, he refused his hostess' offer of more. He took a deep breath as he often did at the beginning of a board meeting, as he had so very often done at those board meetings when Hugo Crouch pressed insistently for staff raises.

"My dear Elizabeth," he began, "my dear Hugo, I know why you asked me here tonight and what you've been hinting at ever since I arrived. And because I want to enjoy your very delightful company without any more awkwardness, I'm going to do here and now what you very obviously want me to do—that is, explain just how it happened that I suggested Hugo would be happier away from Fraser's."

Elizabeth said, "Now, Duncan—"

"You can say your piece in a moment, Elizabeth. Perhaps you'll be surprised when I admit that I am entirely to blame for what happened. Yes, I admit it, the fault was all mine." He lifted one hand to silence Hugo, who was shaking his head vehemently. "No, Hugo, let me finish. As I said, the fault was mine. I made an error of judgment. Oh, yes, I did. I should have been a better judge of men. I should have been able to see when I promoted you that you weren't up to the job. I blame myself for not understanding—well, your limitations."

They were silent. They didn't look at him or at each other.

"We men in responsible positions," he said, "are to blame when the men we appoint can't rise to the heights we envisage for them. We lack vision, that's all. I take the whole burden of it on my shoulders, you see. So shall we forgive and forget? Let bygones be bygones?"

He had seldom seen people look so embarrassed, so shame-faced. It just went to show they were no match for him. His statement had been the last thing they had expected and it was unanswerable. He handed her his plate with its little graveyard of chicken bones among the potato skins and as she took it he saw a look of balked fury cross her face.

"Well, Elizabeth," he said, unable to resist, "am I forgiven?"

"It's too late now. It's past," she said in a very cold, stony voice. "It's too late."

"I'm sorry if I haven't given you the explanation you wanted, my dear. I've simply told you the truth."

She didn't say any more. Hugo didn't say anything. And suddenly Duncan felt most uncomfortable. Their condemning faces, the way they both seemed to shrink away from him, was almost too much for him. His heart began to pound and he had to tell himself that a racing heart meant nothing, that it was pain and not palpitations he must fear. He reached for one of his little white pills ostentatiously, hoping they would notice what they had done to him.

When still they didn't speak, he said, "I think perhaps I should leave now."

"But you haven't had coffee," said Elizabeth.

"Just the same, it might be better—"

"Please stay and have coffee," she said firmly, almost sternly, and then she forced a smile. "I insist."

Back in the sitting room they offered him brandy. He refused it because he had to drive home, and the sooner he could begin that drive the happier he would be. Hugo had a large brandy which he drank at a gulp, the way brandy should never be drunk unless one has had a shock or was steeling oneself for something. Elizabeth had picked up the evening paper and was talking in a very artificial way about a murder case which appeared on the front page.

"I really must go," said Duncan.

"Have some more coffee? It's not ten yet."

Why did they want him to stay? Or, rather, why did she? Hugo was once more busy with the brandy bottle. He would have thought his company must be as tiresome to them as theirs was to him. They had got what they wanted, hadn't they? He drank his second cup of coffee so quickly that it scalded his mouth, and then he got up.

"I'll get an umbrella. I'll come out with you," said Hugo.

"Thank you." It was over. He was going to make his escape and he need never see them again. And suddenly he felt that he couldn't get out of that house fast enough. Really, since he had made his little speech, the atmosphere had been thoroughly disagreeable.

"Good night, Elizabeth," he said. What platitudes could he think of that weren't too ludicrous? "Thank you for the meal. Perhaps we may meet again someday."

"I hope we shall and soon, Duncan," she said, but she didn't give him her cheek. Through the open door the rain was driving in against her long skirt. She stood there, watching him go out with Hugo, letting the light pour out to guide them round the corner of the house.

As soon as he was round that corner, Duncan felt an unpleasant jerk of shock. The headlights of his car were blazing, full on.

"How did I come to do a thing like that?"

"I suppose you left them on to see your way to the door," said Hugo, "and then forgot to turn them off."

"I'm sure I did *not.*"

"You must have. Hold the umbrella and I'll try the ignition."

Leaving Duncan on the flooded path under the inadequate umbrella, Hugo got into the driver's seat and inserted the ignition key. Duncan, stamping his feet impatiently, watched "Not a spark," said Hugo. "Your battery must be almost dead."

"It *can't* be."

"I'm afraid it is. Try for yourself."

Duncan tried, getting very wet in the process.

"We'd better go back in the house. We'll get soaked out here."

"What's the matter?" said Elizabeth, who was still standing in the doorway.

"His battery's dead. The car won't start."

Of course it wasn't their fault but somehow Duncan felt it was. It had happened at their house to which they had fetched him for a disgraceful purpose. He didn't bother to hide his annoyance. "I shall just have to borrow your car, Hugo."

Elizabeth closed the door. "Hugo's car," she said quietly, "was Fraser's. If you remember, Duncan, he had a firm's car and had to give it back."

Duncan couldn't remember. How could he be expected to have all those minor details at his fingertips? "I see," he snapped. "Then if I might just use your phone I'll ring for a hire car. I've a mini-cab number on me." Her expression told him that wasn't going to be possible either. "Don't tell me your phone also belonged to Fraser's."

"No, but they paid for it," said Hugo, "and we can't afford it any more. I'm sorry, Duncan, I don't know what you can do, but we may as well all go and sit down where it's warmer."

"I don't want to sit down. I have to get home." He shook off the hand Elizabeth had placed on his arm. "I must walk to the nearest house *with* a phone."

Hugo opened the door. The rain was more like a wall of water than a series of falling drops. "In this?"

"Then what am I supposed to do?" Duncan cried fretfully.

"Stay the night," said Elizabeth calmly. "I really don't know what else you can do but stay the night."

The bed was just what he would have expected a bed in the Crouch ménage to be, hard, narrow, and cold. She had given him a hot-water bottle, which was an object he hadn't set eyes on in ten years. And Hugo had lent him a pair of pajamas.

All the time this was going on he had protested that he couldn't stay, that there must be some other way, but in the end he had yielded. Not that they had been welcoming. They had treated the whole thing rather as if—well, how had they treated it? Duncan lay in the dark, the hot-water bottle between his knees, and tried to assess just what their attitude had been. Fatalistic, he thought, that was it. They had behaved as if all this were inevitable, that there was no escape, and here he must stay.

Escape was a ridiculous word, of course, but it was the sort of word you used when you were trapped somewhere for a whole night in the home of people who were obviously antagonistic, if not hostile. Why had he been such a fool as to leave those car lights on? He couldn't remember that he had done so and yet he must have. Nobody else would have turned them on. Why should they?

He wished they would go to bed, too. That they hadn't he could tell by the light, the rectangle of dazzlement, that showed round the frame of his bedroom door. And he could hear them talking below, not the words but the buzz of conversation. These late Victorian houses were atrociously built, of course. You could hear every sound. The rain drumming on the roof sounded as if it were pounding on cardboard rather than on slates.

He didn't think there was much prospect of sleep. How could he sleep with the noise and all that was on his mind, the worry of getting the car moved, of finding some way of getting to the office? And it made him feel very uneasy their staying up like that, particularly as she had said, "If you'll go into the bathroom first, Duncan, we'll follow you."

Follow him! That must have been all of half an hour ago. He pressed the switch of his bedlamp and saw that it was eleven thirty. Time they were in bed if she had to get to her school in the morning and he to his accountancy course.

Once more in the dark, but for that gold-edged rectangle, he considered the question of the car lights again. He was certain he had turned them out. Of course it was hard to be certain of anything when you were so upset. The pressure they had put on him had been simply horrible and the worst moments were those when he had been alone with Hugo while that woman was fishing the ancient pullet she'd dished up to him out of her oven. Really, she had been a hell of a long time getting that main course when you considered what it had amounted to. Could she have . . . ?

Only a madwoman would do such a thing and what possible motive could she have had? But if you lived in a remote place and you wanted someone to stay in your house overnight, if you wanted to *keep* them there, how better than to immobilize the guest's car? He shivered, even while he told himself that such fancies were absurd.

At any rate, they were coming up now. Every floorboard in the house creaked and the stairs played a tune like a broken old violin. He heard Hugo mumble something—the man had drunk far too much brandy—and then she said, "Leave all the rest to me."

Another shiver that had nothing to do with the cold ran through him. He couldn't think why it had. Surely, that was quite a natural thing for a woman to say on going to bed? She only meant, "You go to bed and I'll lock up and turn off the lights." He had often said it when his wife was alive. And yet it was a phrase that was familiar to him in quite another context.

Turning on his side away from the light and into fresh caverns under the icy sheet, he tried to think where he had heard it. A quotation? Yes, that was it. It came from *Macbeth*. Lady Macbeth said it when she and her husband were plotting the old king's murder. And what was the old king's name? Douglas? Donal?

Someone had come out of the bathroom and someone else had gone in. Did they always take such ages getting to bed? The lavatory flush roared and a torrent rushed through the pipes that seemed to pass under his bed. He heard footsteps cross the landing and a door closing. Apparently, they slept in the room next to his.

He turned over, longing for the light to go out. It was a pity there was no key in that lock so that he could have locked his door.

As soon as the thought had formed and been uttered in his brain, he realized how fantastic it was. What, lock one's bedroom door in a private house? Suppose his hostess came in in the morning with a cup of tea? She would think it very odd. And she might come in. She had put this bottle in his bed and had placed a glass of water on the table. Of course he couldn't dream of locking the door, and why should he want to? One of them was in the bathroom *again.*

Suddenly he found himself thinking about one of the men he had sacked and who had threatened him. The man had said, "Don't think you'll get away with this, and if you show your ugly face within a mile of my place you may not live to regret it." Of course he had got away with it and had nothing to regret. On the other hand, he hadn't shown himself within a mile of the man's place.

The light had gone out at last. Sleep now, he told himself. Empty your mind or think about something nice—your summer holiday in the French villa, for instance, think about that.

The gardens would be wonderful with the oleanders and the bougainvillaea. And the sun would warm his old bones as he sat on his terrace, looking down through the cleft in the pines at the blue triangle of Mediterranean which was brighter and gentler than that woman's eyes . . . Never mind the woman, forget her.

Perhaps he should have the terrace raised and extended and set up on it that piece of statuary—surely Roman—which he had found in the pinewoods. It would cost a great deal of money, but it was his money. Why shouldn't he spend his own? He must try to be less sensitive, he thought, less troubled by this absurd social conscience which, for some reason, he had lately developed. Not, he reflected with a faint chuckle, that it actually stopped him from spending money or enjoying himself. It was a nuisance, that was all.

He would have the terrace extended and maybe a black marble floor laid in the salon. Fraser's profits looked as if they would hit a new high this year. Why not get that fellow Church to do all their printing for them? If he was really down on his luck and desperate he would be bound to work at a cut rate, jump at the chance, no doubt . . .

Damn it, it was too much! They were talking in there. He could hear their whisperings, rapid, emotional almost, through the wall. They were an absurd couple, no sense of humor between the pair of them. Intense, like characters out of some tragedy.

"The labor we delight in physics pain"—Macbeth had said that, Macbeth who killed the old king. And she had said it to him, Duncan, when he had apologized for the trouble he was causing. The king was called Duncan, too. Of course he was. Fraser was named Duncan and so was the king and he too, in a way, was an old king, the monarch of the Fraser empire. Whisper, whisper, breathed the wall at him.

He sat up and put on the light. With the light on he felt better. He was sure, though, that he hadn't left those car lights on. "Leave all the rest to me." Why say it that way? Why not say what everyone said, "I'll see to everything"?

Macbeth and his wife had entertained the old king in their house and murdered him in his bed, although he had done them no harm, done nothing to them but be king. So it wasn't a parallel was it? For he, Duncan Fraser, had done something, something which might merit vengeance. He had sacked Hugo Crouch and taken away his livelihood. No, it wasn't a parallel at all.

He turned off the light, sighed, and lay down again. They were still whispering. He heard the floor creak as one of them came out of the bedroom. It wasn't a parallel—it was much more. Why hadn't he seen that? Lady Macbeth and her husband had had no cause, no cause.

A sweat broke out on his face and he reached for the glass of water. But he didn't drink. It was stupid not to but—the morning would soon come. "O, never shall sun that morrow see!" Where did that come from? Need he ask?

Whoever it was in the bathroom had left and gone back to the other one. But only for a moment. Again he heard the floorboards creak, again someone was moving about on that dark landing. Dark, yes, pitch-dark, for they hadn't switched the light on this time. And Duncan felt then the first thrill of real fear which didn't subside after the shiver had died but grew and gripped him in a terror the like of which he hadn't known since he was a little boy and had been shut up in the nursery closet of his father's house.

He mustn't be afraid, he mustn't. He must think of his heart. Why should they want vengeance? He'd explained. He'd told them the truth, taking the full blame on himself.

The room was so dark that he didn't see the door handle turn. He heard it. It creaked very softly. His heart began a slow steady pounding and he contracted his body, forcing it back against the wall.

Whoever it was had come into the room. He could see the shape of him—or her—as a denser blackness in the dark.

"What . . . ? Who . . . ?" he said, quavering, his throat dry.

The shape grew fluid, glided away, and the door closed softly. They wanted to see if he was asleep. They would kill him when he was asleep. He sat up, switched on the light again, and put his face in his hands. "O, never shall sun that morrow see!"

He'd put all that furniture against the door, that's what he'd do—the chest of drawers, his bed, the chair. His throat was parched now and he reached for the water, taking a long draft. It was icy cold.

They weren't whispering any more. They were waiting in silence. He got up and put his coat round him. In the bitter cold he began lugging the furniture away from the walls, lifting the iron bedstead that felt so small and narrow when he was in it but was so hideously heavy.

Straightening up from his second attempt, he felt it—the pain in his chest and down his left arm. It came like a clamp, like a clamp being screwed and at the same time slowly heated red-hot It took his body in hot iron fingers and squeezed his ribs. And sweat began to pour from him as if the temperature in the room had suddenly risen tremendously.

Oh, God, oh, God, the water in the glass! They would have to get him a doctor, they would have to, they couldn't be so pitiless He was old and tired and his heart was bad.

He pulled the coat round the pain and staggered out into th black passage. Their door—where was their door? He found it by fumbling at the walls, scrabbling like an imprisoned animal, and when he found it he kicked it open and swayed on the threshold holding the pain in both his hands.

They were sitting on their bed with their backs to him, not i bed but sitting there, the shapes of them silhouetted against th light of a small low-bulbed bedlamp.

"Oh, please," he said, "please help me. Don't kill me, I beg yo not to kill me. I'll go on my knees to you. I know I've done wrong I did a terrible thing. I didn't make an error of judgment. I sacke Hugo because he wanted too much money for the staff, he wante more money for everyone and I couldn't let them have it. wanted my new car and my holidays. I had to have my villa—s beautiful, my villa, my gardens. Ah, God, I know I was greedy bu I've borne the guilt of it for months, every day—on m conscience—the guilt of it."

They turned, two white faces, implacable, merciless. They ros and came toward him, scrambling across their bed.

"Have pity on me," he screamed. "Don't kill me! I'll give yo everything I've got, I'll give you a million—"

But they had seized him with their hands and it was too lat She had told him it was too late.

"In our house!" she said.

"Don't," said Hugo. "That's what Lady Macbeth said. Wha

does it matter whether it was in our house or not?"

"I wish I'd never invited him."

"Well, it was your idea. You said let's have him here because he's a widower and so lonely. I didn't want him here. It was ghastly the way he insisted on talking about having fired me when we wanted to keep off the subject at any price. I was utterly fed up when he had to stay the night."

"What do we do now?" said Elizabeth.

"Get the doctor, or the police. It's stopped raining. I'll get dressed and go."

"But you're not well! You kept throwing up."

"I'm all right now. I drank too much brandy. It was such a strain, all of it, nobody knowing what to talk about. God, what a business! He was all right when you looked into his room a few minutes ago, wasn't he?"

"Half asleep, I thought. I was going to apologize for all the racket you were making but he seemed nearly asleep. Did you understand any of what he was trying to say when he came in here? I didn't."

"No, it was just gibberish. We couldn't have done anything for him, darling. We did try to catch him before he fell."

"I know."

"He had a bad heart, you know."

"In more ways than one, poor old man," said Elizabeth, and she laid a blanket gently over Duncan, though he was past feeling heat or cold or fear or guilt or anything any more.

THE STAR OF STARZ

by Philip MacDonald

Philip MacDonald's "The Star of Starz" is a remarkable tale. It will amaze and confound you.

Although first published in 1973, the story was written more than a decade ago. The earliest draft was finished late in 1961, and the final revision was made in 1962. It was then sent to Ellery Queen's Mystery Magazine—*in 1962, while President John F. Kennedy was still alive—and frankly we were scared to publish it. Now, with the passage of time, we have decided that the story should not be lost . . .*

THIS story will be difficult to write, but I'm going to take a stab at it. It's about an extraordinary affair I was accidentally mixed up in, and it's difficult to write because the other people concerned held exalted positions, to say the least. So exalted that I won't be able to name names, or give specific dates, or even tell where it happened.

So I'll begin by saying the scene was the private summer residence of a certain Ambassador to a certain island country, and the time was early in the second half of this century, on the first day of a small and I mean select weekend party.

The Incident (I have to give it a capital) involved twelve people, and eleven of them were personages—VIPs. But the twelfth was the merest person, so mere, so obscure, that his name doesn't even have to be changed.

I'm referring to myself, Bradley Webbster; not even a middle initial. I was a week past my twenty-sixth birthday, a fellow countryman of the Ambassador, his wife, and a couple of the guests. And I'd never conceivably have met any of them if I hadn't happened to be doing postgraduate work (biochemistry) at the famous island university where the Ambassador's son (let's call him Victor) was in his third year.

He belonged to one of those blue-book, man-about-town cliques they still have there, and we only knew each other at all because we both belonged to the university chess club and both played first-string tennis. So I was surprised when he phoned me that Friday morning, and more surprised still when I found out what he wanted. It seemed he was in the hospital (quarantined with chicken pox, of all things) and wanted me to pinch hit at a weekend party of his mother's.

He gave me quite a snow job: the family couldn't find anyone else at such short notice; the party wouldn't be any fire dance, but I'd get some pretty fair tennis and maybe some chess; my opposite number was a lot of fun; the other guests were just some visiting firemen from home; and it was a nice drive to his father's place on the river, and of course I must use his car.

It was the car that really sold me; the party seemed innocuous enough, probably some millionaires and a couple of politicians. Of course, if I'd asked more questions I might have spotted the real reason he'd picked on me. It had three prongs to it; the first and second (tennis and chess) he'd actually mentioned. But the third, which he'd carefully avoided, was the fact that I'd recently been double security-checked because of my work.

By noon I was on my way, driving blithely along where no angel in his right mind would ever dream of treading. Having lunched on the way, I arrived at the Ambassador's house by two thirty. I'd have been ten minutes earlier except for a car which slowed me down on the last leg of the trip, a narrow country road. It was a middle-aged, low-priced sedan, sadly in need of a wash, and undistinguished was the word for it. So I was surprised to see it turn in through the wrought-iron gates I was heading for myself.

The house was one of those historic-looking jobs they have all over the island country. There were wooded grounds around it, and gardens full of flowers, and an enormous stretch of emerald-colored lawn which sloped down to a backwater of the river. And there were walks of clipped yew and terraces with peacocks. And eventually a flight of steps where the sedan came to a stop.

As I stopped the convertible at a decent interval behind it, I saw the front door of the house swing open and a man and woman come out, obviously Victor's mother and father, Mr. and Mrs. Ambassador. At the same time three people climbed out of the sedan: a gray-haired man in tweeds, one of those island country matrons, and a girl with a slim backview.

They started up the steps, and I untangled my six-foot-three from the convertible and tagged uncomfortably along behind them. In welcoming attitudes Mr. and Mrs. Ambassador waited at the top. There was more than a dash of deference about them, and it puzzled me, until the man in tweeds happened to glance around and I found myself looking at the island country's Prime Minister.

I gaped at his back. Whatever I'd been expecting, it certainly hadn't included rubbing social shoulders with one of the world's leading statesmen.

By the time I'd looked back at the old sedan—I just couldn't figure it!—the other three had reached the top and greetings were in full blast.

Then it was my turn, and things began to get really embarrassing. Talking fast and making little jokes about chicken pox, Mrs. A. was all over me. Using an outsize trowel, she plastered me with thanks for taking Victor's place, and then outdid herself by describing me as "a *most* brilliant young man"!

And Mr. A., who said nothing at all, didn't make me feel any better. His overfirm handshake and banker-type smile couldn't cover up the dubious look in his eyes.

Altogether, it was a pretty unhappy scion of the Webbsters who presently found himself alone upstairs, pacing a paneled bedroom the size of a three-car garage. I was looking into the immediate future and finding it well on the bleak side. With or without a Prime Minister, it was looming a little too rich for the simple Webbster blood.

But there wasn't anything I could do about it, so I washed my hands and ran a comb through my thatch and took myself downstairs, toying with thoughts of revenge on Victor. On my way I didn't see, or hear, any sign of life; and I was thinking I might go out in the sun and maybe talk to a peacock when I discovered I wasn't alone after all. In the hall, near the fireplace, a girl was lurking in the depths of a wing chair. She looked up at me and said, "Hullo," with a "u," the way her people do. And she smiled.

I replied, "Hi," with warmth if not brilliance. I knew she must be the Prime Minister's daughter, but during the introductions she'd been in dark glasses and I'd been in a sweat, so I wasn't prepared for the effect she had on me now.

It was quite an effect, and by the time she'd suggested showing me around and we were outside, strolling along the upper terrace, it had taken a lot of the edge off my fears of the weekend. And when she happened to remark, for no particular reason, that this party promised to be "even stickier than most of these ghastly get-togethers," I didn't even latch onto this fine opportunity to discover exactly what sort of party it was.

I said, "Oh, I don't know—" and was starting a nice line when she suddenly grabbed my arm. "Oh, oh!" she said. "Let's get out of the way," and she pulled me indoors, through the open French windows of a big L-shaped room with a billiard table in it.

She stayed by the windows, looking out. So I looked, too. I saw a rose garden, a tennis court, and a boathouse on the backwater, with a motorboat nosing up to it. The boat was another undistinguished-looking job, and I suppose I should have thought of the sedan. But somehow I didn't; maybe because all I could see on deck were two undistinguished-looking men and some fishing tackle. I didn't even get it when I saw the Ambassador and the Prime Minister hurrying along a path toward the landing stage.

Beside me, the girl said, "Lights!" And then she said, "Camera! Action! Sound of trumpets off!"

I said, "Huh?" and stared at her; and she began to hum the only national anthem that really sounds like one.

So once more I looked out; and now I saw the P.M. and Mr. A. greeting a man and woman who must have been crowded out of sight in the boat's little cabin. And I caught myself gaping again.

Because here was another of the world's top statesmen. The leader of the island country's neighbor. The Tall General himself. In person!

The four of them started toward the house, managing to look like a procession. I suppose I was still gaping, because I heard the girl say, "What's the matter?" and found her looking at me curiously. "Don't tell me you didn't know who was coming," she said. "You must have!"

"Oh, sure," I said quickly. Too quickly, because now I was trapped. I had to show a reason for being so dumbfounded.

But there was a good one right there, and I grabbed it. "It's the way they're getting here," I said. "Your father in that jalopy. And now *him*"— I used the Tall General's name—"sulking in the bilge of a beat-up launch. You must admit it's pretty wildsville."

"It insures privacy, doesn't it?" She blazed at me. "Or do you want the whole world steamed up? Notes from all nations—questions in Parliament—newsmen and security people all over the place!" She calmed down, and laughed. "Television cables in the bathroom. Flash bulbs in the soup. Policemen under the bed. You ought to try that for what you call wildsville!"

"I guess you're right," I said slowly. "I hadn't thought . . ." I was beginning to worry again; the forty-eight-hour future was looking bleaker and more ominous than ever.

But it didn't take her long to make me forget it. As soon as the coast was clear she dragged me outside and we went on with our grand tour of the property, which had once belonged to some king or queen or other.

We'd reached a first-name basis (I'll give hers here as Pamela) before my worries came back, in spades this time. We were walking up a sloping path at the back of the house, and she looked over the low wall at what was still called the stable yard and suddenly stopped. She laughed; and then pointed. "Here's some more wildsville for you!" she said.

All I could see was a delivery truck pulling into the service entry of a country house. Sure it was undistinguished-looking; but it was just a truck, and on the panels it said, BLEDSOE'S LAUNDRY.

But then Mr. and Mrs. A. came popping out from some side door like figures on a Swiss weather clock. They went into their welcoming attitudes again, and waited while the truck backed up to them with its undistinguished-looking rear end. Two men in coveralls jumped out of the cab, then let down the tailgate, with another man helping them from inside; a man in a dark business suit.

The tail converted into a ramp, and when they'd fixed it up, the three men sort of melted away. And I was left looking into the damnedest truck-interior anyone could ever hope to see. The inside of the panels was covered with a cheerful wallpaper. There was a carpet on the floor. Near the gate was an easy chair; and in the middle, flanked by two more chairs and lighted by a shaded lamp, was a table with cards and a couple of scorepads on it.

The 20-20 Webbster vision absorbed all this at a gulp, then focused on the man and woman who got up from the table and crossed to the ramp and casually walked down it.

By this time I should have been prepared to see my own country's two first citizens. But somehow I wasn't; so there I stood, frozen, staring at the man I'd never regretted voting for.

Pamela nudged my arm. "Feel more at home now?"

"Oh, sure," I said. "Sure." But then I looked at her; and suddenly I felt like telling her the truth. "Tell you what I *do* feel," I said. "I don't think any of this is happening. I've got to be dreaming!"

I went on feeling like that for about forty-five minutes, but then I snapped out of it. I had to; because I was on the tennis court, warming up for a set of mixed doubles, and there was no doubt about it; my partner (Bradley Webbster's partner!) was the wife of my President, and we were playing against the President himself and a girl who was the daughter of our main ally's Prime Minister.

It was a better game than you'd think; they all played over-average club tennis, with my partner a shade the weakest. But I worked like a dog and managed to scrape a narrow win for us in both sets. My partner (she was grand) seemed awfully pleased; and the President said he hadn't enjoyed a game so much in a long time.

So I was feeling pretty good when I left the court. Quite different. So different that while I bathed and changed I realized I didn't want to wring Victor's neck any more; I wanted to give him a medal instead. I even quit worrying about my dinner jacket betraying its non-Webbsterian origins. Because now all I felt about this party was a sense of privilege at being in on it, plus enough curiosity to kill a dozen cats.

And I hadn't been downstairs five minutes when I got more

curious than ever. Because two new arrivals (let's call them the Princess and the Young Pundit) came with the cocktails. They were dinner guests; but they were also dynamite. Their recent engagement had thrown a king-sized wrench into the whole international-policy works, and their marriage would mean a new Eastern alliance that none of the diplomacy boys, or anyone else for that matter, had ever even dreamed of. An alliance that would have to make up its mind, and quick too, which side of the ideological fence it was going to come down on.

"Exotic" is an understatement for the note the two of them struck in these surroundings. This was partly because of their color, of course, but mainly because of their clothes. The Young Pundit's odd-type pants and knee-length coat, which looked all right in news pictures and on TV, seemed really wild in a drawing room. And although the Princess's gown was occidental enough, she'd certainly gone all oriental with the jewelry. With diamonds all over her she looked like some vizier's favorite out of the Arabian Nights—just as beautiful and just as out of place.

I stared at her across the room; every time she moved the diamonds winked at me and I was just wondering how much she was worth as she stood when I heard an astonished whisper from Pamela beside me, "For heaven's sake, *she's got It on!*"

I couldn't think what It could be among so much, and didn't get a chance to ask. But when it was my turn to be presented, I saw. It hit me in the eye, luckily only in a figurative way. It was a diamond, all right, but what a diamond! It must have weighed all of forty-five carats, and was cut like a six-pointed star. It was rose-colored, and the refractions from it looked like flames. It hung on an almost invisible platinum chain, about six inches below a five-strand choker of more ordinary stones, and it sort of nestled, just at the beginning of the royal cleavage.

For some reason it had a strange effect on me. Normally, I'm not interested in precious stones, particularly diamonds, but somehow I couldn't get this one out of my mind. I told Pamela about it a few minutes later, when we'd found a window seat to ourselves. "Funny," I said, "I don't know anything about the thing, and couldn't care less. But somehow it's giving me the damnedest *uncomfortable* sensation."

She seemed interested. "P'raps you're psychic," she said, and proceeded to give me a history of the thing. Including its name, which here I can only give as the Star of Starz.

It was one of those jungle-and-conquest sagas, full of temples and treachery, blood and concubines. Pamela did a good job on it, and I admit I was fascinated. But it didn't give me any clue to the nagging in my mind, the nagging which was beginning to feel like one of those slipping memory cogs.

It wasn't till the middle of dinner that the cog jumped into place, and I almost choked trying not to laugh. I looked at Pamela next to me and said, "It's okay. I just found out what's bugging me, that's all."

She was curious. "About the Star, you mean? Tell me." She was pitching her voice under the general clatter of table talk.

"Oh, it's not so much." I matched my tone to hers. "Just that all this"—I looked round the table—"it's all been done before. It's old hat. I've read it a dozen times, and so have you. So has everybody!"

"What in the world are you talking about?" She stared at me.

"Think a minute." I grinned. "The dinner party—the visiting potentates—the lady with the jewel of jewels, the rock to end all rocks." I was enjoying myself. "Remember now? Halfway through dinner everyone starts talking about the thing. So what does the lady do?"

She said, *"Oh!"* Light was dawning.

"Exactly. She takes it off—"

"—and it's passed round from hand to hand—and they all examine it—"

"That's right. And after x minutes, when she's talking to someone about something else, she suddenly looks around and says may I have my rock back, please—"

"—and it's *gone!*"

Pamela was laughing, but she gave a little shudder, and she couldn't help glancing at the Princess across the table. She said, "What a perfectly awful thought! It terrifies me even to think it!"

"So relax." I gave her a final grin. "It can't happen here, as the fella said." At the other end of the table people started laughing, and I saw the President sitting back, looking happily poker-faced.

"I wish we'd heard that," Pamela said. "He can be awfully amusing sometimes."

"I can imagine," I said; and then, as I looked at the President again, I remembered something. "What's his chess game like?" I asked. "You happen to know?"

"Oh, oh!" She laughed. "Has he booked you already?"

"Nothing definite." I was remembering what he'd said when we left the tennis court. "But he did mention playing tomorrow—"

I stopped, because Pamela had suddenly stiffened in her chair as she looked across the table. She whispered, "Oh, *no!*" and when I looked where she was looking, I saw the Princess with her hands up to her neck—

And less than a minute later she was actually handing the Star of Starz to her dinner partner, the Prime Minister. While he was examining it, fascinated, Madame General leaned in from his other side, gabbling exclamations in her own language. And everybody else stopped talking, all of them focusing on the jewel.

The Princess looked around, smiling. She was really stunning, with that white smile against that copper skin. She said, "Please!" in the same syllable-clipping way the Young Pundit talked. "When Mistah Prime Ministah has fin-ished, will anee-one who wishes take the Star to ex-amine. I would be most happee."

And so, apparently, was everyone else—except me and my partner. I caught myself muttering, "Oh, brother!" and Pamela said, "I hate you! Bringing up that story!"

We knew it was all nonsense, of course, but I'll guarantee neither of us took an eye off the fabulous stone while it made its way around the table, flashing those rose-colored flames with every movement anyone gave it. It was a lovely, unbelievable thing; but I wished it would be lovely and unbelievable somewhere else.

It came to us on Pamela's side. We looked at it together, and I passed it on in the shortest possible time compatible with civility.

Then we went on watching—we couldn't help it—until the Princess fastened the platinum chain around her neck again, and the Star of Starz was back where it belonged.

We relaxed then, and traded smiles. "That's a new ending, isn't it?" Pamela said. "I never thought I'd be so happy to see an anticlimax!"

I laughed. It was a pretty good curtain line, and I told her so. We began to talk about something else, and I put the Star out of my mind. I didn't imagine—why should I?—that it would ever cause me another second's worth of concern.

Which only goes to show! Because I was due for a shock. None of your run-of-the-mill little upsets, but a seismic, shattering, cataclysmic *shock!*

It came about eleven thirty, in the big L-shaped room where Pamela had dragged me to duck the Tall General's arrival.

With that sort of calculated informality which seemed to be the keynote, everybody had gathered in here to say goodbye to the dinner guests. We were all in the larger part of the room until the Princess started looking for her cloak, which she'd put down somewhere after a stroll in the gardens.

One of the men found it for her, on a chair by the billiard table; and as this was in the short arm of the L, they were both out of everybody's line of sight as she went toward him and thanked him.

I was standing pretty close, and something—maybe somebody up there hates me!—made me drop my cigarette lighter. It slid several feet across the carpet, finally stopping right next to the corner of the L. Considerably irked—I was talking to Pamela's mother and trying to be impressive—I went after it. And as I bent to pick it up, I heard the man's voice: "Oh, I'm so sorry! . . . Your hair—caught in my cuff link—"

With the lighter in my fingers I lifted my head—and found myself looking straight at the Princess and the man, who had just put the cloak around her shoulders. Their backs were to me, and he was holding his right hand awkwardly high, close to the back of the Princess's head, which was turned toward it.

I saw it all, every lightning movement of it—the fingers of the man's right hand moving very, very slightly as they tweaked at the royal hair in a classic piece of misdirection; the man's left hand, a glint of metal in it, flashing a series of movements out of the royal line of sight; first to the left side of the royal throat, then to the level of the royal ribcage, finally to the handkerchief pocket of the dinner jacket.

It was so fast, so neat, that I might not have known what was going on if the Star hadn't given one last fiery flash as it dropped into the man's pocket, its chain following like a comet's tail.

Somehow—I'll never quite know how—I managed to straighten myself and move back, a fraction of a second before the Princess turned and came out into general view, her cloak drawn around her. The man was beside her, and she was laughing at something he was saying.

People are always writing about minds "reeling," but I'd never understood what they meant before. I did now—because this smooth, slick prestidigitator of a Raffles was the President! The man I'd never regretted voting for!

If I was paid, I couldn't give any coherent account of what went on for the next half hour or so. In my head, Bradley Webbster was wrestling with Bradley Webbster, and getting nowhere slowly. All that either of me knew was that the Princess had left, without realizing she was minus one forty-five-carat national heirloom. Every minute carried her another mile or so away; and while this took a lot of heat off the thief, it was having the reverse effect on the only eyewitness.

I found myself on one of the lower terraces, pacing about. I was on a sort of mental treadmill, thinking that all I *could* do was wonder what I *should* do. What I needed, desperately, was someone to talk to. But the obvious person was the last one I could even approach. Whatever I thought of her personally, it didn't change the fact that she was the daughter of another country's Prime Minister.

So what I needed was a compatriot, and a sympathetic one. The Ambassador was out to start with, and Mrs. A. wasn't any better—

I'd got that far when my mind began to function again, and a new thought came. Why talk at all, to anyone? Wouldn't it be best to do nothing? To say nothing, to think nothing? In short, to keep my lowly nose well out of the whole affair?

The answer was a resounding *Yes,* and I began to feel better—so much better that I started up the steps toward the house.

I was almost at the top when a new thought stopped me cold. Suppose some mental aberration had been behind the theft? Suppose there was a well-hidden family history of kleptomania? Suppose, in fact, that at the time of the theft the thief hadn't been responsible for his actions?

I don't know how long I stood there, wrestling with Bradley Webbster again. This time we didn't have any problem to solve, we just had to stop me from chickening out. Because although I knew I did have to talk after all, and who it was I had to talk to, believe me the assignment was a little on the rugged side.

I found him in the hall, standing by the fireplace, talking to the Ambassador. From what I could hear, it seemed to be about some political mix-up at home, and it was obvious they wouldn't have much use for an interruption.

There was a lot of jelly in my legs, but I went right up to both men, with a smile that must have looked like a death rictus. And my voice came out a couple of semitones high, "Excuse me for butting in, Mr. President," I said, "but how about that game of chess?"

The Ambassador went dark red in the face, and you could have lighted a cigarette on the look he gave me. But before he could speak, the President said, "Oh, I think not tonight," and gave me a polite smile. "Tomorrow for sure, though."

I could feel clammy sweat on my forehead, but I couldn't quit now. "No time like the present, sir," I said. I couldn't keep my eyes from flickering a glance at his handkerchief pocket.

The Ambassador's face wasn't red any more, it was a sort of livid puce. He was so mad that when he tried to speak all that came out was a little hissing noise. But the President looked at me. "Maybe you have something there," he said slowly.

And then he said to the Ambassador, "Let's get together in the morning," and put a hand on my arm and steered me across the hall and along a passage. He opened a door, and we were in a sort of study-type room, very comfortable, with a chess table set up in one of the window alcoves. He'd been chatting all the way, but I hadn't heard a word of it.

He was still at it as we went across to the chess table, and so I had to plunge. I said, "Sir!" but it came out in a high thin squeak, and he didn't seem to hear. He'd picked up a knight from the board and was looking at it. He said, "Nice carving," and held it out for me to see—

But it wasn't in his hand any more. It had gone.

I blinked, and he smiled apologetically, opening his other hand to reveal the thing. "Childish hobby of mine," he said, and dropped into one of the chairs at the table.

I took the other chair, and tried again. I said, "Sir—" this time in a booming bass. But again it didn't take.

"I've been wondering," he said with a friendly smile, "just what sort of impression this little gathering has made on an intelligent, highly educated young man like you." He laughed. "Depressing, I imagine. And disillusioning to discover the world's being run by a collection of stuffed shirts and oddballs."

"Sir!" I was getting really desperate. "There's something I have to ask—"

"Plenty, I should think." The President chuckled. "Actually, you know, these off-the-record meetings were started by my predecessor. He was a great advocate of something he called 'human contact.' I suppose he believed it's easier to do business with a man when you know him personally."

"*Sir!*" I found myself on my feet; they were getting colder by the minute, and it was now or never.

"Sir," I said again. "I know what's in your pocket!" I pointed to it. "And I know how it got there!"

The President sighed. "I was afraid of that," he said. He looked up at me. "You poor chap, what a terrible spot to be in!"

"Yes, sir." I was way off balance. "But—but—"

"This is very difficult, isn't it?" He sighed again. "Would it help if I reminded you that neither I nor my family is noticeably short of money? Or told you that my wife abhors the ostentatious, particularly in jewelry?" He smiled. "Or assured you I have no tendency, latent or otherwise, toward kleptomania?"

I gulped. "I—I don't know, sir. I—"

He studied me. "No help, huh?" He was silent for a moment; then he said suddenly, "Look, my friend: besides myself, you are the only person—repeat *only*—who knows what happened. Could you do me a personal favor?"

I was really sweating now. "If you mean could I forget all about it—how could I, sir? I keep thinking what's going to happen when she finds it's gone! Surely all hell's going to break loose!"

"No doubt about that." He shrugged. "In fact, looking at the immediate future, it's quite an understatement." He kept his eyes squarely on mine. "However, the end results of my little plan should be very different. You see—" He stopped, shaking his head. "No, you don't see." He pushed back his chair and stood up. "So there's only one thing to do—"

"Wh-what's that, sir?" I must have stepped back, because my chair took me behind the knees and I sat down, hard.

"Tell you all about it," said the President. He crossed to the door, and opened it, and looked out. He closed it, and came back to the windows and glanced behind the heavy curtains.

He stood looking down at me. He said slowly, "What I'm going to tell you must be kept to yourself. Completely and permanently. It must never be discussed, or hinted at, or even thought about."

He sat down to face me. "And above all," he said, "it must never be written up . . ."

THE FIVE SENSES OF MRS. CRAGGS

by H. R. F. Keating

Meet a new kind of detective—a charwoman, Mrs. Craggs, whose five senses are especially keen and alert. Perhaps her daily work—cleaning, polishing, dusting, scrubbing in homes, hotels, and public buildings—is what has sharpened her seeing, smelling, touching, hearing, and tasting; if so, it is probably the best training in the world for detecting. But surely Mrs. Craggs possesses a sixth sense that she could only have been born with—as must be true for every detective, in fact and fiction . . .

Would an American author have even thought of making a cleaning woman, a down-to-earth Everywoman, a detective? We wonder. Ah, democracy, and its many faces, seen and unseen . . .

I: *Seeing*

OF all the various cleaning jobs that Mrs. Craggs had had in the course of a long work life, the one at the place they called Murray's House was the one she liked best. Yet she was the person most responsible, when you came down to it, for bringing that job to an end.

Murray's House was a funny old place. It had belonged back in the eighteenth century to old Peter Murray, the inventor and discoverer and gatherer of curiosities, and eventually it had been left to the Borough, who kept it as nearly the way it had been as they could and charged the public to see it. Not that many of the public were willing to pay, but there it was.

Certainly Mrs. Craggs got to like the old place very much. It used to please her to think, when she toiled up the stairs, that she was seeing exactly the same twirls and curls in the banisters that old Peter Murray had seen all those years before. And though she didn't particularly understand many of the curious wooden machines and other things the house was filled with, she liked them all the same. Old Peter Murray had worked on them and put his skill and care into them, and you could tell.

So it was all the more awful when Mrs. Craggs arrived for work one morning, with her friend Mrs. Milhorne, and found that the night porter, old Mr. Berbottle, had been murdered, an event which was to result before long in the final closing of the old house. Thanks to Mrs. Craggs.

Of course everybody said at once that there could be no doubt who had killed Mr. Berbottle: the skinheads—the neighborhood gang of young hooligans. They were always breaking into places and this time poor crotchety, pernickety old Mr. Berbottle must have disturbed them and for that had his head laid open with a piece of lead piping. And all the previous day's receipts, such as they were, had disappeared.

The worst of it was, though, that this had been the first time the money had been left on the premises overnight. Generally, after the manager, Mr. Fingles, had checked it, the money was taken and put in the night safe of the bank by Mr. Tanker, the day porter, a rippling-muscled former bosun of a sail-training ship, who stood for no nonsense from skinheads or anyone else. But Mr. Tanker had been taken ill at lunchtime, and the manager had said there would be no harm in leaving the money in the house for just one night. He and Mr. Berbottle between them were quite capable of looking after it. Only, when it had come to it, Mr. Fingles, who was notorious for liking his half bottle of wine with his dinner, had been so soundly asleep in his comfortable little private flat at the top of the house that he had not heard a thing.

So there the police were all over the place and there was little Mr. Fingles, who had discovered the body when he had come down to collect the mail, in more of a state of agitation than usual, rushing up and down on his little clickety heels and getting in everybody's way. "Like a regular old clockwork doll," Mrs. Craggs had murmured to Mrs. Milhorne, her fellow worker, as they waited for the fingerprint men and the police photographer to finish.

They had a long wait of it too, with nothing more exciting to see for most of the time than the Detective-Superintendent in charge prowling about and looking important, though, as Mrs. Milhorne said, "It isn't as if it's exactly what you'd call a mystery killing, is it?" But at last the Superintendent himself came up to the two of them.

"Very well, ladies," he said, "I shall be here for some time to come, I expect, but there's nothing to stop you two going ahead with your work now. My lads have got everything they want."

And then he paused and became a bit uneasy.

"There is one thing, though," he added. "The porter's room there, where it happened."

"Yes?" said Mrs. Craggs, glancing along to the little room with the ticket window.

"Well," said the Superintendent, still looking uncomfortable, "the fact of the matter is there's—well, there's what you might call traces on the floor in there, and I don't know whether you'd object to—er—dealing with them."

"I couldn't," declared Mrs. Milhorne, with great promptness. "I'm afraid to say I'd come all over queer. I'd be bound to. I've got nerves, you see."

"You don't have to do it," Mrs. Craggs broke in. "The porter's room has linoleum on the floor, and lino polishing's my department, always has been."

She turned to the Superintendent and jerked her head at Mrs. Milhorne.

"She's dusting," she said.

And so off to her dusting went Mrs. Milhorne, though not without putting a hand to her skinny chest and declaring she could "feel the heartbeats something terrible," and Mrs. Craggs matter-of-factly fetched herself a pail of hot water and a scrubbing brush and tackled the porter's room, thinking all the while how old Mr. Berbottle had been so nosey and pernickety and interfering, and how now none of it was doing him any good.

It was only later, when she was on her knees polishing the thin strip of brown linoleum that edged the entrance hall, that she came across something that made her stop suddenly and rise to her feet with a decidedly grim expression on her battered old nut-brown face.

"Mrs. Milhorne, dear," she called to her friend, who was halfway up the stairs, busy doing some fancywork with her duster on the twirls and twiddles of the old banisters.

"Yes, dear?"

"I think I'm just going to have a word with that Superintendent," Mrs. Craggs said. "I want to tell him about this footprint on the lino."

"Footprint on the lino?"

Mrs. Milhorne abandoned her dusting and came down to look. She found her friend standing with sturdy legs wide apart over a footprint, or to be accurate, half a footprint, just on the edge of the lino where it met the broad, but very threadbare, central carpet.

"It's a bare foot," Mrs. Milhorne pronounced after a long inspection. "Looking as if it was on its way to go out by the front door."

"Yes, dear," said Mrs. Craggs.

"And you're going to the Superintendent about it? Well, I know you don't like to have your polish trod on when you've just got it looking all nice, but to go to Scotland Yard about that—well, it beats all."

And Mrs. Milhorne indulged in her favorite trilling laugh.

"He's not Scotland Yard, he's local," said Mrs. Craggs, and off she stumped.

Mrs. Milhorne decided to have a rest from her dusting and stay where she was, by the footprint. To her immense surprise, scarcely ten minutes later Mrs. Craggs came back with the Superintendent. And the great man himself actually squatted down and closely examined the half footprint. Then he pushed himself to his feet and set off up the stairs, looking extremely thoughtful.

At the turn, however, he encountered the manager, coming click-clacking excitedly down. And it was then that Mrs. Milhorne got her biggest surprise of all.

"Mr. Fingles," the Superintendent said to the manager in a voice doom-laden with formality. "I should like you to accompany me to the station, where I have a number of questions I wish to put to you."

It wasn't until the news was in the paper that Mr. Fingles had been charged with the murder that Mrs. Craggs agreed to answer a single one of the many questions Mrs. Milhorne had plagued her with. Then she did explain.

"Clear as the nose on me face really, dear, when you come to think," she said. "Why would a naked footprint be right there on the lino at the edge of the hall?"

"I'm sure I don't know," Mrs. Milhorne replied. "Unless someone just happened to be creeping along there."

"Of course they were creeping, dear. And who would have to creep so as to get right up close to old Mr. Berbottle if it wasn't someone he knew and would wonder what they were doing carrying a piece of lead piping? Especially if it was someone who can't walk about anywhere without making a noise like a little old tip-tapping clockwork doll?"

Mrs. Milhorne pondered over this at length.

"I suppose you're right, dear," she said at last. "But I would've thought a bare footprint like that meant our Mr. Tanker, not Mr. Fingles. Mr. Tanker was always saying how he wore no shoes when he went climbing up all those masts on that ship of his."

"And why would Mr. Tanker want to murder Mr. Berbottle?" Mrs. Craggs demanded.

"I'm sure I don't know, dear. But, come to that, why *did* Mr. Fingles want to murder him?"

"Because of the money, of course," Mrs. Craggs answered. "And Mr. Fingles with his bottles of wine to buy and his nice comfortable flat up there to keep going."

"The money?" Mrs. Milhorne asked.

"Yes. Wasn't this the first time the money had been left here overnight? And wasn't Mr. Berbottle, rest him, just the sort of interfering old fool who would go and check the money against the tickets issued, even though he knew that was Mr. Fingles' job?"

It took Mrs. Milhorne a little time to sort it all out, but she got there in the end.

"You mean Mr. Fingles had been pinching a bit of the takings all along, to help him out, like?" she said. "Now, why couldn't I have seen that?"

Mrs. Craggs gave her a slow smile.

"Because you ain't very keen to get down on your hands and knees, dear," she said, "and see what's in front of your face."

II: *Smelling*

When Mrs. Craggs had the washing-up job at a select residential hotel, she used to allow herself a little treat in the summertime. Between finishing the lunch dishes and beginning on the tea things she took a cup for herself and sat with it in the storeroom. It was not exactly comfortable. Mrs. Craggs had to perch herself on a packing case and there was precious little light.

But it had one distinct advantage as far as Mrs. Craggs was concerned: a row of frosted-glass louver windows high up in one wall that formed the back of the hotel's delightful rose garden. So, in consequence, Mrs. Craggs, sitting on that packing case in the gloom of the storeroom amid a strong smell of soap, was often able to hear the most fascinating conversations.

She was quite unashamed of this. As she said to her friend and coworker, Mrs. Milhorne, to whom she occasionally retailed certain, but not all, of the things she heard, "If they don't know it, then it don't do them no harm. And I think it's interesting." And so, day by day, she contrived to get a notion of almost all the hotel's regular guests, and even visitors who came only for tea often could be added to her bag.

So when, one day, sitting on her accustomed uncomfortable seat, she heard old Mr. Danchflower refer to the elderly visitor with whom he was taking tea as "Lady Etherege," Mrs. Craggs pricked up her ears. Mrs. Milhorne enjoyed feeling she was getting a worm's-eye view of the aristocracy and it did no harm to have a tidbit to feed to Mrs. Milhorne from time to time.

Not that, it soon developed, Lady Etherege was any great shakes when you came down to it. She was blue-blooded all right—you could tell that just by listening to her delicate, tired old voice—but she was far from being rich. Of course, she didn't come right out with that. Not at what was probably the first time she met old Mr. Danchflower who, though he might not be particularly aristocratic, was certainly well off, as you had to be to stay in one of the hotel's best rooms summer and winter alike.

Yet bit by bit, as Mrs. Craggs savored her good, big, strong cup of tea and listened to the two elderly voices floating in through the louver above her, it became quite plain that old Lady Etherege lived like a church mouse.

Mrs. Craggs began to feel really sorry for her. It was all right being poor when you were used to it, but to end your days like that when you'd begun grand as grand, that was hard. Not that Lady Etherege didn't have compensations, it seemed. She even had, so her conversation revealed little by little, an admirer.

Admittedly he was an admirer at a distance. Over in France. And the form his admiration took was no more than sending her for each birthday a bottle of perfume. But what perfume! Mrs. Craggs gathered that the latest bottle had actually been taken, with great reverence, out of Lady Etherege's handbag and that now its stopper was being gently removed and Mr. Danchflower was being permitted a discreet inhalation.

"Oh, excellent," Mrs. Craggs heard him say. "Really, madam, a most delicate scent. What shall I say it reminds me of? Not these roses even. It's far more subtle than that."

"Yes, yes," came Lady Etherege's voice. "It comes from a past age. An age I once knew, let me admit it."

Mrs. Craggs could have sworn she even heard the sigh through the narrow slits of the frosted-glass louver.

"Ah," Lady Etherege added, "there was a time, my dear sir, when I myself had no hesitation in entering a boutique in the Rue St. Honoré and buying perfume at twenty-five pounds a tiny bottle."

"Twenty-five pounds," said old Mr. Danchflower. "I can well believe this cost that much, madam. A most remarkably fine and delicate scent."

"Oh, well," Lady Etherege answered, her simper, too, almost floating through the narrow window, "since we are friends I can tell you that this tiny bottle actually cost even more than that. My dear, dear old admirer accidentally left the bill in the package last year and before I crumpled it up I could not help noticing that the

do roses have a scent?

IT SURELY TAKES AN EGOTISTICAL, COMPETITIVE FART TO KEEP MAKING ABSURD INDICATIONS, OBVIOUSLY A WOMAN.

sum mentioned was the equivalent—you'll hardly believe this, but everything is so very, *very* expensive nowadays—was the equivalent of no less than forty pounds."

"Indeed, indeed, madam. But I do believe it I assure—"

And then through the open louver came what could only be described as a feminine shriek of utter horror, followed an instant later by the small but unmistakable sound of breaking glass.

"Madam, how could I? I—I don't know what I did. I could have sworn the bottle was safe on the arm of the bench, but—"

Old Mr. Danchflower's voice faded into utterly overwhelmed silence. But, rooted on her packing case, Mrs. Craggs could hear all too clearly Lady Etherege's choked sobs, though it was plain she was doing all in her power to restrain them.

And then, seconds later, she heard her own name being loudly called out in the kitchen.

"Mrs. Craggs, Mrs. Craggs! Where is the woman?"

It was Mr. Browne, the under-manager, in even more of a tizzy than usual. Mrs. Craggs slipped down off the packing case, put her teacup where it wouldn't be noticed, and emerged.

"Ah, there you are. There you are. Quick, quick, Mrs. Craggs, out into the rose garden with a bucket and cloth. As fast as you can, as fast as you can. There has been the most terrible disaster."

Mrs. Craggs, without saying she well knew what the disaster was, rapidly filled a bucket with water, seized a floor cloth, and went scuttling round after Mr. Browne.

"It's perfume," Mr. Browne explained, quite unnecessarily since the whole of the garden was now smelling to high heaven of a scent that certainly wasn't that of roses. "A most unfortunate accident. But we must sweep it all away on the instant. On the instant. It must be as if it had never been."

So Mrs. Craggs scarcely looked at the two sad spectators of the tragic scene, Mr. Danchflower standing erect and still deeply blushing and little Lady Etherege beside him, dabbing the daintiest of handkerchiefs to her old tired eyes. Instead Mrs. Craggs swooshed most of the contents of her bucket over the thick oily stain on a large flagstone and then began to mop up as fast as she was able till the pail itself smelled like an oversize bouquet of every flower you could think of.

And, as she worked, Mrs. Craggs heard the two old people talk.

"Madam, may I say again that I cannot think how I could have been so abominably careless. I didn't see the bottle, but I suppose my sleeve must have just caught it."

"It's perfectly all right."

"No. No, madam, it is not all right. You have lost something extremely valuable to you, not only financially but sentimentally. It is not all right, madam."

"It—it was of some sentimental value, yes."

"Madam, that I can never repair. But at least—please be so good as to let me write you a check for forty pounds."

"Oh, no. No, really. Really I could not."

But old Mr. Danchflower had sat down on the bench, taken his check book from his pocket, and was already writing. Lady Etherege sat down beside him.

"No, really, sir," she said. "From an acquaintance of such short standing I could not possibly—"

"Nonsense, madam, nonsense. There, take it!"

"Well. Well, if you insist . . . And there I do believe I see the stopper. I think I will just keep it. You know, a—a souvenir."

Her frail old hand reached down to somewhere near where Mrs. Craggs's floor cloth was at work and the fingers closed round the ornate glass. And then Mrs. Craggs's fingers closed round Lady Etherege's.

"Oh, no, you don't," Mrs. Craggs said loudly.

"Don't? Don't? I do not understand."

Beneath Mrs. Craggs's grasp the thin fingers wriggled hard.

"Oh, yes, you do," said Mrs. Craggs. "You understand quite well that this stopper's got a false compartment in its top. A compartment filled with the delicate scent Mr. Danchflower liked so much, and not with this nasty cheap muck ponging to high heaven."

And then old Lady Etherege dropped the stopper, slid her hand from Mrs. Craggs's grasp, rose in an instant, seized the half-full bucket, emptied its contents all over Mrs. Craggs, and was out of the garden, into the street, and had hopped onto a passing bus before anybody else had time to realize what Lady Etherege had done.

And, as Mrs. Craggs said, "For days and days afterwards you could tell I was coming round the corner yards before I got there. What a niff!"

III: *Touching*

One of the places where Mrs. Craggs once worked as a charwoman was the Borough Museum, and she was there at the time that the celebrated Golden Venus was on a week's loan exhibition. Indeed, she had the honor, obtained not without difficulty, of being allowed to dust this small but extremely ancient and valuable object.

At first, of course, no one had seen the necessity for carrying out such an everyday task. But when the Venus had been on its special display stand surrounded by its own rope barrier for some forty-eight hours, it became evident that even something as precious as this needed the attentions of the duster. Mr. Slythe, the museum's assistant curator, had not been in favor of delegating this task to Mrs. Craggs.

"But the Venus, but a charlady," he had twittered. "What if she did some damage? My mother's dailies are always breaking things. Always."

Mrs. Craggs stood there impassively, waiting to know whether or not she was going to be allowed to get on with it. And it was Mr. Tovey, the curator himself, who gave the final go-ahead.

"Nonsense, man," he said to Mr. Slythe. "The statue's solid metal, unharmed for over two thousand years, and you know how firmly it's fixed to the plinth. We both of us saw to that."

"Ah, well, yes, I suppose so, I suppose so," Mr. Slythe agreed. And then he approached the statue for about the fiftieth time since it had been installed and started once more what Mrs. Craggs called "his cooing act."

"Ah," he said, "the patina, the patina, the inimitable patina of age."

If he'd said that once he'd said it twenty times, Mrs. Craggs thought irritably.

And then Mr. Tovey, not to be outdone, approached the sacred work of art in his turn. And repeated what he had said some twenty times since the piece had been installed.

"The hand of genius, the unmistakable hand of genius. Marvelous, magnificent, absolutely wonderful."

"Shall I do it now, sir?" asked Mrs. Craggs.

"Oh, very well, carry on then. Carry on."

And both Mr. Tovey and Mr. Slythe turned away so as not to see Mrs. Craggs's common yellow duster touch the product of "the unmistakable hand of genius" or "the patina of age." And then they both slewed round again to make sure that, in spite of everything, Mrs. Craggs was not wreaking havoc on the great work.

Indeed, the week of its exhibition was one of considerable strain for both the curator and his assistant. There was not only the public, which would keep coming and looking, attracted in numbers such as the museum had never seen before by stories in the papers about the immense value of the little golden statue, but there was the question of security at night. Of course, a firm of guards had been hired and a pair of them made hourly patrols past the Golden Venus on its plinth while others were on duty at both the front and back doors. But Mr. Tovey had decided this was not enough and had arranged with Mr. Slythe that they should each spend half of every night of the exhibition week on the premises. Both of them took every chance to point out to anybody who would listen, even to Mrs. Craggs if no one better offered, what sacrifices of time they were making, and of saying simultaneously in their different ways that, of course, it was really no sacrifice at all to be able to spend hours in private contemplation either of "the unmistakable hand of genius, coming down to us through the centuries" or of "the patina, the wonderful patina of age, so fine yet so very, very enduring."

So it could hardly be expected that either of them would react with calm when, on the last morning of the Venus' stay in the museum, Mrs. Craggs told them one after the other that the object over which she had just used her common yellow duster was not the genuine Golden Venus but a substitute.

She lay in wait first for Mr. Tovey.

"I'm very sorry to have to tell you, sir," she said when he re-entered the museum, "that is not the same statue as what I dusted yesterday."

"What—what do you mean, woman? Not the same statue?"

"I can tell, sir. I can tell by the touch. I've dusted that five time in all since it's been here and I know the feel of it as well as know the back of me own hand."

"We'll have a look at this," Mr. Tovey declared.

And he took the steps two at a time up to the landing where the Golden Venus stood. He drew a long breath and glared hard at the statue, then rounded on Mrs. Craggs.

"Piffle, my good woman," he said. "Sheer and utter piffle! Why you've only to look to see the hand of genius there, the unmistakable hand of genius."

"And you've only got to lay a duster on it to know it's not the same as what it was yesterday," Mrs. Craggs declared, with equal firmness.

Mr. Tovey drew himself up. But he did not pour forth th torrent of words Mrs. Craggs had braced herself for. Instead he suddenly thrust his big round face close to hers and spoke in a low whisper.

"Now, listen to me, my good woman, you are wrong. Yo cannot be anything else. I have a lifetime of knowledge behind me when I tell you that statue *is* the Golden Venus. But I know wha he press is and what reporters are capable of. So, understand this, ou are not to breathe one word of even the possibility of a theft. Not one word."

Mrs. Craggs looked doubtful. But Mr. Tovey was a persuasive employer and at last she mumbled agreement. Yet, thinking the matter over, she came to the conclusion that his prohibition ought not to include his fellow art expert, Mr. Slythe. So she waited her chance and at last managed to corner him at a spot not far from he Golden Venus, during a slack period in the museum's unaccustomedly busy life.

"Can I have a word?" she asked.

"Yes, yes. What is it? What is it now? Always something. Always some pettifogging detail preventing one from concentrating on one's true work."

"Well, if you say that someone putting a dummy in place f that Golden Venus is a detail," Mrs. Craggs answered, then that's your privilege. But I think it ought to be gone nto."

Mr. Slythe was even more upset than Mr. Tovey. He scooted ver the stone floor toward the statue as if he had been nexpectedly put on roller skates and he peered at it with such earful intensity that he might almost have melted it. And then he eturned, white-faced, to Mrs. Craggs. But not with dismay. With nger.

"You wretched, wretched person," he said. "How dare you? How dare you say a thing like that to me? It's enough to give me a ervous breakdown. Yes, a nervous breakdown."

"Then you don't think it has been changed?" Mrs. Craggs said.

"I do not. Why, anyone with a grain of sensibility could see that *iece* has the patina of age on every inch of it. The unmistakable atina of age. And you tell me that it is a substitute!"

And Mr. Slythe wheeled round and marched away to the anctuary of his private office.

Mrs. Craggs ought to have been convinced. But, if she was, hen why was it that she came to the museum the evening after the immensely successful Golden Venus exhibition had been triumphantly concluded and put in a good many hours of overtime, unpaid? She got out her dustcloths and worked away, rubbing and polishing stairs and corridors, showcases and display rooms. The museum had never gleamed so in all its days.

And at last her prowling duster encountered what she had hoped it would. In next to no time she was out on the steps of the building looking up and down the street, and before long she saw what she was looking for—the local police constable passing on his beat. She beckoned to him.

"I want to report a theft," she said.

The constable hurried in and Mrs. Craggs led him to the place where, dusting and polishing, she had come across a loose tile in the wall decoration of one of the rooms.

"Look," she said.

And she prised out the tile and the one next to it, to reveal a long cavity in which, reposing on a layer of cottonwool, was nothing less than the real Golden Venus.

"It was changed over during one of the gaps between the security patrols," Mrs. Craggs declared.

The constable, who had been aware of the precautions taken over so valuable a piece of property on his beat, saw at once what the situation was.

"It must have been one of them two," he said. "The whatsit—curator, Mr. Tovey, or his Number Two, Mr. Slythe. One of them must have hidden it here till he could slip it out. But—but which? They were each on guard alone half the night. Which could it be?"

"That's simple enough," Mrs. Craggs replied. "They both of them told me I was an old fool for saying it had been changed over. But only one of them made a fuss about not telling anyone else. It's the 'unmistakable hand of genius' you've got to go for, not 'the patina of age.' "

IV: *Hearing*

When Mrs. Craggs first went to work for old Mrs. Proost she rather liked listening to the old lady's music boxes. They were her most cherished possession, left to her by her husband who had died years before and who had devoted his life to the collection. But as time passed and Mrs. Proost insisted on playing one box or another the whole of the time Mrs. Craggs was cleaning in the house, the charwoman began, as she said to her friend Mrs. Milhorne, "To really hate the blessed things."

"I like a good tune," she said, "same as anyone else. But to hear that tinkle, tinkle, tinkle all day and every, why, it's more than human ears can stand." Mrs. Milhorne wondered how the old lady herself could put up with it. "I'll tell you," said Mrs. Craggs. "It's because she doesn't hear a single note."

Why ever not, Mrs. Milhorne wanted to know. It wasn't as if the old lady was deaf, because she'd seen her herself, out doing a bit of shopping and talking with the best "and never a sign of them little things behind your ear."

Mrs. Craggs had smiled at that. "Oh," she said, "she wouldn't let on. Go to any lengths she would to pretend she's heard every word. Nod and smile like an old teetotum. But I know. I can go into that sitting room of hers and so long as I take good care to stand where she can't see me lips, I can say 'Wotcher, me old mate, how's all the little tinkle boxes then?' and she don't take one blind bit of notice."

But Mrs. Craggs put up with the tinkle-tinkling because Mrs. Proost was a nice old thing, even if she was too proud to admit how little she could hear. And all went well. Till the day the old lady asked Mrs. Craggs if, as a special favor, she could come back the next afternoon and serve tea.

"It's my nephew," she said. "My husband's brother's boy, Tony. Such a dear little fellow he used to be, though I'm afraid his parents, poor dear souls, spoiled him dreadfully."

Mrs. Craggs replied that certainly she would come the next day at three and she asked how it was that the young man had never visited his aunt in all the years Mrs. Craggs had been working for her.

"Oh, but you see," said Mrs. Proost, "he's been dreadfully busy. Yes, in the North. He's been away in the North for—oh, for quite eight years now. A most important post."

"What's that then?" asked Mrs. Craggs, opening her lips wide.

"Oh, dear. Well, you will think me silly, but I can't quite recall. It was something to do with aeroplanes, I think. Or was it aerodromes? But it *was* important. I can tell you that."

Mrs. Craggs had been in the kitchen, slicing bread nice and thin for some twenty minutes when the visitor arrived. She answered his ring at the door and showed him into the sitting room. But she was not impressed. Nephew Tony was a good deal older than Mrs. Proost had led her to expect, and he had too travel-worn a look for someone with an important job to do with airplanes, or even airfields. As he walked ahead of her across the hall, she thought she could hear one of the soles of his shoes flapping slightly.

So, instead of retiring discreetly until four o'clock, when it had been agreed she should bring in tea, Mrs. Craggs contrived to stand by the door of the room, as if she was, despite her flowered apron and best hat worn in honor of the event, a sort of footman.

Nephew Tony was very breezy and bold and Mrs. Craggs could see old Mrs. Proost looking at his face carefully as he sat opposite her and so succeeding in answering his hearty remarks about thinking he "wouldn't bother with a taxi from the station, just gave myself a tuppenny bus ride, you know." More like it he walked, thought Mrs. Craggs, even though it was three miles.

But just then Mrs. Proost realized that the charwoman was still hovering over the proceedings.

"Mrs. Craggs," she said, "you may serve tea."

"Bit early, ain't it?" Mrs. Craggs asked, after advancing to where her lips could be read.

"Never mind," Mrs. Proost replied, with a dignity recalling the days when she'd had a real parlormaid in black dress and lace cap. "Master Tony and I will take tea now."

"Very good," said Mrs. Craggs. And so impressed was she with the high tone that her employer had achieved, she added, though rather belatedly, "madam."

But nevertheless out in the kitchen she got the rest of the tea things onto the tray in record time and made the tea itself—in the silver teapot, appearing especially for the occasion—without actually waiting for the pot to warm. And when she entered the sitting room again, she thought she had arrived only just in time.

Nephew Tony was talking about Mrs. Proost's music boxes. And what he was saying sent columns of red anger marching through Mrs. Craggs's head.

"You see, Aunt," he was arguing, "these boxes may be quite valuable and since the truth of it is that, though you play them often enough, you can't really—"

With a fierce jerk of the tea tray between her outstretched arms Mrs. Craggs sent a stream of hot liquid from the spout of the silver pot plummeting straight down onto Nephew Tony's lap.

"Oh, lor, sir, lor," Mrs. Craggs said in instant apology. "What must have come over me? Oh, sir. Sir, you are a mess. Come out to the kitchen right away and I'll sponge you down. We gotter save that nice suit."

And though the suit in fact was of a cut and color that indicated years of service that had begun a long time ago, Nephew Tony did hurry out to the kitchen.

There Mrs. Craggs did nothing at all about sponging the broad spatter of tea. Instead she faced the not so young man with her arms akimbo.

"Now you just listen to me," she said. "I know what you were just going to tell her. And you're not to do it."

"What—what do you mean?" Nephew Tony asked.

"I mean you were going to tell her she's so deaf she can't hear them musical boxes. And I daresay you were going to offer to sell 'em for her. And with a big difference between the price you get and the money you'll give her."

"I don't know what you're talking about," Nephew Tony said. "If I was offering my aunt some good business advice, it's hardly any affair of yours. The money she gets for those boxes would probably be enough to keep her in comfort for the rest of her days."

"She's happy enough as she is, and don't you think nothing else," Mrs. Craggs answered. "She may not hear a single tinkle those blessed boxes make, but she thinks we all believe she does and that's what keeps her going. So don't you try putting your oar in."

Nephew Tony, dabbing for himself at his trousers with a snatched dishcloth, darted the charwoman a glance of fury.

"I'll thank you to keep your interfering nose out of our family business," he said. "I'm going straight back in there and tell my aunt it's plain common sense to sell those boxes, and that I know where I can get a fair price for them."

Mrs. Craggs folded her hands and stood with them in front of her, leaving the way to the kitchen door clear. But there was a look in her eyes that stopped Nephew Tony dead in his tracks.

"What are you looking like that for?" he demanded.

"Because," said Mrs. Craggs, "if you go in there I shall come after you and tell your dear aunt that her nephew's just finished a good spell in quod."

"Prison? How did you know—what do you mean 'prison'?"

"I mean just what I say. That someone who's been out of the way so long he thinks you can still get anywhere on a bus for tuppence hasn't been up in no North of England. He's been inside. I got ears in me head and unless you want me to tell her what I heard, out you go."

"Well," Mrs. Craggs said to Mrs. Proost a few minutes later, taking care to stand where the old lady could see her lips. "Well, I'm sure I don't know where he's gone. Upped and off he did, just like that. 'Spect he remembered an aeroplane he'd got to build or something."

"Yes, yes. I expect that was it," the old lady said. "Young men like him have so much on their minds, you know."

"Yes, dear—yes, madam," said Mrs. Craggs. "That's true enough. And now shall I turn one of your musical boxes on for you? I expect you'd like to hear a nice cheerful tune."

V: *Tasting*

One of the things Mrs. Craggs had to do when she was Mrs. Fitzblaney's daily help was to stay late every Thursday evening and take up supper to Mrs. Fitzblaney's husband, the old Colonel, who was bedridden. "Thirty years between them two if there's a day," Mrs. Craggs used to say to her friend, Mrs. Milhorne. But she got well paid for this extra work, time and a half always. She had been quite firm about that the moment she was first asked, since she well knew there was money and to spare in that household. The Colonel always had the best and liked the best, there was no doubt about that. Though there was doubt about the Colonel himself. The doctor had said years before that he might go any day, and every time that Mrs. Craggs came to the house she half expected to hear the worst.

But every Thursday evening Mrs. Fitzblaney went off to her art class. "And holding hands with the art master, if all I hear's true," said Mrs. Craggs. "Still, that's no business of mine. A little of what you fancy don't do you no harm, that's my motto."

And every week Mrs. Fitzblaney left behind her two ounces of Patna rice to be boiled for ten minutes by the clock and no more and a saucepan of ready-prepared curry to be heated up.

"Fair fussy he is about his curry, the old boy," Mrs. Craggs would say. It had to be cooked in the afternoon by Mrs. Fitzblaney in exactly the way the Colonel liked it, and all Mrs. Craggs had to do was to see that she knocked on the bedroom door, with the tray in her hands, at eight o'clock to the second.

She had been late once, but only once. At half a minute past eight the Colonel's voice, despite his illness, had come roaring down the stairs. "Bearer! Bearer! Where's that blasted bearer? Fellow's late on parade. I won't have it. D'ye hear, damn and blast you? I will not have it." Very much on her dignity Mrs. Craggs had been when she went in with the tray that night.

But being on the dot was not all. That curry had to be hot as well. Not spicy hot. The Colonel liked it that way, but there the doctor had put his foot down. But as near boiling-hot as dammit that curry had to be. There had been trouble about that once too.

"Bearer, what the hell's this? Bloody *ice* pudding? Eh, man? Eh?"

"I do my best," Mrs. Craggs had replied. "And what's more, if I may make so bold as to mention, I am not a man, nor yet a bearer neither, whatever that may be."

But all the same ever afterward she took the precaution of dipping a finger into the saucepan and having a taste, when she thought the curry was ready, to make sure it had reached a really hot heat. The stuff was nasty enough, she thought, but she was not going to be called names at her age.

And then one Thursday came and, as Mrs. Craggs said later to Mrs. Milhorne, "I will not forget, not so long as I has breath in my body to remember by."

At the start it did not seem to be different from any other Thursday evening. Mrs. Craggs, who came to the house to do the cleaning in the afternoon, got through her work as usual. It was the sitting room on Thursdays, and the hall. And at just the usual time Mrs. Fitzblaney came down the stairs dressed as usual in her painting things—"Pair of jeans that should've been in the dustbin years ago," said Mrs. Craggs. "And too tight for her by a long chalk where I won't mention"—and as usual Mrs. Fitzblaney fussed over telling Mrs. Craggs what she knew perfectly well already.

"You won't forget to be on the dot of eight with his supper, will you, Mrs. Er—?" "—Never did have the common decency to get me name right, but that was Mrs. Fitzblaney all over," said Mrs. Craggs—and no sooner had Mrs. Craggs assured her that she had no need to worry about that than it was "Oh, and Mrs. Er—, I forgot to say. You will make quite, quite sure the curry's hot, won't you? The Colonel gets so cross if it isn't just to his liking, you know, and it's terribly bad for him to—to— Well, you know, lose his temper."

"There won't be no cause for complaint from me," said Mrs. Craggs.

And there was not. At seven thirty to the second—she had the radio on "dead quiet" to make sure—onto the stove went the water for the rice and on too went the curry over a nice low heat. And at seven forty-five precisely Mrs. Craggs had the rice dished and waiting and was making doubly sure the curry was really hot. She put her finger in, winced at the heat, but nevertheless lifted a yellowy-brown gob to her lips and bravely tasted it.

"Hot as hot," she said to herself. "Old Blood-and-Guts'll have no complaints tonight." Then she poured the curry with care onto the center of the hollowed-out mound of rice, put the plate on the tray, and carried it upstairs. The Colonel never ate a dessert. "Blasted sweet stuff. Nobody wants to put that in their mouth," he used to say.

Mrs. Craggs knocked at the door of the bedroom just as she heard the church clock strike eight, and "Come in, come in," the Colonel shouted. Mrs. Craggs entered, carried the food over to the bed tray which was already on parade over the Colonel's knees, and set it down.

"Hm," grunted the Colonel. And then he had the grace to add, "Hah. Thank you." Mrs. Craggs knew her services were not required any longer and down she went to the kitchen.

She ought really at this point to have put on her hat and coat and left. The Colonel always pushed aside his tray when he had finished and Mrs. Fitzblaney brought it downstairs when she got back from the art class. That was the regular routine. The Colonel objected to "blasted women always coming in and out of the room like a set of damn railway trains."

But tonight something stopped Mrs. Craggs as she went to take her hat off the peg on the back of the kitchen door. It was not anything particular, just a feeling—a feeling that something was not quite as it ought to be.

For perhaps a full half minute she stood there, nose up against her coat as it hung on the peg, the hat held high in her hand. And then she got it.

"Hot," she said. "It was too hot. Spicy hot as can be." And then she dropped her hat on the floor just where she stood, wheeled round and was out of the kitchen and thumping off up the stairs in as little time as it takes to tell. She got to the top of the stairs. She made for the Colonel's door. She thrust it open without so much as a knock or a word of apology and said, "Stop!"

"Stop? Stop? What the hell d'you mean by 'stop'?"

Afterward Mrs. Craggs said to Mrs. Milhorne that she had never seen a man look so astonished. "You'd have thought it was the Angel Gabriel come in," she said. "You would have, honest."

But at the time Mrs. Craggs failed to answer the Colonel's question. Instead she fired one of her own. "That curry," she said, "have you tasted any of it?"

"Of course I've tasted my bloody curry, woman," the Colonel thundered back. "What's the infernal stuff for if it isn't to be tasted?"

"Then don't you eat one bit more," said Mrs. Craggs.

"What blasted nonsense is this? The first decent hot curry I've had in the last five years and you have the abominable impertinence to come in here and tell me to stop eating it. I'll do no such thing."

And the Colonel plunged his fork deep into the browny-yellow concoction and lifted a gigantic quantity, all dripping, toward his mouth.

It was then that Mrs. Craggs did an unforgivable thing. She

launched herself across the room toward the bed and knocked the Colonel's full fork flying.

"What the—"

Words failed the Colonel.

"Oh, sir," said Mrs. Craggs, "I'm sorry. I really am. I don't know how I even dared to do it, sir."

"And nor do I, you infernal harridan. You're dismissed, d'you hear? Get out, do y'hear me, get out!"

But it was at that moment that the Colonel began to be seriously ill. Mrs. Craggs rolled up her sleeves and set to, and the doctor said afterward that it was solely owing to the sensible way she went about it that the Colonel came out of it as well as he did. But, as she said to Mrs. Milhorne, "I wasn't exactly as calm as a tuppenny cucumber at the time."

In fact, she had gabbled and babbled and said a lot of things that hardly made sense, all of which had had the effect of calming down the old Colonel and probably saving him to live out the rest of his life as the happy resident of a nursing home for ex-officers with proper batmen in attendance.

"It was it being so hot, sir," Mrs. Craggs had babbled that evening. "I mean I know it has to be hot. But not hot like that. And I know Mrs. Fitzblaney knows it mustn't be, 'cos she's always telling me so. And then, when I realized that it was too hot, spicy hot I mean, all of a sudden it came over me why it was. And only why. Poison, I thought. It's to hide the taste of poison. She's done it. She's aiming to be off with that artist fellow and live in comfort on the proceeds. Well, a little of what you fancy does yer good, but there's some things goes too far. And murder's one."

IF IT'S GOT YOUR NUMBER

by Celia Fremlin

The story of a woman shoplifter, of a plump middle-aged woman who has plenty of money—indeed, who has everything she could want in life (everything?)—and still goes shoplifting day after day. But this time she knowingly, deliberately steals a dress four sizes too small and not at all suitable in style . . . This is one of the most unusual shoplifting stories ever written, with the "extra" of Celia Fremlin's distinctive "touch" . . .

JUST catching sight of the woman for a second time didn't prove that she was a store detective. Well, of course it didn't.

Clutching the shopping bag with a hand already slippery with sweat, Martha forced herself to maintain her strolling, leisurely pace, past the glittering racks of cocktail dresses, past the sumptuous evening skirts of velvet and brocade—slowly, slowly does it.

If she once let herself quicken her steps by no matter how small a fraction, she knew she would be lost. Panic would seize her, she would break into a run, make a dash for the escalator, and by that time the whole shop would be after her, not merely this slim elegant woman in the oatmeal trouser-suit.

"*After her!*" How ridiculous! Martha struggled to control her galloping imagination, to think beyond the wild hammering of guilt in her brain, and to consider, coolly, the factual, common-sense reality of her situation.

No one had seen her take the dress. Indeed, in the raucous, blood-red darkness of Young Ideas, with pop music blaring out and the long-haired boys and girls roaming between the clothes like a herd of jungle creatures—in such a setting it would have been hard enough for anyone to notice anything, let alone to bother about such a dull, middle-aged customer as herself.

She had been all alone behind the tight-packed maxi-dresses at the far end of the room, out of sight of everyone, and even with time to make her choice. No one had seen her, either, as she slipped out from behind the rack with her spoils; and now here she was, already half the length of the store away from the scene of her crime, in a different department altogether.

And as for the woman in the oatmeal suit—why, it was coincidence, sheer coincidence, that she should have turned up in this department as well. She wasn't even looking in Martha's direction—hadn't been, either, on that earlier occasion, when they'd passed each other on the way out of Young Ideas.

What would the woman have seen, anyway, even if she *had* looked? Just one more plump, smartly dressed, middle-aged woman strolling through Cocktail and Evening Wear with a shopping bag in her hand. Exactly like all the other middle-aged women who had come shopping this winter Thursday afternoon. All of them smart, all of them with shopping bags in their hands, and all of them—well, an awful lot of them, anyway—with lines of tension round their mouths and a look of furtive anxiety in their eyes, even though they hadn't (well, Martha presumed they hadn't) stolen anything at all.

So there was nothing to mark her out from the rest of them. Absolutely nothing. Stupid to allow her heart to race like this, her hands to sweat! All she had to do was to keep dawdling along—she was in Day Dresses now—pausing to examine a neckline here, a price tag there, just to keep her nerve, and all would be well.

At last the escalator! As she set foot on the moving track and saw the ground floor gliding up to meet her, Martha felt the kind of thankfulness and gratitude that the pilot of a damaged plane must feel as he catches sight of the perfect spot for an emergency landing. For the crowd down there on the ground floor was so large, and packed so tight in all the aisles, that surely all possibility of detection would soon be over.

Down, down she sailed, diving toward that milling anonymous sea of humanity like a fish escaping back into its native element.

Safe! Safe! In her relief Martha almost skipped off the end of the escalator, and as she began to battle her way through the crowd toward the main entrance, she was aware of an exultation that went far beyond the satisfaction of having successfully acquired an £8.50 dress without paying for it. It was as if what she had done was some kind of victory of the human spirit, a slap in the face of middle age. It was even an argument, of sorts—a clinching final argument in the dreary long-drawn-out conflict with her husband.

"*See*, Leonard?" her theft seemed to be saying to him, in gleeful triumph. "*See? That'll* show you!"—though *what* he was to "see," and how the theft was going to "show" him, she had no idea.

Especially since, God willing, Leonard was never going to know anything about it at all.

Already the entrance doors were in sight. Beyond them she could see the glittering dusk of Oxford Street, lit up like fairyland against the coming night. "I've done it, I've done it!" she found herself exulting, in wordless joy, as she pushed and squeezed her way toward the jam-packed entrance. "It's worked, it's succeeded!"—and in that very moment, just as the revolving doors were drawing her in, she became aware of the woman in the oatmeal suit, not a yard away from her.

Martha did not know how far along Oxford Street she had been running before her breath gave out. Not very far, probably, for her muscles and her wind were not what they had once been. Not what they had been before—well, before security and Leonard and a nice home had got their grip on her. Before television and chocolates and over-lavish cocktail parties had become the pattern of her days.

"Everything a woman could want!" Leonard had once launched this hackneyed reproach at her in the course of one of their weary rows, and of course he had been right. She *had* everything—and how, over the years, it had sucked the strength out of her muscles, the zest out of her soul. The strength and the zest which once, long ago . . .

"Excuse me, madam."

Maybe the words were not addressed to Martha at all. Or maybe, even if they were, it was only some stranger asking the way to Selfridge's. She would never know. For before the sentence could be completed she was off and away, battering once more through the crowds, pushing, dodging, worming her way through the interstices of this human maze until, at last, she found herself at the entrance to an Underground station.

Which station it was she did not know and did not care. Headlong she plunged into its seething, anonymous security; and in almost no time at all, it seemed, she was on the train, standing, wedged tight against her fellow passengers, and with the shopping bag still clutched grimly in her left hand.

But the sense of exultation was gone now. The triumph, the exhilaration, the excitement, had all drained out of her, and she felt sanity returning, like a recurrent illness.

Why? *Why* had she done it? She'd had plenty of money in her purse—Leonard had never been mean. It wasn't as if she'd even *wanted* the dress—it was ridiculous, four sizes too small at least, and years and years too young for her, with its frilly, scooped-out neckline and little puff sleeves.

Why had she done such a thing?—risking the career of her hard-working lawyer husband, at the same time possibly bringing total, irremediable humiliation on herself. She could almost see the headlines in the papers: *Wife of Well-Known Barrister in Court for Shoplifting*—and she could almost quote the story which would follow: "victim of a neurotic compulsion . . ." "psychiatric treatment" . . . "not uncommon symptom among women who feel themselves useless and unloved."

Useless and unloved. If any of the neighbors didn't know it already, they would know it now. Or would, if she wasn't very, very careful. Rousing herself, Martha glanced along the car to reassure herself that there was no oatmeal trouser-suit in sight, no official-looking person peering covertly in her direction.

She was surprised, faintly, to notice how much the rush-hour crowd had already thinned out. There were even some seats vacant. Thankfully, still clutching her shopping bag, Martha sank into the nearest empty seat. Only now had she become aware of how tired she was, how much her feet hurt. Indeed, her whole body ached with tiredness after her day's shopping—if "shopping" was the word. She leaned back, gratefully, on the upholstered seat and closed her eyes . . .

Had she dozed off? Martha sat up with a jolt, and with an uneasy feeling that a long, long time had passed. Where had they got to? Had they passed Hammersmith Broadway, where she had to change?

Peering out through the grimy window, she caught a momentary glimpse of an ill-lit platform, dingy and narrow, and crowded with a confusion of people; but before she had been able to ascertain the name of the station, it was gone, and they were thundering on into the darkness.

They must have passed Hammersmith long ago. That grimy, poorly lit station they had just left was wholly unfamiliar. They must be nearing the end of the line—or an even more disturbing thought—maybe she was traveling in the wrong direction altogether. Maybe, in her state of confusion and panic, she had got onto an east-bound train by mistake.

Yes, that must be it. How infuriating! Now she would have to cross over to the other side of the line and perhaps wait ages for a return train. She would be late getting home, that was certain! Leonard would be home before her; he would be waiting, irritable, wanting to know where she'd been, what had kept her so long.

Clutching her guilty shopping bag, would she be able to answer him brightly, convincingly? Or would she find herself blushing and stammering and watching the weary suspicion growing in his cool appraising eyes?

The train was slowing down now, and gathering her things together Martha prepared to leave. Funny how few people there were on the train now. Just a small group of soldiers, and an old man slumped as if in sleep. The lighting was strange, too, so feeble and dim. Something must have gone wrong, but at this point in her thoughts the train came to a halt and the doors slid open.

"Please, what station is this?" she asked the man who was pushing past her into the train; but to her surprise he merely laughed.

"Not much odds, is it, sweetheart?" he remarked jocosely. "So's you're a hundred feet down, that's all you want to worry about, a night like this! Hell, it's bloody murder up there!"—and he passed, whistling, into the train.

"Well!" Martha stood on the platform, speechless, as the train drew away. The cheek of the fellow! Was he a nut or something? And only now did she turn and really look at her surroundings . . .

It was all exactly as she remembered it. The rolls of bedding, the deck chairs, the snug little family parties, with a blanket outspread to mark their territory on the platform, with Mum in the middle dispensing sandwiches and cups of tea, for all the world as if this was a seaside outing. And the old men playing Housey Housey, and the kids larking about, much too near the edge of the platform, the Shelter Wardens shouting at them good-humoredly. And Charlie. Yes, there was Charlie in his usual place at the end of the platform, just tuning up on his accordion.

"You're new here, ain't you, sister?" a kindly, middle-aged man addressed her, and Martha started, as if awakened from sleep. "Me? Oh!" She stopped. "No, I'm old, old!" had been the reply on the tip of her tongue. "I've been here more than thirty years!"—but of course she mustn't disconcert him with such incomprehensible nonsense.

"N-no, I'm not staying, I'm on my way home," she stammered, a strange and incredulous joy growing in her as she spoke. "I have to go—" but as she moved toward the exit, the man laid a friendly, restraining hand on her shoulder.

"I'd stop down here for a bit if I were you, sister," he advised. "Old Jerry ain't half going it tonight! Ain't 'e, Sid?" He appealed for confirmation to an older man, perched on a roll of bedding at their feet and sucking at his pipe.

" 'S'right!" agreed this new contributor to the discussion. " 'S' a real bad 'un tonight! I said it'd be bad, din' I, when them sirens went early? Not five o'clock, it wasn't—I 'adn' 'ad me tea. I don' like it, I says. When them sirens goes early, it means a rough night, I says. 'E only starts up that early when 'e's got a real packet for us! Like that Wednesday when—"

A clatter of running feet along the platform interrupted him. Two youths, rosy with danger, alight with glory from the terrible Outside, were racing along the platform, drunk with news.

"The Ship's got it!" they yelled, in that strange ecstasy of disaster that Martha remembered so well. "Yeah, the Shipton Arms—a direct hit. You can't see it no more, it's all nothin', just bricks an' smoke an' all. Yeah, we seen it! We was right there!"

This was happiness! This was glory! This was living! Martha could see it in the lads' eyes, hear it in their voices, feel it in their gestures. This was the happiness that she, too, had known—she and Basil, glorying in their young daring and in the young strength of their limbs as they raced hand in hand through the gunfire in the empty, blacked-out streets, along a razor edge of death, experiencing such an ecstasy as she would never know again . . .

Unless? This very night? Just once more? Would this dream, this magic, whatever it was—would it last just long enough for that? Were the gods indeed granting her, after thirty stagnant years, another chance?

"I must go," she repeated, almost choking with hope. "My boy friend's waiting for me"—and brushing aside the kindly protests of the shelterers, she set off running up the long, long spiral stairs that led to the outside world.

Yes, running. If she had not guessed it already, from the tremulous joy in her heart, she knew now, for certain, that she was young again. These winding, endless flights of steps meant nothing to her young limbs as she skipped and bounded upward, the stolen dress bumping and swinging against her as she ran.

So *this* was why she had chosen it—a dress for a young girl, so slim, so gay, so daring! She had known all along that it was right for her, for her real, true self.

Faster she ran, and faster; up and up the echoing spiral curves, up and up, on and on, tireless as a mountain deer, knowing that there, at the top, Basil would be waiting.

Every evening since the beginning of the Blitz he had waited for her up there. Night after night he would come rushing from his job in the West End, all the way out here, just to meet her as she came out of the tube, and to escort her safely along the Mile End Road to her home. Together they would race through the black deserted streets, the crack of gunfire in their ears, and the shrapnel clattering on the pavements before and behind.

They met no one—the empty, perilous streets belonged only to them; and as they tore through the whistling death-ridden dark, Martha had realized, even at the time, that she would never know such happiness again.

"You shouldn't!" she sometimes said to Basil, as she came out of the tube station into his waiting arms. "You shouldn't! You should stop up West, it's safer up there." But always he just laughed, as of course she had known he would.

"Don't worry, love!" he would answer, his strong arms encircling her in the savage dark. "Don't worry, I'm as safe here as I'd be anywhere. What I always say is, if it's got your number on it, you'll get it, no matter *where* you are!"

How wrong he was!

She was nearing the top of the stairs now. Faint gleams of blueish light from the ticket office were beginning to play dimly on the curve of the wall, and she was becoming aware of sounds from the outside world. The crackle of gunfire; the clatter of a warden's boots, running; and in the ensuing silence, she became aware of a tension, a sense of approaching climax, which was the only memory she had of that last night. The only *clear* memory, anyway—the rest had been a blur of all-enveloping horror. What *had* happened, exactly?

She had been nearing the top of these spiral steps, she remembered, just as she was now—the lifts were always put out of action as soon as the sirens went on, and so climbing up these spiral stairs when she came home from work had become a familiar routine.

Yes, she had been just at the top of the flight, just coming out into the station entrance, when she had known, suddenly, that something was going to happen. She did not know how she knew, for there was no sound, no explosion, no ominous whistling of an approaching bomb.

She learned afterward that when a bomb is coming *really* near, right on top of you, you don't hear the whistling. But she didn't know this at the time. All she was aware of, in those last moments before the end, was a peculiar, waiting stillness. The whole sky seemed to be leaning outward, somehow, the air was opening out silently, like a flower, and then a voice—the ticket collector it must have been—was screaming at her.

"Get down! Get down!" he had yelled, pushing her back.

But he couldn't have forced her back if she hadn't let him. Already she had glimpsed Basil running across the street toward her, and she could, if she had chosen, have run forward to meet him, not back into the safety of the stairs.

But back, in fact, she had run; down and down, round and round, spiraling down, down, down into safety, while outside the earth rocked to such an explosion as she had never dreamed, and that her mind could not grasp. Her ears were deafened, and her mind was blacked out, and afterward she could remember almost nothing of how it had been.

People were very kind. "How dreadfully sad!" they said, and "You mustn't reproach yourself, there was nothing you could have done to save him." And of course they were right.

Or were they? How could they *know?* How could *anyone* know? If just one person, once, in the whole history of the world, had done just one thing differently from the way he or she in fact had done it, who could say that it would not have changed the whole future of mankind? Who could tell whether, if Martha had run forward toward Basil instead of backward into safety—who could tell if, locked in each other's arms, they might not have had one of those miraculous escapes, some bizarre fluke of blast hurling them somehow into safety? One read of such things. Who could tell? Who can ever, anywhere, say with certainty what *would* have happened *if* . . .

If she had pushed past the well-meaning ticket man. *If* she had defied all her own instincts of self-preservation. *If* she had raced out into the black jaws of death, crying "Basil! Basil! I'm here!"

"Ticket, please."

Martha stared, stupidly, as the man at the barrier waited, hand outstretched. Outside, the commonplace light of peacetime gleamed on the wet streets, and she could feel the weight of her fifty-five years in every limb.

"I—I'm sorry!" she muttered, fumbling in her bag, searching, trying to remember if she had even bought one.

Soon, though, the small fuss was over—she could tell from the man's bored, patronizing manner that he wasn't going to honor with serious reproof such an idiot criminal as this—one who didn't even know which station she'd got on at, let alone which station she was at now. So he shrugged, charged her twenty p. and let her go, out into the wet alien night, thirty years and more away from home.

She was late getting home, of course, just as she had feared, and Leonard was angry. He was angrier still when, later that evening, the store manager phoned him about the dress. The man was less apologetic this time about bothering so important a person as Leonard, and less inclined to hush the whole thing up.

"I'm sorry, sir," he said, "but I'm afraid it can't go on. Yes, I know you always see to it that we get the goods back or pay for it, and—yes, yes, I know, but that's not quite the point, is it? I do appreciate your position, and you have my sympathy, but all the same next time I'm afraid it will be my duty . . ."

Martha, listening in on the bedroom extension, heard her husband slam down the receiver, and she waited, crouched against the pillows, for the familiar storm to break. Leonard's face, as he entered the bedroom, was angrier than she could ever remember.

It came to an end, though, at last. Even the most blazing row cannot go on forever. It ended, as it always did, with Martha in tears and making hysterical promises never to do it again.

But this time, with a sort of weary contempt in his voice that Martha had never heard before, Leonard extracted from her a further promise—not merely never to do it again, but actually never to go shopping by herself again.

"Do you understand, Martha? You can go into Town only if someone will go with you—your sister, or one of your bridge friends—but you are *not* to go to the West End shops by yourself any more. Do you understand?"

And Martha, still sniffling, said she did. She promised to do exactly as he said, and the next morning, the moment he had left the flat, she set off for the West End.

Not for the shops, though. Oh, no, she had an errand now a thousand times more important than going to any shop, and a thousand times more exciting. Somehow, somewhere, she must find once more the magic tube station, the gateway into the world of her youth, the world where she belonged, the only place where she had ever truly lived.

It must be somewhere! All that day—and the next, and the next—she traveled up and down the Central Line, getting out at this station and at that, randomly, but nowhere could she find the station of her dreams.

She did not despair. It *must* be somewhere, it *must!* Perhaps the magic only worked if you got *on* at the right station as well as getting off at the right one. Which station *had* she got on at, that fateful night? Oxford Circus? Bond Street? Marble Arch? It might be any of them—or even Tottenham Court Road, or Holborn.

This added alarmingly to the possible permutations and combinations, but Martha was not disheartened. Each evening, when she got home from her fruitless search, she would lock herself in her room and plan out her next day's itinerary: start from Marble Arch this time and get off at Bow; then back to Marble Arch and start again, this time getting off at East Ham.

Leonard noticed the strange, furtive eagerness about her these days, the secret purposefulness, and at first it worried him; but as the days went by and there were still no phone calls from any of the stores he began to relax. Perhaps, after all, she was keeping her promise. Perhaps she had even reformed.

It was at the end of the third week that the call came; and when, with weary dread, he picked up the phone, it wasn't a store manager on the line at all. It was the police. His wife, they were sorry to tell him, had been killed in an accident just outside Mile End Station. A quite extraordinary accident—at the moment, it all seemed quite impossible to explain—

It remained impossible to explain. Police, doctors, forensic experts were all equally at a loss. What sort of vehicle could it have been, and traveling at what sort of speed, to have inflicted the extraordinary injuries sustained by the deceased?

There seemed to be no clues at all. And of all the people who must have been present at the time of the accident—it was during the evening rush hour—only one came forward as a witness, the ticket collector at Mile End Station. And, really, he might as well have saved himself the trouble, so nonsensical was the story he had to tell, and so unhelpful to the serious investigation that was being undertaken.

On the night of the tragedy, he claimed, he had noticed this woman coming up off the train. She was plump, middle-aged, in no way remarkable; and the only reason he had noticed her was that she was running at top speed right toward the barrier. Thinking she was trying to get through without a ticket, he had reached out and grabbed her arm; accustomed though he was to fare dodgers of all sorts, he had been amazed by the violence of her struggles.

"Let me go! Let me go!" she had screamed. "It's got my number on it!"

Thinking she must be referring to some sort of season ticket or special pass, he had relaxed his grip for a moment, expecting her to produce such a document; and in that split second she had broken free, charged through the barrier, and was out into the street.

And then? Well, all he could say was what he had actually seen with his own eyes; let them make of it what they could. As the woman ran, still at full speed, across the pavement outside the station, she had fallen in pieces. Yes, in pieces.

No, nothing had hit her. She hadn't tripped or stumbled. She had simply fallen in pieces while he watched. Her whole body had quietly disintegrated into a dozen bits that scattered this way and that across the pavement.

And from this statement the ticket collector would not budge.

The police could make nothing of it. And poor Leonard, when he arrived on the scene, was just as baffled. Lawyer though he was, he didn't even make a very good job of identifying the body. It should have been easy for him, because, as it chanced, the head and face had escaped all damage.

"I—I suppose it must be her," he said slowly, staring down at the familiar features.

Familiar, and yet wholly unfamiliar. As he gazed into his wife's dead face, Leonard wondered, in his clear, precise, legal mind, where all that beauty had been hidden during their marriage, and all that happiness on her face.

PROOF OF GUILT

by Bill Pronzini

"Proof of Guilt" is not one of Bill Pronzini's private-eye stories. It's about a pair of big-city detectives who are confronted by what looks like an impossible crime—yes, a locked-room mystery, but with a "difference." The author called it "a very special case of murder"—and we think you will agree . . .

I'VE been a city cop for thirty-two years now, and during that time I've heard of and been involved in some of the weirdest, most audacious crimes imaginable—on and off public record. But as far as I'm concerned, the murder of an attorney named Adam Chillingham is *the* damnedest case in my experience, if not in the entire annals of crime.

You think I'm exaggerating? Well, listen to the way it was.

My partner Jack Sherrard and I were in the Detective Squadroom one morning last summer when this call came in from a man named Charles Hearn. He said he was Adam Chillingham's law clerk, and that his employer had just been shot to death; he also said he had the killer trapped in the lawyer's private office.

It seemed like a fairly routine case at that point. Sherrard and I drove out to the Dawes Building, a skyscraper in a new business development on the city's south side, and rode the elevator up to Chillingham's suite of offices on the sixteenth floor. Hearn, and a woman named Clarisse Tower, who told us she had been the dead man's secretary, were waiting in the anteroom with two uniformed patrolmen who had arrived minutes earlier.

According to Hearn, a man named George Dillon had made a ten-thirty appointment with Chillingham, had kept it punctually, and had been escorted by the attorney into the private office at that exact time. At ten forty Hearn thought he heard a muffled explosion from inside the office, but he couldn't be sure because the walls were partially soundproofed.

Hearn got up from his desk in the anteroom and knocked on the door and there was no response; then he tried the knob and found that the door was locked from the inside. Miss Tower confirmed all this, although she said she hadn't heard any sound; her desk was farther away from the office door than was Hearn's.

A couple of minutes later the door had opened and George Dillon had looked out and calmly said that Chillingham had been murdered. He had not tried to leave the office after the announcement; instead, he'd seated himself in a chair near the desk and lighted a cigarette. Hearn satisfied himself that his employer was dead, made a hasty exit, but had the presence of mind to lock the door from the outside by the simple expediency of transferring the key from the inside to the outside—thus sealing Dillon in the office with the body. After which Hearn put in his call to Headquarters.

So Sherrard and I drew our guns, unlocked the door, and burst into the private office. This George Dillon was sitting in the chair across the desk, very casual, both his hands up in plain sight. He gave us a relieved look and said he was glad the police had arrived so quickly.

I went over and looked at the body, which was sprawled on the floor behind the desk; a pair of French windows were open in the wall just beyond, letting in a warm summer breeze. Chillingham had been shot once in the right side of the neck, with what appeared by the size of the wound to have been a small-caliber bullet; there was no exit wound, and there were no powder burns.

I straightened up, glanced around the office, and saw that the only door was the one which we had just come through. There was no balcony or ledge outside the open windows—just a sheer drop of sixteen stories to a parklike, well-landscaped lawn which stretched away for several hundred yards. The nearest building was a hundred yards distant, angled well to the right. Its roof was about on a level with Chillingham's office, it being a lower structure than the Dawes Building; not much of the roof was visible unless you peered out and around.

Sherrard and I then questioned George Dillon—and he claimed he hadn't killed Chillingham. He said the attorney had been standing at the open windows, leaning out a little, and that all of a sudden he had cried out and fallen down with the bullet in his neck. Dillon said he'd taken a look out the windows, hadn't seen anything, checked that Chillingham was dead, then unlocked the door and summoned Hearn and Miss Tower.

When the coroner and the lab crew finally got there, and the doc had made his preliminary examination, I asked him about the wound. He confirmed my earlier guess—a small-caliber bullet, probably a .22 or .25. He couldn't be absolutely sure, of course, until he took out the slug at the post-mortem.

I talked things over with Sherrard and we both agreed that it was pretty much improbable for somebody with a .22 or .25 caliber weapon to have shot Chillingham from the roof of the nearest building; a small caliber like that just doesn't have a range of a hundred yards and the angle was almost too sharp. There was nowhere else the shot could have come from—except from inside the office. And that left us with George Dillon, whose story was obviously false and who just as obviously had killed the attorney while the two of them were locked inside this office.

You'd think it was pretty cut-and-dried then, wouldn't you? You'd think all we had to do was arrest Dillon and charge him with homicide, and our job was finished. Right?

Wrong.

Because we couldn't find the gun.

Remember, now, Dillon had been locked in that office—except for the minute or two it took Hearn to examine the body and slip out and relock the door—from the time Chillingham died until the time we came in. And both Hearn and Miss Tower swore that Dillon hadn't stepped outside the office during that minute or two. We'd already searched Dillon and he had nothing on him. We searched the office—I mean, we *searched* that office—and there was no gun there.

We sent officers over to the roof of the nearest building and down onto the landscaped lawn; they went over every square inch of ground and rooftop, and they didn't find anything. Dillon hadn't thrown the gun out the open windows then, and there was no place on the face of the sheer wall of the building where a gun could have been hidden.

So where was the murder weapon? What had Dillon done with it? Unless we found that out, we had no evidence against him that would stand up in a court of law; his word that he *hadn't* killed Chillingham, despite the circumstantial evidence of the locked room, was as good as money in the bank. It was up to us to prove him guilty, not up to him to prove himself innocent. You see the problem?

We took him into a large book-filled room that was part of the Chillingham suite—what Hearn called the "archives"—and sat him down in a chair and began to question him extensively. He was a big husky guy with blondish hair and these perfectly guileless eyes; he just sat there and looked at us and answered in a polite voice, maintaining right along that he hadn't killed the lawyer.

We made him tell his story of what had happened in the office a dozen times, and he explained it the same way each time—no variations. Chillingham had locked the door after they entered, and then they sat down and talked over some business. Pretty soon Chillingham complained that it was stuffy in the room, got up, and opened the French windows; the next thing Dillon knew, he said, the attorney collapsed with the bullet in him. He hadn't heard any shot, he said; Hearn must be mistaken about a muffled explosion.

I said finally, "All right, Dillon, suppose you tell us why you came to see Chillingham. What was this business you discussed?"

"He was my father's lawyer," Dillon said, "and the executor of my father's estate. He was also a thief. He stole three hundred and fifty thousand dollars of my father's money."

Sherrard and I stared at him. Jack said, "That gives you one hell of a motive for murder, if it's true."

"It's true," Dillon said flatly. "And yes, I suppose it does give me a strong motive for killing him. I admit I hated the man, I hated him passionately."

"You admit that, do you?"

"Why not? I have nothing to hide."

"What did you expect to gain by coming here to see Chillingham?" I asked. "Assuming you didn't come here to kill him."

"I wanted to tell him I knew what he'd done, and that I was going to expose him for the thief he was."

"You tell him that?"

"I was leading up to it when he was shot."

"Suppose you go into a little more detail about this alleged theft from your father's estate."

"All right." Dillon lit a cigarette. "My father was a hard-nosed businessman, a self-made type who acquired a considerable fortune in textiles; as far as he was concerned, all of life revolved around money. But I've never seen it that way; I've always been something of a free spirit and to hell with negotiable assets. Inevitably, my father and I had a falling-out about fifteen years ago, when I was twenty-three, and I left home with the idea of seeing some of the big wide world—which is exactly what I did.

"I traveled from one end of this country to the other, working at different jobs, and then I went to South America for a while. Some of the wanderlust finally began to wear off, and I decided to come back to this city and settle down—maybe even patch things up with my father. I arrived several days ago and learned then that he had been dead for more than two years."

"You had no contact with your father during the fifteen years you were drifting around?"

"None whatsoever. I told you, we had a falling-out. And we'd never been close to begin with."

Sherrard asked, "So what made you suspect Chillingham had stolen money from your father's estate?"

"I am the only surviving member of the Dillon family; there are no other relatives, not even a distant cousin. I knew my father wouldn't have left me a cent, not after all these years, and I didn't particularly care; but I *was* curious to find out to whom he had willed his estate."

"And what did you find out?"

"Well, I happen to know that my father had three favorite charities," Dillon said. "Before I left, he used to tell me that if I didn't 'shape-up,' as he put it, he would leave every cent of his money to those three institutions."

"He didn't, is that it?"

"Not exactly. According to the will, he left two hundred

thousand dollars to each of two of them—the Cancer Society and the Children's Hospital. He also, according to the will, left three hundred and fifty thousand dollars to the Association for Medical Research."

"All right," Sherrard said, "so what does that have to do with Chillingham?"

"Everything," Dillon told him. "My father died of a heart attack—he'd had a heart condition for many years. Not severe, but he fully expected to die as a result of it one day. And so he did. And because of this heart condition, his third favorite charity—the one he felt the most strongly about—was the Heart Fund."

"Go on," I said, frowning.

Dillon put out his cigarette and gave me a humorless smile. "I looked into the Association for Medical Research and I did quite a thorough bit of checking. It doesn't exist; there *isn't* any Association for Medical Research. And the only person who could have invented it is or was my father's lawyer and executor, Adam Chillingham."

Sherrard and I thought that over and came to the same conclusion. I said, "So even though you never got along with your father, and you don't care about money for yourself, you decided to expose Chillingham."

"That's right. My father worked hard all his life to build his fortune, and admirably enough, he decided to give it to charity at his death. I believe in worthwhile causes, I believe in the work being done by the Heart Fund, and it sent me into a rage to realize they had been cheated out of a substantial fortune which could have gone toward valuable research."

"A murderous rage?" Sherrard asked softly.

Dillon showed us his humorless smile again. "I didn't kill Adam Chillingham," he said. "But you'll have to admit, he deserved killing—and that the world is better off without the likes of him."

I might have admitted that to myself, if Dillon's accusations were valid, but I didn't admit it to Dillon. I'm a cop, and my job is to uphold the law; murder is murder, whatever the reasons for it, and it can't be gotten away with.

Sherrard and I hammered at Dillon a while longer, but we couldn't shake him at all. I left Jack to continue the field questioning and took a couple of men and re-searched Chillingham's private office. No gun. I went up onto the roof of the nearest building and searched that personally. No gun. I took my men down into the lawn area and supervised another minute search. No gun.

I went back to Chillingham's suite and talked to Charles Hearn and Miss Tower again, and they had nothing to add to what they'd already told us; Hearn was "almost positive" he had heard a muffled explosion inside the office, but from the legal point of view, that was the same as not having heard anything at all.

We took Dillon down to Headquarters finally, because we knew damned well he had killed Adam Chillingham, and advised him of his rights and printed him and booked him on suspicion. He asked for counsel, and we called a public defender for him, and then we grilled him again in earnest. It got us nowhere.

The F.B.I. and state check we ran on his fingerprints got us nowhere either; he wasn't wanted, he had never been arrested, he had never even been printed before. Unless something turned up soon in the way of evidence—specifically, the missing murder weapon—we knew we couldn't hold him very long.

The next day I received the lab report and the coroner's report and the ballistics report on the bullet taken from Chillingham's neck—.22 caliber, all right. The lab's and coroner's findings combined to tell me something I'd already guessed: the wound and the calculated angle of trajectory of the bullet did not entirely rule out the remote possibility that Chillingham had been shot from the roof of the nearest building. The ballistics report, however, told me something I hadn't guessed—something which surprised me a little.

The bullet had no rifling marks.

Sherrard blinked at this when I related the information to him.

"No rifling marks?" he said. "Hell, that means the slug wasn't fired from a gun at all, at least not a lawfully manufactured one. A homemade weapon, you think, Walt?"

"That's how it figures," I agreed. "A kind of zipgun probably. Anybody can make one; all you need is a length of tubing or the like and a bullet and a grip of some sort and a detonating cap."

"But there was no zipgun, either, in or around Chillingham's office. We'd have found it if there was."

I worried my lower lip meditatively. "Well, you can make one of those zips from a dozen or more small component parts, you know; even the tubing could be soft aluminum, the kind you can break apart with your hands. When you're done using it, you can knock it down again into its components. Dillon had enough time to have done that, before opening the locked door."

"Sure," Sherrard said. "But then what? We *still* didn't find anything—not a single thing—that could have been used as part of a homemade zip."

I suggested we go back and make another search, and so we drove once more to the Dawes Building. We re-combed Chillingham's private office—we'd had a police seal on it to make sure nothing could be disturbed—and we re-combed the surrounding area. We didn't find so much as an iron filing. Then we went to the city jail and had another talk with George Dillon.

When I told him our zipgun theory, I thought I saw a light flicker in his eyes; but it was the briefest of reactions, and I couldn't be sure. We told him it was highly unlikely a zipgun using a .22-caliber bullet could kill anybody from a distance of a hundred yards, and he said he couldn't help that, *he* didn't know anything about such a weapon. Further questioning got us nowhere.

And the following day we were forced to release him, with a warning not to leave the city.

But Sherrard and I continued to work doggedly on the case; it was one of those cases that preys on your mind constantly, keeps you from sleeping well at night, because you know there has to be an answer and you just can't figure out what it is. We ran checks into Chillingham's records and found that he had made some large private investments a year ago, right after the Dillon will had been probated. And as George Dillon had claimed, there was no Association for Medical Research; it was a dummy charity, apparently set up by Chillingham for the explicit purpose of stealing old man Dillon's $350,000. But there was no definite proof of this, not enough to have convicted Chillingham of theft in a court of law; he'd covered himself pretty neatly.

As an intelligent man, George Dillon had no doubt realized that a public exposure of Chillingham would have resulted in nothing more than adverse publicity and the slim possibility of disbarment—hardly sufficient punishment in Dillon's eyes. So he had decided on what to him was a morally justifiable homicide. From the law's point of view, however, it was nonetheless Murder One.

But the law still had no idea what he'd done with the weapon, and therefore, as in the case of Chillingham's theft, the law had no proof of guilt.

As I said, though, we had our teeth into this one and we weren't about to let go. So we paid another call on Dillon, this time at the hotel where he was staying, and asked him some questions about his background. There was nothing more immediate we could investigate, and we thought that maybe there was an angle in his past which would give us a clue toward solving the riddle.

He told us, readily enough, some of what he'd done during the fifteen years since he'd left home, and it was a typical drifter's life: lobster packer in Maine, ranch hand in Montana, oil worker in Texas, road construction in South America. But there was a gap of about four years which he sort of skimmed over without saying anything specific. I jumped on that and asked him some direct questions, but he wouldn't talk about it.

His reluctance made Sherrard and me more than a little curious; we both had that cop's feeling it was important, that maybe it was the key we needed to unlock the mystery. Unobtrusively we had the department photographer take some pictures of Dillon; then we sent them out, along with a request for information as to his whereabouts during the four blank years, to various law-enforcement agencies in Florida—where he'd admitted to being just prior to the gap, working as a deckhand on a Key West charter-fishing boat.

Time dragged on, and nothing turned up, and we were reluctantly forced by sheer volume of other work to abandon the Chillingham case; officially, it was now buried in the Unsolved File. Then, three months later, we had a wire from the Chief of Police of a town not far from Fort Lauderdale. It said they had tentatively identified George Dillon from the pictures we'd sent and were forwarding by airmail special delivery something which might conceivably prove the nature of Dillon's activities during at least part of the specified period.

Sherrard and I fidgeted around waiting for the special delivery to arrive, and when it finally came I happened to be the only one of us in the Squadroom. I tore the envelope open, and what was inside was a multicolored and well-aged poster, with a picture of a man who was undeniably George Dillon depicted on it. I looked at the picture and read what was written on the poster at least a dozen times.

It told me a lot of things all right, that poster did. It told me exactly what Dillon had done with the homemade zipgun he had used to kill Adam Chillingham—an answer that was at once fantastic and yet so simple you'd never even consider it. And it told me there wasn't a damned thing we could do about it now, that we couldn't touch him, that George Dillon actually had committed a perfect murder.

I was brooding over this when Jack Sherrard returned to the Squadroom. He said, "Why so glum, Walt?"

"The special delivery from Florida finally showed up," I said, and watched instant excitement animate his face. Then I saw some of it fade while I told him what I'd been brooding about, finishing with, "We simply can't arrest him now, Jack. There's no evidence, it doesn't exist any more; we can't prove a thing. And maybe it's just as well in one respect, since I kind of liked Dillon and would have hated to see him convicted for killing a crook like Chillingham. Anyway, we'll be able to sleep nights now."

"Damn it, Walt, will you tell me what you're talking about!"

"All right. Remember when we got the ballistics report and we talked over how easy it would be for Dillon to have made a zipgun? And how he could make the whole thing out of a dozen or so small component parts, so that afterward he could break it down again into those small parts?"

"Sure, sure. But I still don't care if Dillon used a hundred components, we didn't find a single one of them. Not one. So what, if that's part of the answer, did he do with them? There's not even a connecting bathroom where he could have flushed them down. What did he do with the damned zipgun?"

I sighed and slid the poster—the old carnival side-show poster—around on my desk so he could see Dillon's picture and read the words printed below it: STEAK AND POTATOES AND APPLE PIE IS OUR DISH; NUTS, BOLTS, PIECES OF WOOD, BITS OF METAL IS HIS! YOU HAVE TO SEE IT TO BELIEVE IT: THE AMAZING MR. GEORGE, THE MAN WITH THE CAST-IRON STOMACH.

Sherrard's head jerked up and he stared at me open-mouthed.

"That's right," I said wearily. "He *ate* it."

THE SIX SUSPECTS

by Isaac Asimov

Here is one of the most puzzling problems ever to challenge the collective wits of the Black Widowers Club, that eclectic (and often electric) secret society consisting of patent attorney Geoffrey Avalon, code expert Thomas Trumbull, writer Emmanuel Rubin, organic chemist James Drake, artist Mario Gonzalo, and mathematician Roger Halsted . . . and by the way, the author was on the cruise that witnessed, from off the Florida coast, the Apollo moon shot referred to in the story. Isaac Asimov has used the event and the cruise background brilliantly . . .

THE monthly banquet of the Black Widowers had reached the point where little was left of the mixed grill except an occasional sausage and a markedly untouched piece of liver on the plate of writer Emmanuel Rubin—and it was then that voices rose in Homeric combat.

Rubin, undoubtedly furious by the serving of liver at all, was saying, even more flatly than was usual for him, "Poetry is *sound.* You don't *look* at poetry. I don't care whether a culture emphasizes rhyme, alliteration, repetition, balance, or cadence, it all comes down to sound."

Roger Halsted, mathematician and composer of limericks, never raised his voice, but one could always tell the state of his emotions by the color of his high forehead. Right now it was a deep pink, the color extending past the line that had once marked hair. He said, "What's the use of making generalizations, Manny? No generalization can hold generally without an airtight system of axiomatics to begin with. Literature—"

"If you're going to tell me about figurative verse," said Rubin hotly, "save your breath. That was Victorian nonsense."

"What's figurative verse?" asked artist Mario Gonzalo. "Is he making that up, Jeff?" He added a touch to the tousled hair in his careful caricature of the banquet guest, Waldemar Long, who, since the dinner had begun, had eaten in somber silence, but was obviously following every word.

"No," said Geoffrey Avalon, the patent lawyer, "though I wouldn't put it past Manny to make something up if that were the only way he could win an argument. Figurative verse is verse in which the words or lines are arranged typographically in such a way as to produce a visual image that reinforces the sense. 'The Mouse's Tail' in *Alice in Wonderland* is perhaps the best-known example."

Halsted's soft voice was unequal to the free-for-all and he methodically beat his spoon against a water goblet till the decibels simmered down.

He said, "Let's be reasonable. The subject under discussion is not poetry in general, but the limerick as a verse form. My point is this—I'll repeat it, Manny—that the worth of a limerick is not dictated by its subject matter. It's a mistake to think that a limerick has to be dirty to be good. It's easier—"

James Drake, the organic chemist, stubbed out his cigarette, twitched his small grizzled mustache, and said in his hoarse voice, "Why do you call a dirty limerick dirty? The Supreme Court will get you for that."

Halsted said, "Because it's a two-syllable word with a meaning you all understand. What do you want me to say? Sexual-blasphemous-and-generally-irreverent?"

Avalon said, "Go on, Roger. Make your point and don't let them needle you." And from under his luxuriant eyebrows he frowned austerely at the others. "Let him talk."

"Why?" said Rubin. "He has nothing to— Okay, Jeff. Talk, Roger."

"Thank you all," said Halsted, in the wounded tone of one who has finally succeeded in having his wrongs recognized. "The worth of a limerick rests in the unpredictability of the last line and in the cleverness of the final rhyme. In fact, off-color content may seem to have value in itself and therefore require less cleverness—but it produces a less worthwhile limerick. Now it is possible to have the rhyme masked by the orthographical conventions."

"The what?" said Gonzalo.

"Spelling," said Avalon.

"And then," said Halsted, "in seeing the spelling and having that instant of delay in getting the sound, you intensify the enjoyment. But under those conditions you have to *see* the limerick. If you just recite it, the excellence is lost."

"Suppose you give us an example," said Drake.

"I know what he means," said Rubin. "He's going to rhyme M.A. and C.D.—Master of Arts and Caster of Darts."

"That's an example that's been used," admitted Halsted, "but it's extreme. It takes too long to catch on and amusement is drowned in irritation. As it happens, I've made up a limerick while we were having the argument—"

And now for the first time Thomas Trumbull, the code expert, entered the discussion. His tanned and wrinkled face twisted into a dark scowl and he said, "The hell you did. You made it up yesterday and you engineered this whole silly discussion just so you could recite it. If it's one of your *Iliad* limericks, I'll personally—"

"It's not the *Iliad*," said Halsted. "I haven't been working on that recently. It's no use my reciting this one, of course. I'll write it down and pass it around."

He wrote in large block letters on an unused napkin:

YOU CAN'T CALL THE
BRITISH QUEEN MS.
'TAIN'T AS NICE AS
ELIZABETH IS.
BUT I THINK
THAT THE QUEEN
WOULD BE EVEN LESS KEEN
TO HAVE HERSELF
MENTIONED AS LS.

Gonzalo laughed aloud when it came to him. He said, "Sure, if you know that MS is pronounced Miz, then you pronounce LS as Liz."

"To me," said Drake scornfully, "LS would have to stand for 'lanuscript' if it's going to rhyme with MS."

Avalon pursed his lips and shook his head. "Using 'TAIN'T is a flaw. You ought to lose a syllable some other way. And to be perfectly consistent, shouldn't the rhyme word IS be spelled simply S?"

Halsted nodded. "You're quite right, and I thought of doing that, but it wouldn't be transparent enough and the reader wouldn't get it fast enough to laugh. Secondly, it would be the cleverest part of the limerick and would make the LS anticlimactic."

"Do you really have to waste all that fancy reasoning on a piece of nonsense like this?" asked Trumbull.

"I think I've made my point," said Halsted. "That humor can be visual."

Trumbull said, "Well, then, let's drop the subject. Since I'm host this session, that's an order. —Henry, where's the dessert?"

"It's here, sir," said Henry softly. Unmoved by Trumbull's tone, the perennial waiter at the Black Widower banquets deftly cleared the table and dealt out the blueberry shortcake.

The coffee had already been poured and Trumbull's guest said in a low voice, "May I have tea, please?"

The guest had a long upper lip and a long chin. The hair on his head was shaggy but there was none on his face and he had walked with a somewhat bearlike stoop. When he was first introduced, only Rubin had registered any recognition.

Rubin had said, "Aren't you with NASA?"

Waldemar Long had answered with a startled "Yes" as though he had been disturbed out of a half-resentful resignation to anonymity. He had then frowned. He was frowning now again as Henry poured the tea, then melted unobtrusively into the background.

Trumbull said, "I think the time has come for our guest to enter the discussion and perhaps add some sense to what has been an unusually foolish evening so far."

"No, that's all right, Tom," said Long. "I don't mind frivolity." He had a deep and rather beautiful voice that had a definite note of sadness in it. He went on, "I have no aptitude for badinage myself, but I enjoy listening to it."

Halsted, still brooding over the limerick, said with sudden forcefulness, "I suggest Manny *not* be the grillmaster on this occasion."

"No?" said Rubin, his sparse beard lifting belligerently.

"No. I put it to you, Tom. If Manny questions our guest, he will surely bring up the space program since there's a NASA connection. Then we will go through the same argument we've had a hundred times. I'm sick of the whole subject of space and whether we ought or ought not to be on the moon."

"Not half as sick of it as I am," said Long, rather unexpectedly. "I'd just as soon not discuss any aspect of space exploration."

The heavy flatness of the remark seemed to dampen spirits all around. Even Halsted was momentarily at a loss for any other subject to introduce to someone connected with NASA.

Then Rubin stirred in his seat and said, "I take it, Dr. Long, that this is a recently developed attitude of yours."

Long's head turned suddenly toward Rubin. His eyes narrowed. "Why do you say that, Mr. Rubin?"

Rubin's small face came as close to a simper as it ever did. "Elementary, my dear Mr. Long. You were on the cruise that went down to see the Apollo shot last winter. I'd been invited as a literary representative, but I couldn't go. However, I got the promotional literature and noticed you were on the cruise. You were going to lecture on some aspect of the space program, I forget which. So your disenchantment with the subject of space must have arisen in the six months since the cruise."

Long nodded his head slightly a number of times and said, "I seem to be more heard of in that connection than in any other in my life. The damned cruise has made me famous, too."

"I'll go farther," said Rubin, "and suggest that something happened *on* the cruise that disenchanted you with space exploration, maybe to the point where you're thinking of leaving NASA and going into some other field of work altogether."

Long's stare was fixed now. He pointed a finger at Rubin—a long finger that showed no sign of a tremor—and said, "Don't play games." Then, with controlled anger, he rose from his chair and said, "I'm sorry, Tom. Thanks for the meal, but I'll go now."

Everyone rose at once, speaking simultaneously—all but Rubin, who remained sitting with a look of stunned astonishment on his face.

Trumbull's voice rose above the rest. "Now wait a while, Waldemar. Damn it, will all of you sit down? Waldemar, you too. What's the excitement about? Rubin, what *is* all this?"

Rubin looked down at his empty coffee cup and lifted it as though he wished there were coffee in it so that he could delay replying by taking a sip. "I was just making like Sherlock Holmes, simply demonstrating a chain of logic. After all, I write mysteries, you know. But I seem to have touched a nerve." Then gratefully, he said, "Thanks, Henry," as the cup before him sparkled black to the brim.

"What chain of logic?" demanded Trumbull.

"Okay, here it is. Dr. Long said, 'The damned cruise has made me famous, too.' He said 'too' and emphasized the word. That means it did something else for him and since we were talking about his distaste for the whole subject of space exploration, I deduced that the something else was to supply him with that distaste. From his attitude I guessed it was sharp enough to make him want to quit his job. That's all there is to it. As I said, elementary."

Long nodded his head again, in precisely the same slight and rapid way as before, then settled back in his seat. "All right. I'm sorry, Mr. Rubin. I jumped too soon. The fact is I *will* be leaving NASA. To all intents and purposes I *have* left it—and at the point of a shoe. That's all. —We'll change the subject. Tom, you said coming here would get me out of my dumps, but it hasn't worked that way. Rather, my mood has infected you all and I've cast a damper on the party. Forgive me, all of you."

Avalon put a finger to his neat, graying mustache and stroked it gently. He said, "Actually, sir, you have given us something we like above all things—the opportunity to indulge our curiosity. May we question you on this matter?"

"It's not something I'm free to talk about," said Long guardedly.

Trumbull said, "You needn't mention sensitive details and as far as anything else is concerned, everything said in this room is confidential. And, as I always add when I find it necessary to make that statement, the confidentiality includes our esteemed friend, Henry."

Henry, who was standing at the sideboard, smiled briefly.

Long hesitated. Then he said, "Actually, your curiosity is easily satisfied and I guess that Mr. Rubin, at least, with his aptitude for deduction, has already filled in the details. I'm suspected of having been indiscreet, either deliberately or carelessly, and, either way, I may find myself unofficially, but very effectively, blocked from any future position in my field of competence."

"You mean you'll be blackballed?" said Drake.

"That's a word," said Long, "that's never used. But that's what it will amount to."

"I take it," said Drake, "you were not indiscreet."

"On the contrary, I was." Long shook his head. "I haven't denied that. The trouble is they think the story is worse than I admit."

There was another pause and then Avalon, speaking in his most impressively austere tone, said, "Well, sir, *what* story?"

Long passed a hand over his face, then pushed his chair away from the table so that he could lean his head back against the wall.

He said, "It's really so undramatic. I was on this cruise, as Mr. Rubin told you. I was going to give a talk on certain space projects, rather far-out ones, and planned on explaining exactly what was being done in certain fascinating directions. I can't give you *those* details. I found that out the hard way. Some of the stuff had been classified, but I had been told I could talk about it. Then, on the day before I was to give my lecture, I got a radiophone call saying it was all off. There was to be no declassification.

"I was furious. There's no use denying I have a temper and I also have very little gift for extemporaneous or impromptu lecturing. I had carefully written out my talk and had intended to read it. I know that's not a good way of giving a lecture, but it's the best I can do. Now I had nothing left to give to a group of people who had paid considerable money to listen to me. It was a most embarrassing position."

"What did you do?" asked Avalon.

Long shook his head. "I held a rather pathetic question-and-answer session the next day. It didn't go over at all well. It was even worse than just not giving a speech at all. By that time, you see, I knew I was in considerable trouble."

"In what way?" said Avalon.

"If you want the story," said Long, "here it is. I'm not exactly talkative at meals, as you perhaps have noticed, but when I went in to dinner after getting the call, I suppose I put on a passable imitation of a corpse that had died with an angry look on its face. The rest tried to draw me into the conversation if only, I suppose, to keep me from poisoning the atmosphere. Finally one of them said, 'Well, Dr. Long, what will you be talking about tomorrow?' And I blew up and said, 'Nothing! Nothing at all! I've got the paper all written out and it's sitting there on the desk in my cabin and I can't give it because I just found out the material is still classified.' "

"And then the paper was stolen?" said Gonzalo.

"No. Why steal anything these days? It was photographed."

"Are you sure?"

"I was almost sure at the time. When I got back to my cabin after dinner the door was not locked and the papers had been moved. Since then it's become certain. We have proof that the information has leaked."

There was a rather depressed silence at that. Then Trumbull said, "Who could have done it? Who heard you?"

"Everyone at the table," said Long despondently.

Rubin said, "You have a voice that carries, Dr. Long, and if you were as angry as I think you were, you spoke forcefully. Probably a number of people at adjoining tables heard you."

"No," said Long, shaking his head. "I spoke through clenched teeth, not loudly. Besides, you don't realize what the cruise was like. The cruise was badly undersubscribed, you see—poor promotion, mostly. It was carrying only forty percent capacity and the shipping company is supposed to have lost a packet."

"In that case," said Avalon, "it must have been a dreary experience apart from your misadventure."

"On the contrary, up to that point it was very pleasant for me, and it continued to be very pleasant for all the rest, I imagine. The crew nearly outnumbered the passengers, so the service was excellent. All the facilities were available without crowding. They scattered us through the dining room and gave us privacy. There were seven of us at our dining table. Lucky seven, someone said at the beginning." For a moment Long's look of grimness deepened. "None of the tables near us was occupied. I'm quite certain that nothing any of us said was heard anywhere but at our own table."

"Then there are seven suspects," said Gonzalo thoughtfully.

"Six, since you needn't count me," said Long. "I knew where the paper was and what it contained."

"You're under suspicion, too. Or you implied that," said Gonzalo.

"Not to myself," said Long.

Trumbull said peevishly, "I wish you'd come to me with this, Waldemar. I've been worrying over your obviously anxious attitude for months."

"What would you have done if I had told you?"

Trumbull considered. "Damn it, I'd have brought you here. —All right. Tell us about the six other people at the table. Who were they?"

"One was the ship's doctor—a good-looking Dutchman in an impressive uniform."

Rubin said, "He would be. The ship was one of the Holland-American liners, wasn't it?"

"Yes. The officers were Dutch and the crew—the waiters, stewards, and so on—were mostly Indonesian. They'd all had three-month cram courses in English, but we communicated mostly in sign language. I can't complain, though—they were pleasant and hard-working and all the more efficient since there were considerably less than the usual number of passengers."

"Any reason to suspect the doctor?" asked Drake.

Long nodded. "I suspected them all. The doctor was a silent man; he and I were the two silent ones. The other five made continuous conversation, much as you do here at this table. The doctor and I listened. What I've brooded about in connection with him was that it was he who asked me about my talk. Asking a personal question like that was not characteristic."

"He may have been worried about you medically," said Halsted. "He may have been trying to draw you out."

"Maybe," said Long. "I remember every detail of that dinner; I've gone over and over it in my mind. It was an ethnic dinner, so everyone was supplied with little Dutch hats made out of paper and special Indonesian dishes were served. I wore the hat but I hate curried food and the doctor asked about my speech just as a small dish of curried something-or-other was put before me as an appetizer. Between fuming over official stupidity and sickening over the smell of curry, I just burst out. If it hadn't been for the curry, perhaps—

"Anyway, after dinner I discovered that someone had been in my cabin. The contents of the paper weren't so important, classification or not, but what was important was that someone had taken action so quickly. Someone on the ship was part of a spy network and that was more important than the actual coup. Even if the present item were not important, the next one might be. It was vital to report the matter and, as a loyal citizen, I did."

Rubin said, "Isn't the doctor the logical suspect? He asked the question and he would be listening to the answer. The others might not have been listening. As an officer, he would be familiar with the ship, know how to get to your cabin quickly, perhaps even have a duplicate key. Did he have an opportunity to go to your cabin before you did?"

"Yes, he did," said Long. "I thought of all that. The trouble is this. Everyone at the table heard me, because all the rest talked about the system of classification for a while. I kept quiet myself but I remember the matter of the Pentagon Papers came up. And everyone knew where my cabin was because I had given a small party in it for the table the day before. And those locks are easy to open for anyone with a little skill at it—though it was a mistake for the spy not to lock the door again on leaving; but whoever it was had to be in a hurry. And as it happened, everyone at the table had a chance to get to my cabin during the course of the meal."

"Who were the others, then?" asked Halsted.

"Two married couples and a single woman. The single woman —call her Miss Robinson—was pretty, a little on the plump side, had a pleasant sense of humor, but had the bad habit of smoking during meals. I rather think she took a fancy to the doctor. She sat between us—we always had the same seats."

"When did she have a chance to visit your cabin?" asked Halsted.

"She left shortly after I made my remark. I was brooding too deeply to be aware of it at the time but of course I remembered it afterward. She came back before the fuss over the hot chocolate came up because I remember her trying to help."

"Where did she say she went?"

"Nobody asked her at the time. She was asked afterward and she said she had gone to her cabin to go to the bathroom. Maybe she did. But her cabin was close to mine."

"No one saw her at all?"

"No one would. Everyone was in the dining room and to the Indonesians, all Americans look alike."

Avalon said, "What's the fuss over the hot chocolate you referred to?"

Long said, "That's where one of the married couples comes in. Call them the Smiths and the other couple the Joneses. Mr. Smith was the raucous type. He reminded me, in fact, of—"

"Oh, Lord," said Rubin. "Don't say it."

"All right, I won't. He was one of the lecturers—in fact, both Smith and Jones were. Smith talked fast, laughed easily, turned almost everything into a double entendre, and seemed to enjoy it all so much he had the rest of us doing it, too. He was a very odd person—the kind of fellow you can't help but take an instant dislike to and judge to be stupid. But then, as you got used to him, you found that you liked him after all and that under all his surface foolishness he was extremely intelligent. The first evening, I remember, the doctor kept staring at him as if he were a specimen, but by the end of the cruise the doctor had come to like and respect him.

"Jones was much quieter. He seemed horrified at first by Smith's outrageous comments but eventually he was matching him, I noticed—rather, I think, to Smith's discomfiture."

Avalon asked, "What were their fields?"

"Smith was a sociologist and Jones a biologist. The idea was that space exploration should be viewed from the light of many disciplines. It was a good concept but there were serious flaws in the execution. Some of the talks, though, were excellent. There was one on Mariner 9 and the new data on Mars that was superb, but that's beside the point.

"It was Mrs. Smith who created the fuss. She was a moderately tall thin girl. Not very good-looking by the usual standards but with an extraordinarily attractive personality. She was soft-spoken and clearly went through life automatically thinking of others. I believe everyone quickly grew to feel quite affectionate to her and Smith himself seemed devoted. The evening I shot my mouth off, she ordered hot chocolate. It came in a tall glass, very top-heavy and, of course, as a mistaken touch of elegance, it was brought on a tray.

"Smith, as usual, was talking animatedly and waving his arms as he did so. He used all his muscles when he talked. The ship swayed, he swayed—well, anyway, the hot chocolate went into Mrs. Smith's lap.

"She jumped up. So did everyone else. Miss Robinson moved

quickly toward her to help. I noticed that and that's how I know she was back by then. Mrs. Smith waved help away and left in a hurry. Smith, looking suddenly confused and upset, tore off the paper Dutch hat he was wearing and followed.

"Five minutes later he was back, talking earnestly to the head steward. Then he came to the table and said that Mrs. Smith had sent him down to assure the steward she was wearing nothing that couldn't be washed, she hadn't been hurt, that it wasn't anyone's fault, and that no one should be blamed.

"He wanted to assure us she was all right, too. He asked if we could stay at the table till his wife came back. She was changing clothes and wanted to join us again so that none of us would feel as though anything very terrible had happened. We agreed, of course. None of us was going anywhere."

Avalon said, "And that means Mrs. Smith had time to go to your cabin."

Long nodded. "Yes. She didn't seem the type, but I suppose in this game you have to disregard surface appearances."

"And you all waited?"

"Not the doctor. He got up and said he would get some ointment from his office in case she needed it for burns, but he came back before she did by a minute or so."

Avalon said, tapping his finger on the table slowly to lend emphasis, "And he, too, might have gone into your cabin. And Miss Robinson might have when she left before the hot-chocolate incident."

Rubin said, "Where do the Joneses come in?"

Long said, "Let me go on. When Mrs. Smith came back she denied having been burned and the doctor had no need to give her the ointment, so we can't say if he even went to get it. He might have been bluffing."

"What if she had asked for it?" said Halsted.

"Then he might have said he couldn't find what he had been looking for but if she came with him he'd do what he could. Who knows? In any case, we all sat for a while as though nothing unusual had happened and then, finally, we broke up. By that time ours was the last occupied table. Everyone left, with Mrs. Jones and myself lingering behind for a while."

"Mrs. Jones?" asked Drake.

"I haven't told you about Mrs. Jones. Dark hair and eyes, very vivacious. Had a penchant for sharp cheeses, always taking a bit of each off the tray when it was brought round. She had a way of looking at you when you talked that had you convinced you were the only other person in the world. I think Jones was rather a jealous type in his quiet way. At least, I never saw him more than two feet from her, except this one time. He got up and said he was going to their cabin and she said she would join him soon. Then she turned to me and said, 'Can you explain why those terraced icefields on Mars are significant? I've been meaning to ask you all during dinner and didn't get a chance.'

"It had been that day that we'd had the magnificent talk on Mars and I was rather flattered that she turned to me instead of to the astronomer who had given the talk. It seemed as though she were taking it for granted I knew as much as he did. So I talked to her for a while and she kept saying, 'How interesting.' "

Avalon said, "And meanwhile Jones could have been in your cabin."

"Could be. I thought of that afterward. It was certainly atypical behavior on both their parts."

Avalon said, "Let's summarize, then. There are four possibilities. Miss Robinson might have done it when she left before the hot-chocolate incident. The Smiths might have done it as a team after deliberately spilling the hot chocolate. Or the doctor could have done it while supposedly going for the ointment. Or the Joneses could have also done it as a team, with Jones doing the dirty work while Mrs. Jones kept Dr. Long out of action."

Long nodded. "All this was considered and by the time the ship was back in New York, security agents had begun the process of checking the backgrounds of all six. You see, in cases like this, suspicion is all you need. The only way any secret agent can remain undetected is for him or her to remain unsuspected. Once the eye of counterintelligence is on him, he must inevitably be unmasked. No cover can survive an investigation in depth."

Drake said, "Then which one did it prove to be?"

Long sighed. "That's where the trouble arose. None of them. All were clean. There was no way, I understand, of showing any one of them to be anything other than what they seemed."

Rubin said, "Why do you say you 'understand.' Aren't you part of the investigation?"

"At the wrong end. The clearer those six are, the guiltier I appear to be. I told the investigators—I *had* to tell them—that those six are the only ones who could possibly have done it, and if none of them did, they must suspect me of making up a story to hide something worse."

Trumbull said, "Oh, hell, Waldemar. They can't think that. What would you have to gain by reporting the incident if you were responsible?"

"That's what they don't know," said Long. "But the information did leak and if they can't pin it on any of the six, then they're going to pin it on me. And the more my motives puzzle them, the more they think those motives must be very disturbing and important. So I'm in trouble."

Rubin said, "Are you sure those six are really the only possibilities? Are you sure you really didn't mention it to anyone else?"

"Quite sure," said Long dryly.

"You might not remember having done so," said Rubin. "It could have been something very casual. Can you be *sure* you didn't?"

"I can be sure I didn't. The radiophone call came only a few minutes before dinner. There just wasn't time to tell anyone before dinner. And once I got away from the table, I was back in my cabin before I said anything to anybody."

"Who heard you on the phone? Maybe there were eavesdroppers."

"There were ship's officers standing around certainly. However, my boss expressed himself Aesopically. I knew what he meant, but no one else would have understood."

"Did you express *your*self Aesopically?" asked Halsted.

"I'll tell you exactly what I said: 'Hello, Dave.' Then I said, 'Damn it to hell.' Then I hung up. I said those six words. No more."

Gonzalo brought his hands together in a sudden, enthusiastic clap. "Listen, I've been thinking. Why does the job have to be so planned? It could have been spontaneous. After all, everybody knows there's this cruise and people connected with NASA are going to talk and there might be something informative going on. Someone—it could have been anyone—kept searching various rooms during the dinner hour each day and finally came across your paper—"

"No," said Long sharply. "It passes the bounds of plausibility to suppose that someone, by the merest chance, would find my paper just in the hour or two after I had announced that a classified lecture was sitting on my desk. Besides, there was nothing in the paper that would have given any indication of importance to the non-expert. It was only my own remark that would have told anyone it was there and that it was important."

Avalon said thoughtfully, "Suppose one of the people at the table passed on the information, in perfect innocence? In the interval they were away from the table, they might have said to someone, 'Did you hear about poor Dr. Long? His paper was shot out from under him.' Then that someone, anyone, could have done the job."

Long shook his head. "I wish that could be so, but it can't. That would only happen if the particular individual at my table was innocent. If the Smiths were innocent when they left the table, the only thing on their mind would be the hot chocolate. They wouldn't stop to chat. The doctor, if innocent, would be thinking only of getting the ointment. By the time Jones left the table, assuming he was innocent, he would have forgotten about the matter; if anything, he would talk about the hot chocolate, too."

Rubin nodded. "All right. But what about Miss Robinson? She left before the hot-chocolate incident. The only interesting thing in her mind would have been your dilemma. She might have said something."

"Might she?" said Long. "If she is innocent, then she was really doing what she said she was doing—going to the bathroom in her cabin. If she had to desert the dinner table to do so, there would have had to be urgency; and no one under those conditions stops for idle chatter."

There was silence around the table.

Long said, "I'm sure investigation will continue and eventually the truth will come out and it will be clear that I'm guilty of no more than an unlucky indiscretion. By then, however, my career will be down the drain."

"Dr. Long?" said a soft voice. "May I ask a question?"

Long looked up, surprised. "A question?"

"I'm Henry, sir. The gentlemen of the Black Widowers Club occasionally allow me to participate—"

"We sure do, Henry," said Trumbull. "Do you see something the rest of us don't?"

"I'm not certain," said Henry. "I see quite plainly that Dr. Long believes only the six others at the table could possibly be involved, and those investigating the matter apparently agree with him—"

"There's no one else," said Long.

"Well, then," said Henry, "I am wondering if Dr. Long mentioned his views on curry to the investigators."

Long said, "You mean that I didn't like curry?"

"Yes," said Henry. "Did that come up?"

Long spread his hands and then shook his head. "No, I don't think it did. Why should it? It's irrelevant. It's just an additional excuse for my talking like a jackass. I told it to you here in order to get some sympathy, I suppose, but it certainly would mean nothing to the investigators."

Henry remained silent for a moment, and Trumbull said, "Does the curry have meaning to you, Henry?"

"I think it does," said Henry. "I think we are in rather the position Mr. Halsted described earlier in the evening in connection with limericks. Some limericks to be effective must be *seen;* sound is not enough. And some scenes to be effective must be seen."

"I don't get that," said Long.

"Well, Dr. Long," said Henry. "You sat there in the ship's restaurant at a table with six other people and therefore only those six other people heard you. But if we could *see* the scene instead of having you describe it to us, wouldn't we see something that you have omitted?"

"No, you wouldn't," said Long doggedly.

"Are you sure?" asked Henry. "You sit here with six other people at a table, too, just as you did on the ship. How many people have heard your story?"

"Six—" began Long.

And then Gonzalo broke in, "No, seven, counting you, Henry."

"And was there no one serving you at the table, Dr. Long? You said the doctor had asked you about the speech just as a curried dish was put before you and it was the smell of curry that annoyed you to the point where you burst out with your indiscretion. Surely, the curry didn't place itself before you of its own accord. The fact is that at the moment you made your statement, there were six people sitting at the table, and a seventh standing just behind you and out of sight."

"The waiter," said Long in a whisper.

Henry said, "There's a tendency never to notice a waiter unless he annoys you. An efficient waiter is invisible, and you mentioned the excellence of the service. Might it not have been the waiter who carefully engineered the spilling of the hot chocolate to create a diversion, or perhaps took advantage of the diversion, if it were an accident. With waiters many and diners few, it might not be too noticeable if he disappeared for a while. Or he could claim to have gone to the men's room if it were noticed. He would know the location of the cabin as well as the doctor did, and be as likely to have some sort of picklock."

Long said, "But he was an Indonesian. He couldn't speak English."

"Are you sure? He'd had a three-month cram course, you said. And he might have known English better than he pretended. You would be willing to suspect that Mrs. Smith was not as sweet and thoughtful underneath as she was on the surface, and that Mrs. Jones's vivacity was a pretense, and the doctor's respectability, and Smith's liveliness and Jones's devotion and Miss Robinson's need to go to the bathroom. Might not the waiter's ignorance of English also have been a pretense?"

"By God," said Long, looking at his watch, "if it weren't so late I'd call Washington now."

Trumbull said, "If you know some home phone numbers, *do* call now. Your career is at stake. Tell them the waiter ought to be investigated, and for heaven's sake don't tell them you got the notion from someone else."

"You mean, tell them I just thought of it? They'll ask why I didn't think of it before."

"Ask them why *they* didn't. Why didn't *they* think a waiter goes with a table in a dining room?"

Henry said softly, "No reason for anyone to think of it. Only very few are as interested in waiters as I am."

GREEN INK

by William Miller

Voted the best "miniature" of the year . . .

SEBASTIAN SAMPSON liked his name. It was strong and solid. It sounded impressive when spoken and looked positively formidable when written, especially if he made large sweeping S's, or underscored the signature with bold strokes, or tailed it off with a string of exclamation points.

Sebastian Sampson liked his name because he liked himself. And why shouldn't he? At fifty-five he looked upon himself as a splendid example of the self-made man—a little paunchy, perhaps, but well dressed in a conservative style, as befitted the president of the Merchants City Bank.

He took great pride in having reached the top of his profession.

"After all," he once told his first vice-president, "it's not every man who starts as a teller and ends up as president. I've trodden on a few toes to get here, but now I'm here and here I stay."

He ended his brief boastful confession with another extravagant Sampsonian signature on *The Wall Street Journal.*

That evening, as he waited at the station for the commuter train, Sampson felt especially pleased with himself. He had just directed the bank into another lucrative investment that would pay handsome dividends and further consolidate his standing with the stockholders.

Perhaps he should celebrate by going to the theater, he thought, as his eyes rested on a theater poster. It was a brilliant poster with dancing figures.

And then Sampson felt that irresistible urge again—the urge to write his name. To write his name outdoors would be the crowning touch to another successful day.

Sampson glanced to right and left. The other commuters stood with heads buried in their newspapers. Sampson flipped out his pen and in a flourishing hand wrote his signature on the top white margin of the poster. The next moment the train arrived at the station and the buoyant Sampson jostled his way to a seat by the window.

He pressed his face close to the glass, smirking as his eye fastened on the black-inked signature that shrank as the train pulled away from the station.

The following evening Sampson went back to the poster to take a little sly satisfaction in gazing on his handiwork. His smile faded into a look of stunned disbelief.

Beneath his signature someone had added in bright green ink the words: *is an idiot.*

Sampson glowered at the impudent postscript. Who the . . . ?

His mental splutterings were cut short by the arrival of his train.

The next evening Sampson almost tripped in his haste to inspect the poster. A second green-ink comment greeted him.

His brow furrowed in anger as he read the full inscription: *Sebastian Sampson is an idiot and a pompous oaf.*

Snatching out his pen, Sampson fired back with: *And you are a childish scribbler.*

Obsessed now with the exchanges on the poster, Sampson rushed back the next day to find that Green Ink had replied: *Anyone who goes around writing his own name on posters must be a megalomaniac.*

Sampson boiled as he wrote: *At least I'm not a coward. Identify yourself and I'll punch you in the nose.*

When Sampson got back to the poster the next evening he found his challenge accepted.

You're on, Green Ink had replied. *The address is 1873 East 110th Street. Third floor. Second door on the right. Be there at nine tonight.*

The next day the newspapers carried the following story:

"Veteran police officers were scratching their heads today over the antics of a city banker who met his death last night in an abandoned tenement at 1873 E. 110th St.

"Dead is 55-year-old Sebastian Sampson, president of the Merchants City Bank, who, according to a passer-by, ran into the building shortly before nine o'clock last night.

"From a police reconstruction of the incident, it appears the bank president raced up the stairs to the third floor, entered an apartment door, and fell three stories to his death.

"Puzzled police said they have no clue to explain why the banker was in a building already in the process of being demolished in a city wrecking project."

Three mornings later, on the day Sebastian Sampson was to be buried, the man sitting at Sampson's desk said, "How thoughtless of me—I forgot to send a condolence card."

And the first vice-president, who was now the president of the Merchants City Bank, refilled his pen with green ink.

IN THE SECRET HOLLOW

by Florence V. Mayberry

Readers of Ellery Queen's Mystery Magazine *do not have to be reminded that Florence V. Mayberry is a gifted writer. Every one of her stories bears her individual stamp, and it is hard to believe that any of them could have been written by someone else (which is perhaps the ultimate test). In this story she reaches a new height—at least, a different height—a quality of sheer eeriness and horror unmatched in her previous work . . . "a queer prickly nervousness crawling over my skin" . . .*

I CAN'T seem to remember the name of that London theater. Not even that night I went there. It was the one where

The Mousetrap by Agatha Christie played so long, maybe it's still playing; maybe when the world is ended, and all the people are gone, it will still be playing. No, that won't work. I mean, the play will need people in it, scared mousy people to be the mice. That's what a mousetrap is for. Mice.

I love London. Even before Tommy took me to see it six years ago, so we could be married in his favorite city, I loved it as much as he did. Those stories about Sherlock Holmes, I began reading them when I was eight or nine and I was never sure whether it was Holmes and Dr. Watson or just London that I loved. Later all those other stories with London as the background, including some Tommy wrote himself—he writes beautiful, scary mystery stories, and some of them sell. Anyway, I love London. It's such a lovely place to read about, with sinister figures skulking through yellow fog, bobbies thudding out of mists, Fagins and Oliver Twists all over the place.

The night I went to see *The Mousetrap* there wasn't any fog. Just a clear chilly night. Still, it had its own special feel, that night, one you could touch, fondle, possess. Like a soft old shoe made of finest leather and handsewn. But down in its toe was a secret doorway, an Alice in Wonderland doorway; and when its key was found and the doorway opened, mystery was waiting.

It was a game to play, searching for that secret doorway. Touch and fondle London, and perhaps the key would fall into my hand. Then I would find Tommy. He was hiding in London. I knew it. Playing his own game—he loves games, he was the one who taught me to play games. Like the night back in San Francisco when we played hide-and-seek. Only, poor Tommy, he never came to find me.

It was too sad to think about San Francisco. So I stopped. Pretended it went away, who knows where, anywhere, and nothing was real except the two days I had been in London looking for Tommy. Would he be around this corner, or that?

Inside this store, or another? At Buckingham Palace or Madame Tussaud's? Or on one of those red double-decker buses?

That's it! That's what he'd like, I said to myself. Don't take a taxi to the theater, take a bus with lots of people for him to hide behind. I asked the hotel doorman what bus went near the theater, then ran up the street and caught it.

Tommy wasn't on the bus. I looked everywhere, and he wasn't anywhere. A woman with a little pinched face and a big hat with daisies on it looked lonely, so I sat beside her. "I wish Tommy *had* been here," I said to her. "But it doesn't hurt to wish, does it, even if it doesn't come true? It's fun while you're wishing, isn't it?"

She stared a moment, then asked softly, "Do you wish, too? That's a comfort. To know there are others." Then she ducked her face into her coat collar, jumped up, and scurried off the bus like a little mouse. I wished she had stayed, to help me find Tommy. But probably she was already looking for someone else.

The man walking around the crowded square near where I got off the bus, with a tray hanging from his neck, was looking for people, too. To buy the little toy dogs he had on the tray. He set one of them on the pavement for me, and the darling thing walked. So I bought it and gave it back to him so it wouldn't be lonely without the others. "I wish you'd help me, I'm lost," I told him. "I don't see *The Mousetrap* anywhere."

"Mousetrap? Not here, lydy, it's only dogs I've got. And no shops nearby for mousetraps." He cocked his head and grinned. "By the look of you, it's Harrods you'll want. Likely they'll have a gold one set with jools for you."

"Not a real mousetrap. It's a play called *The Mousetrap.* A mystery play. Even the theater's a mystery, because I can't find it."

"Well, you've found Old Jim," he said. "It's wonderful the w'y everyone in trouble finds me. Something tells them, go look up Old Jim, he's been in trouble himself so he'll know how to set you right. Follow me, dearie. No time at all you'll be sitting there at your play with chills up your back."

We marched like a parade around the square, Old Jim asking right and left, "*The Mousetrap*, lads, where's *The Mousetrap*?"

He stopped before a tall elegant woman with pale hair. "Begging your pardon, ma'am, but this little lydy's looking for *The Mousetrap*. Not to catch mice, mind you, it's a pl'y in a theater we can't find. Would you be going there yourself? Show her the w'y?" Apologetically he added, "She's American, y'know. Don't know her w'y about."

The blonde woman smiled. "Neither do I. I'm a stranger too, Swedish. And I'm visiting my daughter in the country, we're just in for the evening. But perhaps all of us together can find the theater for you."

She took my hand, and hers was warm and cozy. "Your hand is so cold," she said. "And your wrap—it's beautiful, but are you sure it is sufficiently warm for London nights? Oh, please, sir—" She stopped a tall man, young and handsome. "One moment, please, will you help this American lady find the theater where *The Mousetrap* is playing?"

But I had already dropped her hand and gone to him. Put my hands on his shoulders, stood on tiptoe, kissed his chin. "Hello, Tommy," I said.

He stepped back quickly. I stumbled forward, my hands grasping at his lapels. "Sorry," he said. "Awf'ly sorry. Some mistake. I mean—well, really—" And he darted away.

"What will I do?" I asked the Swedish lady. "It wasn't Tom again. For two days, ever since I've been in London, some of them look like Tommy. Then they always turn out not to be."

"Poor dear. You've lost someone?" She patted my hand, put her arm around my shoulders. "Are you certain you're warm enough? Perhaps you could change your ticket, come another night with a warmer wrap."

"For a minute he looked like Tom. With the hat covering his

hair. Tommy's hair shines, it's golden red. No, I have to go to the theater, Tommy may be there. He writes mysteries, you know, so he's sure to go to Agatha Christie's play."

"Then we must find it." Old Jim was gone, back in the crowd again. She spoke to the young couple beside her, the girl as blonde and tall as herself. "We must find a theater for this American lady."

"Perhaps I can find a cabbie, he'll take me to the theater."

But there wasn't a cabbie in sight, only people milling about. The young couple grew restless, impatient, whispering to each other. "Don't worry, I'll find *The Mousetrap*," I told my Swedish friend. "Someone will know."

"I will worry."

"Please don't. I found you, didn't I? I'll find someone else."

"That's the difficulty. And he may not be your Tommy. I really wish I could stay with you." She leaned forward and kissed me lightly. "Take care, little one. Do you know your eyes are the color of the North Sea? Not cold, but that same deep molten gray. Not cold, dear, beautiful."

Tommy liked my eyes, too. When we first met he said they were like shadows with the sun hiding behind them. Later, after we were married, he said no, not shadows, they held too much movement for shadows. Their gray was always changing, shifting color, scurrying about like millions of little gray mice running to hide, only they couldn't get away. That's when he stopped calling me Virginia. Called me Mousie. His darling Mousie.

The Swedish lady left with the young couple and I turned down a narrow street looking for *The Mousetrap*.

I passed a restaurant, dim lights shining through murky windows outlining its sign *HAMBURGERS*. It was delightful, it made me laugh to find an American lunch counter in this tucked-away fragment of London. Then I remembered I was hungry, I hadn't eaten since breakfast, walking and searching all day. I turned back and went in.

Inside it wasn't American, it was London. Absolutely lovely.

Two men in splotched white aprons talking in cockney accents, one at the counter, the other cooking. Talking to each other, because I was the only customer.

The hamburger was so un-American, so charred and dry, I had to laugh again. After that I couldn't stop. Laughed and laughed while the two men looked at me kind and careless. Finally the counterman said, "A cuppa tea will help that," and set one before me. Good tea, hot and strong. It stopped the laughing and I was glad, because my insides were beginning to hurt.

"Do you know where *The Mousetrap* is playing?" I asked.

" 'Ow's that? Mousetrap? Pl'ying? Oh, you mean the pl'y no one's to tell the end of. Not far, lydy. Across the street, down a bit past a posh restaurant. Keep on, look to your right, and there it is. Never went to the pl'y myself but I heard you're not to tell the end of it afterwards, takes away the fun for others coming later."

"Maybe there isn't an end, that's why they can't tell it," I said. "Maybe it just keeps on and on, with no end, and that's the secret nobody's to tell, that it never stops, that's why it's been running all those years. It would be a good joke, don't you think? Have you seen my Tom? He loves hamburgers, he'd be sure to come in if he passed by."

The counterman's face remained kind, but it tightened. As though he had put a drawstring around it, pulled it a bit, and was ready to pull more. He looked at the cook. "You see Tom?"

" 'Ow's that? Tom who?"

"Tom Riordan. My husband. He's not in Los Angeles, or Madrid, or Paris. I looked in all those places. So he's certain to be here. We were married in London, you know, I should have looked here first. But there was that trip we'd planned. Madrid, then Paris, then London. Los Angeles first, because he'd sold a story to television there. But I didn't find him, so he's in London. And he's sure to go see *The Mousetrap*—he writes mystery stories, you know."

"I'd never run out on a girl who looked like you," the cook said. "Maybe he's 'urt someplace. Where did you last see him?"

"In his coffin. Back in San Francisco, where we live."

The cook's face got loose. It was so funny I had to struggle not to laugh again, his face so loose and the waiter's getting tighter.

"You see, it was another story he was writing. Seeing how it would be like to be dead. But when I got into the coffin he wasn't there. So I went to the funeral parlor. Tommy loves funeral parlors—he goes to them and watches funerals. For his stories, you know. But he wasn't there. He was just gone. And I never wore widow's clothes or wept or found his grave—not anything—so he couldn't be really dead, could he?"

They looked at each other. "That's something to think on," the waiter said. "P'raps 'e's home by now. Waiting up for you. Ever think of that?"

I shook my head. "No. I telephoned. The maid said—" But it was too terrible to repeat. It was dreadful of her to tell me such a sad thing when I was trying to be happy in London. *Don't you remember, Miss Virginia? He's gone. Don't you remember?*

That's a stupid thing to tell me, I already know that, that's why I'm looking for him. He wasn't in the coffin in his study. Nor at the funeral parlor. Nor at the cemetery, none of the graves had his name on them.

Miss Virginia, please tell me where you are, stop thinking about Mr. Tom. Come—

It was infuriating, so I had told her to shut up. Stubborn, irritating fool! Wouldn't help me find Tommy.

Please come home, Miss Virginia, your brother's half crazy looking for you.

So I hung up.

"Tommy's not home, he's here in London," I told the men. "Hiding, he loves to tease. Teasing is mystery too, isn't it? Never know the truth of teasing until it stops, do you?"

The waiter shook his head. "It's a question, all right. Tell you w'ot, if 'e's not at the theater, you come back and have tea with us, free. You'll need comp'ny."

Such sweet men, real London people, so understanding. I paid my bill, gave them a wave, and headed for *The Mousetrap*.

Across the way, down the street toward the muted colored sign of the posh restaurant. On to the end of the shadowy street. And there it was. Just past the corner, *THE MOUSETRAP* in lights above its entrance. A quiet, dingy little theater on the outside, hiding goodies inside the way the English like to do it. And the goody would be Tommy! My wonderful red-haired wild Tommy!

"Has Tommy come yet?" I asked the girl in the ticket kiosk.

She stared a moment. Then said, "I'm sure I didn't notice, madam."

"Oh, I wish you had. It's been so long since I've seen him."

"Why don't you just go along inside?" she said. "If he's not there, perhaps he'll come after a bit. They usually do."

I went inside, found my seat, and watched the people as they came in. Every one of them. But no Tommy. "Do you suppose my husband is in the play?" I said to the couple beside me. "It could be a trick he's playing—he loves to tease. He might be, mightn't he?"

"Oh, quite," the lady said.

Then the house lights darkened and the play began.

Tommy wasn't in the play. And he wasn't in the audience. I would have known. I would have *felt* him. Besides, who could miss Tommy? Tall, broad-shouldered, and all that shining hair. He was so handsome, people always stopped talking or whatever they were doing and stared at him. Then he would smile, and he had such a lovely grin they had to smile back. Yes, I would have known if Tommy had been in the theater.

So I left. Before the play ended. Before I knew what the mystery was, so I'll never be able to tell it to anyone.

The streets were shadowy, not many people about. Up ahead was a two-decker red bus. I ran, but it ran faster. Gone. And Tommy might have been on it.

Then I knew. Just knew. Suddenly. And began shaking all over, a queer prickly nervousness crawling over my skin. Not inside of me, just on the outside. Inside I felt wonderful, because I was feeling Tommy. Right there, with me. Beside me. No, behind me, slipping from one side to the other every time I turned to catch him. Tease!

"Tommy, shame! Making me search half around the world for you. But I knew I'd find you. In London, just as I thought."

I whirled. Fast. But he was too quick for me. Oh, that character! I didn't want to encourage him by laughing, but I couldn't help it. "Tommy, you're dreadful! Oh, not really, Tommy, I love you just as you are, it's really a good joke. To catch me at *The Mousetrap*. Your little Mousie. But I caught you, too, I knew you'd be here."

I kept whirling, laughing, and whirling in the lovely London night, but I couldn't really catch him. How could Mousie catch that lovely big Tom-Cat with that shining red hair?

Another bus came along and we ran to catch it. I did, but Tommy missed it. He wasn't with me any more when I sat down inside. I began to cry.

"Mum, what's the trouble?" the girl conductor asked.

"I've lost someone. He didn't get on."

"P'raps you'd like to get off? He won't be far behind."

Of course he wouldn't be. I began to laugh again. That shameful man, he'd be running beside the bus, dodging out of sight every time I looked out the window. "No, this time I'll tease him," I told her. "He can just run to catch up with me."

"That's the spirit," the girl said, grinning. "Dries the tears fast, that kind of spunk."

The bus didn't turn toward Paddington Station, near where I'd found a hotel, but wheeled around the other side of Hyde Park.

"But my hotel's not this way," I told the man across the aisle. "I suppose I'd better get off."

"Now's as good a time as any," he said. "We all have to get off sooner or later."

So I did. Almost in front of a huge hotel. "I'm thirsty!" I said. Loud. So Tommy could hear if he'd caught up.

He had, because he whispered, right in my ear, "Let's go in here. It's one of the best."

Tommy behind, me in front, we went into the hotel's lower entrance. He was doing it again. Leaving all the nuisance arrangements to me. Always doing that. I mean, I don't mind the money part, my brother and I were left plenty of that, and Tommy's stories didn't make much. But I don't like calling people, making reservations, bothering with bills and all those crazy papers lawyers have you sign. "Let Tommy sign them for me," I told my lawyer. But the lawyer said Tommy couldn't. It was my money, not Tommy's. So I fooled him. I signed the checks and gave most of the money to Tommy. Lots of times I didn't have any money and neither did Tommy. Then Tommy made me explain to the bill collectors why we weren't paying our bills. If I hadn't been so glad to have Tommy back I would have been cross because he made me ask the doorman where we could get coffee. "Just coffee. Or"—I turned to Tommy, but he scooted out of sight—"Tommy, would you like a sandwich?"

The doorman waited almost a minute before he answered me, just like everyone was doing back in San Francisco. Finally he said, "Madam, you'd best go upstairs to the library. Coffee is served in the library. Or coffee and sandwiches can be sent to your room."

"My husband and I aren't staying here."

"The library is upstairs, madam."

I didn't bother with the elevator. I was onto that trick of Tommy's. I would go into one elevator and he'd catch another, and when we got upstairs he'd take another down and leave me alone. Lots of times he did that. So we walked up.

"The library, please," I said to a bellman.

"This way, madam."

Lovely, lovely, that library. Like being inside an English novel.

Like one of those old men's clubs where only dukes and lords stay. Or retired Army officers. Or something. Old men sunk deep into chairs, papers before their faces, all of them slowly dropping their papers as we came in. As though we'd entered screaming.

Laughter tickled my chest, bubbled in my throat, almost came out but I choked it back. I started to say, "Good evening." But that would have been wrong, like speaking from the audience to the actors on a stage.

The men hid their faces with their papers again and a waiter—no, he must have been a butler, he was so elegant in his swallow-tail coat—came to me. "Do you wish something, madam?"

He gave me chills, he was so superior and proper, with the expression of a schoolteacher who would smack my palms with a ruler even if I was a girl.

"Coffee, please. Cream for my husband, none for me." Tommy, the fink, wouldn't say a word. "I wish sometimes you'd do the ordering," I whispered to him. "And come sit properly beside me."

"I beg pardon, madam?"

"I'm just speaking to my husband, sir," I said coldly. I had to tack on that "sir," he was so terrifying.

"Certainly, madam."

He returned with a silver tray and set it on a low table before the divan. A silver coffee server, two cups beside it, a pitcher of cream, sugar. He poured the coffee, lifted the pitcher, and asked, "How much cream for the gentleman?"

"Just enough for color. No sugar. Mine is black."

He did the cream just right and moved off to one side.

Tommy wouldn't drink his coffee. Because he wasn't there any more. Slipped away. Gone. Probably turned off by that butler.

"Is Madam ill?" the butler asked.

"No. But my husband has left. Now I'll have to look for him all over again."

"Yes, madam."

I drank my coffee, paid the butler, and he bowed me out.

It was quiet outside, no one around, the night so empty the air seemed hollow. How good it would be, I thought, to crawl into that hollow, as an animal crawls into a hollow log. Curl up. Sleep. Rest.

Then I knew. That's where Tommy was hiding. In the hollow. Waiting for me to crawl in beside him. "Like you did in San Francisco," I said loudly so he'd be sure to hear. "Crawl in beside you, like in the coffin, and we'll both go to sleep. Only this time nobody will ever find us and take you away."

Tommy laughed. Deep, sweet, man laugh. "Tommy, darling, help me, how do I get inside the hollow?"

"This way!" Across the street. Toward the shops. Harrods?

"Tommy, you're mad! It's night, the shops aren't open."

"Here!" Farther. Always ahead.

"Are you looking for a present for me? Because you went away and left me alone? You don't need to, Tommy, I only need you."

He was above me, slipping ahead, out of reach. Then he vanished into the hollow, leaving behind only an echo of his laugh to ring in my ears. But I had found him out, now I knew where he was. I lifted my feet and climbed after him into the secret hollow.

Tommy slapped me. Hurt terribly. Gritty hand. Ground into me, scraped my face. But that must be the trick of it, that was how one entered the hollow, for Tommy was calling, "Over herehereHEREHEREHERE!"

"Where?"

"HEREHEREHEREHEREHERE—" Over and over, screaming.

"You never wait for me, not even in your coffin, never."

He kept screaming, screaming. Until at last he picked me up and laid me on a white flat coffin. "Are we going to the funeral parlor now, Tommy?"

"Put another blanket over her, she's going into shock." The voice wasn't Tommy's. It belonged to a stranger. Tommy was gone again. I began to cry. Inside of me, not outside with tears, and the tears cried too because they couldn't get out. Then I climbed into the air again and looked for the hollow and Tommy . . .

They had no business doing it. Putting me in a hospital. Just when I had almost reached Tommy. They made me so cross I wouldn't eat. Covered my head with the sheet. "I'm dead," I told them.

Then they did a worse thing. None of their business. They brought in my brother. Ron. Clear from San Francisco. To sit at my bedside and try to pat my hand and tell me lies. You would think that a boy you had been raised with, and who took care of you after your parents were dead because he was older, wouldn't tell you lies.

"Virginia, dear, this is Ron." I knew that, why wouldn't I know my own brother's voice? "Listen to me. I've come to take you home. You'll be all right now, safe, I'll see to that. Tommy's out of the way."

"You killed him!" I said through the sheet. "I remember now. You took me out of the coffin and threw him in it. I woke up and saw you. But he's not dead, he's alive. I found him here in London."

"Tommy's not in London, baby."

"He is! He wasn't at the funeral parlor, or in any of the graves. I read all those marble slabs, like dead books. But his name wasn't on any of them."

"You're only remembering part of it, Virginia. Try to remember all of it. So you'll get well, get straight in your mind. Tommy was arrested, can't you remember that, too? Tommy tried to kill you. He gave you an overdose of some drug he was fooling with—experimenting for his stories, he claimed. Had you in that damn coffin he kept in his study. With the lid down and a scarf over your face.

"I came to your house that night, to find out why your account at the bank was continually overdrawn and bill collectors were coming to me for payment. I figured Tommy was using up your money. The maid let me in and I went to his study. He was at his desk, typing. Said he'd been looking all over for you, couldn't find you anywhere. That lately you had been strange, wandering on long walks, disappearing for hours. I started to leave and go find you myself. It gave me the creeps, in there with that damn coffin."

Ron tried to pull the sheet from my face. I hung onto it.

"Virginia, you've got to get it straight. Tommy tried to kill you! If I hadn't noticed a scrap of your scarf caught in the hinge of the coffin lid, I would have left. But by the grace of God, I did see it and had a hunch to look in it. I had to unfasten the lid, so you didn't do it by yourself, like he said. And when I lifted the lid, there you were. The scarf covering your face. Unconscious from lack of air and that stuff he'd been giving you."

"Shut up!"

He yelled, like through a tunnel, "I won't! So I knocked him into the coffin, called the doctor and the police. Listen, Virginia, you and I have a lot of money. And your will makes him your principal heir. Face it, Virginia, he—"

I shut out Ron's voice. Left him all by himself in that nasty hospital room. Slipped away into the secret hollow. "Hi," Tommy said when I got there. "That stinker Ron. Always nosing around, not letting us have fun. But it was a good plot, wasn't it, Mousie? Man gives wife overdose of drugs, brother saves her but wife is still kookie, thinks husband is dead, goes to husband's funeral. Only there isn't any funeral, and no grave. Because she was the one supposed to be dead. Amusing type of murder story, don't you think, Mousie?"

"I looked everywhere for you, Tommy. All over London. Then at *The Mousetrap*, I was sure you'd be there. Only you weren't inside, you were waiting outside." Someone laughed. It wasn't Ron, I'd left him back in the hospital. And it was too shrill to be Tommy. I couldn't blame whoever it was for laughing. Because it was really funny. The way I kept looking for it. And hadn't known all along that of course I would be the one inside it. What else are mousetraps for?

Editorial Postscript

We sent advance proofs of Florence V. Mayberry's *In the Secret Hollow* to Dame Agatha Christie and we think you will be interested in her reaction. The following is quoted from Dame Agatha Christie's letter to Ellery Queen:

"I would like you to know the profound impression *In the Secret Hollow* has made upon me. I have first a feeling of definite personal involvement, since the story starts with my play *The Mousetrap*. Also, the roots of it seem to bring back to me various memories of my childhood. Between the ages of five and twelve years old, I led a wonderfully happy life, and I now realise that the reason for that was I created for myself, a self-invented dramatised version of many different ways of life in which I was the central character. Is there perhaps in everyone's life a Secret Hollow created by necessity?

"This author is the only writer I can recall to have demonstrated this. It is one of the most original stories I have come across.

"Mousie needed her Tommy. She created him and wherever *she* is—he also will be there—hiding from her, or looking for her—teasing her. Those two are always in close relationship. They each have their own reality out of this strange love story. What does the final problem of the coffin mean? It is the reader who is left to make the reply. With supreme skill the author has left it that way.

"Is it at the end Mousie's joyous tragedy that she accepts the cold coffin—still laughing as she has laughed throughout? Or is it Tom Cat's victory when he kills the thing he loved and achieves thereby riches and the knowledge and experience he craves? Was Mousie really part of Tom Cat's dream? Or was Tom Cat part of Mousie's dream?

"That perhaps would be Lewis Carroll's question. Anyway—a very remarkable tale and one on which Florence Mayberry should be congratulated. Either Tom Cat or Mousie, one of them created and imagined the other—and so the other came to life. But which way round was it?"

AGATHA CHRISTIE MALLOWAN

THE CORRUPTION OF OFFICER AVAKADIAN

by Stanley Ellin

If a full year passed without our publishing a new story by Stanley Ellin, we'd feel as if somehow during those twelve months we had missed an issue . . .

Stanley Ellin's publication record in Ellery Queen's Mystery Magazine *is extraordinary—there is no other word for it. For the past twenty-seven years—beginning in 1948 with his first published work, "The Specialty of the House," which has become an accepted modern classic in the field—Mr. Ellin has written one story every year especially for* EQMM. *In four of the twenty-seven years he found time to write two stories.*

The 1973 story is one of detection—but of strictly unorthodox detection. It is different from any other Stanley Ellin story we can remember—which shows that Mr. Ellin is still experimenting, still altering the shape and substance of the mystery short story, without ever forgetting that we are living in the 1970s . . .

IN regard to this heated issue of police corruption, I take the position—

No.

What with one thing and another, I believe it would be best to simply describe the curious event which led me to the position I take. And to start with the call received by Officer Schultz and me in our patrol car that night some time ago—I can measure the time by reflecting that two cherubic daughters have since been added to my roster of four sturdy sons, the Avakadians always having been a precocious and prolific breed—because that dispatcher's message was, I now see, the opening curtain on the event.

The call came at one A.M. abruptly breaking the bleak silence in the car. That silence, as we cruised along, was entirely Schultz's doing. I had been expostulating on various aspects of our profession—informatively, I knew; brightly, I hoped—until Schultz said, "Will you kindly shut up, Avakadian?" after which I kept my thoughts entirely to myself.

I suppose that the kindest way to put it was that Schultz was not dedicated to his job. I had graduated with highest honors from Police School, having spent my months there among highly motivated and dedicated men. I had served my probationary period as foot patrolman among several young officers who also demonstrated this spirit. Now, for the first time, I was encountering an entirely different kind of police officer. Indeed, after only three days as Schultz's partner in police patrol car Number 8, I had begun to wonder whether I had been placed in his company to glean the lessons an experienced old hand could provide or whether he had been placed in my company so that a bit of my own keen spit-and-polish attitude, my devotion to the departmental rule book, might not rub off on him.

In that latter case, it was time wasted. Schultz was only a few months from retirement, a bloated old time-server who seemed to make up his own rules as he went along. He was slovenly of person—his uniform jacket always appeared to be buttoned at the wrong buttons—and worse than that, he was slovenly in manner and attitude, always more willing to expend his scant energies in crawling through loopholes in the rule book than in carrying them out to the letter.

Despite his uncongenial manner toward me, I believe he did have a grudging respect for what I represented. This surfaced briefly when, during our first tour of duty together, he suddenly asked me—and there was genuine wonderment in his tones—"Were you always like this, Avakadian?" To which, in honest response, I explained that in my youth I had been the youngest Eagle Scout in the history of my troop and that before I set my course by the departmental rule book, I had steered it by nothing else than the Boy Scout Handbook. I even recited for him from memory the Scout Laws on being trustworthy, loyal, helpful, friendly, courteous, kind, obedient, cheerful, thrifty, brave, clean, and reverent, to which he only said in quick retreat to his curmudgeon role, "And how did friendly get in there?"

That stung me a little, though I well understood the reasons for it. As for example, any snacks we had during our tour of duty Schultz apparently regarded as gifts from the proprietors of the hamburger stands we stopped at, but I had insisted we pay in full for them, even though this procedure seemed to bewilder and alarm those proprietors. And twice, when we had caught up with traffic violators who were as transparently eager to buy their way out of trouble as Schultz was to take their money, my stern insistence on writing out the ticket made any such transaction impossible.

So in answer to his gibe, all I said was, "Remember, Schultz, friendliness does not mean condoning moral laxity." He had no answer to that, of course.

But, not to digress, that night in question we were cruising along sharing a bleak silence when the dispatcher's voice was heard. "Car eight. Householder at 77 Pineview, northwest," to which Schultz responded, as was his wont, "Yeah, sure," so that I, as I was invariably forced to do, had to take the speaker from Schultz's hand before he could hang it up and crisply reply to the dispatcher, "Ten-four," the only proper response.

I then remarked to Schultz—and it was not the first time I had been forced to do so—that since we were now on call, both the flasher and the siren had to be put into operation.

"Why?" Schultz said. "Why, Avakadian? Take a look. There isn't any traffic. Why do we have to make a circus of every call?"

"Because, Schultz, the rules prescribe it. And if you want the number of the exact rule—"

"Forget it," Schultz snarled, but willy-nilly he did turn on flasher and siren.

The northwest district was and is an area of luxurious homes, each surrounded by beautifully tended lawns. The door of Number 77 was already ajar as Schultz and I approached it along a flagstoned path, and when we reached the door I saw on the wall beside it a brass plaque inscribed *Cyrus Cahoon, M.D.* No surprise, that, since many of the finest properties in these parts were owned by members of the medical profession.

The tall aristocratic woman in robe and slippers who stood in the doorway motioned us inside the house. There, on one side of the foyer we entered, open doors revealed a waiting room and medical examining room. On the other side was a living room where a man dressed in a rather rumpled suit stood regarding us from beneath lowering brows. The woman pointed at him and said, "This is my husband, Dr. Cyrus Cahoon. He wishes to report an atrocious crime."

"I wish to report nothing, Florence," said Dr. Cahoon. "You were the one who invited these men here. Now do me the favor of inviting them out."

"Yeah, sure," Schultz said, and was already preparing to depart when Mrs. Cahoon grasped his arm firmly. "Officer," she said, "my husband may choose to stand mute, but if kidnaping is a crime, I cannot."

"It's a crime," Schultz said uncomfortably, and I must admit I felt an excitement at what I was hearing. My third day on this detail, and here I was confronted by one of the most heinous and dramatic of all felonies. I could only regret that I was not yet in detective grade where the task of handling the case would be mine. It was incredible that Schultz should manage to remain so stolid as he put the question, "Who's been kidnaped?"

Mrs. Cahoon again leveled a forefinger at her husband. "He was."

"He looks all right to me," Schultz said.

"I am all right," Dr. Cahoon said.

Schultz tried to detach his arm from Mrs. Cahoon's grip. He said, "Lady, if you and your husband would settle it between yourselves and then let us know how it came out—"

Mrs. Cahoon hung onto his arm. "It has been settled. My husband was kidnaped by a gang of criminals, do you hear? And he cannot deny it."

Plainly, Schultz wanted nothing more than to make a quick exit. Even more plainly, leaving now would be gross neglect of duty. At the very least, information on the crime had to be entered into our notebooks; the detective squad would have to be informed. So, although I had been advised by the department to follow Schultz's lead in all calls, I saw that, so to speak, I must now take the bit between my teeth.

I pulled out my notebook and pencil. I said to Dr. Cahoon, "Sir, what is the problem here? Are you afraid of reprisals if you take proper action against your alleged kidnapers?"

Dr. Cahoon regarded me steadily for a few moments. Then he looked at Schultz. "Is he for real?" he asked.

Happily, Mrs. Cahoon recognized the authority in my tone. She released Schultz's arm and turned to me. "I want you to write all this down," she said.

I held up my notebook and pencil to indicate that I was more than ready to do my duty.

"Oh, hell," Dr. Cahoon said.

"Officer," Mrs. Cahoon said, "an hour ago I woke from a sound sleep wondering why it was suddenly so light in the bedroom. Then I saw this woman standing there with a gun pointed at me. Then I saw another woman on the other side of the bed pointing a gun at my husband, and a man getting some of my husband's clothing from the closet. It was horrible. It was like a bad dream."

"I have survived the experience," Dr. Cahoon said.

Mrs. Cahoon disregarded this. "The man told my husband to put on his suit over his pajamas. My husband will not admit it but he was very much shaken. He offered the man all the money we had in the house, and the man said, 'No. We want you.' "

"Three of them," I said. "Can you describe them?"

"Yes," said Mrs. Cahoon. "The women wore housedresses. The one pointing the gun at me was short and stout. At least a size eighteen. She had curlers in her hair. Large pink plastic rollers. The other woman could have been a size twelve. She had gray hair done in a very unattractive permanent. The man was gray-haired, too. Medium height, medium weight, totally undistinguished in appearance. Then two of them removed my husband from the room—"

"I removed myself from the room," Dr. Cahoon said. "I left under my own power, putting one foot ahead of the other in the customary fashion."

"With a gun at your head," Mrs. Cahoon pointed out.

"That I cannot deny."

"And where were you taken?" I asked.

"Downstairs to my examining room."

"And then?" I said encouragingly.

"Then I was asked to produce my medical bag, which I did, and to submit to having my eyes blindfolded by a length of bandage. And since there seems to be no way of turning off your tape, Officer, I will tell you that I was then conducted to a car and driven for about ten or fifteen minutes to some location where I was led indoors. When the blindfold was removed I saw that I was in a rather poorly furnished bedroom. A young man was in bed there, apparently suffering acute pain, and a young woman whom I took to be his wife was also there, hysterically sympathizing with him."

Inspiration struck me. I said, "That young man was suffering a gunshot or knife wound, wasn't he? And you were expected to treat him without informing the authorities."

"The young man," Dr. Cahoon said, "was suffering what in layman's language is called a sprained ankle, although it was his impression, and his wife's, that the ankle was broken. After diagnosing the condition, I gave him a sedative, bound the ankle properly, advised bed rest. By now I imagine he is sound asleep, his pain eased."

"Well, mine isn't," Mrs. Cahoon said sharply. "After what I went through when they hauled you away—"

"Yes?" I prompted.

"That horrible little fat woman stayed right here with me all that time. She plunked herself down on the chair next to my bed and kept that gun pointed at me. She said to me, 'Just keep cool, sister,' and in the most threatening way."

"That's all she said?" I asked. "Nothing about what her accomplices were up to?"

"Nothing," said Mrs. Cahoon. "Later on she did ask me about my bedroom drapes."

"Your bedroom drapes?"

"Yes. She asked how much they cost, and when I told her, she said in a very sneering manner, 'They really took you, didn't they?' But every time I asked about my husband she just stared at me with those beady little eyes and wouldn't say a word."

Schultz stirred himself. He said to Dr. Cahoon, "But they brought you back okay, didn't they?"

"Yes," Dr. Cahoon said. "They also paid me." He dug into a pocket and held up a twenty-dollar bill to our view. "The wife, or whoever she was, gave it to me before I was blindfolded again and led away. She said, 'That should take care of it, Doc,' and since I was in no position to negotiate at length, I said yes, it did."

Schultz drew a long slow breath as if to fill his lungs for an ordeal ahead. He pointed at a chair. "Can I sit down?" he said.

"My home is your home," Dr. Cahoon said.

Schultz sat down and stretched out his legs. I was dismayed to see that this glaringly exposed to all his scuffed shoes and bedraggled socks. He said to Dr. Cahoon, "You don't make house calls, do you?"

"I used to," the doctor said. "But you understand that my practice now—"

"Yeah, sure," Schultz said, and then remarked complainingly, "When I was a kid, doctors made house calls. Even this time of night."

"And what," demanded Mrs. Cahoon, justifiably angry, "does that have to do with the crime committed against us?"

Schultz made no effort to answer this unanswerable question. Instead, he said to Dr. Cahoon, "You know there's been other cases like this lately? Other doctors being snatched?"

From Mrs. Cahoon's expression I saw that she was as astonished by this as I was. I was even more astonished to hear Dr. Cahoon say, "Yes. So some of my colleagues have been saying."

"What!" Mrs. Cahoon said explosively. "And not a word of it getting out? I don't believe it!"

"Lady, you can believe it," Schultz advised. "As for no word getting out, I guess all those other doctors got hit this way feel like your husband does about it. They'd kind of like to keep it strictly in the family."

"Do you hear that, Florence?" Dr. Cahoon said. He said to Schultz, "I tried to explain this to her. Maybe you'll have better luck at it than I did."

"Yeah, sure," Schultz said. He shook his head reproachfully at Mrs. Cahoon. "You see, lady, if we turn in a report on this, tomorrow you won't be able to walk out of your door what with all the reporters and TV guys there. And all of them looking to play it for comedy."

"Comedy?" Mrs. Cahoon said. "A crime like this?"

"Well, nobody got hurt, did they? And Doc here got paid for the job, just like all the others did. Now what do you make of a kidnaping where it's the victim that gets paid off? And let's face it, lady, the public will not be with you. Same goes for any jury that gets this case. Push the wrong button right now, and next thing you'll be a coast-to-coast joke."

Plainly, Mrs. Cahoon was hard hit by this. She stared at Schultz, her mouth opening and closing in a rather fishlike way. At last she found her voice. "Incredible," she said weakly.

"A coast-to-coast joke, Florence," Dr. Cahoon said. "Yes, indeed, the whole medical profession will have much to thank you for."

"Incredible," Mrs. Cahoon said again. She grasped the back of a chair and managed to seat herself. Her eyes remained glassily fixed on a far wall of the room. "Incredible."

Dr. Cahoon said to Schultz, "I think you have made your point, Officer. Thank you for that. Now if you gentlemen would like a drink before you leave—"

"Well—" Schultz said, hauling himself out of his chair; then he glanced my way. "No, not while we're on duty."

One does not enter into a confrontation with a fellow officer before the public. I maintained a tight-lipped silence until we were seated in the patrol car. I made an effort to keep my voice level. "Schultz," I said, "are you aware that a felony must be placed on record, however the complainant may feel about it?"

"Yeah, sure. So we'll put this down as a prowler who took off when we came around."

"You may do that, Schultz. I, however, am going to enter a detailed report on everything I have just seen and heard, including the unpleasant fact that a kidnap ring is being allowed to operate with impunity right under the department's nose."

"Yeah," Schultz said. "Well, you're way off base, Avakadian."

"If you are suggesting that the exposure of a crime wave—"

"I already exposed it, Avakadian. Unofficial like. On my own, see? I figured out after the first few snatches that it had to be that phone-answering service all these doctors use that was behind it. It was the one thing tied in with all of them. And that's what it was. Some nice old lady on the night switchboard there got so upset by doctors turning down house calls that she got some friends of hers to do something about it. That way, at least, they can take care of anybody they know personally and can count on not to spill the beans. And the guns are toy guns."

"Schultz, hasn't it entered your mind that your nice old lady is guilty of at least a dozen felonies?"

"I know. But if everybody wants it hushed up, why make trouble? And I'll let you in on something good, Avakadian, if you forget the book for once. I got a deal with that old lady, so any time me or the family needs a doctor she sees to it one shows up quick. Say the word, and she'll sign you on with the rest of the department."

"Do you mean that the whole department is in on this?"

"Sure. They're practically all family men, ain't they? Look at you, Avakadian, with a wife and four kids. How many times did you get turned down so far when you wanted a doctor to come fix one of them up?"

My mind was whirling, part of it doing painful arithmetic in answer to that question, part of it recoiling in horror from the proposition being cold-bloodedly offered me. But the arithmetic seemed to be submerging all other thoughts.

"Schultz," I said at last, "do you absolutely guarantee that those were only toy guns?"

"Absolutely," said Schultz.

And now, looking back, I must say that things have worked out very well, especially during influenza epidemics.

Which is why I take the position in regard to police corruption that one must not be too inflexible. Let us face one indisputable fact. The rule book serves well in most cases, but it does not bring healing.